THE FIFTH OMNI BOOK OF
SCIENCE FICTION

Here are fourteen remarkable stories from the pages of OMNI Magazine. All powerfully written, these stories reflect the talent and vision of some of today's science fiction writers. From grandmaster Robert Silverberg to the fresh young voice of Nebula and Hugo award winner William Gibson, these authors provide you with the stories that you love to read — and with the quality that you've come to expect from OMNI.

THE FIFTH
OMNI

BOOK OF
SCIENCE FICTION

Edited by Ellen Datlow

ZEBRA BOOKS
KENSINGTON PUBLISHING CORP.

ZEBRA BOOKS

are published by

Kensington Publishing Corp.

OMNI is a registered trademark of Omni Publications International, Ltd.

Table of Contents

THE FIFTH

OMNI

BOOK OF

SCIENCE FICTION

INTRODUCTION

As a result of the enormous popularity of the first four OMNI BOOKS OF SCIENCE FICTION, there will be many more volumes. This is quite heartening news. I happen to love the short story form, and I think that it's crucial for publishers and editors to support this literary genre.

Most science fiction writers begin their careers writing short stories—simply for the reason that they *are* short, and therefore less of an investment in time than a novel. Writing stories is excellent training. And because of their length, established writers can continue to experiment with style or structure. To realize you've failed in intent after thirty pages is a lot less devastating than after several hundred pages.

Short story editors have more of a leeway than book editors in buying and publishing something unconventional or difficult. Magazine editors, like myself, are putting together a package, and each story we buy does not make or break our magazine (or anthology). On the other hand, book editors have less literary license. Each and every book must be viewed as a money-maker or loser. The market for science fiction stories whether in magazines or anthologies, has always been better than for mainstream short stories. A long tradition has developed which continues to this day.

Like most editors, I have certain writers whom I publish regularly—people I affectionately refer to as my stable. These are the writers whom I can consistently count on for the kind of story I want in OMNI. Some of those writers are included in this book. Robert Silverberg, the consummate professional, is one of the few established novelists I know who still writes several short stories a year (more than I can publish). But OMNI does not only publish grand masters like Silverberg. William Gibson is one of the most promising young writers in science fiction today, and OMNI took a strong interest in helping him develop his talent. His first novel, NEURO-MANCER, won the Nebula and Hugo Awards. Now, Gibson is being wooed away by book publishers, so that I have to charm, cajole, threaten and just plain drive him crazy in order to keep him writing short fiction for OMNI. Howard Waldrop is another young writer. He is at his best with short fiction, and writes wonderful quirky little stories like the one included here. Marc Laidlaw was a very persistent teenager from whom I finally bought "400 Boys" after several complete overhauls. It was the first story I bought from him, and judging from his other stories of the past few years, his versatility is startling. Gregg

Keizer's first story was published in OMNI in 1982, and I've bought three more since then. The last piece in the book, "Lunatic Bridge," is a novelette by Pat Cadigan, who is another regular OMNI contributor. It has never been published before.

The only thing these fourteen stories have in common is that they are all quite powerful in very different ways. I believe they prove how important the science fiction story continues to be, not only within the genre, but to literature.

Ellen Datlow
Fiction Editor
January 1987

MULTIPLES

By Robert Silverberg

There were mirrors everywhere, making the place a crazy house of dizzying refraction: mirrors on the ceiling, mirrors on the walls, mirrors in the angles where the walls met the ceiling and the floor, even little eddies of mirror dust periodically blown on gusts of air through the room so that all the bizarre distortions, fracturings, and dislocations of image that were bouncing around the place would from time to time coalesce in a shimmering haze of chaos right before your eyes. Colored globes spun round and round overhead, creating patterns of ricocheting light. It was exactly the way Cleo had expected a multiples club to look.

She had walked up and down the whole Fillmore Street strip, from Union to Chestnut and back again, for half an hour, peering at this club and that before finding the courage to go inside one that called itself Skits. Though she had been planning this night for months, she found herself paralyzed by fear at the last minute: afraid they would spot her as a fraud the moment she walked in, afraid they would drive her out with jeers and curses and cold, mocking laughter. But now that she was within, she felt fine—calm, confident, ready for the time of her life.

There were more women than men in the club, something like a seven-to-three ratio. Hardly anyone seemed to be talking to anyone else. Most stood alone in the middle of the floor, staring into the mirrors as though in trance.

Their eyes were slits, their jaws were slack, their shoulders slumped forward, their arms dangled. Now and then, as some combination of reflections sluiced across their consciousnesses with particular impact, they would go taut and jerk and wince as if they had been struck. Their faces would flush, their lips would pull back, their eyes would roll, they would mutter and whisper to themselves; then after a moment they would slip back into stillness.

Cleo knew what they were doing. They were switching and doubling. Maybe some of the adepts were tripling.

Her heart rate picked up. Her throat was very dry. What was the routine here? she wondered. Did you just walk right out onto the floor and plug into the light patterns, or were you supposed to go to the bar first for a shot or a snort?

She looked toward the bar. A dozen or so customers were sitting there, mostly men, a couple of them openly studying her, giving her that new-girl-in-town stare. Cleo returned their gaze evenly, coolly, blankly. Standard-looking men, reasonably attractive, thirtyish or early fortyish, business suits, conventional hairstyles: young lawyers, executives, maybe stockbrokers—successful sorts out for a night's fun, the kind of men you might run into anywhere. Look at that one—tall, athletic, curly hair, glasses. Faint, ironic smile, easy, inquiring eyes. Almost professional. And yet, and yet—behind that smooth, intelligent forehead, what strangenesses must teem and boil! How many hidden souls must lurk and jostle! Scary. Tempting.

Irresistible.

Cleo resisted. Take it slow, take it slow. Instead of going to the bar, she moved out serenely among the switchers on the floor, found an open space, centered herself, looked toward the mirrors on the far side of the room. Legs apart, feet planted flat, shoulders forward. A turning globe splashed waves of red and violet light, splintered a thousand times over into her upturned face.

Go. Go. Go. Go. You are Cleo. You are Judy. You are Vixen. You are Lisa. Go. Go. Go. Go. Cascades of iridescence sweeping over the rim of her soul, battering at the walls of her identity. *Come, enter, drown me, split me, switch me. You are Cleo and Judy. You are Vixen and Lisa. You are Cleo and Judy and Vixen and Lisa. Go. Go. Go.*

Her head was spinning. Her eyes were blurring. The room gyrated around her.

Was this it? Was she splitting? Was she switching? Maybe so. Maybe the capacity was there in everyone, even her, and all that it would take was the lights, the mirrors, the right ambience, the will.

I am many. I am multiple. I am Cleo switching to

Vixen. I am Judy, and I am—

No. I am Cleo.

I am Cleo.

I am very dizzy, and I am getting sick, and I am Cleo and only Cleo, as I have always been. I am Cleo and only Cleo, and I am going to fall down.

"Easy," he said. "You okay?"

"Steadying up, I think. Whew!"

"Out-of-towner, eh?"

"Sacramento. How'd you know?"

"Too quick on the floor. Locals all know better. This place has the fastest mirrors in the west. They'll blow you away if you're not careful. You can't just go out there and grab for the big one—you've got to phase yourself in slowly. You sure you're going to be okay?"

"I think so."

He was the tall man from the bar, the athletic, professorial one. She supposed he had caught her before she had actually fallen, since she felt no bruises.

His hand rested easily now against her right elbow as he lightly steered her toward a table along the wall.

"What's your name?" he asked.

"Judy."

"I'm Van."

"Hello, Van."

"How about a brandy? Steady you up a little more."

"I don't drink."

"Never?"

16

"Vixen does the drinking," she said.

"Ah. The old story. She gets the bubbles, you get her hangovers. I have one like that too, only with him it's hunan food. He absolutely doesn't give a damn what lobster in hot and sour sauce does to my digestive system. I hope you pay her back the way she deserves."

Cleo smiled and said nothing.

He was watching her closely. Was he interested, or just being polite to someone who was obviously out of her depth in a strange milieu? Interested, she decided. He seemed to have accepted that Vixen stuff at face value.

Be careful now, Cleo warned herself. Trying to pile on convincing-sounding details when you don't really know what you're talking about is a sure way to give yourself away sooner or later.

The thing to do, she knew, was to establish her credentials without working too hard at it; sit back, listen, learn how things really operate among these people.

"What do you do up there in Sacramento?"

"Nothing fascinating."

"Poor Judy. Real-estate broker?"

"How'd you guess?"

"Every other woman I meet is a real-estate broker these days. What's Vixen?"

"A lush."

"Not much of a livelihood in that."

Cleo shrugged. "She doesn't need one. The rest of us support her."

"Real estate and what else?"

She hadn't been sure that multiples etiquette included talking about one's alternate selves. But she had come prepared. "Lisa's a landscape architect. Cleo's into software. We all keep busy."

"Lisa ought to meet Chuck. He's a demon horticulturalist. Partner in a plant-rental outfit—you know, huge dracaenas and philodendrons for offices, so much per month, take them away when they start looking sickly. Lisa and Chuck could talk palms and bromelaids and cacti all night."

"We should introduce them."

"We should, yes."

"But first we have to introduce Van and Judy."

"And then maybe Van and Cleo," he said.

She felt a tremor of fear. Had he found her out so soon? "Why Van and Cleo? Cleo's not here right now. This is Judy you're talking to."

"Easy. Easy!"

But she was unable to halt. "I can't deliver Cleo to you just like that, you know. She does as she pleases."

"Easy," he said. "All I meant was, Van and Cleo have something in common. Van's into software, too."

Cleo relaxed. With a little laugh she said, "Oh, not you, too! Isn't everybody nowadays? But I thought you were something in the academic world. A university professor or something like that."

"I am. At Cal."

"Software?"

"In a manner of speaking. Linguistics. Metalinguistics, actually. My field is the language of language—the basic subsets, the neural coordinates of communication, the underlying programs our brains use, the operating systems. Mind as computer, computer as mind. I can get very boring about it."

"I don't find the mind a boring subject."

"I don't find real estate a boring subject. Talk to me about second mortgages and triple-net leases."

"Talk to me about Chomsky and Benjamin Whorf," she said.

His eyes widened. "You've heard of Benjamin Whorf?"

"I majored in comparative linguistics. That was before real estate."

"Just my lousy luck," he said. "I get a chance to find out what's hot in the shopping-center market and she wants to talk about Whorf and Chomsky."

"I thought every other woman you met these days was a real-estate broker. Talk to them about shopping centers."

"They all want to talk about Whorf and Chomsky. More intellectual."

"Poor Van."

"Yes. Poor Van." Then he leaned forward and said, his tone softening, "You know, I shouldn't have made that crack about Van meeting Cleo. That was very tacky of me."

"It's okay, Van. I didn't take it seriously."

"You seemed to. You were very upset."

"Well, maybe at first. But then I saw you were just horsing around."

"I still shouldn't have said it. You were absolutely right: This is Judy's time now. Cleo's not here, and that's just fine. It's Judy I want to get to know."

"You will," she said. "But you can meet Cleo, too, and Lisa and Vixen. I'll introduce you to the whole crew. I don't mind."

"You're sure of that?"

"Sure."

"Some of us are very secretive about our alters."

"Are you?" Cleo asked.

"Sometimes. Sometimes not."

"I don't mind. Maybe you'll meet some of mine tonight." She glanced toward the center of the floor. "I think I've steadied up now. I'd like to try the mirrors again."

"Switching?"

"Doubling," she said. "I'd like to bring Vixen up. She can do the drinking, and I can do the talking. Will it bother you if she's here, too?"

"Won't bother me unless she's a sloppy drunk. Or a mean one."

"I can keep control of her when we're doubling. Come on, take me through the mirrors."

"You be careful now. San Francisco mirrors aren't like Sacramento ones. You've already discovered that."

"I'll watch my step this time. Shall we go out there?"

"Sure," he said.

As they began to move out onto the floor a slender, T-shirted man of about thirty came toward them. Shaven scalp, bushy mustache, medallions, boots. Very San Francisco, very gay. He frowned at Cleo and stared straightforwardly at Van.

"Ned?"

Van scowled and shook his head. "No. Not now."

"Sorry. Very sorry. I should have realized." The shaven-headed man flushed and hurried away.

"Let's go," Van said to Cleo.

20

This time she found it easier to keep her balance. Knowing that he was nearby helped. But still the waves of refracted light came pounding in, pounding in, pounding in. The assault was total: remorseless, implacable, overwhelming. She had to struggle against the throbbing in her chest, the hammering in her temples, the wobbliness of her knees. And this was pleasure for them? This was a supreme delight?

But they were multiples, and she was only Cleo, and that, she knew, made all the difference. She seemed to be able to fake it well enough. She could make up a Judy, a Lisa, a Vixen, assign little corners of her personality to each, give them voices of their own, facial expressions, individual identities. Standing before her mirror at home, she had managed to convince herself. She might even be able to convince him. But as the swirling lights careened off the infinities of interlocking mirrors and came slaloming into the gateways of her reeling soul, the dismal fear began to rise in her that she could never truly be one of these people after all, however skillfully she imitated them in their intricacies.

Was it so? Was she doomed always to stand outside their irresistible world, hopelessly peering in? Too soon to tell—much too soon, she thought, to admit defeat.

At least she didn't fall down. She took the punishment of the mirrors as long as she could stand it, and then, not waiting for him to leave the floor, she made her way—carefully, carefully, walking a tightrope over an abyss—to the bar. When her head had begun

21

to stop spinning she ordered a drink, and she sipped it cautiously. She could feel the alcohol extending itself inch by inch into her bloodstream. It calmed her. On the floor Van stood in trance, occasionally quivering in a sudden, convulsive way for a fraction of a second. He was doubling, she knew: bringing up one of his other identities. That was the main thing that multiples came to these clubs to do. No longer were all their various identities forced to dwell in rigorously separated compartments of their minds. With the aid of the mirrors and lights the skilled ones were able to briefly to fuse two or even three of their selves into something more complex. When he comes back here, she thought, he will be Van plus X. And I must pretend to be Judy plus Vixen.

She readied herself for that. Judy was easy. Judy was mostly the real Cleo, the real-estate woman from Sacramento, with Cleo's notion of what it was like to be a multiple added in. And Vixen? Cleo imagined her to be about twenty-three, a Los Angeles girl, a one-time child tennis star who had broken her ankle in a dumb prank and had never recovered her game afterward, and who had taken up drinking to ease the pain and loss. Uninhibited, unpredictable, untidy, fiery, fierce: all the things that Cleo was not. Could she be Vixen? She took a deep gulp of her drink and put on the Vixen face: eyes hard and glittering; cheek muscles clenched.

Van was leaving the floor now. His way of moving seemed to have changed: He was stiff, almost awkward, his shoulders held high, his elbows jutting oddly. He looked so different that she wondered whether he was still Van at all.

"You didn't switch, did you?"

"Doubled. Paul's with me now."

"Paul?"

"Paul's from Texas. Geologist, terrific poker game, plays the guitar." Van smiled, and it was like a shifting of gears. In a deeper, broader voice he said, "And I sing real good too, ma'am. Van's jealous of that, because he can't sing worth beans. Are you ready for a refill?"

"You bet," Cleo said, sounding sloppy, sounding Vixenish.

His apartment was nearby, a cheerful, airy, sprawling place in the Marina district. The segmented nature of his life was immediately obvious: The prints and paintings on the walls looked as though they had been chosen by four or five different people, one of whom ran heavily toward vivid scenes of sunrise over the Grand Canyon, another to Picasso and Miró, someone else to delicate, impressionist views of Parisian street scenes and flower markets. A sun room contained the biggest and healthiest houseplants Cleo had ever seen. Another room was stacked with technical books and scholarly journals, a third was equipped with three or four gleaming exercise machines. Some of the rooms were fastidiously tidy, some impossibly chaotic. Some of the furniture was stark and austere; some was floppy and overstuffed. She kept expecting to find roommates wandering around. But there was no one here but Van. And Paul.

Paul fixed the drinks, played soft guitar music, told

23

her gaudy tales of prospecting on the West Texas mesas. Paul sang something bawdy sounding in Spanish, and Cleo, putting on her Vixen voice, chimed in on the choruses, deliberately off-key. But then Paul went away, and it was Van who sat close beside her on the couch. He wanted to know things about Judy, and he told her a little about Van, and no other selves came into the conversation. She was sure that was intentional. They stayed up very late. Paul came back toward the end of the evening to tell a few jokes and sing a soft late-night song, but when they went into the bedroom, she was with Van. Of that she was certain.

And when she woke in the morning she was alone. She felt a surge of confusion and dislocation, remembered after a moment where she was and how she happened to be there, sat up, blinked. Went into the bathroom and scooped a handful of water over her face. Without bothering to dress she went padding around the apartment looking for Van.

She found him in the exercise room, using the rowing machine, but he wasn't Van. He was dressed in tight jeans and a white T-shirt, and he looked somehow younger, leaner, jauntier. There were fine beads of sweat along his forehead, but he did not seem to be breathing hard. He gave her a cool, distantly appraising, wholly asexual look as though it was not in the least unusual for an unknown naked woman to materialize in the house and he was altogether undisturbed by it. "Good morning. I'm Ned. Pleased to know you." His voice was higher than Van's, much higher than Paul's, and he had an odd, overprecise way of shaping each syllable.

Flustered, suddenly self-conscious and wishing she had put her clothes on before leaving the bedroom, she folded one arm over her breasts, though her nakedness did not seem to matter to him at all. "I'm — Judy. I came with Van."

"Yes, I know. I saw the entry in our book." Smoothly he pulled on the oars of the rowing machine, leaned back, pushed forward. "Help yourself to anything in the fridge," he said. "Make yourself at home. Van left a note for you in the kitchen."

She stared at him: his hands, his mouth, his long muscular arms. She remembered his touch, his kisses, the feel of his skin. And now this complete indifference. No. Not *his* kisses, not *his* touch. Van's. And Van was not here now. There was a different tenant in Van's body, someone she did not know in any way and who had no memories of last night's embraces. *I saw the entry in our book.* They left memos for one another. Cleo shivered. She had known what to expect, more or less, but experiencing it was very different from reading about it. She felt almost as if she had fallen in among beings from another planet.

But this is what you wanted, she thought. *Isn't it?* The intricacy, the mystery, the unpredictability, the sheer weirdness? A little cruise through an alien world because her own had become so stale, so narrow, so cramped. And here she was. *Good morning. I'm Ned. Pleased to know you.*

Van's note was clipped to the refrigerator by a little yellow magnet shaped like a ladybug. DINNER TONIGHT AT CHEZ MICHEL? YOU AND ME AND WHO KNOWS WHO ELSE. CALL ME.

That was the beginning. She saw him every night

25

for the next ten days. Generally they met at some three-star restaurant, had a lingering, intimate dinner, went back to his apartment. One mild, clear evening they drove out to the beach and watched the waves breaking on Seal Rock until well past midnight. Another time they wandered through Fisherman's Wharf and somehow acquired three bags of tacky souvenirs.

Van was his primary name—she saw it on his credit card one night—and that seemed to be his main identity, too, though she knew there were plenty of others. At first he was reticent about that, but on the fourth or fifth night he told her that he had nine major selves and sixteen minor ones. Besides Paul, the geologist, Chuck, who was into horticulture, and Ned, the gay one, Cleo heard about Nat, the stock-market plunger—he was fifty and fat, made a fortune every week, and divided his time between Las Vegas and Miami Beach; Henry, the poet, who was shy and never liked anyone to read his work; Dick, who was studying to be an actor; Hal, who once taught law at Harvard; Dave, the yachtsman, and Nicholas, the cardsharp.

And then there were the fragmentary ones, some of whom didn't have names, only a funny way of speaking or a little routine they liked to act out.

She got to see very little of his other selves, though. Like all multiples he was troubled occasionally by involuntary switching. One night he became Hal while they were making love, and another time he turned into Dave for an hour, and there were momentary flashes of Henry and Nicholas. Cleo perceived it right away whenever one of those switches came: His voice, his movements, his entire manner and personality changed immediately. Those were startling, exciting moments for her, offering a strange exhilaration. But generally his control was very good, and he stayed Van, as if he felt some strong need to experience her as Van, and Van alone. Once in a while he doubled, bringing up Paul to play the guitar and sing or Dick to recite sonnets, but when he did that the Van identity always remained present and dominant. It appeared that he was able to double at will, without the aid of mirrors and lights, at least some of the time. He had been an active and functioning multiple for as long as he could remember — since childhood, perhaps even since birth — and he had devoted himself through the years to the task of gaining mastery over his divided mind.

All the aspects of him that she came to meet had basically attractive personalities: They were energetic, stable, purposeful men who enjoyed life and seemed to know how to go about getting what they wanted. Though they were very different people, she could trace them all back readily enough to the underlying Van from whom, so she thought, they had all split. The one puzzle was Nat, the market operator. It was hard for Cleo to imagine what he was like when he was Nat — sleazy and coarse, yes, but how did he manage to make himself look fifteen years older and forty pounds heavier? Maybe it was all done with facial expressions and posture. But she never got to see Nat. And gradually she realized it was an oversimplification to think of Paul and Dick and Ned and the others as mere extensions of Van into different modes.

Van by himself was just as incomplete as the others. He was just one of many that had evolved in parallel, each one autonomous, each one only a fragment of the whole. Though Van might have control of the shared body a greater portion of the time, he still had no idea what any of his alternate selves were up to while they were in command, and like them he had to depend on guesses, fancy footwork, and such notes and messages as they bothered to leave behind in order to keep track of events that occurred outside his conscious awareness. "The only one who knows everything is Michael. He's seven years old, as smart as a whip, and keeps in touch with all of us all the time."

"Your memory trace," Cleo said.

Van nodded. All multiples, she knew, had one alter with full awareness of the doings of all the other personalities — usually a child, an observer who sat back deep in the mind and played its own games and emerged only when necessary to fend off some crisis that threatened the stability of the entire group. "He's just informed us that he's Ethiopian," Van said. "So every two or three weeks we go across to Oakland to an Ethiopian restaurant that he likes, and he flirts with the waitresses in Amharic."

"That can't be too terrible a chore. I'm told Ethiopians are very beautiful people."

"Absolutely. But they think it's all a big joke, and Michael doesn't know how to pick up women anyway. He's only seven, you know. So Van doesn't get anything out of it except some exercise in comparative linguistics and a case of indigestion the next day. Ethiopian food is the spiciest in the world. I can't

28

stand spicy food."

"Neither can I," she said. "But Lisa loves it. Especially Mexican. But nobody ever said sharing a body is easy, did they?"

She knew she had to be careful in questioning Van about the way his life as a multiple worked. She was supposed to be a multiple herself, after all. But she made use of her Sacramento background as justification for her areas of apparent ignorance of multiple customs and the everyday mechanics of multiple life. Though she too had known she was a multiple since childhood, she said, she had grown up outside the climate of acceptance of the divided personality that prevailed in San Francisco, where an active subculture of multiples had existed openly for years. In her isolated existence, unaware that there were a great many others of her kind, she had at first regarded herself as the victim of a serious mental disorder. It was only recently, she told him, that she had come to understand the overwhelming advantages of life as a multiple: the richness, the complexity, the fullness of talents and experiences that a divided mind was free to enjoy. That was why she had come to San Francisco. That was why she listened so eagerly to all that he was telling her about himself.

She was cautious, too, in manifesting her own multiple identities. She wished she did not have to pretend to have other selves. But they had to be brought forth now and again, if only to maintain Van's interest in her. Multiples were notoriously indifferent to singletons. They found them bland, overly simple, two-dimensional. They wanted the excitement of embracing one person and discovering another, or two or three. So she gave him Lisa, she gave him Vixen, she gave him the Judy-who-was-Cleo and the Cleo-who-was-someone-else, and she slipped from one to another in a seemingly involuntary and unexpected way, often when they were in bed.

Lisa was calm, controlled, straitlaced. She was totally shocked when she found herself, between one eye blink and the next, in the arms of a strange man. "Who are you?—where am I?" she blurted, rolling away and pulling herself into a fetal ball.

"I'm Judy's friend," Van said.

She stared bleakly at him. "So she's up to her tricks again."

He looked pained, embarrassed, solicitous. She let him wonder for a moment whether he would have to take her back to her hotel in the middle of the night. Then she allowed a mischievous smile to cross Lisa's face, allowed Lisa's outraged modesty to subside, allowed Lisa to relent and relax, allowed Lisa to purr—

"Well, as long as we're here already—what did you say your name was?"

He liked that. He liked Vixen, too—wild, sweaty, noisy, a moaner, a gasper, a kicker and thrasher who dragged him down onto the floor and went rolling over and over with him. She thought he liked Cleo, too, though that was harder to tell, because Cleo's style was aloof, serious, baroque, inscrutable. She would switch quickly from one to another, sometimes running through all four in the course of an hour. Wine, she said, induced quick switching in her. She let him know that she had a few other identities, too, fragmentary and submerged. She hinted that they were troubled, deeply neurotic, self-destructive: They were under control, she said, and would not erupt to cause woe for him, but she left the possibility hovering over them to add spice to the relationship and plausibility to her role.

It seemed to be working. His pleasure in her company was evident. She was beginning to indulge in little fantasies of moving down permanently from Sacramento, renting an apartment, perhaps even moving in with him, though that would surely be a strange and challenging life. She would be living with Paul and Ned and Chuck and the rest of the crew, too, but how wondrous, how electrifying.

Then on the tenth day he seemed uncharacteristically tense and somber. She asked him what was bothering him, and he evaded her, and she pressed, and finally he said, "Do you really want to know?"

"Of course."

"It bothers me that you aren't real, Judy."

She caught her breath. "What the hell do you mean by that?"

"You know what I mean," he said quietly, sadly. "Don't try to pretend any longer. There's no point in it."

It was like a jolt in the ribs.

She turned away and was silent a long while, wondering what to say. Just when everything was going so well, just when she was beginning to believe she had carried off the masquerade successfully.

"So you know?" she asked timidly.

"Of course I know. I knew right away."

She was trembling. "How could you tell?"

31

"A thousand ways. When we switch, we *change*. The voice. The eyes. The muscular tensions. The grammatical habits. The brain waves, even. An evoked-potential test shows it. Flash a light in my eyes and I'll give off a certain brain-wave pattern, and Ned will give off another, and Chuck still another. You and Lisa and Cleo and Vixen would all be the same. Multiples aren't actors, Judy. Multiples are separate minds within the same brain. That's a matter of scientific fact. You were just acting. You were doing it very well, but you couldn't possibly have fooled me."

"You let me make an idiot of myself, then."

"No."

"Why did you—how could you—"

"I saw you walk in that first night, and you caught me right away. I watched you go out on the floor and fall apart, and I knew you couldn't be multiple, and I wondered, What the hell's she doing here? Then I went over to you, and I was hooked. I felt something I haven't ever felt before. Does that sound like the standard old malarkey? But it's true, Judy. You're the first singleton woman who's ever interested me."

"Why?"

He shook his head. "Something about you—your intensity, your alertness, maybe even your eagerness to pretend you were a multiple—I don't know. I was caught. I was caught hard. And it's been a wonderful week and a half. I mean that."

"Until you got bored."

"I'm not bored with you, Judy."

"Cleo. That's my real name, my singleton name. There is no Judy."

"Cleo," he said, as if measuring the word with his lips.

"So you aren't bored with me even though there's only one of me. That's marvelous — tremendously flattering. That's the best thing I've heard all day. I guess I should go now, Van. It *is* Van, isn't it?"

"Don't talk that way."

"How do you want me to talk? I fascinated you, you fascinated me, we played our little games with each other, and now it's over. I wasn't real, but you did your best. We both did our best. But I'm only a singleton woman, and you can't be satisfied with that. Not for long. For a night, a week, two weeks maybe. Sooner or later you'll want the real thing, and I can't be the real thing for you. So long, Van."

"No."

"No?"

"Don't go."

"What's the sense of staying?"

"I want you to stay."

"I'm a singleton, Van."

"You don't have to be," he said.

The therapist's name was Burkhalter, and his office was in one of the Embarcadero towers. To the San Francisco multiples community he was very close to being a deity. His specialty was electrophysiological integration, with specific application to multiple-personality disorders. Those who carried within themselves dark and diabolical selves that threatened the stability of the group went to him to have those selves purged or at least contained. Those who sought

33

to have latent selves that were submerged beneath more outgoing personalities brought forward into a healthy functional state went to him also. Those whose life as a multiple was a torment of schizoid confusions instead of a richly rewarding contrapuntal symphony gave themselves to Dr. Burkhalter to be healed, and in time they were. And in recent years he had begun to develop techniques for what he called personality augmentation. Van called it "driving the wedge."

"He can turn a singleton into a multiple?" Cleo asked in amazement.

"If the potential is there. You know that it's partly genetic: The structure of a multiple's brain is fundamentally different from a singleton's. The hardware just isn't the same, the cerebral wiring. And then, if the right stimulus comes along, usually in childhood, usually but not necessarily traumatic, the splitting takes place, the separate identities begin to establish their territories. But much of the time multiplicity is never generated, and you walk around with the capacity to be a whole horde of selves yet never know it."

"Is there reason to think I'm like that?"

He shrugged. "It's worth finding out. If he detects the predisposition, he has effective ways of inducing separation. Driving the wedge, you see? You do *want* to be a multiple, don't you, Cleo?"

"Oh, yes, Van. Yes!"

Burkhalter wasn't sure about her. He taped electrodes to her head, flashed bright lights in her eyes, gave her verbal-association tests, ran four or five different kinds of electroencephalograph studies, and still he was uncertain. "It is not a black-and-white matter," he said several times, frowning, scowling. He was a multiple himself, but three of his selves were psychiatrists; so there was never any real problem about his office hours. Cleo wondered if he ever went to himself for a second opinion. After a week of testing she was sure that she must be a hopeless case, an intractable singleton, but Burkhalter surprised her by concluding that it was worth the attempt. "At the very worst," he said, "we will experience spontaneous fusing in a few days, and you will be no worse off than you are now. But if we succeed—"

His clinic was across the bay, in a town called Moraga. She spent two days undergoing further tests, then three days taking medication. "Simply an anticonvulsant," the nurse explained cheerily. "To build up your tolerance."

"Tolerance for what?" Cleo asked.

"The birth trauma," she said. "New selves will be coming forth, and it can be uncomfortable for a little while."

The treatment began on Thursday. Electroshock, drugs, electroshock again. She was heavily sedated. It felt like a long dream, but there was no pain. Van visited her every day. Chuck came too, bringing her two potted orchids in bloom, and Paul sang to her, and even Ned paid her a call. But it was hard for her to maintain a conversation with any of them. She heard voices much of the time. She felt feverish and dislocated, and at times she was sure she was floating eight or ten inches above the bed. Gradually that sensation subsided, but there were others nearly as odd. The voices remained. She learned how to hold conversations with them.

35

In the second week she was not allowed to have visitors. That didn't matter.

She had plenty of company even when she was alone.

Then Van came for her. "They're going to let you go home today," he said. "How are you doing, Cleo?"

"I'm Noreen," she said.

There were five of her apparently. That was what Van said. She had no way of knowing, because when they were dominant she was gone—not merely asleep, but *gone*, perceiving nothing. But he showed her notes that they wrote, in handwritings that she did not recognize and indeed could barely read, and he played tapes of her other voices: Noreen, a deep contralto; Nanette, high and breathy; Katya, hard and rough New York; and the last one, who had not yet announced her name, a stagy, voluptuous, campy siren voice.

She did not leave his apartment the first few days, and then she began going out for short trips, always with Van or one of his alters close beside. She felt convalescent. A kind of hangover from the drugs had dulled her reflexes and made it hard for her to cope with traffic, and also there was the fear that she would undergo a switching while she was out. Whenever that happened it came without warning, and when she returned to awareness afterward she felt a sharp discontinuity of memory, not knowing how she suddenly found herself in Ghirardelli Square or Golden Gate Park or wherever it was that the other self had taken their body.

36

But she was happy. And Van was happy with her. One night in the second week, when they were out, he switched to Chuck — Cleo knew it was Chuck coming on, for now she always knew right away which identity had taken over — and he said, "You've had a marvelous effect on him. None of us have ever seen him like this before — so contented, so fulfilled —"

"I hope it lasts, Chuck."

"Of course it'll last! Why on earth shouldn't it last?"

It didn't. Toward the end of the third week Cleo noticed that there hadn't been any entries in her memo book from Noreen for several days. That in itself was nothing alarming: An alter might choose to submerge for days, weeks, even months at a time. But was it likely that Noreen, so new to the world, would remain out of sight so long? Lin-lin, the little Chinese girl who had evolved in the second week and was Cleo's memory trace, reported that Noreen had gone away. A few days later an identity named Mattie came and went within three hours, like something bubbling up out of a troubled sea. Then Nanette and Katya disappeared, leaving Cleo with no one but her nameless, siren-voiced alter and Lin-lin. She was fusing again. The wedges that Dr. Burkhalter had driven into her soul were not holding; her mind insisted on oneness and was integrating itself; she was reverting to the singleton state.

"All of them are gone now," she told Van disconsolately.

"I know. I've been watching it happen."

"Is there anything we can do? Should I go back to Burkhalter?"

37

She saw the pain in his eyes. "It won't do any good," he said. "He told me the chances were about three to one this would happen. A month, he figured; that was about the best we could hope for. And we've had our month."

"I'd better go, Van."

"Don't say that."

"No?"

"I love you, Cleo."

"You won't. Not for much longer."

He tried to argue with her, to tell her that it didn't matter to him that she was a singleton, that one Cleo was worth a whole raft of alters, that he would learn to adapt to life with a singleton woman. He could not bear the thought of her leaving now. So she stayed: a week, two weeks, three. They ate at their favorite restaurants. They strolled hand in hand through the cool evenings. They talked of Chomsky and Whorf and even of shopping centers. When he was gone and Paul or Chuck or Hal or Dave was there she went places with them if they wanted her to. Once she went to a movie with Ned, and when toward the end he felt himself starting to switch she put her arm around him until he regained control so that he could see how the movie finished.

But it was no good. He wanted something richer than she could offer him: the switching, the doubling, the complex undertones and overtones of other personalities, resonating beyond the shores of consciousness. She could not give him that. He was like one who has voluntarily blindfolded himself in order to keep a blind woman company. She knew she could not ask him to live like that forever.

And so one afternoon when Van was somewhere else she packed her things and said good-bye to Paul, who gave her a hug and wept a little with her, and she went back to Sacramento. "Tell him not to call," she said. "A clean break's the best." She had been in San Francisco two months, and it was as though those two months were the only months of her life that had had any color in them, and all the rest had been lived in tones of gray.

There had been a man in the real-estate office who had been telling her for a couple of years that they were meant for each other. Cleo had always been friendly enough to him: They had done a few skiing weekends in Tahoe the winter before; they had gone to Hawaii once; they had driven down to San Diego. But she had never felt anything particular when she was with him. A week after her return she phoned him and suggested that they drive up north to the redwood country for a few days. When they came back she moved into the condominium he had just outside town.

It was hard to find anything wrong with him. He was good-natured and attractive, he was successful, he read books and liked good movies, he enjoyed hiking, rafting, and backpacking, he even talked of driving down into the city during the opera season to take in a performance or two. He was getting toward the age where he was thinking about marriage and a family. He seemed very fond of her.

But he was flat, she thought. Flat as a cardboard cutout: a singleton, a one-brain, a no-switch. There was only one of him, and there always would be. It was hardly his fault, she knew. But she couldn't settle for someone who had only two dimensions. A terrible restlessness went roaring through her every evening, and she could not possibly tell him what was troubling her.

On a drizzly afternoon in early November she packed a suitcase and drove down to San Francisco. She checked into one of the Lombard Street motels, showered, changed, and walked over to Fillmore Street. Cautiously she explored the strip from Chestnut down to Union, from Union back to Chestnut. The thought of running into Van terrified her. Not tonight, she prayed. Not tonight. She went past Skits, did not go in, stopped outside a club called Big Mama, shook her head, finally entered one called The Side Effect. Mostly women inside, as usual, but a few men at the bar, not too bad-looking. No sign of Van.

She bought herself a drink and casually struck up a conversation with a short, curly-haired, artistic-looking type.

"You come here often?" he asked.

"First time. I've usually gone to Skits."

"I think I remember seeing you there. Or maybe not."

She smiled. "What's your now-name?"

"Sandy. Yours?"

Cleo drew her breath down deep into her lungs. She felt a kind of light-headedness beginning to swirl behind her eyes. *Is this what you want?* she asked herself. *Yes. Yes. This is what you want.*

"Melinda," she said.

40

Man-Mountain Gentian

By Howard Waldrop

Just after the beginning of the present century, it was realized that some of the wrestlers were throwing their opponents from the ring without touching them."
—*Ichinaga Naya,* Zen-Sumo: Sport and Ritual, *Kyoto, All-Japan Zen-Sumo Association Books, 2014.*

It was the fourteenth day of the January Tokyo tournament. Seated with the other wrestlers, Man-Mountain Gentian watched as the next match began. Ground Sloth Ikimoto was taking on Killer Kudzu. They entered the tamped-earth ring and began their *shikiris*.

Ground Sloth, a *sumotori* of the old school, had changed over from traditional to Zen-sumo four years before. He weighed one hundred eighty kilos in his *mawashi*. He entered at the white-tassle salt corner. He clapped his huge hands, rinsed his mouth, threw salt, rubbed his body with tissue paper, then began his high leg lifts, stamping his feet, his hands gripping far down his calves. The ring shook with each stamp. All the muscles rippled on his big frame. His stomach, a flesh-colored boulder, shook and vibrated.

Killer Kudzu was small and thin, weighing barely over ninety kilos. On his forehead was the tattoo of his homeland, the People's Republic of China, one large star and four smaller stars blazing in a constellation. He also went into his ritual *shikiri*, but as he clapped he held in one hand a small box, ten centimeters on a side, showing his intention to bring it into the match. Sometimes these were objects for meditation, sometimes favors from male or female lovers, sometimes no one knew what. The only rule was that they could not be used as weapons.

The wrestlers were separated from the onlookers by four clear walls and a roof of plastic. Over this hung the traditional canopy and tassles, symbolizing heaven and the four winds.

Through the plastic walls ran a mesh of fine wiring, connected to a six-volt battery next to the north-side judge. This small charge was used to contain the pushes of the wrestlers and to frustrate help from outside.

A large number of 600x slow-motion video cameras were strategically placed around the auditorium to be used by the judges to replay the action if necessary.

Killer Kudzu had placed the box on his side of the

line. He returned to his corner and threw more salt onto the ground, part of the ritual purification ceremony.

Ground Sloth Ikimoto stamped once more, twice, went to his line, and settled into position like a football lineman, legs apart, knuckles to the ground. His nearly bare buttocks looked like giant rocks. Killer Kudzu finished his *shikiri* and squatted at his line, where he settled his hand near his votive box and glared at his opponent.

The referee, in his ceremonial robes, had been standing to one side during the preliminaries. Now he came to a position halfway between the wrestlers, his war fan down. He leaned away from the two men, left leg back to one side as if ready to run. He stared at the midpoint between the two and flipped his fan downward.

Instantly sweat sprang to their foreheads and shoulders, their bodies rippled as if pushing against great unmoving weights, their toes curled into the clay of the ring. The two of them stayed tensely immobile on their respective marks.

Killer Kudzu's neck muscles strained. With his left hand he reached and quickly opened the votive box.

Man-Mountain Gentian and the other wrestlers on the east side of the arena drew in their breath.

Ground Sloth Ikimoto was a vegetarian and always had been. In training for traditional sumo, he had shunned the *chunkonabe*, the communal stew of fish, chicken, meat, eggs, onions, cabbage, carrots, turnips, sugar, and soy sauce.

Traditional *sumotori* ate as much as they could hold twice a day, and their weight gain was tremendous.

Ikimoto had instead trained twice as hard, eating
only vegetables, starches, and sugars. Meat and eggs
had never once touched his lips.

What Killer Kudzu brought out of the box was a
cheeseburger. With one swift movement he bit into it
only half a meter from Ground Sloth's face.

Ikimoto blanched and started to scream. As he did,
he lifted into the air as if chopped in the chest with an
ax, arms and legs flailing, a wail of revulsion coming
from his emptied lungs.

He passed the bales marking the edge of the ring —
one foot dragging the ground, upending a boundary
bale — and smashed to the ground between the ring
and the bales at the plastic walls.

The referee signaled Killer Kudzu the winner. As he
squatted the *gyoji* offered him a small envelope
signifying a cash prize from his sponsors. Kudzu, left
hand on his knee, with his right hand made three
chopping gestures from the left, right, and above —
thanking man, earth, and heaven. Kudzu took the
envelope, then stepped through the doorway of the
plastic enclosure and left the arena to rejoin the other
west-side wrestlers.

The audience of eleven thousand was on its feet as
one, cheering. Across Japan and around the world,
two hundred million viewers watched television.

Ground Sloth Ikimoto had risen to his feet, bowed,
and left by the other door. Attendants rushed in to
repair the damaged ring. Man-Mountain Gentian
looked up at the scoring clock. The entire match had
taken a mere 4.1324 seconds.

It was three-twenty in the afternoon on the four

teenth day of the Tokyo invitational tournament.

The next match would pit Cast Iron Pekowski of Poland against the heavily favored Hokkaidan, Typhoon Takanaka.

After that would be Gentian's bout with the South African, Knockdown Krugerrand. Man-Mountain Gentian stood at 13-0 in the tournament, having defeated an opponent each day so far. He wanted to retire as the first Grand Champion to win six tournaments in a row, undefeated. He was not very worried about his contest with Knockdown Krugerrand slated for later this afternoon.

Tomorrow, though, the last day of the January tournament, his opponent would be Killer Kudzu, who after this match also stood undefeated at 14-0.

Man-Mountain Gentian was 1.976 meters tall and weighed exactly two hundred kilos. He had been a *sumotori* for six years, had been *yokozuna* for the last two of those. He was twice holder of the Emperor's Cup. He was the highest paid, most famous *Zensumotori* in the world.

He was twenty-three years old.

He and Knockdown Krugerrand finished their *shi-kiris*. They got on their marks. The *gyoji* flipped his fan.

The match was over in 3.1916 seconds. He helped Krugerrand to his feet, accepted the envelope and the thunderous applause of the crowd, and left the reverberating plastic enclosure.

* * *

45

"You are the wife of Man-Mountain Gentian?" asked a voice next to her.

Melissa put on her public smile and turned to the voice. Her nephew, on the other side, leaned around to look.

The man talking to her had five stars tattooed to his forehead. She knew he was a famous *sumotori*, though he was very slim and his *chon-mage* had been combed out and washed, and his hair was now a fluffy explosion above his head.

"I am Killer Kudzu," he said. "I'm surprised you weren't at the tournament."

"I am here with my nephew, Hari. Hari, this is Mr. Killer Kudzu." The nephew, dressed in his winter Little League outfit, shook hands firmly. "His team, the Mitsubishi Zeroes, will play the Kawasaki Claudes next game."

They paused while a foul ball caused great excitement a few rows down the bleachers. Hari made a stab for it, but some construction foreman of a father came up grinning triumphantly with the ball.

"And what position do you play?" asked Killer Kudzu.

"Utility outfield. When I get to play," said Hari sheepishly, averting his eyes and sitting back down.

"Oh. How's your batting average?"

"Pretty bad. One twenty-three for the year," said Hari.

"Well, maybe this will be the night you shine," Killer Kudzu said with a smile.

"I hope so," said Hari. "Half our team has the American flu."

"Just the reason I'm here," said Kudzu. "I was to

46

meet a businessman whose son was to play this game. I find him not to be here, as his son has the influenza also."

It was hot in the domed stadium, and Kudzu insisted they let him buy them Sno-Kones. Just as the vendor got to them, Hari's coach signaled, and the nephew ran down the bleachers and followed the rest of his teammates into the warm-up area under the stadium.

Soon the other lackluster game was over, and Hari's team took the field.

The first batter for the Kawasaki Claudes, a twelve-year-old built like an orangutan, got up and smashed a line drive off the Mitsubishi Zeroes' third baseman's chest. The third baseman had been waving to his mother. They carried him into the dugout. Melissa soon saw him up yelling again.

So it went through three innings. The Claudes had the Zeroes down by three runs, 6-3.

In the fourth inning, Hari took right field, injuries having whittled the flu-ridden team down to the third-stringers.

One of the Kawasaki Claudes hit a high looping fly straight to right field. Hari started in after it, but something happened with his feet; he fell, and the ball dropped a meter from his outstretched glove. The center fielder chased it down and made the relay, and by a miracle they got the runner sliding into home plate. He took out the Zeroes' catcher doing it.

"It doesn't look good for the Zeroes," said Melissa.

"Oh, things might get better," said Killer Kudzu. "Didn't you know? The opera's not over till the fat lady sings."

"A diva couldn't do much worse out there," said Melissa.

"They still don't like baseball in my country," he said. "Decadent. Bourgeois, they say. As if anything could be more decadent and middle-class than China."

"Yet, you wear the flag?" She pointed toward the tattoo on his head.

"Let's just call it a gesture to former greatness," he said.

Bottom of the seventh, last inning in Little League. The Zeroes had the bases loaded, but they incurred two outs in the process. Hari came up to bat.

Things were tense. The infield was back, ready for the force-out. The outfielders were nearly falling down from tension.

The pitcher threw a blistering curve that got the outside. Hari was caught looking.

From the dugout the manager's voice saying unkind things carried to the crowd.

Eight thousand people were on their feet.

The pitcher wound up and threw.

Hari started a swing that should have ended in a grounder or a pop-up. Halfway through, it looked as if someone had speeded up a projector. The leisurely swing blurred.

Hari literally threw himself to the ground. The bat cracked and broke neatly in two at his feet.

The ball, a frozen white streak, whizzed through the air and hit the scoreboard one hundred ten meters away with a terrific crash, putting the inning indicator out of commission.

Everyone was stock-still. Hari was staring. Every

48

player was turned toward the scoreboard.

"It's a home run, kid," the umpire reminded Hari.

Slowly, unbelieving, Hari began to trot toward first base.

The place exploded, fans jumping to their feet. Hari's teammates on the bases headed for home. The dugout emptied, waiting for him to round third.

The Claudes stood dejected. The Zeroes climbed all over Hari.

"I didn't know you could do that more than once a day," said Melissa, her eyes narrowed.

"Who, me?" asked Kudzu.

"You're perverting your talent," she said.

"We're *not* supposed to be able to do that more than once every twenty-four hours," said Kudzu, flashing a smile.

"I know that's not true, at least really," said Melissa.

"Oh, yes. You are *married* to a *sumotori*, aren't you?"

Melissa blushed.

"The kid seemed to feel bad enough about that fly ball he dropped in the fourth inning. Besides, it's just a game."

At home plate, Hari's teammates congratulated him, slapping him on the back.

The game was over, the scoreboard said 7–6, and the technicians were already climbing over the inning indicator.

Melissa rose. "I have to go pick up Hari. I suppose I will see you at the tournament tomorrow."

"How are you getting home?" asked Killer Kudzu.

"We walk. Hari lives near."

"It's snowing."

"Oh."

"Let me give you a ride. My electric vehicle is outside."

"That would be nice. I live several kilometers away from —"

"I know where you live, of course."

"Fine, then."

Hari ran up. "Aunt Melissa! Did you see? I don't know what happened! I just felt, I don't know, I just hit it!"

"That was wonderful." She smiled at him. Killer Kudzu was looking up, very interested in the stadium support structure.

The stable in which Man-Mountain Gentian trained was being entertained that night. That meant that the wrestlers would have to do all the entertaining.

Even at the top of his sport, Man-Mountain had never gotten used to the fans. Their kingly prizes, their raucous behavior at matches, their donations of gifts, clothing, vehicles, and in some cases houses and land to their favorite wrestlers. It was all appalling to him.

It was a carry-over from traditional sumo, he knew. But Zen-sumo had become a worldwide, not just a national, sport. Many saved for years to come to Japan to watch the January or May tournaments. People here in Japan sometimes sacrificed at home to be able to contribute toward new *kesho-mawashis*, elaborate, heavy brocade and silk aprons used in the wrestlers' ring-entering ceremonies.

Money, in this business, flowed like water, appearing in small envelopes in the mail, in the locker room, after feasts such as the one tonight.

Once a month Man-Mountain Gentian gathered them all up and took them to his accountant, who had instructions to give it all, above a certain princely level, away to charity. Other wrestlers had more, or less, or none of the same arrangements. The tax men never seemed surprised by whatever amount wrestlers reported.

He entered the club. Things were already rocking. One of the hostesses took his shoes and coat. She had to put the overcoat over her shoulders to carry it into the cloakroom.

The party was a haze of blue smoke, dishes, bottles, businessmen, wrestlers, and funny paper hats. Waitresses came in and out with more food. Three musicians played unheard on a raised dais at one side of the room.

Someone was telling a snappy story. The room exploded with laughter.

"Ah!" said someone. "*Yokozuna* Gentian has arrived."

Man-Mountain bowed deeply. They made two or three places for him at the low table. He saw that several of the host party were Americans. Probably one or more were from the CIA.

They and the Russians were still trying to perfect Zen-sumo as an assassination weapon. They offered active and retired *sumotori* large amounts of money in an effort to get them to develop their powers in some nominally destructive form. So far, no one he

51

knew of had. There were rumors about the Brazilians, however.

He could see it now, a future with premiers, millionaires, presidents, and paranoids in all walks of life wearing wire-mesh clothing and checking their Eveready batteries before going out each morning.

He had been approached twice, by each side. He was sometimes followed. They all were. People in governments simply did not understand.

He began to talk, while sake flowed, with Cast Iron Pekowski. Pekowski, now 12-2 for the tournament, had graciously lost his match with Typhoon Takanaka. (There was an old saying: In a tournament, no one who won more than nine matches ever beat an opponent who has lost seven. That had been the case with Takanaka. Eight was the number of wins needed to maintain current ranking.)

"I could feel him going," said Pekowski, in Polish. "I think we should talk to him about the May tournament."

"Have you mentioned this to his stablemaster?"

"I thought of doing so after the tournament. I was hoping you could come with me to see him."

"I'll be just another retired wrestler by then."

"Takanaka respects you above all the others. Your *dampatsu-shiki* ceremony won't be for another two weeks. They won't have cut off all your hair yet. And while we're at it, I still wish you would change your mind."

"Perhaps I could be Takanaka's dew sweeper and carry his ceremonial cloth for him when he enters his last tournament. I would be honored."

"Good! You'll come with me then, Friday morning?"

"Yes."

The hosts were much drunker than the wrestlers. Nayakano the stablemaster was feeling no pain but still remained upright. Mounds of food were being consumed. A businessman tried to grab-ass a waitress. This was going to become every bit as nasty as all such parties.

"A song! A song!" yelled the head of the fan club, a businessman in his sixties. "Who will favor us with a song?"

Man-Mountain Gentian got to his feet, went over to the musicians. He talked with the samisen player. Then he stood facing his drunk, attentive audience.

How many of these parties had he been to in his career? Two, three hundred? Always the same, drunkenness, discord, braggadocio on the part of the host clubs. Some fans really loved the sport, some lived vicariously through it. He would not miss the parties. But as the player began the tune he realized this might be the last party he would have to face.

He began to sing.

"I met my lover by still Lake Biwa
just before Taira war banners flew . . ."

And so on through all six verses, in a clear, pure voice belonging to a man half his size.

They stood and applauded him, some of the wrestlers in the stable looking away, as only they, not even the stablemaster, knew of his retirement plans and what this party probably meant.

He went to the stablemaster, who took him to the

club host, made apologies concerning the tournament and a slight cold, shook hands, bowed, and went out into the lobby, where the hostess valiantly brought him his shoes and overcoat. He wanted to help her, but she reshouldered the coat grimly and brought it to him.

He handed her a tip and signed the autograph she asked for.

It had begun to snow outside. The neon made the sky a swirling, multicolored smudge. Man-Mountain Gentian walked through the quickly emptying streets. Even the ever-present taxis scurried from the snow like roaches from a light. His home was only two kilometers away. He liked the stillness of the falling snow, the quietness of the city in times such as these.

"Shelter for a stormy night?" asked a ragged old man on a corner. Man-Mountain Gentian stopped.

"Change for shelter for an old man?" asked the beggar again, looking very far up at Gentian's face.

Man-Mountain Gentian reached in his pocket and took out three or four small ornate paper envelopes that had been thrust on him as he left the club.

The old man took them, opened one. Then another and another.

"There must be more than eight hundred thousand yen here," he said, very quietly and very slowly.

"I suggest either the Imperial or the Hilton," said Man-Mountain Gentian, then the wrestler turned and walked away.

The old man laughed, then straightened himself with dignity, stepped to the curb, and imperiously summoned an approaching pedicab.

Melissa was not home.

He turned on the entry light as he took off his shoes. He passed through the sparsely furnished, low living room, turned off the light at the other switch.

He went to the bathroom, put depilatory gel on his face, wiped it off.

He went to the kitchen, picked up half a ham, and ate it, washing it down with three liters of milk. He returned to the bathroom, brushed his teeth, went to the bedroom, unrolled his futon, and placed his cinder block at the head of it.

He punched a button on the hidden tape deck, and an old recording of Kimio Eto playing "Rukodan" on the koto quietly filled the house.

The only decoration in the sleeping room was Shuncho's print *The Strongest and the Most Fair*, showing a theater-district beauty and a *sumotori* three times her size; it was hanging on the far wall.

He turned off the light. Instantly the silhouettes of falling snowflakes showed through the paper walls of the house, cast by the strong streetlight outside. He watched the snowflakes fall as he listened to the music, and he was filled with *mono no aware* for the transience of beauty in the world.

Man-Mountain Gentian pulled up the puffed cotton covers, put his head on the building block, and drifted off to sleep.

They had let Hari off at his house. The interior of the runabout was warm. They were drinking coffee in the near-empty parking lot of Tokyo Sonic #113.

"I read somewhere you were an architect," said Killer Kudzu.

"Barely," said Melissa.

"Would you like to see Kudzu House?" he asked.

For an architect, it was like being asked to one of Frank Lloyd Wright's vacation homes or one of the birdlike buildings designed by Eero Saarinen in the later twentieth century. Melissa considered.

"I should call home first," she said after a moment.

"I think your husband will still be at the Nue Vue Club, whooping it up with the money men."

"You're probably right. I'll call him later. I'd love to see your house."

The old man lay dying on his bed.

"I see you finally heard," he said. His voice was tired.

Man-Mountain Gentian had not seen him in seven years. He had always been old, but he had never looked this old, this weak.

Dr. Wu had been his mentor. He had started him on the path toward Zen-sumo (though he did not know it at the time). Dr. Wu had not been one of those cryptic koan-spouting quiet men. He had been boisterous, laughing, playing with his pupils, yelling at them, whatever was needed to get them to see.

There had been the occasional letter from him. Now, for the first time, there was a call in the middle of the night.

"I'm sorry," said Man-Mountain Gentian. "It's snowing outside."

"At your house, too?" asked Dr. Wu.

Wu's attendant was dressed in Buddhist robes and seemingly paid no attention to either of them.

"Is there anything I can do for you?" asked Man-Mountain Gentian.

"Physically, no. This is nothing a pain shift can help. Emotionally, there is."

"What?"

"You can win tomorrow, though I won't be around to share it."

Man-Mountain Gentian was quiet a moment. "I'm not sure I can promise you that."

"I didn't think so. You are forgetting the kitten and the bowl of milk."

"No. Not at all. I think I've finally come up against something new and strong in the world. I will either win or lose. Either way, I will retire."

"If it did not mean anything to you, you could have lost by now," said Dr. Wu.

Man-Mountain Gentian was quiet again.

Wu shifted uneasily on his pillows. "Well, there is not much time. Lean close. Listen carefully to what I have to say.

"The novice Itsu went to the Master and asked him, 'Master, what is the key to all enlightenment?'

" 'You must teach yourself never to think of the white horse,' said the Master.

"Itsu applied himself with all his being. One day while raking gravel, he achieved insight.

" 'Master! Master!' yelled Itsu, running to the Master's quarters. 'Master, I have made myself not think about the white horse!'

" 'Quick!' said the Master. 'When you were not thinking of the horse, where was Itsu?'

57

"The novice could make no answer.

"The Master dealt Itsu a smart blow with his staff.

"At this, Itsu was enlightened."

Then Dr. Wu let his head back down on his bed.

"Good-bye," he said.

In his bed in the lamasery in Tibet, Dr. Wu let out a ragged breath and died.

Man-Mountain Gentian, standing in his bedroom in Tokyo, began to cry.

Kudzu House took up a city block in the middle of Toyko. The taxes alone must have been enormous.

Through the decreasing snow, Melissa saw the lights. Their beams stabbed up into the night. All that she could see from a block away was the tangled kudzu.

Kudzu was a vine, originally transplanted from China, raised in Japan for centuries. Its crushed root was used as a starch base in cooking; its leaves were used for teas and medicines; its fibers, to make cloth and paper.

What kudzu was most famous for was its ability to grow over and cover anything that didn't move out of its way.

In the Depression Thirties of the last century, it had been planted on road cuts in the southeastern United States to stop erosion. Kudzu had almost stopped progress there. In those ideal conditions it grew runners more than twenty meters long in a single summer, several to a root. Its vines climbed utility poles, hills, trees. It completely covered other vegetation, cutting off its sunlight.

58

Many places in the American south were covered three kilometers wide to each side of the highways with kudzu vines. The Great Kudzu Forest of central Georgia was a U.S. national park.

In the bleaker conditions of Japan the weed could be kept under control. Except that this owner didn't want it to. The lights playing into the snowy sky were part of the heating and watering system that kept vines growing year-round. All this Melissa had read. Seeing it was something again. The entire block was a green tangle of vines and lights.

"Do you ever trim it?" she asked.

"The traffic keeps it back," said Killer Kudzu, and he laughed. "I have gardeners who come in and fight it once a week. They're losing."

They went into the green tunnel of a driveway. Melissa saw the edge of the house, cast concrete, as they dropped into the sunken vehicle area.

There were three boats, four road vehicles, a Hovercraft, and a small sport flyer parked there.

Lights shone up into a dense green roof from which hundreds of vines grew downward toward the light sources.

"We have to move the spotlights every week," he said.

A butler met them at the door. "Just a tour, Mord," said Killer Kudzu. "We'll have drinks in the sitting room in thirty minutes."

"Very good, sir."

"This way."

Melissa went to a railing. The living area was the size of a bowling alley, or the lobby of a terrible old hotel.

The balcony on the second level jutted out from the east wall. Killer Kudzu went to a console, punched buttons.

Moe and the Meanies boomed from dozens of speakers.

Killer Kudzu stood snapping his fingers for a moment. "Oh, send me! Honorable cats!" he said. "That's from Spike Jones, an irreverent American musician of the last century. He died of cancer," he added.

Melissa followed him, noticing the things everyone noticed—the Chrome Room, the Supercharger Inhalorium, the archery range ("the object is *not* to hit the targets," said Kudzu), the Mososaur Pool with the fossils embedded in the sides and bottom.

She was more affected by the house and its overall tawdriness than she thought she would be.

"You've done very well for yourself."

"Some manage it, some give it away, some save it. I *spend* it."

They were drinking kudzu-tea highballs in the sitting room, which was one of the most comfortable rooms Melissa had ever been in.

"Tasteless, isn't it?" asked Killer Kudzu.

"Not quite," said Melissa. "It was well worth the trip."

"You could stay, you know," said Kudzu.

"I thought I could." She sighed. "It would only give me one more excuse not to finish the dishes at home." She gave him a long look. "No, thank you. Besides, it wouldn't give you an advantage in the match."

"That really never crossed my mind."

"I'm quite sure."

60

"You are a beautiful woman."

"You have a nice house."

"Hmmm. Time to get you home."

"I'm sure."

They sat outside her house in the cold. The snow had stopped. Stars peeped through the low scud.

"I'm going to win tomorrow, you know," said Killer Kudzu.

"You might," said Melissa.

"It is sometimes possible to do more than win," he said.

"I'll tell my husband."

"My offer is always open," he said. He reached over and opened her door on the runabout. "Life won't be the same after he's lost. Or after he retires."

She climbed out, shaking from more than the cold. He closed the door, whipped the vehicle in a circle, and was gone down the crunching street. He blinked his lights once before he drove out of sight.

She found her husband in the kitchen. His eyes were red, he was as pale as she had ever seen him.

"Dr. Wu is dead," he said, and wrapped his huge arms around her, covering her like an upright sofa.

He began to cry again. She talked to him quietly.

"Come to bed. Let's try to get some sleep," she said.

"No, I couldn't rest. I wanted to see you first. I'm going down to the stable." She helped him dress in his warmest clothing. He kissed her and left, walking the

61

few blocks through the snowy sidewalks to the training building.

The junior wrestlers were awakened at four A.M. They were to begin the day's work of sweeping, cleaning, cooking, bathing, feeding, and catering to the senior wrestlers. When they came in they found him, stripped to his *mawashi*, at the three-hundred-kilo push bag, pushing, pushing, straining, crying all the while, not saying a word. The floor of the arena was torn and grooved.

They cleared up the area for the morning workouts, one junior wrestler following him around with the sand trowel.

At seven A.M. he slumped exhausted on a bench. Two of the *juryo* covered him with quilts and set an alarm clock beside him for one in the afternoon.

"Your opponent was at the ball game last night," said Nayakano the stablemaster. Man-Mountain Gentian sat in the dressing room while the barber combed and greased his elaborate *chon-mage*. "Your wife asked me to give you this."

It was a note in a plain envelope, addressed in her beautiful calligraphy. He opened and read it.

Her letter warned him of what Kudzu said about "more than winning" the night before, and wished him luck.

He turned to the stablemaster.

"Had Killer Kudzu injured any opponent before he became *yokozuna* last tournament?" Man-Mountain asked.

Nayakano's answer was immediate. "No. That's unheard of. Let me see that note." He reached out.

Man-Mountain Gentian put it back in the envelope, tucked it in his *mawashi*.

"Should I alert the judges?"

"Sorry, I shouldn't have mentioned it," said Man-Mountain Gentian.

"I don't like this," said the stablemaster.

Three hefty junior wrestlers ran in to the dressing room carrying Gentian's *kesho-mawashi* between them.

The last day of the January tournament always packed them in. Even the *maegashira* and *komusubi* matches, in which young boys threw each other, or tried to, drew enough of an audience to make the novices feel good.

The call for the *ozeki*-class wrestlers came, and they went through the grandiose ring-entering ceremony, wearing their great *kesho-mawashi* aprons of brocade, silk, and gold, while their dew sweepers and sword-bearers squatted to the sides.

Then they retired to their benches, east or west, to await the call by the falsetto-voiced *yobidashi*.

Man-Mountain Gentian watched as the assistants helped Killer Kudzu out of his ceremonial apron, gold with silk kudzu leaves, purple flowers, yellow stars. His forehead blazed with the People's Republic of China flag.

He looked directly at Gentian's place and smiled a broad, crooked smile.

There was a great match between Gorilla Tsunami

63

and Typhoon Takanaka, which went on for more than thirty seconds by the clock, both men straining, groaning, sweating until the *gyoji* made them stop, and rise, and then get on their marks again.

Those were the worst kinds of matches for the wrestlers, each opponent alternately straining, then bending with the other, neither getting advantage. There was a legendary match five years ago which took six thirty-second tries before one wrestler bested the other.

The referee flipped his fan. Gorilla Tsunami fell flat on his face in a heap, then wriggled backwards out of the ring.

The crowd screamed and applauded Takanaka.

Then the *yobidashi* said, "East — Man-Mountain Gentian. West — Killer Kudzu."

They hurried their *shikiris*. Each threw salt twice, rinsing once. Then Man-Mountain Gentian, moving with the grace of a dancer, lifted his right leg and stamped it, then his left, and the sound was like the double echo of a cannon throughout the stadium.

He went immediately to his mark.

Killer Kudzu jumped down to his mark, glaring at his opponent across the meter that separated them.

The *gyoji*, off guard, took a few seconds to turn sideways to them and bring his fan into position.

In that time, Man-Mountain Gentian could hear the quiet hum of the electrical grid, hear muffled intake of breath from the other wrestlers, hear a whistle in the nostril of the north-side judge.

"Huuu!" said the referee, and his fan jerked.

Man-Mountain Gentian felt as though two freight trains had collided in his head. There was a snap as his muscles went tense all over and the momentum of the explosion in his brain began to push at him, lifting, threatening to make him give or tear through the back of his head.

His feet were on a slippery, sandy bottom, neck-high wave crests smashed into him, a rip tide was pushing at his shoulder, at one side, pulling his legs up, twisting his muscles. He could feel his eyes pushed back in their sockets as if by iron thumbs, ready to pop them like ripe plums. His ligaments were iron wires stretched tight on the turnbuckles of his bones. His arms ended in strands of noodles, his face was soft cheese.

The sand under him was soft, so soft, and he knew that all he had to do was to sink in it, let go, cease to exist.

And through all that haze and blindness he knew what it was that he was not supposed to think about.

Everything quit: He reached out one mental hand, as big as the sun, as fast as light, as long as time, and he pushed against his opponent's chest.

The lights were back, he was in the stadium, in the arena, and the dull pounding was applause, screams.

Killer Kudzu lay blinking among the ring bales.

"Hooves?" Man-Mountain Gentian heard him ask in bewilderment before he picked himself up.

Man-Mountain Gentian took the envelope from the referee with three quick chopping motions, then made a fourth to the audience, and they knew then and only then that they would never see him in the ring again.

The official clock said 0.9981 second.

"How did you do it, Man-Mountain?" asked the Tokyo paparazzi as the wrestler showered out his *chon-mage* and put on his clothes. He said nothing.

He met his wife outside the stadium. A lone newsman was waiting for her, "Scoop" Hakimoto.

"For old times' sake," begged Hakimoto. "How did you do it?"

Man-Mountain Gentian turned to Melissa. "Tell him how I did it," he said.

"He didn't think about the white horse," she said. They left the newsman standing there, staring.

Killer Kudzu, tired and pale, was getting in his vehicle. Hakimoto came running up. "What's all this I hear about Gentian and a white horse?" he asked.

Kudzu's eyes widened, then narrowed.

"No comment," he said.

That night, to celebrate, Man-Mountain Gentian took Melissa to the Beef Bowl.

He had seventeen orders and helped Melissa finish her second one.

They went back home, climbed onto their futons, and turned on the TV.

Gilligan was on his island. All was right with the world.

RETURNING HOME

By Ian Watson

Thank God, the runway was clear. An Aeroflot crew had apparently touched down just moments before a radiation bomb went off overhead. But the pilot's nervous system lasted long enough for him to steer his plane off the concrete onto grass—unless he had merely swerved.

Anyway, our landing was a pushover. As well it needed to be, with upwards of thirty million displaced Americans pushing behind us. There were two hundred of us packed into our plane—with a second Ilyushin to follow some hours later.

Most wonderful of all, there was no reception committee of Chinese waiting for us. So those Canadian bastards hadn't been lying after all. The Chinese hadn't flooded over the frontier to fill up this spur of the Soviet Union. And yet somehow we hadn't *believed* that the Chinese would. It was as if the spirit that impelled us toward the East had promised us this

67

land and had preserved it for us.

Leaving Group Red at the airport, the rest of us rounded up some brand-new buses, got them going, and drove in convoy into downtown Khabarovsk— ending up outside the Far East Hotel on Karl Marx Street, which seemed as good a place as any other to billet ourselves for the time being.

There weren't too many shriveled mummies in the streets. The streets themselves were reasonably clean and neat. The human animal seemed to prefer to die in its burrow, if it could get there in time.

I'd just told Hank Sullivan to take a fatigue squad round the hotel to clear all the bodies they found into a single room and was getting the others organized, when Mary cried out, "Greg, come over here."

She was waving the handset of an old-fashioned-looking telephone, farther down the lobby.

I hadn't been meaning to bring Mary in on the first flight. Strictly the two hundred of us were a technical spearhead, and Mary wasn't a sailor or mechanic or locomotive driver. But she was a fine survivor, and if dishing up fish and chipmunk stew or nettle-and-mushroom soup without a single pot or stove isn't a technical accomplishment, then I don't know what is.

So when she'd insisted, we'd compromised by leaving little Suzie in good hands up in Magadan for later delivery, and Mary came along as our provisions officer. She was still looking fairly gaunt—as were we all—and her blond hair had all grown out a mousy brown. But I loved her even more dearly after all that we'd been through.

"What is it?"

"The phone *works*, Greg."

I ran to her, while everyone turned to watch us, and it was then—when I got my hands on that phone and heard it humming—that it really all came home to me: *We had won through.*

Because the goddamn lovely old phone was receiving power. No doubt from some hydroelectric scheme that was still churning out electricity automatically.

"Hey, Billy Donaldson," I called across the lobby, "get your ass behind that check-in desk and find another phone along there. Call out your number."

Hitching up his Soviet Army greatcoat, redheaded Billy stepped over the assorted wizened corpses in their crumpled, dusty suits and dresses, careful not to soil the garments with his boots.

As the first pioneer group to cross the Bering Strait, we'd all got rid of our bark-and-straw boots and our stinking dog- and cowhide coats as soon as we reached the first Soviet outpost. The other scraggy survivors still converging on the tip of Alaska, this summer after the War, would have to wait just a little longer for proper clothes.

The phone box had a slot for two-kopeck pieces, but I guessed that you didn't need money for a call inside the hotel—almost as if the phone was telling me how to use it.

Billy bawled out a number, and I dialed.

"Hullo? Can you hear me, Billy?" I said.

"Sure thing."

And I saluted the phone. This was a real fantasy moment. I could almost believe that I was phoning home to the States. Only, of course, there were no phones left over there. Or cities, for that matter. But still!

69

"General Greg Berry reporting. We've reached Khabarovsk. We're on the route of the Trans-Siberian Railway! Group Red will set up an air shuttle service to Magadan tomorrow. Group White will take a train down to Vladivostok, and if there aren't any Chicoms there, either — and, so help me, I know so deep down in me there won't be any, it's as though God has told me Himself — then Group White'll sail the biggest warship they can handle out of the navy yards up to the Bering Sea. And Group Blue will get the locos rolling across the Siberian railroad. We're in business!"

We horsed around on the phone for a while like a couple of kids. But of course every word of it was true. As Mary watched, the first grin in ages appeared on her face.

It was a damned shame about last year's war, but at least now we knew that we'd won it — and forever.

As the culmination of the U.S. government's search for nondestructive nuclear weapons, which wouldn't wipe out the treasures of the world, we'd just deployed the Super-Radiation Bomb — which was as much an advance upon the neutron bomb of the Eighties as the neutron bomb was upon the unwieldly hydrogen bomb.

The SRB produced hardly any blast or heat damage; if air-burst correctly, none at all. But its short-term radiation yield was incredible — and without any residual radioactivity. One single SRB detonated over Moscow would kill every living thing in the city and its environs — apart from cockroaches and such — and

70

it would leave all the factories and apartment blocks, all the offices and shops, all the museums and churches, in perfect condition.

The Soviets, of course, denounced this at once as the "Super-Capitalist Bomb," because it respected property but not persons. And they in turn unveiled their own secretly developed superweapon, which they called the "Socialist Bomb." We called it the "SOB."

The Devil himself must have had a hand in the design of this Socialist Bomb. Its effects were far more cruel.

How exactly it did it, I don't know for sure, and we never had time fully to suss out the theory, but basically it generated a sub-atomic vibration field, perhaps at the quark level, that affected any inanimate matter that had in any way been manufactured, worked, or tailored by man, leaving a particular "signature" written in it. The SOB had no effect at all on living tissue, or landscape, or minerals in the ground, or even foodstuffs — though it put paid to the containers. But it burst the continuum, for any "made" or "shaped" article within its field. It rapidly transformed the particles in any target object into "virtual" particles so that they slipped out of existence, perhaps reemerging somewhere else in our universe, or in some parallel universe. Within minutes a thing grew soft, then foggy, then vanished away.

In other words, drop an SOB on New York City and very soon you would have no New York City at all, only an empty space with millions of people wandering around stark-naked. Yes, we would be naked to our enemies, forced to accept occupation and emergency aid.

Those of us, that is, who didn't get killed when things grew foggy. The Soviets had said that we would have about four minutes to get clear, but how could that help the crew and passengers on an airliner? They would rain down from the stratosphere. Or the office staff on the fiftieth floor of a skyscraper? They would find themselves with no floors beneath their bare feet. Or sailors, pitched into the ocean as their ship dissolved? Or the engineer of a speeding train?

These could amount to millions.

And there the cruelty was only just beginning. How many more would die in the following weeks of cold or hunger—as food rotted away—or from lack of medical attention, or from a hundred other things?

And they had the gall to call it a "humane" bomb! Even though it would destroy all civilization we knew, all the paintings in the great collections, all the highways and gas stations, all the space launch vehicles. Every laboratory, every hospital, every surfboard, oil refinery, and shopping mall, every can of Budweiser and every TV set. The Statue of Liberty, the Golden Gate Bridge, Disneyland, the lot.

Who started the War? The Soviets, without a doubt. They must have thought they could sneak up on us.

In less than an hour the U.S.A. and the USSR exchanged their entire arsenals of Radiation Bombs and SOBs.

And the Soviets were all dead.

But we were left naked, without a single possession, except what we could make with our hands subsequently from the countryside.

And nobody came to help us. God, how they must have hated us, for years! The rest of the world shunned us. They treated us as a nation of murderers, when so many of us were dying, too. No foreign ships arrived on our bare shores. No airplanes landed on our fields. The Mexicans spurned us, I hear. The Canadians fenced off their border and built a wide electrified corridor running all the way up through British Columbia into Alaska, like a double Berlin Wall. They told us to get lost.

But God has got to have been on our side. *Something*, some divine force, clearly put it into all of our heads just what we had to do, and how.

You take a nation without a penny to its name. You take that, and you take a vast country that's been completely cleaned out of people, full of empty cities and factories, airports and harbors.

You put the two things together, and what do you get?

You get a whole population marching in the only direction possible—to recover the goods they need to carry on.

You get a shivering, starving nation, dressed in dog skins and such, hauling logs north to build rafts and dugouts to cross the Bering Strait and bring back some real ships from the other side—while the first pioneers press on south, by boat or light plane or four-wheel drive, to get to *somewhere* half-decent and firm up and supply the route for all those who would follow. You get the greatest human migration ever.

And, as with animal migrations, there's an instinctive, almost *guided* aspect to it — as if our destination has been broadcasting to us. As well as broadcasting to everyone else. To leave it be! So, like superstitious peasants, it seems the Chinese have kept out of the USSR. Vladivostok is even closer to China than Khabarovsk is, but for sure we would find Vladivostok empty, too. I admit that I couldn't be one hundred percent positive of this till we arrived in Khabarovsk. But now — as I said earlier in the hotel — I felt as sure as if God had whispered in my heart. This land was reserved for us, the victors, from one shining ocean, the Pacific, to the shining Baltic Sea.

Later, since it was a golden evening and we'd all done as much as we reasonably could, I decreed four hours R and R.

Billy, Hank, and I removed a bottle of Stolichnaya vodka from the hotel kitchen and wandered out to hit the town. Mary declared she was exhausted and could do with an early night, but I think she just said so to give us boys a chance to get roaring drunk.

So we capered up Lenin Avenue to Lenin Square, admiring the silliest things: toy pedal cars on a lane around the weedy flowerbeds, abandoned ice-cream carts, rows of bright red fruit-drink machines with the syrupy goo all dried up in them, and of course a statue of *that man* with his worker's cloth cap, leaning forward into the future and looking aggressive. Hank climbed up the statue and sat piggy-back on his metal shoulders, urging him on.

We took in another public park, behind the Dynamo Football Stadium, but the mosquitoes drove us out of there. So we went window-shopping instead—which may seem a little weird for three grown men, especially as the goods in the shop windows were few and poor stuff. But, my God, actual shop windows—with *things* in them!

One of the shops was a grocer's. A *gastronom*. We were getting pretty good at picking out names of streets and buildings in the crazy Russian characters.

"I've never tasted caviar," said Billy.

"So let's find some cans of caviar," I said.

In we went. A mummy, which we took to be a shopgirl's, lay pointing a bare finger bone up at approximately the right shelf. Other mummies, in suits and raggy coats and uniforms, lay piled up against the liquor counter, and behind it; so we avoided that area. Hank scooped up half a dozen little cans, which was all there were.

"Thank you, Miss," Billy giggled nervously; so I handed him the vodka bottle to kill it. As he grabbed it, he hiccuped.

We took the cans off to a restaurant, where there weren't many corpses, and switched on the lighting, which worked, as the phone had worked, though the result was disconcertingly bright. The Russians must have like to chat to one another with searchlights shining on their faces. We sat tipsily contemplating the cans and a hand-scrawled menu, written in pencil.

"Service is sure slow," Hank joked. Producing a hook of a can opener from his Soviet uniform, he tossed this on the tablecloth for us. "I'm going to find something to wash these down." He headed for the kitchen.

Billy picked up the menu while I was working on

75

the cans. His eyes blinked like an owl's.

"*Borsch*," he pronounced in a puzzled voice, as if that menu scribbled by a drunken spider was telling him what it said. "*Salat eez Krab*. We'd better get good at this, eh, Greg? If we're going to be living in Russia for the rest of our lives."

"You know, old buddy, you're right." I nodded. "We aren't going to be able to alter all the signs and notices—"

"And diagrams and lists and warnings and instructions—"

"And *et cetera*. We aren't going to be able to change them all over into English very quickly. If ever."

Hank returned, triumphantly cradling another bottle with a red skyscraper on the label. Very like a picture of some Nineteen-thirties building in New York, except that the skyscraper was probably some state office block in Moscow, and Moscow still existed.

We caroused awhile till we heard horns hooting along the street. So we piled outside. A victory parade was heading our way. I spotted Dave Weinstock at the wheel of the leading vehicle, thumping on the horn, and glanced at my watch. Obviously Dave was heading back toward the Far East Hotel as per instructions, and he had had the bright idea of rounding up a few extra vehicles as well as sounding a bugle recall on the horns.

There were buses and trucks and a couple of private automobiles, too. I guess their radiators hadn't cracked during the previous winter. Or maybe they had, but since they were being driven only a little way round town, this wouldn't hurt them. There was quite a bit of fixing up to be done if we were going to own Volgas and Zhigulis, the way we had owned Chevys and Mustangs until last summer.

The parade was as noisy as a Fourth of July celebration.

Hank grinned. "Loud enough to wake the dead, eh?"

This made me frown. I was feeling just a little maudlin now, on account of the drink, in what I felt sure was a very Russian way. But I perked up as soon as we joined the parade, scrambling up onto a truck.

I took the bottle from Hank and waved it grandly.

"Here's a toast, you guys! To prosperity, again!"

"To railroads and liquor!" Billy shouted. "To TV sets and cigarettes. To chairs and sausages. To . . . to . . . cornucopia! To the horn of plenty!"

I didn't know that my friend Billy knew words like *cornucopia*. It sounded like a Russian word, the way he said it.

"To civilization!"

I caught hold of Billy by the lapels and gripped him tight. The streetlights had come on automatically awhile back, and Billy's big hairy face gleamed with sweat.

"We beat the Commies, Billy. The Commies took away all our property, but we took away their lives! We beat them!"

Then we laughed and wept and hugged one another. I think Major Billy Donaldson even kissed me on both cheeks, but charitably I attributed this to the drink.

77

Next morning we all assembled outside the hotel. Our numbers had been swollen overnight by the arrival of two hundred souls on the second Ilyushin. (The Ilyushin we'd come in, and a Tupolev, had already flown back north to Magadan.) The pilot of the second Ilyushin, a Captain Tom Quinn, had come into town to see the place and get some sleep. This rather annoyed me, since he should have stayed at the airport, but his sheer boyish exuberance won me over.

"It's like landing on Mars! Yes, sir, on the red planet itself! You know," he confided, "I was a bit nervous, piloting that Commie crate. But it was just as if that old plane *flew herself*. Cooool." He was wearing some dead Soviet pilot's uniform, with the Order of Soviet Aviation pinned to its breast.

"That's very nice, Captain. Now please get the hell back to the airport, would you?"

Today was railroad day. The Trans-Siberian called us. So we all piled into trucks and buses and headed off up Karl Marx Street toward Khabarovsk's train station.

As we rode, somebody started singing "When the Saints Come Marching In," and everyone joined in. Then, as our convoy was crossing Lenin Square, somehow the song changed itself into "Maryland, My Maryland." Everyone seemed to have forgotten the words and just carried on humming the tune loudly in harmony.

Oh Mary, my Mary! Mary had done wonders with our breakfasts. And the hot coffee . . . I kissed my fingers.

". . . people's flag is deepest red!" I heard a single

78

voice sing out amidst the humming. I glared at the man, and he shut up.

There were a lot of red flags hanging about. I presumed all that kind of paraphernalia would have to stay around for a while. And this set me to thinking about melting down all the statues of *that man* into something useful, such as coins, and about how good it would be to have change jingling in my pocket again, even though everything was free for the time being.

"Hey, Hank," I called. "What do you suppose we're going to do about money?"

Hank pulled out a bundle of rouble notes from his pocket. He laughed.

"Use these, eh?"

"But what about *dollars* and *cents*, for Christ's sake? Why not use *our* money?"

"Have you got any cents to make dies from? Have you got any Treasury plates to print dollars off?"

"There'll still be billions of dollars abroad."

"Electronic money, a lot of it. Anyway, it'll be worth nothing now. The foreigners aren't speaking to us, remember? And as for here" — he chuckled — "somebody seems to have hung up a real Iron Curtain, or else the whole place would be swarming."

"Maybe there's been a United Nations resolution — to quarantine the USSR?" Billy suggested.

"Just like everyone quarantined America!" Hank snapped bitterly.

"Maybe they're all scared of some smart computer firing off more Socialist Bombs?"

Hank leaned close to Billy.

"Nobody can breathe the air here but us. I *know*

79

it." He flourished the Russian money. "So I figure we'll use this stuff as soon as we get organized. We can *call* the roubles bucks and the kopecks cents."

"Be easier to call them roubles and kopecks," Billy observed. "After all, that's what's printed on them. Don't want to confuse the growing kids."

Billy was in sheer ecstasy as soon as we climbed aboard one of the green passenger cars of the *Vostok*, sitting on the southbound track in the cavernous train station. We'd worried that a lot of trains might have been in transit at the time the radiation bombs went off and had run on mindlessly through the steppes and forests. But here was the *Vostok*, just waiting for us.

And opulent wasn't the word. This was a veritable mobile palace of the tracks. Solid brass fittings everywhere. Mahogany woodwork. Thick Turkish carpets on the floors. Golden curtains hanging at the windows. Red plush seats—even the swingdown ones along the corridors.

"Holy Moses! It's like some giant Cunard liner from the Nineteen-twenties or Thirties! Group White's going to ride into Vladivostok in style."

Billy fingered everything rapturously. Well, so did I. Here was everything that we'd been dreaming about, in a crazed way, for months. All here, just waiting for us to use.

"Of course," I had to remind Billy gently, "the whole USSR isn't *all* like this . . ."

"Well, hell, but even so! I mean, things, things, lovely *things*! It's Las Vegas and Hollywood and—everything they took away from us!"

Finally Billy tore himself away from the passenger

accommodation, and we were able to go up front to get a report on the Czech diesel loco.

Group White, with Billy in command, trundled out of Khabarovsk station a couple of hours later, the CHS4 that pulled the cars hooting deliriously. By then we had manned the switch tower with — well, I was going to say with a skeleton crew. But it already had that, of course. Once out of Khabarovsk, Group White would have to stop and switch any points themselves.

Getting the Khabarovsk station running again was all suddenly so easy. Murphy's Law seemed to fly right out the window. The machinery practically *told* us what we were supposed to do with it.

That was all four heroic months ago.

It's been an unexpectedly long summer and unseasonably benign fall in the north of the world, and what we've accomplished matches the building of the Trans-Siberian Railway itself — or the construction of the great hydroelectric scheme at Bratsk.

We've ferried fifty million-plus survivors down to Vladivostok in the superb Soviet Navy ships. (And late stragglers were still turning up at Nome, Alaska, till quite recently. No doubt there'll be another, smaller flood into Alaska next season.)

We've settled them in Vladivostok itself, and here in Khabarovsk, and down river at Komsomolsk, and along the railroad line as far out as Chita and Ulan-Ude and Irkutsk, near the shore of Lake Baikal, and up around Bratsk. Some have even got as far as Tomsk and Novosibirsk.

Of course, everybody has to work damn hard, each according to his or her capacity. But we've all put on weight — or fat, at any rate. And we've put on a different style of clothing, too, now that the Siberian winter's here at last. We stride, or waddle about, bundled in long, thick coats, with fur hats on our heads, and earmuffs.

We've managed to reestablish a money economy, and we *are* having to use these darned kopecks and roubles.

We drink vodka and sweet champagne, since that's what the distilleries turn out. We eat black bread and pickled sturgeon and red cabbage and such, since that's what appears on the shelves these days.

I'm stamping up and down the platform in Khabarovsk station, waiting to meet the "nine-thirty-five P.M." train from Irkutsk. Mary, whom I've begun calling Mariya lately, has a very useful and quite easy job as a conductress. (Little Sasha's in the crèche; we'll collect her soon.) There's snow on the tracks, and the air is full of white flakes.

Like a storm of souls blowing about.

Here she comes: the pride of Russia, headlamps aglow through the blizzard.

By my watch it's exactly four-thirty-five A.M.. As usual, the train's exactly on time.

That's Moscow time, of course. The Trans-Siberian line has always run according to Moscow time. We haven't gone as far as Moscow yet, but this fact reminds us of Moscow, and the West, awaiting us.

The *Rossiya* glides to a silent halt.

Mariya lets down the steps of her carriage, and the passengers stumble off, their breath clouding the air like so many mobile samovars. They're clutching cardboard suitcases and huge food packages tied with string. As soon as Mariya's replacement has clambered on board, she herself descends.

Beaming, though shivering somewhat in her railway uniform, she waddles to me.

"Grigori! Grigorooshka!"

Ghosts . . .

Suddenly I'm terrified, as if the snow has abruptly parted, right up to the heavens, and I have seen the skull of the moon rushing down to Earth to crush us.

For when the bomb exploded at Hiroshima, many people's silhouettes were etched into walls, as if the shadows of the dead were photographed by the fireball.

And everything around us—railroad engines, oil refineries, lumber mills, dams and turbines, bakeries and distilleries—is likewise imprinted invisibly by the radiation, with all the Soviets dead. I *know*—for a fleeting moment—that every building and machine and thing we use is alive, possessed. Locomotives, *gastronoms*, buses and tractors, offices and ice-cream carts and rouble notes, all tell us what to do, and the way to do it. The whole environment, of Russian making, sucked up their souls for safekeeping, and now they have entered us, like dybbuks. Why else the craze among us for Russian words and phrases, and the way these seem to well up, and link up, almost spontaneously?

That's why no Chinese came here. The land didn't want them. It wanted us, so that we could have a long time to repent.

Only there aren't enough of us to go round. So we'll have to work hard to build up our great nation.

This brief waking nightmare fades as soon as Mariya crushes me to her in her stout arms.

Drawing back, she peers at me, a concerned look on her face.

"*Shto svami*, Grigorishka?"

"Nothing's the matter, Mariya. *Nichivo!*"

Farther down the train, the driver leans from his cab.

"So long, there!" he calls along to my wife. "*Dasvidaniya, tovarich!*" Good-bye, comrade.

America is as wild and empty and far away as it was a hundred thousand years ago before any Asians first traversed the Bering Strait to roam the American plains as Indians. America is a forgotten country. Mother Russia is our land, and we are hers.

Good-bye, several hundred million dead souls. Good-bye, and hullo.

Mariya links arms with me, and off we march. Like two puppets on a stage. But no strings dangle from the roof, directing us. By now the strings are in our muscles and our nerves. And in our minds.

TRICERATOPS

By Kono Tensei

English translation by David Lewis

The father and son were returning from cycling. They had set out together on a Sunday of deepening autumn, heading for the cycling course along the river. On the way back they had been forced to burrow through the exhaust and dust of the national highway before finally reaching the residential area a mile from home. Their house lay beyond this slightly aging neighborhood, on the other side of the small hill, in the new subdivision.

It was only a little past seven, but the autumn sun was sinking quickly and darkness had begun to gather about them. The father and son stopped their bikes beneath the yellow light of the streetlamps and breathed the cool air in deeply.

"Are you okay, Dad?"

"My knees are ready to fall apart. Let me rest a minute."

"I don't feel a thing."

"I guess you wouldn't," said the father. He smiled wryly as he lit a cigarette.

"Somebody's making curry!" his son cried suddenly. "I'm starving to death. Can't we go now? It's just a little bit farther."

"I guess so."

The father crushed out the cigarette with the tip of his shoe and put his hands back on the black handlebars. It was at the instant the father and son had put one foot to the pedals, at the instant they were looking down the road ahead of them, were beginning to gather momentum, a huge shadow darted across the intersection no more than five or six meters away, shaking the very earth as it passed.

It had the feeling of mass, of power, of a bulldozer, of a ten-ton truck.

Though its passage took but an instant, it indelibly burned on their eyes an image of thick, clearly animal skin, an almost slimy sheen, the quiver of flesh and muscle.

Hands still tightly gripping the handlebars, the father and son lowered their feet from the pedals and stared.

Thick dust swirled beneath the streetlamps. The tremors gradually subsided.

It seemed a subterranean rumbling still growled about them.

Then, quite abruptly, even that rumbling stopped.

It stopped with a slightly unnatural air, almost as though a tape recording had been suddenly switched off, but in any case it had ceased, and their surroundings filled again with crying babies, the smell of dinner cooking, raucous TV commercials.

Shall we . . . ?

The father asked with his eyes, and his son nodded.

They stopped their bikes at the intersection and looked ahead.

A scattering of streetlamps threw down hazy light. Traces of gas and watermain work were everywhere around them. The road stretched on with its splitting asphalt, returned to silence.

"Where'd it go?" the son asked.

"Aaah."

The father shook his head.

The two of them were silent for a while.

"Dad, what do you think it was?"

"I don't know."

"I almost thought it was a rhinoceros. It was too big to be a cow. It looked seven or eight meters long. And if my eyes weren't fooling me, it was twice as high as this fence. That would make it three meters, uh-uh, even taller."

"Aaah," said the father again. "I guess a rhino might get loose from the zoo sometimes. It's not impossible. But didn't you see two horns on that thing's head?"

"Horns? Yeah, it did look like two horns."

"So it couldn't be a rhinoceros."

"So it was a cow after all? A bull?"

"It must be. You don't see many of them anymore, but it's my guess a bull got loose from some farm or pasture near here."

"Yeah."

"Well, if it keeps on like that, there's going to be one whale of an accident when it meets a truck."

"Yeah."

The father and soon looked back down the road. They listened. But aside from the cheerful night noises with their tales of domestic peace and tranquillity, there were no hints of anything amiss in the town.

Almost as though it never happened.

The father shook his head.

If I'd been alone, I'd have thought I was hallucinating.

After a long while the father and son pedaled silently and hurried along the road home. The street began its gradual ascent, and they stopped several times to rest.

The town spread out behind them. They turned and looked back, but there were no signs of anything unusual, no accusing shadows, and nowhere a trembling of the earth, a rising plume of dust.

"Dad, did you see the tail?" the son asked suddenly.

"Mmmm, what about it?"

"Didn't you see it? A superfat tail?"

The father and son reached the crest of the hill and passed through the last sparse copse of trees.

Suddenly their own subdivision lay before them.

The lights were on in all the new houses of the new town, but somehow—perhaps because of the sharp glare of the scattered mercury-vapor lamps—the homes seemed to hunch stockily against the earth.

The mother had dinner ready for them.

"Oh, come on now. Was it really that big?"

Chopsticks in midair, the mother eyed the father

and son across the dinner table.

"It was! It was so big I thought it was a rhino."

"Well, it's terrible if it's true. The whole town must be in an uproar."

"Actually there wasn't any at all. Even the running noise stopped, just like that."

"That's right. It stopped like we'd never heard a thing."

"But that's impossible. Oh, I see now. That's why you two were so interested in the news all of a sudden. And did they say anything about it on the news?"

"Not a thing. But it may be too early, too soon, for it to get on the news."

"Boy, it's gotta get on the news! Look, it's seven, eight meters long for sure, and at least three meters high."

"I think you're just exaggerating. Really, have you ever seen or even heard of a cow that big? This isn't a joke, is it? You're not playing games with me?"

"We are not. Anyway, we saw it for sure. Didn't we, Dad?"

"Absolutely. If that was a cow, it'd be a cinch there'd be steaks for five hundred people or more."

"Oh, stop it this instant! You *are* joking."

The mother laughed shrilly, and the father and son looked at each other, their expressions strangely vague.

After a while the father also laughed, dryly, shortly.

"Well, it hardly matters. There was a little earthquake; then that thing went zipping by. So we got a good shock out of it. Maybe the shadows threw us off, made it look bigger than it was. All that's really certain is that it wasn't a dog or a pig or some animal like that, but a really big rascal, right?"

"Yeah." The son nodded, still not quite satisfied, and began to work his chopsticks.

A variety show was on the television screen. A skimpily clad Eurasian girl was weaving her arms and legs as she sang, almost howled, in a strange, strained voice. The wife laughed shrilly again.

"What is it?"

"The singer, she just blew her nose!"

"Her nose?"

"Oh, come on! You were just telling me about it yesterday, weren't you? You said this girl sometimes blows her nose when she's straining too hard. I thought I'd never heard anything so stupid in my life, but really just now she blew her nose. I, oh, it's too *funny*!"

The mother rolled with laughter again.

The father and son smiled tightly and lowered their eyes.

The father stayed up nearly half that night, drinking. His wife and son had gone to bed, but he, somehow unable to sleep, rose and, putting his legs up to the electric heater in the living room, propped himself up on one arm and began to drink leisurely away at the whiskey he poured little by little into his glass. The last news of the day started on the television, left on since early evening, but, as expected, there was no mention of the shadow they had seen.

Were they really just seeing things?

The alcohol seeped through every cell in his aching

90

muscles, slowly tanning his exhausted body like leather. At least that was how it felt to the father as he continued to watch the shifting screen.

At some point he dozed off.

Someone was blowing his nose. Gradually the noise grew rougher, increasing in violence until it sounded like bellows. *This is no joke. No singer's going to blow her nose like that. This is one heck of a dream.* Half-asleep, half-awake, his mind spun idly.

Eventually the noise was joined by a low moan, shameless and huge, as though echoing from inside a mammoth cave. *No way. This isn't that singer's voice. What's going on?*

His eyes snapped open.

A moan.

A noise like a bellows.

And the sounds continued.

He looked at the television set. The station was already off the air, and the screen held a sandstorm of cracking light. He turned it off and listened.

The noise was coming from outside.

The father peered through a crack in the curtains.

Scraggly potted plants filled the little garden, no larger than a cat's forehead. Beyond the hedge loomed a huge black shadow, with an eye that glittered piercingly in the dark.

It did look a little like a rhinoceros.

But the horn on its nose was even sharper than a rhino's, and beneath it the mouth curved like a raptor's beak, and from that mouth puffed violent white breath like a steam locomotive.

The head was fully a third the size of the body, resembling a buffalo's. Two long horns jutted out like spears, but the turned-up, helmetlike shield between the head and abdomen was like that of no other animal he had ever seen.

A door opened.

The father turned to find his son standing in the room. The boy had pulled his trousers on over his pajamas, and he looked soberly at his father as he pushed one arm into his sweater.

"Is it there?" the son asked in a low voice.

"Yes."

The father jerked his jaw in the direction of the shadow outside.

The mammoth animal scratched the fence twice, three times with the tips of its horns, then slowly swung its side toward them. It began to walk. Like a heavy tank moving out for a night battle.

The dark brown back, the hips, the thick, heavy tail like a giant lizard's trailing down from those hips, all these passed slowly through their field of vision. The quiver of muscle beneath thick skin.

"That's not a cow or rhino," said the son, his voice sticking in his throat.

"It seems to be a dinosaur. That's all I can think of."

"If it's really a dinosaur, then I've seen it in my books. It's a famous one. Not *Allosaurus*, not *Stegosaurus*—"

"This one's beak is pointed, but its teeth don't look like much."

"It has a mouth like a beak?"

"That's right."

"Then it's *Triceratops*! Isn't that right, Dad! *Triceratops*. It means the three-horned dinosaur. The nose horn and two on its forehead, that makes three, right!"

"Then that's it. *Triceratops*."

Triceratops, living and fighting and fighting again in an endless struggle for survival in the late Cretaceous, Mesozoic world seventy million years before, domain of history's most savage beast, the carnivorous monster *Tyrannosaurus rex*. *Triceratops*, that massive herbivore, possessing the most powerful armament of any animal ever known. Triceratops, *that* triceratops, was even now walking leisurely down the road before their very eyes.

"Shall we go outside?"

"Sure!"

Father and son slipped through the entrance door of their home. It was chilly outside, but there was no wind.

Ten meters away the small mountains of triceratop's hips swayed steadily forward, dragging a tail like a telephone pole. They couldn't see the beast's face beyond the expansive sweep of the shield. But from triceratop's posture they could well imagine its cautious advance, front legs crouched, head lowered, body in readiness for the slightest sign of danger.

At last triceratops reached the end of the street. Before it stood a stone fence and to the left and right, walls of brick and stone.

He'll head back this way.

Father and son drew back between the gateposts, but in the next instant they stopped, rooted speechless in their tracks.

Triceratops did not stop. It put its head up against the stone wall and sank smoothly into the hard

93

surface. The shield vanished, the front legs and the slice of backbone above them vanished, the hips and hind legs vanished, the tail from base to tip, inch by steady inch, simply disappeared.

Morning came, and the father, setting off to work, and the son, setting off for school, both left the house at the same time.

The father and son exchanged glances and walked to the stone fence at the end of the road. The wall stood solidly, blocking their way.

They fingered it, but found nothing unusual.

Nor was there a single break in the mortar-painted sides, the window glass of the house beyond the wall.

"I've read about dimensional faults and stuff like that," the son said.

"Mmmm. But those are all just theories."

"Theories?"

"When you say that something you can't prove might be this way or that way, that's a theory."

"So there aren't any dimensional faults?"

"Well, someone just thought them up. They might really exist, and they might not. If you figure they exist, then the surface of this wall must be right about the fault line. Between our world and the world of *Triceratops*, seventy million years ago. But really you can try explaining it just about any way you please."

"For instance?"

"For instance, you could think that our world and *Triceratops*'s world exist simultaneously. Instead of popping in and out of a fault line every now and then, we're really both here all the time with just a bit

94

of a lag in between. That would explain why we can somehow look through into that other world, and they can look through to us. It'd be just that fine a difference."

"Huh?"

"I started thinking about it when there was a thick, warm animal smell in the house this morning. And this isn't the first time, you know. It's been like this for at least two or three months now. The people living here must be experiencing the same thing."

"Triceratops went inside their house?"

"You've got it now."

"So can they see it, too? Just like us?"

"Maybe. But you know how people's heads are. We try to deny things that we think are impossible. It's a kind of protective instinct. So even if we somehow do see it, or feel it, we usually just shut it out automatically, choose not to see it, not to do it. If we see it again, two, three times maybe, then common sense comes to the rescue and we laugh it off. 'Nerves.' 'Boy, what a crazy idea!' And that's the end of it."

"And if it still doesn't stop?"

"Then people stop accepting you. You can't live a productive social life anymore."

The boy shook his head lightly from side to side, then laughed.

"What's so funny?"

"Nothing much. I was just thinking about Mom. I didn't tell her what I saw last night. Can you guess what would happen to me if I did?"

The father laughed, too.

"Well, she'd sure put you on the rack. That is, if it wasn't right after she'd just seen the same thing

95

herself."

"I guess I can't tell any of my friends about it, either."

"Of course not. Now let's get going. We can talk it over when we get home."

The father and son started walking.

Occasionally speaking and laughing happily together.

And every time they met a neighbor:

"Good morning!"

"Good morning!"

Scattering high-spirited greetings all about them.

The father and son often saw dinosaurs after that.

Sometimes, glancing up at the sunset, they'd glimpse the shadow of a huge winged creature like *Pteranodon*, weaving across the sky. But the only earth-hugging dinosaurs they saw were triceratopses.

Apparently the local habitat was best suited to *Triceratops*. The beast asleep in the garage, its head so perfectly aligned with the family car that it seemed a strange horned automobile was snoring humorously away, the huge dinosaur passing over the head of a small child crying fretfully by the roadside, all these apparitions were triceratopses.

Sometimes the father and son would even see them—though only transparently—walking the sun-bathed road in full daylight.

Nor was it only what they could see. The cloying animal smell, the low grunting. Running nonstop to the station on ice-stretched, frigid mornings as they gasped and choked on impossible flower pollen.

Listening to the distant, bassoonlike cries of a female triceratops in heat, howling through the long night.

You and your dad seem awfully close these days. Anything special going on?

There were days when his mother would badger him, but the son simply grinned.

"Nothing special," was all he'd say.

It was on one of those days, yet another Sunday evening when they had gone cycling about the neighborhood, though not as far as on the day they first met triceratops. After passing through the copse on the top of the hill and coming out above their subdivision, the father and son came to a stop, finding themselves speechless and unable to move.

A triceratops huddled superimposed over every house in the town, their skin — brilliant green beneath the mercury lamps — gently rising and falling with their breathing. Occasionally one would open its eyes in a narrow slit, and every time the lids raised, the pupils would glitter in brilliant rose, perhaps because of rhodopsin pigment like that found in some species of crocodile.

It was a scene of phantasmal beauty, like the winking of giant fireflies.

"Do you suppose the land over there's the same as the town?"

"Maybe they can see us and feel us like we feel them. Maybe they're just trying to keep warm."

"You may be right."

"Isn't it a weird feeling? Everyone's going to work or leaving for school from a dinosaur's belly, and they're coming home to the belly, eating dinner, watching TV."

"But that's how it is."

"Hey, my room's in its butt."

"Don't let it get to you."

"But it's really peaceful somehow, isn't it? They may look fierce, but I've never seen a triceratops fighting."

"They hardly ever run, either."

"Yeah, that's right. Just the one we saw that first time, in the other town."

"I wonder what he was running for."

"Anyway, it's peaceful enough today."

"There's nothing better than peace."

The peace did not last long.

It was a day when yellow sand blown from the continent filled the air and turned the sun the color of blood, a harsh, unpleasant day.

It was the day that the son, looking casually toward the national highway from the hilltop while returning from a friend's house, saw a dozen dinosaurs running on strange hind legs—like ostriches—long tails held high, kicking up clouds of dust.

"Those were tyrannosauruses for sure. Superfat back legs and little skinny front ones like decorations. Pointed mouths. Anyway, tyrannosauruses. And they were really moving fast. They came running at least as far as the station."

"We're just a little way from the station here, but I didn't feel anything like tyrannosaurus when I was coming home just now. Even the triceratops in the garage just opened his eyes a bit and stared at me like he always does."

"But I really did see them."

"Maybe they ran right through town and went somewhere else?"

"But I wonder why they would do that. They went out of sight near the station."

"Hmmm."

The father crossed his arms.

"In that case maybe they're still milling around there somewhere. Or maybe—"

"Let's go see," said the son.

"You two are up to something again, aren't you?"

The mother shouted after them. The father and son smiled, waved, and mounted their bicycles.

They went as far as the station, but there was no trace of any tyrannosauruses. After watching the station plaza for a while, they turned leisurely back home.

A small creek flowed close to the station, completely covered with concrete. There was a playground built on top of it. The long, covered drain formed a second road, stretching almost to their subdivision.

"Let's go back this way."

The father and son pedaled their bicycles slowly over the concrete plating. The tires bounced heavily every time they jumped a gap between the plates.

Their front lights waved widely.

Before long they became aware of a strange noise. It sounded like rapid water and, an octave lower, the grunting of countless pigs. Moments later they felt the earth begin to rumble.

And suddenly they looked down at their feet. And ran to the metal lid of an air vent.

They were running beneath the metal mesh of the

lid, fiercely kicking up the water as they ran. Their wet hides glistened; their necks were outstretched. The pack of tyrannosauruses dashed for the subdivision like a conveyor belt, a never-ending stream.

They had been following the watercourse. The group near the national highway had been but a single part, a flying column, and had merged with the main group at the station.

"This is bad."

It hardly mattered if they hurried, yet the father and son began to pedal furiously.

As they neared the subdivision, countless tyrannosauruses danced up through the concrete sheeting ahead of them, looking like a geyser of muddy water.

All the houses on the slanting slope of the subdivision heaved up their roofs and began to move.

The triceratops had risen.

The fighting began.

Before their eyes, a triceratops, head lowered, charged forward and plunged sharp horns into the carotid artery of an attacking tyrannosaurus. The carnivore, its blood fountaining into the air like water from a fire hose, fell back, lashed its long tail, and leaped hugely, gouging out the triceratop's eyes with a single sweep of the key-shaped claws on its forelegs.

Three more tyrannosauruses swooped onto the mammoth body of the triceratops, crumpled just six meters in front of their home. The huge reptiles plunged razor teeth into the belly meat, already ripped apart by their claws. The surroundings were flooded in a murky river of blood.

"Isn't that our triceratops?" cried the boy, his voice shaking.

"You're right."

A tyrannosaurus had fallen in front of the entrance-way. The father and son warily watched its huge blood-shot eyes, the convulsive contractions of its belly, as they wheeled their bikes up the driveway.

The fighting lasted throughout the night.

Even at the height of the raucous laughter of a televised singing contest, the father and son could hear the war cries, could feel the thick hide splitting, the shrieks of the hour of death.

By morning the combat had almost ended, and the countless corpses of triceratopses and tyrannosauruses, some still barely twitching the tips of their tails, some dragging the ripped tatters of their stomachs, lay tumbled across the landscape.

Almost without exception, the corpses of triceratopses had their entrails dug out, their ribs laid bare, and their neck shields chopped into ribbons. But most of the tyrannosauruses showed only deep puncture wounds in their necks and bellies, escaping utter destruction.

There were even a few scattered survivors. But none had escaped unscathed. All had lost the energy to keep on fighting.

One tyrannosaurus, his flung-out leg half mincemeat from the thigh down, continued to drag out and gobble the guts of the triceratops he had slaughtered.

Behind him sprawled the body of one of his comrades, a gaping hole bored through its neck, its body clotted with dried blood, while no more than five meters away a triceratops grazed silently on the grass, blood still seeping from one of its eyes.

Every now and then the tyrannosaurus would raise its head and glare—though perhaps this was only their

101

fancy—balefully at the grazing triceratops.

If you eat that crud, why'd you kill us?

The father and son almost felt they could hear that voice.

If there's too much to eat, why did you keep on butchering us?

The triceratops's unbloodied eye seemed to ask that back.

The father and son watched as they walked slowly to the station. The corpses that weren't dripping were at least tolerable. But even they were brought up short where the large intestines of a tyrannosaurus lay heaped across the road, as if they had sprung writhing from the animal's torn-open belly. After a moment's pause they edged by on the side of the street.

A woman in fashionable white slacks passed through the blood-smeared landscape, her shoes clicking loudly, her eyes suspiciously watching father and son.

A microbus filled with kindergarteners passed through that landscape, bearing its load of lively chatter.

An elementary-school student passed through that landscape, singing a jingle.

Skylark dancing to the sky
God is reigning in the sky
The world, the world's a trifle.

NEW ROSE HOTEL

By William Gibson

Seven rented nights in this coffin, Sandii. New
Rose Hotel. How I want you now. Sometimes I hit
you. Replay it so slow and sweet and mean, I can
almost feel it. Sometimes I take your little automatic
out of my bag, run my thumb down smooth, cheap
chrome. Chinese .22, its bore no wider than the
dilated pupils of your vanished eyes.

Fox is dead now, Sandii.

Fox told me to forget you.

I remember Fox leaning against the padded bar in
the dark lounge of some Singapore hotel, Bencoolen
Street, his hands describing different spheres of influ-
ence, internal rivalries, the arc of a particular career,
a point of weakness he had discovered in the armor of

some think tank. Fox was point man in the skull wars, a middleman for corporate crossovers. He was a soldier in the secret skirmishes of the zaibatsus, the multinational corporations that control entire economies.

I see Fox grinning, talking fast, dismissing my ventures into intercorporate espionage with a shake of his head. The Edge, he said, have to find that Edge. He made you hear the capital *E*. The Edge was Fox's grail, that essential fraction of sheer human talent, nontransferable, locked in the skulls of the world's hottest research scientists.

You can't put Edge down on paper. Fox said, can't punch Edge into a diskette.

The money was in corporate defectors.

Fox was smooth, the severity of his dark, French suits offset by a boyish forelock that wouldn't stay in place. I never liked the way the effect was ruined when he stepped back from the bar, his left shoulder skewed at an angle no Paris tailor could conceal. Someone had run him over with a taxi in Berne, and nobody quite knew how to put him together again.

I guess I went with him because he said he was after that Edge.

And somewhere out there, on our way to find the Edge, I found you, Sandii.

The New Rose Hotel is a coffin rack on the ragged fringes of Narita International. Plastic capsules a meter high and three long, stacked like surplus Godzilla teeth in a concrete lot off the main road to the airport. Each capsule has a television mounted flush with the ceiling. I spend whole days watching Japanese game shows and old movies. Sometimes I have your gun in my hand.

Sometimes I can hear the jets, laced into holding patterns over Narita. I close my eyes and imagine the sharp, white contrails fading, losing definition.

You walked into a bar in Yokohama, the first time I saw you. Eurasian, half gaijin, long-hipped and fluid in a Chinese knock-off of some Tokyo designer's original. Dark European eyes, Asian cheekbones. I remember you dumping your purse out on the bed, later, in some hotel room, pawing through your makeup. A crumpled wad of New Yen, dilapidated address book held together with rubber bands, a Mitsubishi bank chip, Japanese passport with a gold chrysanthemum stamped on the cover, and the Chinese .22.

You told me your story. Your father had been an executive in Tokyo, but now he was disgraced, disowned, cast down by Hosaka, the biggest zaibatsu of all. That night your mother was Dutch, and I listened as you spun out those summers in Amsterdam for me, the pigeons in Dam Square like a soft, brown carpet.

I never asked what your father might have done to earn his disgrace. I watched you dress; watched the swing of your dark, straight hair, how it cut the air.

Now Hosaka hunts me.

The coffins of New Rose are racked in recycled scaffolding, steel pipes under bright enamel. Paint flakes away when I climb the ladder, falls with each step as I follow the catwalk. My left hand counts off the coffin hatches, their multilingual decals warning of fines levied for the loss of a key.

I look up as the jets rise out of Narita, passage

home, distant now as any moon.

Fox was quick to see how we could use you, but not sharp enough to credit you with ambition. But then he never lay all night with you on the beach at Kamakura, never listened to your nightmares, never heard an entire imagined childhood shift under those stars, shift and roll over, your child's mouth opening to reveal some fresh past, and always the one, you swore, that was really and finally the truth.

I didn't care, holding your hips while the sand cooled against your skin.

Once you left me, ran back to that beach saying you'd forgotten our key. I found it in the door and went after you, to find you ankle deep in surf, your smooth back rigid, trembling; your eyes far away. You couldn't talk. Shivering. Gone. Shaking for different futures and better pasts.

Sandii, you left me here.

You left me all your things.

This gun. Your makeup, all the shadows and blushes capped in plastic. Your Cray microcomputer, a gift from Fox, with a shopping list you entered. Sometimes I play that back, watching each item cross the little silver screen.

A freezer. A fermenter. An incubator. An electrophoresis system with integrated agarose cell and transilluminator. A tissue embedder. A high-performance liquid chromatograph. A flow cytometer. A spectrophotometer. Four gross of borosilicate scintillation vials. A microcentrifuge. And one DNA synthesizer, with in-built computer. Plus software.

Expensive, Sandii, but then Hosaka was footing our bills. Later you made them pay even more, but you were already gone.

Hiroshi drew up that list for you. In bed, probably. Hiroshi Yomiuri. Maas Biolabs GmbH had him. Hosaka wanted him.

He was hot. Edge and lots of it. Fox followed genetic engineers the way a fan follows players in a favorite game. Fox wanted Hiroshi so bad he could taste it.

He'd sent me up to Frankfurt three times before you turned up, just to have a look-see at Hiroshi. Not to make a pass or even to give him a wink and a nod. Just to watch.

Hiroshi showed all the signs of having settled in. He'd found a German girl with a taste for conservative loden and riding boots polished the shade of a fresh chestnut. He'd bought a renovated townhouse on just the right square. He'd taken up fencing and given up kendo.

And everywhere the Maas security teams, smooth and heavy, a rich, clear syrup of surveillance. I came back and told Fox we'd never touch him.

You touched him for us, Sandii. You touched him just right.

Our Hosaka contacts were like specialized cells protecting the parent organism. We were mutagens. Fox and I, dubious agents adrift on the dark side of the intercorporate sea.

When we had you in place in Vienna, we offered them Hiroshi. They didn't even blink. Dead calm in an L.A. hotel room. They said they had to think about it.

Fox spoke the name of Hosaka's primary competitor in the gene game, let it fall out naked, broke the protocol forbidding the use of proper names.

They had to think about it, they said.

Fox gave them three days.

I took you to Barcelona a week before I took you to Vienna. I remember you with your hair tucked back into a gray beret, your high Mongol cheekbones reflected in the windows of ancient shops. Strolling down the Ramblas to the Phoenician harbor, past the glass-roofed Mercado selling oranges out of Africa.

The old Ritz, warm in our room, dark, with all the soft weight of Europe pulled over us like a quilt. I could enter you in your sleep. You were always ready. Seeing your lips in a soft, round O of surprise, your face about to sink into the thick, white pillow — archaic linen of the Ritz. Inside you I imagined all that neon, the crowds surging around Shinjuku Station, wired electric night. You moved that way, rhythm of a new age, dreamy and far from any nation's soil.

When we flew to Vienna, I installed you in Hiroshi's wife's favorite hotel. Quiet, solid, the lobby tiled like a marble chessboard, with brass elevators smelling of lemon oil and small cigars. It was easy to imagine her there, the highlights on her riding boots reflected in polished marble, but we knew she wouldn't be coming along, not this trip.

She was off to some Rhineland spa, and Hiroshi was in Vienna for a conference. When Maas security flowed in to scan the hotel, you were out of sight.

Hiroshi arrived an hour later, alone.

Imagine an alien, Fox once said, who's come here to identify the planet's dominant form of intelligence. The alien has a look, then chooses. What do you think he picks? I probably shrugged.

The zaibatsus, Fox said, the multinationals. The blood of a zaibatsu is information, not people. The structure is independent of the individual lives that comprise it. Corporation as life form.

Not the Edge lecture again, I said.

Maas isn't like that, he said, ignoring me.

Maas was small, fast, ruthless. An atavism. Maas was all Edge.

I remember Fox talking about the nature of Hiroshi's Edge. Radioactive nucleases, monoclonal antibodies, something to do with the linkage of proteins, nucleotides . . . Hot, Fox called them, hot proteins. High-speed links. He said Hiroshi was a freak, the kind who shatters paradigms, inverts a whole field of science, brings on the violent revision of an entire body of knowledge. Basic patents, he said, his throat tight with the sheer wealth of it, with the high, thin smell of tax-free millions that clung to those two words.

Hosaka wanted Hiroshi, but his Edge was radical enough to worry them. They wanted him to work in isolation.

I went to Marrakech, to the old city, the Medina. I found a heroin lab that had been converted to the extraction of pheromones. I bought it, with Hosaka's money.

I walked the marketplace at Djemaa-el-Fna with a sweating Portuguese businessman, discussing fluorescent lighting and the installation of ventilated specimen cages. Beyond the city walls, the high Atlas. Djemaa-el-Fna was thick with jugglers, dancers, storytellers, small boys turning lathes with their feet, legless beggars with wooden bowls under animated holograms advertising French software.

We strolled past bales of raw wool and plastic tubs of Chinese microchips. I hinted that my employers planned to manufacture synthetic beta-endorphin. Always try to give them something they understand.

Sandii, I remembered you in Harajuku, sometimes. Close my eyes in this coffin and I can see you there— all the glitter, crystal maze of the boutiques, the smell of new clothes. I see your cheekbones ride past chrome racks of Paris leathers. Sometimes I hold your hand.

We thought we'd found you, Sandii, but really you'd found us. Now I know you were looking for us or for someone like us. Fox was delighted, grinning over our find: such a pretty new tool, bright as any scalpel. Just the thing to help us sever a stubborn Edge, like Hiroshi's, from the jealous parent-body of Maas Biolabs.

You must have been searching a long time, looking for a way out, all those nights down Shinjuku. Nights you carefully cut from the scattered deck of your past.

My own past had gone down years before, lost with all hands, no trace. I understood Fox's late-night habit of emptying his wallet, shuffling through his identification. He'd lay the pieces out in different patterns, rearrange them, wait for a picture to form. I knew what he was looking for. You did the same thing with your childhoods.

In New Rose, tonight, I choose from your deck of pasts.

I choose the original version, the famous Yokohama hotel-room text, recited to me that first night in bed. I choose the disgraced father, Hosaka executive. Hosaka. How perfect. And the Dutch mother, the summers in Amsterdam, the soft blanket of pigeons in the Dam Square afternoon.

I came in out of the heat of Marrakech into Hilton air conditioning. Wet shirt clinging cold to the small of my back while I read the message you'd relayed through Fox. You were in all the way; Hiroshi would leave his wife. It wasn't difficult for you to communicate with us, even through the clear, tight film of Maas security; you'd shown Hiroshi the perfect little place for coffee and kipferl. Your favorite waiter was white haired, kindly, walked with a limp, and worked for us. You left your messages under the linen napkin.

All day today I watched a small helicopter cut a tight grid above this country of mine, the land of my exile, the New Rose Hotel. Watched from my hatch as its patient shadow crossed the grease-stained concrete. Close. Very close.

I left Marrakech for Berlin. I met with a Welshman in a bar and began to arrange for Hiroshi's disappearance.

It would be a complicated business, intricate as the brass gears and sliding mirrors of Victorian stage magic, but the desired effect was simple enough. Hiroshi would step behind a hydrogen-cell Mercedes and vanish. The dozen Maas agents who followed him constantly would swarm around the van like ants; the Maas security apparatus would harden around his point of departure like epoxy.

They know how to do business promptly in Berlin.

111

I was even able to arrange a last night with you. I kept it secret from Fox; he might not have approved. Now I've forgotten the town's name. I knew it for an hour on the autobahn, under a gray Rhenish sky, and forgot it in your arms.

The rain began, sometime toward morning. Our room had a single window, high and narrow, where I stood and watched the rain fur the river with silver needles. Sound of your breathing. The river flowed beneath low, stone arches. The street was empty. Europe was a dead museum.

I'd already booked your flight to Marrakech, out of Orly, under your newest name. You'd be on your way when I pulled the final string and dropped Hiroshi out of sight.

You'd left your purse on the dark, old bureau. While you slept I went through your things, removing anything that might clash with the new cover I'd bought for you in Berlin. I took the Chinese .22, your micro-computer, and your bank chip. I took a new passport, Dutch, from my bag, a Swiss bank chip in the same name, and tucked them into your purse.

My hand brushed something flat. I drew it out, held the thing, a diskette. No labels.

It lay there in the palm of my hand, all that death. Latent, coded, waiting.

I stood there and watched you breathe, watched your breasts rise and fall. Saw your lips slightly parted, and in the jut and fullness of your lower lip, the faintest suggestion of bruising.

I put the diskette back into your purse. When I lay down beside you, you rolled against me, waking, on your breath all the electric night of a new Asia, the future rising in you like a bright fluid, washing me of everything but the moment. That was your magic, that you lived outside of history, all now.

And you knew how to take me there.

For the very last time, you took me.

While I was shaving, I heard you empty your makeup into my bag. I'm Dutch now, you said, I'll want a new look.

Dr. Hiroshi Yomiuri went missing in Vienna, in a quiet street off Singerstrasse, two blocks from his wife's favorite hotel. On a clear afternoon in October, in the presence of a dozen expert witnesses, Dr. Yomiuri vanished.

He stepped through a looking glass. Somewhere, offstage, the oiled play of Victorian clockwork.

I sat in a hotel room in Geneva and took the Welshman's call. It was done, Hiroshi down my rabbit hole and headed for Marrakech. I poured myself a drink and thought about your legs.

Fox and I met in Narita a day later, in a sushi bar in the JAL terminal. He'd just stepped off an Air Maroc jet, exhausted and triumphant.

Loves it there, he said, meaning Hiroshi. Loves her, he said, meaning you.

I smiled. You'd promised to meet me in Shinjuku in a month.

Your cheap, little gun in the New Rose Hotel. The chrome is starting to peel. The machining is clumsy, blurry Chinese stamped into rough steel. The grips are red plastic, molded with a dragon on either side. Like a child's toy.

Fox ate sushi in the JAL terminal, high on what we'd done. The shoulder had been giving him trouble, but he said he didn't care. Money now for better doctors. Money now for everything.

Somehow it didn't seem very important to me, the money we'd gotten from Hosaka. Not that I doubted our new wealth, but that last night with you had left me convinced that it all came to us naturally, in the new order of things, as a function of who and what we were.

Poor Fox. With his blue oxford shirts crisper than ever, his Paris suits darker and richer. Sitting there in JAL, dabbing sushi into a little rectangular tray of green horseradish, he had less than a week to live.

Dark now, and the coffin racks of New Rose are lit all night by floodlights, high on painted metal masts. Nothing here seems to serve its original purpose. Everything is surplus, recycled, even the coffins. Forty years ago these plastic capsules were stacked in Tokyo or Yokohama, a modern convenience for traveling businessmen. Maybe your father slept in one. When the scaffolding was new, it rose around the shell of some mirrored tower on the Ginza, swarmed over by crews of builders.

The breeze tonight brings the rattle of a pachinko parlor, the smell of stewed vegetables from the push-carts across the road.

I spread crab-flavored krill paste on orange rice crackers. I can hear the planes.

Those last few days in Tokyo, Fox and I had adjoining suites on the fifty-third floor of the Hyatt. No contact with Hosaka. They paid us, then erased us from official corporate memory.

But Fox couldn't let go. Hiroshi was his baby, his pet project. He'd developed a proprietary, almost fatherly, interest in Hiroshi. He loved him for his Edge. So Fox had me keep in touch with my Portuguese businessman in the Medina, who was willing to keep a very partial eye on Hiroshi's lab for us.

When he phoned, he'd phone from a stall in Djemaa-el-Fna, with a background of wailing vendors and Atlas panpipes. Someone was moving security into Marrakech, he told us. Fox nodded. Hosaka.

After less than a dozen calls, I saw the change in Fox, a tension, a look of abstraction. I'd find him at the window, staring down fifty-three floors into the Imperial gardens, lost in something he wouldn't talk about.

Ask him for a more detailed description, he said, after one particular call. He thought a man our contact had seen entering Hiroshi's lab might be Moenner, Hosaka's leading gene man.

That was Moenner, he said, after the next call. Another call and he thought he'd identified Chedanne, who headed Hosaka's protein team. Neither had been seen outside the corporate arcology in over two years.

By then it was obvious that Hosaka's leading researchers were pooling quietly in the Medina, the black executive Lears whispering into the Marrakech airport on carbon-fiber wings. Fox shook his head. He was a professional, a specialist, and he saw the sudden accumulation of all that prime Hosaka Edge in the Medina as a drastic failure in the zaibatsu's tradecraft.

Christ, he said, pouring himself a Black Label, they've got their whole bio section in there right now. One bomb. He shook his head. One grenade in the right place at the right time . . .

I reminded him of the saturation techniques Hosaka security was obviously employing. Hosaka had lines to the heart of the Diet, and their massive infiltration of agents into Marrakech could only be taking place with the knowledge and cooperation of the Moroccan government.

Hang it up, I said. It's over. You've sold them Hiroshi. Now forget him.

I know what it is, he said. I know. I saw it once before.

He said that there was a certain wild factor in lab work. The edge of Edge, he called it. When a researcher develops a breakthrough, others sometimes find it impossible to duplicate the first researcher's results. This was even more likely with Hiroshi, whose work went against the conceptual grain of his field. The answer, often, was to fly the breakthrough boy from lab to corporate lab for a ritual laying on of hands. A few pointless adjustments in the equipment, and the process would work. Crazy thing, he said, nobody knows why it works that way, but it does. He grinned.

But they're taking a chance, he said. Bastards told us they wanted to isolate Hiroshi, keep him away from their central research thrust. Balls. Bet your ass there's some kind of power struggle going on in Hosaka research. Somebody big's flying his favorites in and rubbing them all over Hiroshi for luck. When Hiroshi shoots the legs out from under genetic engineering, the Medina crowd's going to be ready.

He drank his scotch and shrugged.

Go to bed, he said. You're right, it's over.

116

I did go to bed, but the phone woke me. Marrakech again, the white static of a satellite link, a rush of frightened Portuguese.

Hosaka didn't freeze our credit, they caused it to evaporate. Fairy gold. One minute we were millionaires in the world's hardest currency, and the next we were paupers. I woke Fox.

Sandii, he said. She sold out. Maas security turned her in Vienna. Sweet Jesus.

I watched him slit his battered suitcase apart with a Swiss army knife. He had three gold bars glued in there with contact cement. Soft plates, each one proofed and stamped by the treasury of some extinct African government.

I should've seen it, he said, his voice flat.

I said no. I think I said your name.

Forget her, he said. Hosaka wants us dead. They'll assume we crossed them. Get on the phone and check our credit.

Our credit was gone. They denied that either of us had ever had an account.

Haul ass, Fox said.

We ran. Out a service door, into Tokyo traffic, and down into Shinjuku. That was when I understood for the first time the real extent of Hosaka's reach.

Every door was closed. People we'd done business with for two years saw us coming, and I'd see steel shutters slam behind their eyes. We'd get out before they had a chance to reach for the phone. The surface tension of the underworld had been tripled, and everywhere we'd meet that same taut membrane and be thrown back. No chance to sink, to get out of sight.

Hosaka let us run for most of that first day. Then they sent someone to break Fox's back a second time.

I didn't see them do it, but I saw him fall. We were in a Ginza department store an hour before closing, and I saw him arc off that polished mezzanine, down into all the wares of the new Asia.

They missed me somehow, and I just kept running. Fox took the gold with him, but I had a hundred New Yen in my pocket. I ran. All the way to the New Rose Hotel.

Now it's time.

Come with me, Sandii. Hear the neon humming on the road to Narita International. A few late moths trace stop-motion circles around the floodlights that shine on New Rose.

And the funny thing, Sandii, is how sometimes you just don't seem real to me. Fox once said you were ectoplasm, a ghost called up by the extremes of economics. Ghost of the new century, congealing on a thousand beds in the world's Hyatts, the world's Hiltons.

Now I've got your gun in my hand, jacket pocket, and my hand seems so far away. Disconnected.

I remember my Portuguese business friend forgetting his English, trying to get it across in four languages I barely understood, and I thought he was telling me that the Medina was burning. Not the Medina. The brains of Hosaka's best research people. Plague, he was whispering, my businessman, plague and fever and death.

Smart Fox, he put it together on the run. I didn't even have to mention finding the diskette in your bag in Germany.

118

Someone had reprogrammed the DNA synthesizer, he said. The thing was there for the overnight construction of just the right macromolecule. With its inbuilt computer and its custom software. Expensive, Sandii. But not as expensive as you turned out to be for Hosaka.

I hope you got a good price from Maas.

The diskette in my hand. Rain on the river. I knew, but I couldn't face it. I put the code for that meningial virus back into your purse and lay down beside you.

So Moenner died, along with other Hosaka researchers. Including Hiroshi. Chedanne suffered permanent brain damage.

Hiroshi hadn't worried about contamination. The proteins he punched for were harmless. So the synthesizer hummed to itself all night long, building a virus to the specifications of Maas Biolabs GmbH.

Maas. Small, fast, ruthless. All Edge.

The airport road is a long, straight shot. Keep to the shadows.

And I was shouting at that Portuguese voice, I made him tell me what happened to the girl, to Hiroshi's woman. Vanished, he said. The whir of Victorian clockwork.

So Fox had to fall, fall with his three pathetic plates of gold, and snap his spine for the last time. On the floor of a Ginza department store, every shopper staring in the instant before they screamed.

I just can't hate you, baby.

And Hosaka's helicopter is back, no lights at all, hunting on infrared, feeling for body heat. A muffled whine as it turns, a kilometer away, swinging back toward us, toward New Rose. Too fast a shadow, against the glow of Narita.

It's alright, baby. Only please come here. Hold my hand.

ADAGIO

By Barry B. Longyear

Tobias sat on the red-stone grave marker on the side of Graveyard Hill and watched as Forrest tortured the rocks with the portable generator he had taken from the cargo bay. Torture is what Lady Name called Forrest's game. Lady Name was convinced that Forrest was insane.

Tobias raised a grimy hand and rubbed his eyes. Hell, Lady Name was wig-picker bait herself. That's why she was called Lady Name. It was a temporary label for the woman until she could figure out just who the hell she was. Or at least until she would say who she was. Cage and Forrest thought she had amnesia. Tobias didn't buy that, but he didn't care.

He lowered his hand and let his gaze wander past the main shelter dome until it came to rest upon the remains of the ship. Three kilometers behind the cargo vessel was the jagged ledge that had ventilated the command module as the ship ground to a stop. Through the rents in the command module, he could see Lady Name. She was silently watching Forrest. Motionless.

It was entirely possible that Lady Name would kill Forrest. A matter of indifference to Tobias. Somewhere below her in the twisted metal, Cage would be nervously working on the computer. Death still seemed to matter to Cage. His nerves were the direct result of Lady Name frequently sitting just out of his field of vision, staring at him, sharpening her knife upon one of the dead red stones.

The dried and cracked crust that had formed over the surface of the red dust when it last rained was almost all gone. The little bit of wind, the motion of the rocks, the feet of the humans had eroded the crust. And it had been such a long time since it had rained. When they had constructed the main shelter dome from the cargo-bay supplies, it had been gleaming white. Now it was covered with dull-red dust.

It seemed like years had passed since they had put up the dome and installed the nutrition system. Twenty meters in diameter, it was large enough to shelter all five of them. Lady Name was the first one to move out and erect an individual shelter. There had been fifty of the plastic-plank shelter kits in the cargo bay. Now they each had one, only meeting in the dome to eat. The fact was that they could no longer stand each other.

The whisper of feet dragging in the dust interrupted Tobias's thoughts. Tillson. The footsteps stopped.

"Is it possible, Tobias, that God has done this to us

to provide us with a challenge against which to test our virtue?"

Tobias turned to his left and glared up at the chaplain. Tillson was naked again. "Stick it up your ass, Howard."

Chaplain Howard Tillson nodded gravely. "You are right, of course. You are very wise, Tobias. Very wise."

The chaplain turned and stumbled his way down the back of Graveyard Hill, his droopy buns jiggling with each step.

Tobias again pondered the fact that Tillson had a woman's ass. Another fact to ponder was that rescue had best happen before Tillson's ass got to look much better. He hollered down the hill at the jiggling ass, "Tillson, put some clothes on!"

The chaplain stopped, turned, looked up at Tobias, and nodded. "You are right, of course. You are always right, Tobias."

Placing his hands upon his knees, Tobias pushed himself to his feet and dusted off the seat of his flight suit. He turned and looked down at the grave marker he had been sitting on. Osborn's marker. It was a smooth, red stone just like Mikizu's.

They had to use only the red stones for grave markers. They didn't walk off.

The gray stone Tobias had originally used to mark Osborn's grave was now several meters downslope, running like hell, Forrest claimed. It had taken the gray stone five of the planet's month-long days to race the short distance. Gray stones, white stones, green stones, black stones. They littered the red landscape. They were alive. The red ones didn't move.

They were dead.

Osborn was dead. And Mikizu. He let his gaze wander two meters to the left to another red stone. When Mikizu had piloted the ship, shearing it off that ledge, he had lost his head. Tobias knew because he had carried that head to the grave while Forrest and Cage carried the pilot's remainder.

Too quick, Tobias thought. Too quick and clean a death for you, Mikizu. Tobias unsealed his suit and pissed on the pilot's grave. When he was finished he stumbled down the hill, entered his individual shelter, and flopped down on his cot. He closed his eyes thinking of dead red grave markers.

Osborn was dead. Mikizu was dead. Mikizu was no loss. If it hadn't been for him they wouldn't be stranded. But Osborn. Tobias wished Osborn were still alive. He'd know what to do. But Osborn had to be a hero. . . .

He had sat in the sputtering flashes of the emergency lights, watching Osborn's eyeballs leak. The chief engineer was in the wreckage of the engineering deck, inhaling vacuum, the seat of his trousers puddling with piss and blood, the fluid from his eyeballs dribbling down his cheeks.

There had been plenty of time for Osborn to get on his suit. The hull damage in aft engineering had dumped only the pressure from that compartment. The rest of the ship lost pressure only because of the warped bulkhead seals. It took minutes for the ship to lose cabin pressure. But Osborn wanted to flick switches, punch buttons, and twirl knobs. The rest of

124

them probably owed him their lives. The asshole.

"Tobias?" The headset in his suit spoke. It was the pilot, Mikizu. "Engineering? Osborn? Tobias?"

Tobias answered. "What?"

"Osborn?"

"Osborn's dead."

A brief pause. "Tobias, I need to know the power situation."

Through his suit's faceplate, he glanced at the remains of the engineering board. "I can't help but believe, Mikizu, that you know just about as much as I do about that."

"The bridge panel is dead."

"No shit." He leaned back against the bulkhead, glanced at Osborn, and closed his eyes. "We're all dead back here, too."

"I need power if we're going to go down."

"Is there any point?"

"Forrest thinks so."

Forrest. Second pilot. A little bastard but smart. Tobias shook his head to clear it. Time to knock off the smartmouth.

"Main and auxiliary plants are down. Whatever it was that came flying through the hull took out the engines. I couldn't sell what's left of them for scrap."

Another pause, this one longer. "What about the fuel cells?"

"They're okay. Osborn got the lines shut down before too much fuel escaped. What's Forrest got in mind?"

Forrest's voice entered his helmet. "We can try for a dead-stick landing. If you can rig the steering jets, Tobias, the computer says we have a chance of making it through the atmosphere."

"How much of a chance?"

Forrest laughed. "Don't ask." He became quiet. "We have a better chance at making a landing than we have trying to stay alive up here. Can you rig something?"

Tobias looked around the engineering deck, the challenges of practical necessity temporarily crowding out projections of disaster and demise. With the board shot there would be some wiring to do. He'd have to work off the batteries. And some plumbing, not to mention readjusting the steering jets to use main-plant fuel. He didn't really know if that could be done. But there was something else. The entry heat would turn aft engineering into a furnace.

"Forrest, I can make a try at the steering jets, but something has to be done about those holes in the hull."

"Get to work on the jets. When you're ready, I'll help you with the holes. We can snatch some plate from somewhere."

Tobias pushed up and began working his way toward aft engineering. He loved doing wiring in atmospheric longjohns. It was like doing watch repair while wearing a pair of boxing gloves. The failing gravity would just make it interesting.

He punched the switch, and the hatch swung slightly open and jammed. With his foot he kicked it the rest of the way open. He stood in the hatch and looked into the darkness of the engine room.

The only light came from the holes in the hull. Tobias knew that some of those flickers were stars, but most of them were too bright for that. The bright ones were the remains of the crumbled planets that formed the Oids Belt in orbit around a sun called Mantchee.

Merchant crews don't like the Oids Belt and never go there. The union even got it in the contract. Asteroids, planetoids, and paranoids. Tobias still had one of the buttons that says I AVOID THE OIDS.

But there were passengers and parts to pick up and deliver to strange and wonderful places, and a pilot who believed in shortcuts more than he did in minimum safety or union contracts. Tobias swore that if he and the pilot managed to live through the landing, Tobias's first planet-side act would be to murder Mikizu.

First things first.

He returned, grabbed Osborn, and dislodged the engineering chief's body from the rapidly freezing fluids that were pinning his ass to the deck.

Pulling the body to the hatch, Tobias pushed it toward the large hole at his feet.

The still form somersaulted slowly toward the hole and jerked to a halt. Tobias pulled the light from his belt and aimed the beam at the opening.

The back of Osborn's head had been speared and snagged by the hole's ragged edge. One of the thick splinters of metal protruded from Osborn's left eye.

Someday the geniuses will figure out how to puke in a space suit. He turned away.

"this thing will serve us if we obey it"
"how will it serve"
"it will stop pain and death"
"this thing brought us pain

127

and death"
"we must obey"
"this thing now wants us to kill"

"Forrest is still torturing the rocks." It was Lady Name's voice.

Tobias buried his head more deeply into his pillow. "If you don't get out of here, I'll rip out your spine and strangle you with it."

No footsteps moving away. He could feel the woman's hurt gaze on his back. The flimsy shelter almost radiated with terminal sulk. Tobias chased away his nightmares and rolled over on his cot. "Go away, Lady. Take up a hobby, go play with yourself, anything. Anything but tattling on Forrest. I don't find forty-year-old children amusing."

"I am not tattling, Tobias. I am reporting. One of your men is torturing the rocks. Those rocks are alive."

"Lady, first, they are not my men. If anyone is in charge, it's Forrest. Second, I don't care about the rocks. I really don't. My only problem is keeping sane until someone picks up our signal. Rescue, Lady. Think rescue."

"No one will pick up the signal. Forrest told you it can't get through the radiation."

"You don't know that. Forrest doesn't know that for certain. There's a chance."

She stared at him for a moment, almost looking sane, then nodded toward the shack's doorway. "What are you going to do about Forrest?"

He turned his back and burrowed into his pillow. "Nothing."

128

Footsteps, finally.

The beacon signal would get through. It had to. Then a curious thought entered his mind. He felt he *should* be rooting for the beacon signal's success. A moral thing. What generations of humans would say was the thing he should be doing right then. The curious thought was that he didn't really care whether the signal got through or not.

"soon the dark"
"soon we kill"
"it is the wish of this thing"

Mantchee rode half-hidden by the horizon. Tobias entered the main shelter, the red glare of the week-long sunset casting the interior of the dome in blood.

They were all seated around the low table. Lady Name, as usual, was watching Forrest. Forrest was entertaining himself with his own thoughts while Tillson struggled, probably uncomfortable with the unfamiliar feeling of wearing clothes. Nelson Cage was heavily into a wiring diagram, the symbols and the problems their relationships represented providing as much entertainment for him as the rocks did for Forrest.

As he pulled a ration pack from the dispenser, Tobias heard Cage announce. "I have the computer working."

Tillson: "God doesn't like computers."

Lady Name: "What are you going to kill time with now, Cage?"

Forrest: "Break it, Cage. Break the computer and fix it again."

129

Cage's face flushed red. "I don't know what's wrong with you people. After five months of hard work I've managed to—"

Forrest leaned forward holding a finger before his lips. "Shhh." He brought his finger down and smiled. "No one cares, Cage."

Tobias lowered himself into the chair to Forrest's right, sipped at the acid-tasting hot beverage, and gnawed on a nutribar as Cage leaned back, his voice becoming brittle. "We can use the computer—"

"For what?" Tobias shook his head as he bit again at the nutribar. "Except for getting rescued, all our solvable problems are solved. We have oxygen, water, rations, and a livable temperature spread. The only things in short supply are patience and sanity. Do you have any games you can play on that thing? We could use some entertainment."

Cage snorted and sat back in his chair. "Games," he repeated in disgust. He looked over at Lady Name. "At least I know who you are now."

She looked away from Forrest for a split second. As she resumed her watch on the pebble persecutor she replied, "Cage, you haven't a clue who I am."

Cage smirked. "Barbara Striker. *Doctor* Barbara Striker. I managed to retrieve the passenger manifest. It says you are Doctor Barbara Striker, a biologist formerly with the Dison System colonization effort, currently relieved of your post because you are a fucking crazy."

"Words." She slowly turned her head toward Cage. "I'll be using the computer."

"You will not! I just finished repairing it."

Lady Name grinned as she stood and walked from

the dome, obviously headed for the wreck and the computer. Cage leaned toward Tobias. "You must do something!"

Forrest chuckled and shook his head. "Calm down. Let her play with the machine. It's got to be better than having her perched like a vulture on my shoulder all the time."

"What if she breaks it?"

"Then you can fix it again. It really isn't very important."

Cage stood abruptly and walked rapidly from the dome. Again Forrest chuckled. "Cage is on his way to the ship to lay down the law to Lady Name."

"Yeah, and when she flashes that blade of hers he'll be back with a wet crotch." Tobias pointed with his thumb toward the door. "How come you aren't out playing with your rocks?"

"Things are arranged."

"What's that mean?"

"I have initiated certain things out there. I'm teaching them to serve. When it becomes light again you should be able to see how my subjects have responded."

Tobias finished off the remaining portion of his nutribar and tossed the wrapper on the plastic floor. *If Forrest wants to play god, at least he doesn't make a lot of noise. But they're all crazy*, he thought. *Every single last one of them. Am I?*

There was a scream from the wreckage, and a moment later Cage could be seen, holding his arm, running toward his individual shelter. Forrest nodded, his eyes still closed. "It looks as though they've decided that Lady Name gets to use the computer."

131

He opened one eye and aimed it at Tobias. "Is it true that you piss on Mikizu's grave?"

Tobias finished his beverage and placed the cup on the table. He sat back, clasped his hands over his belly, and watched Mantchee slip a little lower behind the horizon. "Every chance I get."

"now we kill"
"the not green should know why we kill"
"tell them to ask this thing"

The dark came. Tobias tossed beneath his thermal blanket, trying to sleep, flying in the face of the fact that he was all slept out. Had been slept out for hours. Probably days—those twenty-four-hour spans of time they call days on a planet whose memory had grown dim. Back on a planet in a time when there was youth, ideals, dreams, plans. The excitement of school and training.

The monotony of space. All of it reduced to keeping the power plants in second-rate ships coughing along in exchange for a paycheck and a pension that he didn't think he'd live long enough to collect—

"To hell with this." Long ago Tobias had lost the ability to entertain himself with his own company.

He sat up, still wearing his filthy flight suit, and slipped his feet into his icy boots. The smell of his own body hung around him like a curse. There would be enough light from the Oids to make it to the place where the stream was aboveground if he wanted to take a bath. He shivered at the thought. What the hell. Everyone was being tracked by his own shadow of funk.

Keeping the thermal blanket wrapped around his shoulders, Tobias stepped outside. The Oids were bright in the night sky. Maybe they should use the computer to plot the Oids. There was a lot of crap out there, all in the same orbit. Some fine day maybe one of those three-hundred-kilometer-long chunks of rock might slam into the middle of their camp. He spat on the ground. "And if we knew, what could we do about it?"

There was a light on in the wreckage of the ship. Tobias began moving his feet in that direction. The other individual shelters were dark. The main shelter had a light on, but no one was inside the dome. The open cargo hatch in the belly of the ship glowed with a dim red. Whoever was in the ship, it wouldn't be Cage. The computer man had a thing about conserving the ship's batteries. He would never leave on a light that wasn't needed. As though it made any difference. The batteries would outlive them all.

Tobias entered the cargo bay and began working his way around and through the jumble of opened containers and their scattered contents.

Most of it had been destined for a low-budget evaluation mission on some steamy planet out there somewhere. Everything anyone would need to learn the learnable about a planet and then screw it up. They had found the shelters and rations there.

Forward of the cargo hatch another light burned above a stack of strange equipment that Tobias had never seen before. Must have come from the cargo. Cables ran from the stack through the crew's quarters toward the cockpit. He entered the corridor to the crew's quarters, his mind thumbing through the obvious as he trudged up the slight incline to the cockpit. *If a full crew had been on board, maybe. If Mikizu hadn't overestimated his and his ship's abilities, maybe. If they'd followed company policy and stayed the hell out of the Oids, maybe. If they hadn't been ordered out of their way to pick up the passengers, maybe. Maybe. If. If ending it on this dreary rock wasn't such a fitting end to a dreary life. If.*

He could hear no sound forward except for the almost inaudible whine of the power converter. He stopped at the hatch to the cockpit and peered in.

Lady Name's back was toward him. She was sitting back, watching, almost hypnotized by the patterns appearing upon the display. Every few moments the image would switch to columns of figures and then back to the patterns.

He stepped into the cockpit. "Hey, Lady. What're you up to?"

She whirled about, the needle-pointed blade in her right hand. As he froze, a slow grin appeared on her face. "You shouldn't sneak up on me that way, Tobias. You almost got to do your pension as a eunuch." She lowered the blade. "Why are you here?"

His gaze still fixed on the knife, Tobias worked his way to the commo station couch and sat down. "I couldn't sleep anymore. Thought Cage's machine might have something to read."

She turned back to the display over the keyboard. "This terminal is busy."

"Are any of the other stations hooked up?"

She didn't answer. He watched her for a moment, then turned his attention to the display. "Does that have anything to do with the gear you've hooked up in

134

the cargo bay?"

She nodded toward the display. "Those are the thought patterns of one of the green rocks. I have one of the small ones in a sensory chamber. When I can get the main sensors hooked up, I'll be able to receive from any rock in sight."

Turning her head away from the screen, she fixed Tobias with a hate-filled glare. "You refused to do anything about Forrest. Now I'm taking matters into my own hands."

Tobias shook his head. "You be real careful, Lady Name. You keep this up and you just might buy a real case of the crazies." He nodded once toward the screen. "Once you have all of that data, what are you going to be able to do with it?"

"Communicate, Tobias. Communicate."

"Talk with the rocks? Hell, if they communicate at the same rate that they move, you'll be an old woman before you can get a hello back. And if you can communicate with them, so what?"

"It looks as though they conceptualize and communicate faster than they move." She faced the display. "Forrest is doing terrible things to the rocks. I've been watching him. On a primitive pain-pleasure level, he has divided some of the rocks into armies. And he is forcing them into situations where they must fight each other."

"Fight?" Tobias burst out in laughter. "That has to be the action event of the century. Hell, Lady, I've been here just as long as you, and I don't see any war going on."

"It's there all the same. Once I can communicate with the rocks, I'm going to teach them how to fight

Forrest."

Tobias glanced at the other terminal in the cockpit and decided that trying to read in the same compartment with Lady and her shiv would not exactly be the ultimate in relaxation. There was another terminal in engineering. The ghosts in engineering, however, had been sufficient to keep Tobias out of there since he and Forrest had dragged Osborn's remains from the compartment. Suddenly he felt very tired. Perhaps even tired enough to sleep. He got to his feet and slowly made his way out of the ship.

As he stood in the dim, red light outside the cargo hatch, he noticed one of the white rocks. It was rounded and about the size of a pillow. It had been there ever since—

No, he thought. *It's closer to the hatch now. When we landed it was farther away.* He shook his head. Another recruit for Lady Name's liberation army. He muttered as he walked toward his shelter, "Enlist now. Avoid the rush later."

As he passed the main shelter, he glanced in and froze as he saw Tillson's naked body hanging by its neck from a piece of cargo line tied to the dome's center brace.

He entered the shelter and lowered himself into a chair as a feeling of absolute desolation invaded his soul. *What's the point? What is the point of any of it?*

"Isn't that just a tad ghoulish for entertainment, Tobias?" It was Forrest's voice. He was standing in the doorway. Forrest nodded toward the body. "Just look at that. The man was totally incompetent. Look at the way he placed that noose, straight up the back."

Tobias closed his eyes and leaned his head against the back of his chair. "It seems to have done what it was intended to do."

"True. But old Tillson must have done quite a mambo before he died. His neck isn't broken, Tobias. He danced. He danced for a long time."

"I guess Tillson just wasn't much of a hangman."

Forrest snorted out a laugh. "He wasn't much of a chaplain, either. He just wasn't much of anything."

There were sounds coming from behind Forrest. He turned and Cage pushed past him and came to a halt as the body came into his view. "For God's sake." Cage looked first at Forrest and then at Tobias seated in the chair. "For God's sake, cut him down!" He moved toward the body.

Forrest studied Tillson's still form. "Wouldn't it be amusing to leave him there for Lady Name? We'd all be eating our rations as though nothing were out of the ordinary, and in she'd come. What would she do?"

Cage finished righting the overturned chair next to the hanging corpse. "Give me a hand, someone."

Tobias pushed himself to his feet and headed toward the door. He paused next to Forrest. "Help him. Help him you sonofabitch, or I'll kill you."

A breath of amusement passed over Forrest's face as he walked over to Cage and began helping him take down the body.

Outside, walking rapidly away from the camp, Tobias felt the angry sickness forcing its way through his wall of control. He began running into the dark.

"why must I die"
"ask this thing"
"i asked this thing and no answer"
"ways of this thing are mysterious—die"

The second Earthday into the new sunrise. Tobias stood on Graveyard Hill next to Tillson's grave marker, staring at the long shadows cast by the rocks below. One of the shadows moved. His gaze traced along the shadow to its source. It was Forrest moving among the rocks.

Tobias squatted, leaned his forearms upon his knees, and clasped his hands together. Curious that no one had questioned whether Tillson's suicide was in fact a suicide. The body had been taken down, planted, and never mentioned again.

Tillson's mind had gone, no question about that. His shelter had been littered with incoherent scribblings. Mostly theological squirrel droppings, a rambling eternal justification of the author's existence. There were occasional moments of apparent lucidity. Relative lucidity. All things being relative.

Most of Tillson's lucid moments were crowded with the pain and anguish of a man who knows he is losing his mind. Fragments still teased Tobias's mind.

"Forrest explained that each rock is a small community of the creatures. A community of individuals bound by their physical nature and shared nervous systems to act for the community's welfare, much like the cells of a human body. Each rock, then, can be treated as an individual. The rock color is a genetic

138

thing and has no other significance. The rocks cannot perceive anything that doesn't stay still for at least the equivalent of nine Earth days.

"He dispenses pain and death to the rocks according to whether the rocks have acted in accordance with the signs he has made. It must be terrifying to the creatures. Signs suddenly appearing out of nowhere. Signs that, if they are disobeyed, instantly reap horrible consequences. The creatures must believe themselves to be in the grip of spirits — terrible gods.

"Forrest is teaching them good and evil. Doing what Forrest signs is the good; disobeying Forrest is the evil. Before Forrest these creatures had no conception of good and evil. The horrors of moral commandments whose reasons for existence must be taken on blind faith. I wonder if the rocks will survive morality as long as humans have.

"A few moments ago Forrest showed me something. It was a green pebble the size of a blueberry. It seems that several of the rocks, acting in concert, prepared a platform and placed this pebble upon it. Then they left the platform. It must have taken many weeks. But there it is. The faithful tithing to their god. They prepared an altar and placed one of their members upon it. A gift. A virgin thrown into the volcano. A lamb pumping out its blood in the temple. The rocks have learned how to sacrifice.

"I am an obscenity."

There was no possible way of knowing how long after writing those words that the chaplain had

139

hanged himself. Or had been murdered.

"I am an obscenity."

Tobias looked down at Tillson's grave marker. "This is a hell of a place to try and judge an entire life, Howard."

A whoop of joy came from below. Tobias turned his head to see Forrest running among the rocks. And the rocks he was running among were of only two colors, green and red. Everywhere else there was a fairly even mix of white, green, gray, and black, as well as dead red ones. But in Forrest's little community the only ones left living were green. The green rocks, in accordance with their god's wish, had killed those who were not green. There had indeed been a war.

Tobias reached down and picked up a small white rock. The terror, the passion that must exist in those very slow creatures. The pain of those who sacrificed one of their own number to Forrest. It wouldn't be a sacrifice without the pain of loss. And the pain couldn't exist without some form of love.

What about that little green pebble? The article of sacrifice? If the others had time enough to move away from the platform, so did the pebble. It had been green. Alive. It had faced the horror of the unknowable. And it had stood there, waiting for Forrest.

Courage?

He suddenly felt guilty about holding the white rock and tried to replace it exactly from where it had come. But he couldn't remember which side had been up. He stood, wondering how he would feel if the next instant he found himself standing on his head.

He headed for the ship, being careful where he

140

placed his feet.

"the green kills ours — why"
"the gray must kill the green — how"
"this thing serves the green"
"this thing will serve the gray if the gray obeys this thing"

Tobias sat in the commo couch and watched Lady Name alternately punch buttons and refer to the notes that she kept on slips of paper in her right breast pocket. The sensors he had installed above the cockpit seemed to be working, whatever it was that they did.

"There." She pointed at the incomprehensible scramble of numbers on the display. "That's the key. We'll be able to talk to them in a bit."

"Forrest can already do that."

"Our way will be much faster. We won't have to fuck them over and wait for them to deduce the message. Direct communication." She faced Tobias. "Did you find the portable units?"

He nodded toward the rear of the cockpit, where two heavy-looking, brown metal cases stood. "What do we need those for?"

She turned back to the display. "As soon as Forrest figures out what we're doing in here he'll turn this computer into rubble. Once I have the data milked and processed through this thing, we won't need it anymore. I'll enter the translation codes into the portable units, and we can use them. I hope they're still working."

"They don't look damaged." Tobias looked back at

141

the units as he felt himself squirm in his chair. Lady Name's use of the pronoun we made Tobias more than a bit uncomfortable. After all, she was crazy.

"Why don't we just kill Forrest and be done with it?"

"We aren't murderers, Tobias. We are the good guys." Tobias glanced at the knife resting on her lap and raised an eyebrow. She nodded and reached for the keyboard. "Hide the soft suits and portable units while I try it out and see what happens."

"the gray also seeks the signs of this thing"

"this thing serves the green—we obeyed"

"still the gray seeks the signs"

"this thing will not betray the green"

"This thing will betray you."

"who signs"

"Truth."

"we obey this thing"

"this thing will not betray us"

"This thing will betray you."

"who signs"

"Truth."

"truth is what"

"I am."

"does truth serve the green"

"Truth serves truth. Will the green serve truth?"

"the green serves this thing"

"The gray serves this thing. Truth is stronger. Serve me."

"truth what have we done"

"what have we done"

Lady had been right about Forrest going after the

computer. While they had been pulling down rations in the dome, the circuits had been trashed. Shortly after, Cage wandered off in the distance beyond the ship. Tobias had followed the man's footsteps in the red ash, between and around the endless rocks, until he came to a bottomless chasm. It was an opening that looked as though real gods had scarred the floor of the plain with a huge razor. The footsteps went to the edge, and that was that.

So long Cage.

From the entrance to the dome, Tobias watched Forrest study his subjects in the dying light at the end of another week-long sunset. He was seated on top of one of the large red stones. Surrounding him were nothing but red rocks. All quite alive.

Lady Name had told them: "You must fight this thing, not each other."

"how to fight this thing"

"Play dead."

Tobias chuckled as he gnawed at his rations. Forrest's new army, as well as his original force, were immobilized. They wouldn't fight. Lady Name had given the green the command to tell the gray about truth. The word had even spread to the white and the black. If you don't fight, you don't have to kill. If you don't fight, you don't have to die.

Tobias laughed out loud. Play dead; turn red. It would be a simple task for the rocks, requiring only the sacrifice of each rock's surface members. The surface dies, but inside they live. And growth takes place against the ground.

He saw Forrest's head turn slowly in his direction. The small man studied him, his face as expressionless as one of the rocks. He called out, "Tobias!" He held up the current generator. "Tobias, what if I kill them all? What if I just go from stone to stone and give each a little shot?"

"Then you'd have nothing left to play with except your radish, Forrest. Your game would be over."

He lowered his shock stick and grinned. "You joined the wrong side, Tobias."

Tobias laughed and turned into the dome. He finished off his nutribar, tossed the wrapper on the floor, and flopped down in a chair facing the doorway. He had taken to sitting and sleeping facing doorways. When someone's out to get you, paranoia is just practical thinking.

He glanced at the position of Mantchee and frowned. Lady Name was going to meet him to explain the new sequence they were going to initiate. She had determined that the rocks had the ability to excrete their waste products in the form of a highly corrosive vapor. It wouldn't kill the rocks. Their ability to obtain what they needed from the atmosphere wouldn't be affected. Creatures with lungs, however, would die.

The soft suits and respirators would leave only Forrest inhaling acid. The only real problem was trying to convince the rocks to do it. Lady Name suspected that for some reason, the rocks might object to wandering around in a cloud of their own shit.

The doorway darkened. It was Forrest, and he was holding something in his hands. He squatted in the

144

doorway.

"You know, Tobias, there were many times in my life when I thought I had all my ducks in a row. When I thought I was on top of everything. It wasn't always true."

Tobias hooked another chair with the toe of his boot and pulled it closer to him, crossing his legs at the ankles upon it. "Welcome to the club."

Forrest looked down at what was in his hands. "It might not be true for you."

"Just stop fucking with the rocks, Forrest, and it'll be all over."

He glanced up and grinned. "You think so?" He placed what was in his hands upon the floor, stepped upon it with one foot, and lifted as the sound of a sharp crack reverberated around the dome.

He stood and tossed the object across the space that separated them. Tobias caught it with his left hand as Forrest turned and left the doorway empty.

It took a moment, but Tobias recognized the object. It was the hilt of Lady Name's knife.

"there is a new one"
"it is this thing"
"it signs as truth signs"
"it is this thing stronger"
"there is a sign"
"truth do you sign"
"Truth is dead."
"truth cannot die"
"Call truth and see."
"we call truth—truth see our sign—truth"
"Truth does not see your sign. Truth is dead."

"who do we serve now"
"You know me."
"this thing"
"must we again kill and die to serve"
"You know me."
"we know you"

By the light of the Oids he had found her among the mountain of red rocks beyond the ship, on the way to Cage's Chasm. That's where she had stashed her half of the equipment. Her soft suit had been slashed, her respirator broken. Her portable communication unit was missing. She was dead. Tobias extinguished his light and turned away. Forrest must have taken some time to multilate Lady Name's body.

Had Forrest found the other suit and communication unit? Tobias looked back toward the gentle silver gleam of the ship. To Hell with it. Let Forrest play with the damned rocks if that's what he wanted. What did Tobias care? Keep going with the rations, stay out of Forrest's way. Wait for rescue. Simple.

He turned back, knelt on both knees next to her body, and clumsily began pushing the red ash over her. "You dumb bitch. You dumb crazy bitch."

"what must we do to atone"
"There is another. Kill it."
"to kill what we cannot see—how"
"Find a way."

The edge of another new sunrise. Tobias looked through the dome window at the pink of the slow dawn. How long had it been since he had seen

Forrest? Back when the man had broken Lady Name's knife. He frowned. Had only one night passed, or was it two? Or three?

He sipped at his steaming beverage, lowered his cup, and looked at it. Somewhere back on Earth there was a person with a degree in nutrition who had never stepped outside of his or her environmentally controlled city. That person had invented N-669 Beverage, Survival, Hot. More than likely that person had never tasted N-669 Beverage, Survival, Hot. At odd moments Tobias had a fantasy about finding that person, cramming a funnel down his or her throat, and pouring in ten or twelve liters of N-669 Beverage, Survival, Hot.

A sound. He slowly looked up and turned.

The sound had been something between a groan and a creak. He looked up at the inside of the dome. No problem there that he could see. His head turned toward the doorway. As he took a step toward it, half of the dome came crashing down to the floor next to him; it knocked him clear across to the wall of the undamaged half.

Another crash. Another.

He cleared his head, opened his eyes, and watched the open sky in horror as a ten-meter column of rocks teetered, then came falling toward him.

He scrambled to his feet and leaped into the rubble to escape, a deafening roar and a choking cloud of dust overtaking him.

The sounds stopped, and the dust settled. He opened his eyes and chanced a glance at his surroundings. The dome was nothing but rubble crisscrossed by collapsed columns of rocks. He pulled himself to his feet, climbed up the rocks and rubble until he stood on top. Except for where he was standing, the landscape was unchanged, the long shadows of the morning pointing away from the bit of Mantchee that showed over the horizon.

"Forrest!" Forrest was nowhere to be seen. "Forrest!"

Tobias took several deep breaths and looked down at the destruction of the dome. Without the dispenser what rations he could rescue from the wreckage would last only a few days—Earth days at that. Without the dispenser . . . he looked at the empty cup still gripped in his hand. So long N-669 Beverage, Survival, Hot. There were no more dispensers or rations in the ship's cargo hold. The equipment used to tap into the groundwater supply had been crushed along with the dispenser.

Tobias began gathering up the few nutribars he could find and reach. Already his mind was planning what he would do once he broke out his own portable communication unit and set up his command post. There still remained Lady Name's stunt with the corrosive vapor. Tobias didn't wonder about being able to figure out how to get the rocks to do it. He *had* to. But first there was food, water, shelter to arrange. Time. It would take time. But he had nothing but time. He spoke in mutters as he worked.

"I'll get you, Forrest. You miserable little son of a bitch. I'll get you."

"we have found truth"
"is truth dead"
"truth is dead—it is a strange creature truth—soft

small and made of food"

"what of the other this thing wants us to kill"

"we do not know—some toward the beginning of the new light sign about another there far below the surface dead—in the mound are the two who appeared when this thing first appeared—they are dead"

"four of them—still there is this thing"

"there is a sign"

"Forrest. Answer if you're reading. Forrest."

"who signs"

"I look for the one called this thing."

"truth is dead—you are not this thing"

"are you the other"

"I am God. Where is this thing?"

"who is god"

"I am. God rules all."

"are you like truth or like this thing"

"No. I have more power."

"even we can see this thing"

"If you cannot see this thing we have more power than god"

"Serve God or you will suffer."

"this thing already provides us with what you offer us god—we serve this thing"

"You must serve me."

"Communicate. I am stronger than this thing. Answer. Answer. Answer."

From the top of Graveyard Hill, Tobias surveyed the results of his efforts. He was standing in the center of a circular enclosure of red rocks, a triangular piece of the dome serving as a roof. Inside were some cushions from the dome and a panel he had grabbed from the ship. The panel controlled the array of debris-impregnated seismic charges surrounding his position on the hill. If Forrest or any of his followers wanted to get at him, they'd need a guide to get through the fireworks.

Next to the cushions was a stack of the seismic charges rigged with adjustable time-delay triggers. They were in case Forrest told his rocks to do the falling-column bit again. The soft suit and respirator were still in their containers, in case Tobias ever got some of the rocks to see things his way. Next to the soft suit were his container of water lugged from the surface stream and his supply of ration bars. In addition to the ration bars, he had managed to salvage four containers of the powder that the dispenser used to make up good old N-669 Beverage, Survival, Hot. Vitamins, minerals, and old underwear. He wondered what N-669 would taste like cold.

Next to the rations, on the other side of the cushions, stood the portable communication unit. Tobias bit the skin on the inside of his lower lip. *What did the rocks mean when they said they could see Forrest?*

He leaned his forearms upon the edge of the red wall and scanned the area behind Graveyard Hill. Forrest was nowhere around. Not even a footprint. And for the rocks to see Forrest, he would have to stay substantially in one place for the better part of nine Earth days. Tobias looked farther to the right, moving his position until he was overlooking the camp. The shelters had been in place long enough to be seen. And the graves. The ship.

He studied the wreckage of the ship. To the rocks it

must have appeared out of nowhere. Huge, gleaming. Silver. A color the rocks had never seen before. And then they began getting signs. Certain actions in relation to the signs brought death. Other actions did not. They learned the penalty of disobedience. Good and evil came to stay. And it all began after the ship appeared.

Tobias nodded and sat on his cushions, energizing the portable communications unit. "Oh, Forrest, old buddy. Do I have a numnum for you."

"who signs"

"God."

"we serve this thing"

"I have found this thing. If I kill this thing, will you serve me?"

"we see this thing—this thing now sees what we think"

"I see what you think. Will you serve me?"

"we see this thing"

"I will kill this thing and appear to you. Then you will serve me."

"we wait"

The directional indicator on the portable unit and a quick move enabled him to triangulate the positions of two of the rocks with which he had been communicating. After marking them, it took only minutes to rig the ship. Remote-controlled seismic charges next to the half-full fuel cells. Tobias quickly searched the crew's quarters and scanned the cargo hold for anything additional that he might be able to use. There was a three-wheeled motorized "mule." He energized

151

it and drove it over and around the mess in the hold until he was outside, next to the marked rocks. He worked the forks of the mule beneath first one rock and then the next. With the rocks secured, he drove them to the top of Graveyard Hill and parked them where they could see both the ship and the inside of his bunker. Moving the rocks would add some time to the demonstration, but he would be too vulnerable in the open.

His preparations completed, he sat down and waited. If he stayed in the same place, in the same position, with only brief absences to piss on Mikizu's grave, the rocks would see him shortly after they were able to perceive the ship. The only problem was boredom. But there were entertainments. Keeping alert for an attack of some kind by Forrest. That and the voices he was beginning to hear.

All a part of going crazy, he reminded himself. Still he wished the voices were loud enough for him to understand. Who knows? His insanity might have something interesting to say.

He sat back and stared at the two green rocks he was trying to convince. A thought passed his attention, and he began laughing, "Talk about your hard sells!"

When he calmed down, he began to wait.

"who signs"
"God. I have moved you."
"your power is great"
"Do you see this thing?"
"we see this thing"
"Do you see me?"

152

"we see you god — you are very small — this thing is much larger"

"My power is greater."

"this thing has moved us without us seeing the move — what you have done is no more"

"Will you serve me on faith, or must I kill this thing?"

"you must kill this thing"

Mantchee was slowly moving toward sunset, but enough time remained. Tobias pressed the remote trigger and watched as the ship disappeared in a sheet of light and sound. Too bad, he thought as he watched the heat carry the flames and black smoke high into the shimmering red of the sky. It's too bad that it happens so quickly. If they could see it, the flaming death of this thing would impress the rocks.

He sat back to wait. It would take another nine days for the rocks to see that this thing was destroyed.

The portable communication unit began making strange buzzing sounds. He looked at the operation panel inside the case. The only image on the screen above the tiny keyboard was an instructional line: SWITCH FUNCTION TO NORMAL RECEIVE.

He did as instructed and sat back in shock, withdrawing his hand as though it had been burned, as an angry, deep snarl came from the unit's speaker.

"Tobias! Tobias, I'm coming for you! Do you hear me?"

After his shock passed, Tobias grinned. "Is something wrong, Forrest?"

"The ship! Why did you blow the ship?"

"I think you know, old thing. Shall I put on a nice,

153

hot cup of N-669 when you come calling? By the way, old thing, what are you using for food these days?"

The unit was silent. Tobias laughed as he switched the function selector back to the rock channel. It didn't seem so long a time. The nine days. The voices provided some entertainment. Still, they were muddy, too distant. But at times they even seemed to sing. Especially toward the end. Strange songs. Forrest never did show.

"It is time to decide."
"this thing brings us pain and death — god what do you bring us"
"The good."
"god we will serve you"
"And now will you have faith in me?"
"god we will have faith in you"
"Tell the others. All must serve God."
"god we will tell the others"

Does perception of time adjust to the local framework of time? Tobias let the thought sit just behind his eyes as he made his weary way to the stream. There didn't seem to be enough time in the day to do everything. Lug water, eat, talk to the rocks, and try to get them to understand about the acid vapor. He had gone back and dug up Lady Name's body, hoping there would be some clue in her notes. She must have had some idea about how to get the rocks to expel the vapor. But her breast pocket was empty. If anyone had those notes, it was Forrest.

But it was the feel of the dead breast behind that pocket that captured his attention. Hard. Unyielding.

154

He uncovered it and found it to be made of gray stone. Her entire body had been replaced by the gray. Back at Graveyard Hill, he uncovered part of Osborn's body. He had been replaced by gray and green. He didn't bother to check out Mikizu. Whatever the rocks were doing, they were only doing it to the dead. That was none of his concern. Not yet.

He came to the bank of the stream and lowered his containers to the ground. The stream was dry. He climbed down the bank and dug at the cracked surface of the bed with his hands. Dry.

He sat back on his heels, his gaze resting on the distant hills. *That's where the water comes from*, he thought. *And that's where Forrest is. That's where he cut it off.*

And that's where I'm going to kill you.

The light and the dark. Days. It seemed that so much time had passed that he ought to have forgotten what he was trying to do. At moments he would forget.

He finished securing the portable communication unit to the mule next to the driver's seat. In the vehicle's tiny cargo bay were the remainder of his rations, the water containers, his soft suit and respirator, and his supply of bombs. He looked back at the two green rocks that had been keeping him company for—

How long? He looked at the communication unit. There was a date- and time-indicator function. He didn't know the date. For some reason it seemed important to know.

155

He opened the unit, energized it, and switched the function selector to date/time. The figures were unreadable, a smear of flashes, as though the indications had been recorded in time lapse and replayed at normal speed.

The reflection of his image in the screen showed the face of an old man.

"god"

"What?" Tobias looked up and around. He looked back at the communication unit. The function selector was still on date/time. The voices again?

"god"

He looked again at the two green rocks.

"What?"

"take me with you"

"Why?"

"there is a new one more powerful than this thing"

The rock on the right. He didn't know how, but he knew that was the one that was talking to him. *Have I slowed down that much,* he wondered, *or have the rocks finally gotten it into high gear? Or have I lost my mind?*

"god bring me"

"Why?"

"i can help you"

"Help me to do what?"

"i can help you fight lucifer"

So Forrest is calling himself Lucifer. Tobias leaned against the mule and looked toward the hills. He nodded. "Sure. You come."

And he saw the rock move.

It seemed to flow across the red dust. A balloon filled with water. Light and dark. Rapidly shifting shadows. Time. Again light, the dark, light. The rock was now next to the mule.

He watched Mantchee streak across the sky, leaving him not in day or night but in half-light. That fast, he wondered, or have I become that slow.

"Am I seeing this as you see it?"

"i do not know how god sees"

Tobias pulled himself into the driver's seat. The brace he had grabbed came away in his hand. The metal of the mule was pitted, corroded, like lace. The supplies, the soft suit, the water containers — all dust.

He stood naked, a film of gray over his skin. He sank down next to the green rock. "I can't make it. Too tired. Too old."

"we will carry you"

Tobias watched the landscape move. Green, gray, black, and white globes flowing around the red. Rapid rivers of shapes. He felt himself lifted and carried. In the sky Mantchee was an even bar of yellow light against the dim pink.

As he was moved along, floating upon that softly undulating river of life, the edge of a thought — *what would he do when he met Forrest?* — came and left many times. *My mind*, he said to himself, *really is going. But Forrest will be just as old, if he's still alive.*

He was at the hills. He could not push himself up to look. The rocks rose beneath his head and shoulders.

"Forrest."

There was no answer, except for the stinging pain all over his body. He watched his skin peel and blacken, curling away to expose the bones beneath. The acid. Forrest taught them to shit acid.

157

"I can't fight him. I am dying."

"god you must live — become as lucifer"

"I am God. Good cannot become as Lucifer. I am good."

"lucifer says he is the evil — is good less powerful than lucifer"

"I cannot change my purpose."

"change not purpose — change form — become as lucifer"

The thread of a thought spoke to him. *Lucifer has no protection against the acid. Then what has Lucifer become? And what must I become to live?*

"I am afraid."

"god — you want us to have faith in you — have faith in us — become as lucifer"

There was not enough tissue left to force air through vocal cords that no longer existed. His thought was his response. *Very well. I will become as Lucifer.*

He stood, his height above the crest of the hills, his reach wider than the plain beneath his feet. Beyond the hills a massive head leered back at him. The face was rot, corruption, evil.

"You are God," it hissed.

"Lucifer."

A glow invaded the engineer's heart. He reached out his great arms and wrapped his fingers around the monster's throat.

When they came to investigate the weak, garbled signal from the Oids Belt, they quickly located the beacon. It was from a type of commercial cargo ship that hadn't been in use for over a century. Of the ship, passengers, and crew, the only trace remaining was a curious statue of two naked human men, in mortal combat, standing upon the bodies of five other humans, the sculpture surrounded by a wall of red masonry. The local life form informed them that the statue was titled "Equilibrium."

TRACK OF A LEGEND

By Cynthia Felice

Christmas started at school right after we returned from Thanksgiving holiday and took down the paper turkeys and pilgrims from the windows. The teacher sang "Jingle bells, Santa smells, Rudolph laid an egg" all the while that he was supposed to be reprogramming my December reading assignment, and the computer printed out MERRY CHRISTMAS every time I matched a vowel sound with the right word, and BAH, HUMBUG whenever I was wrong. And it said BAH, HUMBUG a lot and didn't light up the observation board. We used the gold math beads as garlands for the tree because we ate most of the popcorn, and paper chains were for kindergarteners who weren't smart enough to scheme to get out of lessons. Still, we had to listen to civic cassettes so that we would know it was also the anniversary of the Christmas Treaty of '55 that brought peace to all the world again. And to top it off, on the very last day before

Christmas our teacher improvised a lecture about how whole stations full of people had nowhere to go but back to Earth, their way of life taken from them by the stroke of a pen. The cassettes didn't mention that part. I didn't think Earth was such a bad place to go, but I didn't speak up because I was eager to cut out prancing, round-humped reindeer with great racks of antlers from colored construction paper. I put glitter that was supposed to be used on the bells on the antlers and hooves, and the racks were so heavy that my reindeer's heads tore off when I hung them up. After lunch teacher said he didn't know why we were sitting around school on Christmas Eve day when it was snowing, and he told us to go build snowmen, and he swept up the scraps of construction paper and celluloid and glitter alone while we put our Christmas stars in plastic sacks and tucked them into our jackets so that our hands would be free to make snowballs.

My best friend, Timothy, and I took some of the gingerbread cookies sprinkled with red sugar to leave in the woods for Bigfoot, then ran out the door and got pelted with snowballs by upper-graders who must have sneaked out earlier.

Timothy and I ran over the new-fallen snow in the playground to duck behind the farthest fence, where we scooped up snow and fired back. We were evenly matched for a while, snowballs flying thick and heavy. Then the little kids came out of school and betrayed us by striking our flanks.

"The little brats," Timothy muttered, throwing down a slushball. I suspect he was less upset that the little ones had decided to team up with the big kids

162

than that one of them was crying and making his way to the school building, and someone was sure to come checking to see who was making ice balls. "Come on," he said, still feigning disgust. "Let's go build our own fort and get ready for Bigfoot."

The creature of yore was not so legendary in our parts, where we kids often found footprints in mud after rainstorms and in the snows of winter, especially in the woods surrounding the school. The grown-ups just shook their heads and said someone was playing a joke, that nobody wore shoes that big and that a real Bigfoot would be barefoot, like in the video show. But no one really knew what Bigfoot's toes looked like. My dad said even the video maker just guessed. We kids figured Bigfoot's foot was full of matted hair or lumpy skin that left those strange-looking ridges. And we just knew that Bigfoot came out in the dark storms looking for a stray child to eat, and that gingerbread cookies merely whetted the creature's appetite.

Leaving the school behind us, we made our way toward the greenway along the hoverpath, where the freighters sprayed us with a blizzard of snow when they whooshed by.

"Look here," Timothy shouted, tugging at something he'd stepped on in the snow. Both of us scratched at the snow and pulled until we freed a great piece of cardboard. It was frozen stiff.

"Let's go to the hill," I said.

Dragging our cardboard sled behind us, we trudged along Bigfoot's own trail through the woods. You could tell the creature had passed here from time to time because branches were broken back wider than any kid could cause, and the path circled the hill outside a wire-and-picket fence, and the gate was always locked to keep Bigfoot and everyone else out. The hill was treeless, acres of grass manicured by robots with great rotary blades in summer and smooth as a cue ball in winter. Perfect for sledding. The only trouble with the hill was that Timothy's aunt lived in the shiny tin-can-lying-on-its-side house at the top. I knew she was weird because Timothy said she never came outside or went anywhere, and my parents would shake their heads when they talked about her. But we had the cardboard sled in our hands, and he was pulling strongly; so I guess he didn't care about his weird aunt.

The fence might keep clumsy Bigfoot out but delayed us only a few seconds when we snagged a ragged edge of the cardboard on it and had to stop to free it. Then we climbed what seemed to be fourteen thousand one hundred ten meters of elevation to a place a little below the odd house, where we finally rested, breathing as hard as ancient warriors who'd just dragged their elephant up the Alps.

Timothy's aunt's house whirred and clicked, and I looked up. There were no windows, but it had a thousand eyes hidden in the silver rivets that held the metal skin over tungsten bones.

In the white snow it looked desolate, save for a trickle of smoke.

"Hey, your aunt's house is on fire," I said.

Timothy gave me a look that always made me feel stupid. "Her heat exchanger's broken. She's burning gas," he said. "I know because she asked my dad to get her a new one before Christmas."

"Does she come to your house for Christmas?"

"Nah. Sometimes she comes video, just like she used to when she lived up there." He gestured skyward, where snowflakes were crystallizing and falling on us, but I knew he meant higher, one of the space stations or orbiting cities. "It's better now because there's no delay when we talk. It's like she was in Portland or something."

"What's she like?" I said, suddenly wondering about this peculiar person who had been a fixture in my community since I was little, yet whom I'd never seen.

Timothy shrugged. "Like an aunt . . . always wanting to know if I ate my peas." Warrior Timothy was patting the cardboard elephant sled, making ready to resume our journey in the Alps.

"Why doesn't she come out of there?"

"My dad says she's got a complex or something from when she lived up there." He gestured skyward again.

"What's a complex?"

For a moment Timothy looked blank, then he said, "It's like what Joan-John and Lester-Linda Johnson have."

"You mean she goes to the clinic and comes back something else?" I said, wondering if his aunt used to be his uncle.

"I mean she doesn't go anywhere."

"But like to the consumer showcases down in the mall and the restaurant. She goes there, doesn't she?"

"Nope. Last year when her mux cable got cut and her video wasn't working she practically starved to death."

"But why? Is she crippled or something?" The teacher had said he knew a spacer who spent most of his time in a swimming pool, and when he did come out he had to use a wheelchair because he was too old to get used to gravity again.

"No, she's not crippled."

"What's she look like?"

"My mother."

Timothy's mother was regular looking; so whatever a complex was, it had nothing to do with getting ugly. The Johnsons weren't ugly either, but they went through what my dad called phases, which he said was all in their heads. Maybe Timothy's aunt's complex was like Lester Johnson's Linda phase, but that didn't seem right because Lester-Linda came outside all the time and Timothy's aunt never did.

"What does she do inside all the time?"

"Works."

I nodded, considerably wiser. The old public buildings were down in the woods with the school, mostly monuments to waste of space ever since we got our mux cable that fed into every building in the community. Most of the grown-ups stopped *going* to work, and they stopped coming to school on voting day, but we still had to go, and not just on voting day.

"Come on," Timothy said.

But the smoke fascinated me. It puffed out of a silver pipe and skittered down the side of the house as if the fluffy falling snow was pushing it down. It smelled strange. I formed a snowball, a good solid one, took aim at the silver pipe, and let it fly.

"Missed by at least a kilometer," Timothy said, scowling.

166

Undaunted I tried another, missed the pipe, but struck the house, which resounded with a metallic thud. I'd closed one of the house's eyes with a white patch of snow. Timothy grinned at me, his mind tracking with mine. She'd have to come out to get the snow off the sensors. Soon we had pasted a wavy line of white spots about midway up the silver wall.

"One more on the right," commanded Timothy. But he stopped midswing when we heard a loud whirring noise. Around the hill came a grass cutter, furiously churning snow with its blades.

"Retreat!" shouted Attila the Hun. Timothy grabbed the frozen cardboard sled.

We leaped aboard and the elephant sank to its knees. I didn't need Timothy to tell me to run.

At the fence we threw ourselves over the frozen pickets, miraculously not getting our clothes hung up in the wires. The grass cutter whirred along the fenced perimeter, frustrated, thank goodness, by the limits of its oxide-on-sand mind.

"Ever seen what one of those things does to a rabbit?" he asked me.

"No."

"Cuts them up into bits of fur and guts," Timothy said solemnly.

"Your aunt's weird," I said, grateful to be on the right side of the fence.

"Uh oh. You lost a glove," Timothy said.

I nodded unhappily and turned to look over at the wrong side of the fence. Shreds of felt and wire and red nylon lay in the grass cutter's swath.

We walked on, feeling like two dejected warriors in the Alpine woods without our elephant and minus one almost-new battery-operated glove until we spied Bigfoot's tracks in the snow—big, round splots leading up the side of the wash. Heartened by our discovery, we armed ourselves properly with snowballs and told each other this was the genuine article. The snowfall was heavier now, really Bigfoot weather, and we knew how much Bigfoot liked storms, or we'd find tracks all the time.

We followed the footprints all the way to the Wigginses' house, only to find little Bobby Wiggles in them, hand-me-down boots overheating and making great puddles with each step.

Bobby stood looked at us, cheeks flushed from heat or stinging wind. Then he or she—I couldn't tell if Bobby Wiggles was a boy or a girl—giggled and went running into the house.

Timothy and I stayed out in the snow searching for Bigfoot tracks but found only rabbit tracks, which we followed in hopes that Bigfoot might do likewise, since aside from children there was nothing else for it to eat in our neighborhood, and no children had ever been reported eaten. Bigfoot may not have been hungry, but we had had only a few gingerbread cookies since noon; so when the rabbit tracks zagged near my house, we didn't turn again. We forgot the rabbit and Bigfoot and walked the rest of the way through the ghost-white woods to my front door, where we kicked off our boots and threw down our jackets and gloves. Mom and Dad were in the media room in front of the kitchen monitor, checking the Christmas menu.

"Go back and plug your gloves into the recharger," Dad said without glancing up.

But Mom must have looked up because she said right away, "Both of them."

"I lost one," I said.

"Go back and find it."

Timothy and I looked at each other.

Mom was still watching me. "It won't do any good," I said finally. "We were up on the hill, and Timothy's aunt sicced the grass cutter on us."

"Why would she do a thing like that?"

Timothy and I shrugged.

"Well, I'll call her and ask her to let you get your glove," Dad said, rolling his chair to the comm console.

"The grass cutter got it," I said, more willing to face punishment for losing a glove than what might happen if Dad found out the day before Christmas that we'd closed her house's eyes.

"I told you she was getting crazier by the minute," Dad said.

"She isn't dangerous."

"How do you know that? The grass cutter, of all things."

"She has too much dread to be deliberately mean. I don't doubt for a second that she knew a couple of kids could outrun the grass cutter, and what else could she do? Go outside and ask them to go away?" Mom shook her head. "Her heart would stop from the anxiety of leaving her little sanctuary."

"She left the clinic fast enough when it caught on fire, and when she first came back that was as much her sanctuary as her spaceship house is now."

"You can't expect her to have enough energy to treat every minor day-to-day incident like an emer-

169

gency."

"I think she should go back where she came from."

"Hush, dear. We voted for the treaty."

"They ought to have sent them to L-5."

"Couldn't, and you know—"

Timothy and I left them talking about his aunt, but I knew I'd probably not heard the end of the glove. That was the problem with sexagenarian parents; they knew all the tricks from the first set of kids, and they had very good memories.

In the kitchen we had hot chocolate, slopping some on the puzzle my big sister had broken back into a thousand pieces before she gave it to me.

"What are you getting for Christmas?" Timothy asked me, his cheeks still pink from being outdoors and his eyes as bright as tinsel fluttering in the warm convection currents of the house.

I shrugged. My parents were firm about keeping the Christmas list up-to-date, and that started every year on December twenty-sixth. I still wanted the fighting kite I'd keyed into the list last March, and the bicycle sail and the knife and the Adventure Station with vitalized figures and voice control. I also wanted the two hundred and eighty other items on my list and knew I'd be lucky if ten were under the tree tomorrow morning and that some of them would be clothes, which I never asked for but always received. "An Adventure Station," I finally said, more hopeful than certain. It was the one thing I'd talked about a lot, but Dad kept saying it was too much like the Hovercraft Depot set I'd gotten last year.

"Me too," Timothy said, "and a sled. Which should we play with first?"

A sled! I didn't have to go to the terminal and ask for a display of my Christmas list to know that a sled was not on it. My old one had worked just fine all last winter, but I'd used it in June to dam up Cotton Creek to make a pond for my race boats, and a flood had swelled the creek waters and carried it off and busted the runners. Too late to be remembering on Christmas Eve, because I didn't believe in Santa Claus or Kris Kringle. Only in Bigfoot, because I had seen the footprints with my own eyes.

"We should play with the sleds first," Timothy said, "before the other kids come out and ruin the snow."

"I'm going to get a knife with a real L-5 crystal handle."

Timothy shrugged. "My aunt's going to give me one of hers someday. She has lots of stuff from when she was a spacer."

"Yeah, but my knife will be new. Then I'd like to see Bigfoot get away from me!"

"We can bring Bigfoot back on my sled," Timothy said excitedly. He chugalugged the rest of his chocolate. "Early, right after presents. Meet me at the hill."

"Why at the hill?" I said suspiciously. But Timothy was already heading for the door and pulling on his boots.

"Best place for sledding."

"But what about your aunt's mower?" I said, whispering now.

"Early," he reminded me as he stepped out into the snow. I followed him, holding the door open. "And bring your sled."

"What time do you open presents?" I said. But if Timothy answered, I didn't hear.

The snow was falling in fat flakes, and the wind had come up and the snow was starting to drift over the hedges. Funny how it wasn't really dark with all that white around, and funny, too, how I wasn't so glad that it was coming down. What good was it without a sled? I could use the cardboard if I could find it again, which I doubted, for I could tell that if it kept snowing at the rate I was seeing from my doorway, there would be half a meter or more by morning, which also meant the grass cutter would get clogged before it got five meters from Timothy's crazy aunt's house. Timothy would let me try his sled if I pulled it up the hill, 'cause if he didn't I wouldn't let him hold my L-5 crystal-handled knife . . . if I got one.

"Close the door!" my father shouted, and I closed it and went to bed early, knowing I couldn't sleep but wanting to because morning would come sooner if I did, and when it did I would not have a sled—maybe not even an L-5 crystal-handled knife—only an old Adventure Station that Timothy didn't want to play until after lunch, and who cared about snow anyhow, even if it did come down so fast and hard that it was catching on my bedroom window like a blanket before my sleepy eyes.

I woke to silence and the sure knowledge that it was Christmas morning. I didn't know whether to look out the window or check under the tree first, until I heard my sister in the hall and made a dash to beat her to the living room, where my parents had piled all the packages, with their red bows and wrappings, under the tree.

The big one wrapped in red plastic had to be the

Adventure Station, though my parents were famous for putting little items like L-5 crystal-handled knives in packages the size of CRTs, complete with rocks to weigh it down so you couldn't tell. I couldn't wait to find out for sure what was in it, but I had to because my parents came in muttering about coffee and asking if it was even dawn and not caring that it wasn't when they had their coffee and I put their first presents to open in their laps. I wanted to open the red plastic-covered package, but I couldn't tear the plastic, and my big sister was hogging the slitter; so I opened a smaller one with my name on it. A shiny blue crystal that was almost mirror bright but not quite, so I could see the steel blade was in the package, and suddenly I felt good about the snow, too, and about looking for Bigfoot even if we did have to carry it back on Timothy's sled. I got the slitter away from my sister and sliced open the Adventure Station, only it wasn't. I looked at my parents in complete amazement and saw that they both had that special knowing twinkle in their eyes that parents get when they've done something you don't expect them to do. In the packing popcorn was a new sled, the collapsible kind with a handle for carrying it back up the hill and a retractable towing cord and three runner configurations so that it could be used on hard-packed snow or powder. I extended it to its full length right there in the living room, awed by its metallic gleam and classy black racing stripes.

And then with my knife strapped around the outside of my jacket and my sled in hand, I was off to meet Timothy, determined to have Bigfoot in tow before lunchtime. The going was slow because the drifts were tall and I loved to break their peaks and feel the stuff collapse beneath my feet and to stand under the tallest pines and shake the snow off the branches, as if I were in a blizzard and not in the first sparkling rays of sunshine. I went the long way to the hill, sure I would find traces of Bigfoot so early in the morning, and I did. Huge prints that were bigger than I could make, even though they were filled in with new snow, and the stride sure wasn't kid-size. Besides, what grown-up would walk through the woods on Christmas Eve during a snowstorm? I'd follow them, I decided, until I had to turn off for the hill, then Timothy and I would come back and follow the tracks to Bigfoot's lair. But I didn't have to turn off. The fat tracks headed right off through the woods along the same shortcut Timothy and I had used yesterday.

Timothy wasn't there yet, and because I couldn't wait to try my sled on the hill and not because I was afraid to follow the tracks alone, I stopped at the place we'd climbed over yesterday. The snow had drifted along the inside of the fence, almost hiding the pickets from view. I figured that with just a little more accumulation it would have covered the top, then my silver sled could carry me all the way from the top of the hill, over the fence, and deep into the woods, where the trees would provide a test of steering skill or a fast stop. I climbed the fence, sled in hand, then carried armfuls of snow to the highest drift, scooping and shoving until the tops of the pickets were covered. When I was satisfied the sled would glide over, I looked around for Timothy, who might still be opening his presents for all I knew, then

I started to the top of the hill. I was only a little bit wary about the grass cutter, for I figured it would get clogged if it came out in the snow, but you never know what else a crazy lady who sent out grass cutters to hack up kids might have. But the little house at the top was almost completely snow covered, and there was no sign of smoke. Either Timothy's father got her that new heat exchanger or she froze.

At the top of the hill, not too close to the house in case she was just sleeping and not dead, I extended the sled, putting the runners in their widest configuration to keep me atop the deep snow. I climbed on and took off, the Teflon bottom gliding like ice on ice, and the wind stinging my face, and my heart beating with joy at the sled's speed on its very first trial run. Only trouble was that the wide runners didn't steer very well as I picked up speed, and there being no beaten path in the snow, I wasn't completely certain I'd be on target to make my fence jump. I pulled hard to the right, and the sled came with it sluggishly, but enough so I started to think again that I would make the jump. I could see the pickets on either side, and those would make a painful stop, but I was going to make it and know what it was like to fly on a sled for a few meters, or I would have known if I hadn't overcorrected just before hitting the big drift. The sled skidded along the downside of the drift and into a hole. I hit on something that sent me flying. I came down hard, hurt and crying, upside down.

It took me a minute to realize that I wasn't badly hurt, just scraped and bumped here and there, and stuck. My head felt funny, almost like someone was choking me and pressing against my skull, but it wasn't so bad that I couldn't see once I stopped crying. But I couldn't get loose. I could get hold of the fence and turn a bit but not enough to unhook my foot, which was firmly wedged between two pickets as far as it could go. Try as I would, as nimble as I was, and as desperate in knowing that I was quite alone and there was no one to send for help, I could not get loose. I shouted for Timothy, prayed he would come out of the woods and get me loose, but he never came. I cried again, and my tears froze, and the plug in my mitten power pack must have come loose, because my fingers were cold, too. The woods were things with icy tentacles frozen to the sky, and the sun reflected brightly off the snow-topped world and made me cry again. The wide expanse of sky looked vast and forbidding and somehow confirmed my worst fears that there was no one but me within a million klicks. And I wondered how long a person could live upside down. Didn't they do that all the time out in space? It had made Timothy's aunt weird but, oh, Timothy's aunt! Maybe her house had ears as well as eyes, and I shouted and shouted, promising I'd never throw snowballs at her house again. I thought that all the blood in my body was pooled behind my eyeballs, and if I cried again my tears would be blood, and I wanted to cry again because I knew that Timothy's aunt never would come because she never went anywhere.

And then in the stillness of the morning, when there was nothing to hear in the snowpacked world but my crying, I heard what sounded like an animal breathing into a microphone—a very powerful microphone or a very big animal.

I held my breath and listened carefully, watching the woods, terrified that the creature was lurking there behind the snow-covered bushes. But I was hanging upside down, and it took me a moment to realize that the sound was coming from behind me, closer now, hissing. I turned wildly and pressed my face against the pickets to see what was on the other side.

A towering hulk.

Shoulders like a gorilla.

White as the snow.

Breath making great clouds.

Feet leaving massive tracks.

There wasn't a doubt at all in my mind that I'd finally found Bigfoot, and it was more awful than anything I had imagined.

I screamed and struggled, quite willing to leave my foot behind in the fence, if only that were possible. I tried to unsheathe my knife, and I dropped it in the snow. It was within reach, and I might have retrieved it, but the massive creature grabbed me by my coat-tails and hefted me up. With my foot free I kicked blindly, and I must have hurt it because it finally put me down. The fence was between us, but its hand still gripped me by the shoulders—smooth hands without fur, white and slightly slick looking, except there were wrinkles where the joints ought to have been, and those were like gray accordion pleats. I stood, dazed and dizzy from being on my head so long, staring up at Bigfoot's shiny eye. Her face was featureless but for the eye, and she still hissed angrily, and she had a vapor trail drifting out from her backside.

She let go of me, reached over to pick up the L-5 knife, and twirled it between her thumb and forefinger. The crystal flashed in the sunlight, just like the ads they'd filmed on L-5. She flipped it, and I caught it two-handed. I backed away toward where my sled lay, didn't bother to collapse it, but grabbed the cord. I ran for the woods.

When I looked back, Bigfoot was gone, but her tracks left a clear trail to the desolate little house at the top of the hill, where Christmas was wholly a video event, where Timothy's crazy aunt would rather starve to death than come out for food. And sometimes when it snowed, especially when it snowed on Christmas Day, I climbed over the fence of her universe to wipe the drifts of snow off the eyes of her house. It fell like glittering Christmas stars, peaceful again for all the world.

PRIME TIME

By Norman Spinrad

Edna chose to awake this morning to good old breakfast loop A. John was reading a newspaper over pancakes and sausages in the kitchen of their old home. The kids were gulping the last of their food and were anxious to be on their way to school.

After yesterday's real-time-shared breakfast with John, she really felt she needed the soothing old familiar tape from her files today. It might have been shot way back during the 1987–88 television season on a crude home deck, it might be snowy and shaky, but Edna still ran it three or four mornings a week in preference to the breakfast soaps or more updated domestic footage. Somehow it captured what prime breakfast time with John and the kids had really been like, and somehow that made it her prime breakfast programming choice.

Edna: Now, Sammy, you finish the rest of your

milk before you run outdoors!
Sammy: (slugging down the rest of his milk) Aw, Ma, I'm gonna be late!
Edna: Not if you don't take your usual shortcut past the candy store.

Of course the old tape hadn't been shot from her stereo perspective, and there *was* something strange about seeing yourself in your own domestic programming, and it certainly wasn't as well written as a breakfast soap, but then none of the soaps were personalized and none of her other domestic tapes with John had footage of the kids at grade-school age.

John was always after her to share real-time programming with him. He'd voice her over on the communication channel and show her tapes he had made for himself with her in them, or he'd entice her with shared domestic tapes, or he'd bombard her with porn-channel footage.

But the domestic tapes he programmed for them to share all took place in exotic locales, and the story lines were strictly male-type fantasies—John's idea of suitable real-time programming for the two of them to share ran to camel caravans across the desert, spaceship journeys to strange planets full of weird creatures, sailing the South Seas, discovering lost cities, fighting in noble wars. And her viewpoint role was usually a cross between Wonder Woman and Slave Girl. Well, that might be how John wished to real-time-share with her, but Edna preferred her soaps and romantic historicals, which John categorically refused to real-time-share with her under any circumstances.

As for the porn channels that he wanted to real-time-share with her, the only word was *disgusting*.

Still, he *was* her husband, and she felt she had to fulfill her conjugal obligations from time to time; so five or ten times a season she gritted her teeth and real-time-shared one of his crude male porn channels in the sex-object role. Less frequently he consented to time-share a historical X with her, but only because of the implied threat she'd withhold her porn-channel favors from him if he didn't.

So by and large it was mealtime program sharing that was their least distasteful channel of contact and the one that saw most frequent use.

John: (wiping his lips with his napkin) Well, honey, it's off to the salt mines. Ready to go, Ellie?
Ellie: I got to make wee-wee first.

TOTAL TELEVISION HEAVEN 60-SECOND SPOT #12 FINALIZED BROADCAST VERSION HARD CUT FROM BACK

A series of low, pink buildings, emphasizing sunrise through the palm trees.

Announcer's voice-over: (medium hard sell) Total Television Heaven, the ultimate retirement community for Electronic Age seniors . . .

A rapidly cut montage from the adventure channels, the porn channels, the soaps, etc. Make it the

most colorful and exciting footage we've got and emphasize expensive crowd scenes and special effects.

Announce's voice-over: (orgasmic) Twenty full channels of pornography, thirty-five full channels of adventure, forty channels of continuing soaps—live, full-time, in over a hundred possible realities, produced by the finest talents in Hollywood . . .

CLOSE-UP ON A MAN'S HEAD

Intelligent, with neat, dignified, gray hair. As hands fit stereo TV goggles over his eyes. (Earphones already in place.)

Announcer's voice-over: (institutional) You live as the viewpoint character in a wonderland of sex and adventure through the electronic magic of total stereo TV!

MEDIUM SHOT ON A FAMOUS OLD ACTOR

Cast someone with recognition value who's willing to sign up for a two-hundred-year annuity.

Famous Old-Actor: And that's not all! Tape your family! Tape your friends! Take your loved ones with you to Total Television Heaven and keep them with you forever!

CAMERA PULLS BACK FOR A FULL SHOT

We see that the Famous Old Actor is being helped into a glass amnion tank. He keeps talking and smiling as the attendants strap him to the couch, fit the earphones and stereo TV goggles, hook up his breathing mask and waste tube, and begin filling the tank with fluid.

Famous Old Actor: A vast tape library. Custom-cut programs to your order! I wish I'd signed up years ago!

The throat mike is attached, his hand is taped to the tuner knob, the nutrient tube is inserted in his arm (no on-camera needle penetration, please), the amnion tank is topped off and sealed. The camera moves in for a close-up on the face of the Famous Old Actor, seen floating blissfully in his second womb.

Famous Old Actor: (filtered) I'm never coming out—and I'm glad!

DISSOLVE TO: SUNSET OVER TOTAL TELEVISION HEAVEN

The sun sinks into the sea in speeded-up time over the pink pastel client-storage buildings, and a glorious, star-filled sky comes on like an electronic billboard.

Announcer's voice-over: (transcendent) No man knows God's intent for the hereafter, but at Total Television Heaven modern biological science

183

guarantees you a full two hundred years of electronic paradise in the safety and comfort of your own private tank. And a full annuity costs less than you think!

FADE-OUT

John: Maybe we can make it out to the lake this weekend.
Edna: Supposed to be clear, in the seventies, I heard on the weather . . .

This season John had been acting stranger and stranger, even during their mealtime sharing. His conversation was becoming more and more foul-mouthed and even incoherent. He had taken to appearing in elaborate character roles even over breakfast, and yesterday's real-time-shared breakfast had been just about more than Edna could take.

He'd voiced her over the night before and invited her to breakfast the next morning in Hawaii, where they had real-time-shared their honeymoon in the dim, distant past — so many seasons ago that no recording tape of it existed; none had been made way back then, before anyone had even dreamed of retiring to Total Television Heaven. It had been a very long time indeed since John had invited her to real-time-share their past at all, even in a reconstructed version, and so when he told her he had custom-programmed breakfast on the beach in Hawaii, Edna had been so thrilled that she agreed to time-share his breakfast program against what had lately been becoming her better judgment.

The program wakened her to sunrise on the beach, the great golden ball rising out of the dark sea in speeded-up stop-motion animation like a curtain going up, illumining the bright blue sky that suddenly flared into existence as she found herself lying on the sand beneath it.

This to the theme of an ancient primetime show called *Hawaii Five-O*, as a majestic breaker rolled and broke, rolled and broke, again and again, in a closed loop beyond the shoreline foam.

John appeared in the role of a tanned, blond, muscled Adonis wearing a ludicrously short grass skirt. A breakfast table was set up at the edge of the sea itself, in the foot-high wash of foam kicked up by the eternal rolling wave that towered and broke, towered and broke, above them.

Naked, godlike Polynesians—a youth for her, a maiden for John—helped them to their feet and escorted them to the wicker peacock chairs on either side of the strange table. The table was a block of polished obsidian on Victorian-looking brass legs; there was a depression in the center, out of which a grooved channel ran to the seaside edge of the table-top.

This was certainly not their Hawaiian honeymoon as Edna recollected it, and she didn't need a tape in order to be sure of that!

"Welcome, O love goddess of the north, to my groovy pad," John crooned in a strange, cracked voice. He clapped his hands. "An oblation in thine honor."

The naked maiden produced a squealing piglet, which she pressed into the pit in the center of the table. The naked youth handed John a huge machete. "Hai!" John screamed, hacking the piglet in half with a swipe of his blade. Blood pooled in the pit in the table, then ran down the groove to the edge and dripped off into the sea. As the first drops of blood touched the ocean, the water abruptly changed color, and for a few moments a towering wave of blood arched over them.

A few moments later, when the eternal wave was blue water again and Edna's viewpoint angle returned to a shot on the table, the gory mess had been replaced by a white tablecloth, two plates of ham and eggs, a pot of coffee, and a bottle of dark island rum.

"Oh, John," she said disgustedly, "it's all so . . . so—"

"Eldritch? Excessive? Demented?" John said petulantly, crotchety annoyance cracking his handsome, twenty-year-old features. "You're such a timid bird, Edna. No sense of fun. No imagination."

"Killing things is not my idea of either fun or imagination," Edna retorted indignantly.

John laughed a weird, nervous laugh. A whale breached not far offshore, and immediately a giant squid wrapped tentacles around it. A fight to the death began. "Killing things?" John said. "But there's nothing alive here to kill!" This is Heaven, not Earth, and we can do anything we want without consequences. What else can we do?"

"We can have a normal, civilized breakfast like decent human beings."

"Normal, civilized breakfast!" John shouted. "Decent human beings!" A volcano erupted somewhere inland. Terrified natives fled before a wall of fiery lava. "Who cares about being decent human beings when we're not even alive, my princess?"

"I haven't the faintest idea what you're talking about," Edna said primly. But of course some small part of her did, and that part was chilled to the core.

"Sure and begorra, you do, Edna!" John said mockingly. "Avast, matey, what makes you so sure we're still alive? For lo, how many television seasons has it been since we retired? A hundred? Two hundred? Verily and forsooth, time out of mind. Can you even guess, my slave girl? I can't."

Edna blanched. She didn't like this kind of talk at all. It was worse than his machismo adventure programs, worse than the porno programming he enjoyed putting her through, worse on a whole other level she had trained herself not to contemplate.

"Of course we're alive," she said. "We're real-time-sharing now, aren't we?"

Bathing beauties water-skied in a chorus line through the curl of the wave. A flying saucer buzzed the beach. A giant crab seized their servants in its pincers. It whisked them away as they screamed.

"Ah, mine Aphrodite, how can we be sure of that? Thou couldst be croaked and I could be tuning in to an old tape where you still lived. Har-har, I could be dead except in this program of yours."

"This is certainly no program of mine, John Rogers!" Edna shouted. "Only *you* could have invited me to a breakfast program like this!"

"I stink, therefore I am," John cackled. Lightning rattled. Schools of porpoises leaped in and out of the great wave.

And so it had gone. Nubian slaves lighting ciga-

187

rettes. Dancing gulls. An orgy sequence. And all throughout it, John babbling and ranting like a demented parrot in his beachboy body. Only one thing had kept Edna from tuning him out and tuning in a breakfast soap, and that was the dim, distant thought that to do so might precipitate the final break between them, the break between her and something that she could no longer conceptualize clearly.

John: (rising from the table) What's for dinner tonight, by the way?
Edna: Roast chicken with that corn bread stuffing you like.

He kisses her briefly on the lips.

John: Mmmmm . . . ! I'll try to pick up a bottle of that German wine on the way back from work if I'm not too late.

He opens the door, waves, and exits.

Edna: Have a good day.

But now, while she watched her image bid good-bye to John as he left for work on that dim, fuzzy old tape she found so soothing, Edna wondered how long it would be before she would consent to real-time-share a meal with the "real" John again, a John she no longer recognized as the husband in her domestic tapes, a John she was not sure she wanted to know about.

After all, she thought, turning to *Elizabeth the*

188

Queen, her favorite historical romance of this season, too much of that could ruin her domestic tapes with John for her, and then where would she be if she could no longer live comfortably in her past?

Right now she was seated on her throne in the early evening light, and Sir Walter Raleigh was bowing to her with a boyish twinkle in his eye that made her quiver.

Rolling among naked teen-aged girls in a great marbled Roman bath. Popping off Indians with his Remington repeater. Swinging on a vine through a jungleful of dinosaurs. Leading the pack around the last turn at the Grand Prix de Monaco.

Boring, boring, boring! Irritably John flipped through the broadcast channels, unable to find anything capable of holding his attention. What a lousy season this was, even worse than the last! There wasn't a single adventure program that had any originality to it; the porno channels made him think of Edna and her damned disapproval of anything still capable of turning him on; and old domestic tapes, he knew, would just make him furious.

Of course he had a big file of classic recordings and custom-programmed favorites to draw upon when real-time programming got boring, and so he started flipping through his videx, desperately looking for something to fill this time slot.

Flying his one-man space fighter low over an alien glass city, shattering the crystal towers with his shock wave as he rose to meet the bandits. Chasing a fat merchantman under a full head of sail: Avast, me hearties, prepare a broadside! Auctioned as a sex slave to a mob of horny women. Doing a smart left bank around a skyscraper, with Lois Lane in his arms.

He really had some choice footage in his tape library, but he had run all of it so often down through the long seasons that every bit of it seemed engraved in his real-time memory. He had lost the ability to surprise himself, even with how gross he could get, and he had to go further and further out to avert . . . to avert . . . to avert . . .

Onward, the Light Brigade! Thousands of screaming teen-aged groupies mobbed the stage, grabbed his guitar, tore off his clothes. "Frankly, Scarlett," he said, as she sank to her knees, "I don't give a damn."

If only Edna had the gumption to be a real wife to him! Lord knew, he tried to be a real husband to her. Didn't he regularly invite her to real-time-share the porn channels with him, and didn't he take pains to choose the most far-out sex programming available? Didn't he invite her to all his best adventure programs? Didn't he invite her to the best mealtime custom programming instead of the same old domestic tapes?

He did his best to make her programming day interesting and surprising, and what did he get from her in return? A lot of whining about his dirty mind, a determination to get him caught in one of those saccharine historical X's with her, and a dreary desire to mealtime-share the same musty old domestic tapes over and over again. What was the purpose of retiring to Total Television Heaven in the first place if you were afraid of grossness, if you insisted on realism, if all you wanted was to watch endless reruns of the same old, boring past?

Striding through the jungle, a great, hairy gorilla beating his chest while the natives flee in terror. Executing a snappy Immelmann and coming up on the Red Baron's tail, machine guns blazing. Getting head from the legendary Marilyn Monroe.

Damn it, retiring to Total Television Heaven before either of them was sixty-five had been Edna's idea in the first place, John told himself, though a part of him knew that wasn't exactly totally true. With the kids at the other end of the continent and the economy in such bad shape and nothing interesting going on in their real-time lives, it was only his job that had kept them from trading in their Social Security equity for a two-hundred-year annuity to Total Television Heaven. He figured that if he could work another ten years and save at the same rate, it would enable them to buy an extra fifty years of Heaven. But when the cost of living rose to the point where he wasn't saving anything . . . well, at that point he hadn't really needed that much convincing, especially since there was a rumor that Social Security was about to go bust and the smart thing to do was get into Heaven while you could.

But what good was two hundred and ten years in Total Television Heaven if your wife insisted on living in her tape loops of the past? How much fun could you have if all you had to rely on was the broadcast programmers and your own imagination?

Making love to a fair rescued damsel on the steaming corpse of a slain dragon. The image began to flicker. Diving out of an airplane, spreading his arms and flying like a bird; the air seemed to turn to a thick, choking fluid. Tarzan of the Apes, making love to an appreciative lioness, felt an uncomfortable pressure against his eyeballs.

Oh, God, it was happening again! For some time now something had been corroding John Rogers. He could feel it happening. He didn't know what it was, but he knew that he didn't *want* to know what it was.

I'm just sick and tired of having to fill every time slot in my programming day with something I have to choose myself, he told himself nervously. Sure, he could time-share with Edna and let her fill some time slots for him, but her idea of programming made him want to puke.

In fact, the lover of the insatiable Catherine the Great felt a bubble of nausea rising within him even as the beautiful czarina crawled all over him. Napoleon's mind felt a nameless dread even as he led the triumphal march through Paris. Because the thought that had intruded unbidden into his mind was, What would happen if he didn't choose anything to fill the time slot? Was it possible? Would he still be there? Where *was* there?

And questions like those brought on the leading edge of an immense, formless, shapeless, choking dread that took him out of the viewpoint character and made him see the whole thing as if through the eyes of a video camera: lines of dots, pressure against his eyeballs . . .

He shuddered inwardly. Convulsively he switched to a domestic porno tape of himself and Edna making love in the grass on the slope of a roaring volcano. She screamed and cursed and moaned as he stuck it to her, but . . . but . . .

Edna, I've got to get out of here!

But what can I possibly mean by that?

Frantically he voiced her over. "Edna, I've got to real-time-share with you," he said shrilly. "Now!"

"I'm tuned in to *China Clipper* now, and it's my favorite historical X," her voice-over whined as he continued to pound at her under the volcano.

"Please, Edna, porn channel Eight, real-time-share with me now, if you don't . . . if you don't . . ." A wave of molten lava roared and foamed down the mountain toward them as Edna moaned and swore toward climax beneath him.

"Not now, I'm enjoying my program," her distant voice-over said.

"Edna! Edna! Edna!" John shrieked, overcome with a terror he didn't understand, didn't want to understand.

"John!" There was finally concern in her voice, and it seemed to come from the Edna who thrashed and moaned beneath him in orgasm as the wave of lava enfolded them in painless fire.

"John, you're disgusting!" she said at the height of the moment. "If you want to time-share with me, we'll have to go to a domestic tape *now*. Loop E."

Raging with fear, anger, and self-loathing, he followed her to the domestic tape. They were sitting on the back porch of their summer cabin at the lake, overlooking the swimming raft, where the kids were playing a ragtag game of water polo. *Oh, Jesus . . .*

"Now what's got you all upset, John?" Edna said primly, pouring him a glass of lemonade.

John didn't know what to say. He didn't know how

to deal with it. He didn't even want to know what he was dealing with. He was talking to a ghost. He was talking to his wife talking to a ghost. He . . . he . . .

"We've got to do more real-time-sharing, Edna," he finally said. "It's important. We shouldn't be alone in here all the time."

"I haven't the faintest idea what you're babbling about," Edna said nervously. "As for more real-time-sharing, I'm perfectly willing to share mealtimes with you on a regular basis if you behave yourself. Here. At the house. On our honeymoon. Even in a good restaurant. But not in any of your disgusting programming, John, and that goes double for the porn channels. I don't understand you, John. You've become some kind of pervert. Sometimes I think you're going crazy."

A burst of multicolored snow flickered the old tape. Edna sipped her lemonade. His eyes ached. He was choking.

"I'm going crazy?" John cried thickly. "What about you, Edna, living back here and trying to pretend we're really still alive back then, instead of here in . . . in—"

"In Total Television Heaven, John," Edna said sharply. "Where we're free to program all our time slots to suit ourselves. And if you don't like my programming, you don't have to time-share it. As for your programming, I don't know how you stand it."

"But I can't stand it!" John shouted as a water-skier was drawn by a roaring speedboat past their porch. "That's what's driving me crazy." From somewhere came the sounds of a softball game. A 747 glided by overhead.

194

"Daddy! Daddy!" the kids waved at him.

"But this is worse!" he screamed at Edna, young and trim in her two-piece-bathing suit. A neighbor's dog came up, wagging its tail, and she gave it her hand to lick. "This isn't real, and it's not even an honest fantasy; you're dead inside of here, Edna, living through your old tape loops, floating in . . . floating in . . ."

He gagged. An image of a fetus faded in, faded out, faded in again. He felt something pressing against his face like an ocean of time drowning him, pulling him under. Nothing was real. Nothing but whatever Edna had become speaking through her long-dead simulacrum near the lake.

"Stop it, John! I won't listen to such filth!"

"Oh, Jesus, Edna, we're dead, don't you see? We're dead and drifting forever in our own tape loops, and only—"

"Good-bye, John," Edna said frostily, taking another sip of lemonade. "I much prefer the way you were to this!"

"Edna! Edna! Don't break the time-share! You're all that's left!"

Edna: Say, honey, why don't we go inside and make a little love in the afternoon.

A thunderclap rends the sky. It begins to rain. Edna laughs and undoes the halter of her swimsuit.

Edna: Oh, I'm getting wet. Why don't you grab a towel and dry me off.

She gets up, giggling, takes John's hand, and leads him inside.

"Oh, no, no!" John shouted as his viewpoint followed her. For she was no longer there, and he remembered every scene, every angle, every special effect of this program. Something inside him snapped. He had to get out of here. He switched his videx to rapid random scan, unable to think of choosing a program to fill his time slot.

Getting head from Marilyn Monroe sailing the Spanish Main—fetus floating in the eternal amnion—a giant gorilla chasing dusky natives from dinner with Edna and the kids in the dining room of their house—a million flickering electronic dots against his eyeballs—flying like a bird through the towers of New York around the Eiffel Tower—choking in the sea of time—leading the cavalry charge to plant the flag on Iwo Jima—lungs straining for a surface that wasn't there—stepping out of the air lock under triple suns—trapped in syrupy quicksand forever—arriving at the sultan's harem in King Arthur's squad car—

Awake, aware, alive for a long, horribly lucid moment—floating and choking in the amniotic quicksand with meaningless images attacking his eyeballs—waking up from a long suffocation dream into a long suffocation dream that wouldn't go away, couldn't go away, or there'd be—

Dueling with the musketeers swinging on a vine through the jungle of the Great Barrier Reef with

Edna in a hammock screaming orgasm in the harem with a dozen houris soaring through space screaming around great ringed Saturn screaming against the dead cold black phosphor-dotted everlasting void drowning choking screaming god oh god oh oh oh—

As she faded out of the viewpoint character of Elizabeth the Queen, Edna thought of John. How long ago had that terrible final real-time sharing taken place? Was it still the same television season?

It was time for dinner, and she programmed dinner loop C. She, John, and the kids were seated at Thanksgiving dinner. She was wearing her Sunday best, the kids were neat and combed, and John was wearing a suit.

John: This stuffing is delicious, honey!
Sammy: Can I have the other drumstick?
Ellie: Pass the cranberry sauce.
Edna: It's wonderful to have a quiet Thanksgiving dinner just for the four of us, isn't it, John?

Edna felt so contented, so at peace with herself and her family, so right with the world. *I really should invite John to real-time-share this wonderful Thanksgiving*, she thought maternally. *I really ought to give him one last chance to be a proper father to the kids and husband to me.*

Filled with Christian charity, she voiced over to his channel. "John?" she said, scooping up mashed yams with brown sugar and passing the salt to her beaming husband, who planted a little kiss on her wedding

197

ring *en passant*. "I'm having Thanksgiving dinner with you and the kids, and I'd like you to be a good father and real-time-share with us."

There was nothing on the voice-over channel for a moment as John handed the drumstick to Sammy. Then, as Sammy took it from him and bit into it with boyish gusto, John screamed.

An endless, ghastly, blubbering shriek that rattled Edna's teeth and poisoned the moment with unremitting horror.

"John Rogers, you're an animal. I don't know you anymore, and I don't want to!" she shouted back at the horrid sound and broke the connection once and for all.

John: Don't gobble your food, Sammy, or you'll turn into a turkey.
Sammy: (turkey sound) Gobble, gobble!

All four of them laugh heartily.

John: Please pass me some more of the peas, honey. What do you say, kids, isn't your mother the best cook in the world?
Sammy and Ellie: Yay, Mom!

Edna beamed as she handed John the bowl of creamed peas. He smiled at her. Edna relaxed. How good it was to have a nice, civilized Thanksgiving dinner with your husband and your family just the way you liked it. Peaceful and loving and together forever.

She decided to play a romantic porn program after

198

dinner. She would meet John in an elegant café in old Vienna, a waltz in a grand ballroom, share a bottle of champagne on a barge in the Seine, and then make love on a bear rug in front of a roaring fireplace. She knew that everything would be just perfect.

EDGES

By Gregg Keizer

From the corner of my eye I watch Marart's death. I have my own rigging to work, meters to keep in sight; so all I can do is watch him from the corner of my eye. I think I see a line fluttering where one should be taut, and he is off balance as he leans over the deck of his clipper. I feel little for him. My heart pounds wildly and I cannot forget that he tried to force me onto a cairn of rocks moments before.

My clipper is functioning perfectly, coming abeam of his again, and though my sight is drawn to the smoothness of the salt that streams beneath me, I *have* to look and watch Marart. There is nothing else I can do, even if I wished, for it would take kilometers to slow and stop my clipper. By then he would be a dwindling speck on the horizon of the Flats.

I look up to starboard and see the shifting and dancing image we chase. I try to focus on it, but it remains blurred, a yellow stain that flickers in the heat waves. Although it is only half a kilometer away, it is on the other side of the Edge, the blackened land that seems to swallow the very light that refracts and bounces off the Flats. I cannot see an end to the darkened salt that was fused into a sort of chipped glass by the megaton bombs centuries ago. No one sails on the Edge; no one crosses the line between shimmering white and light-sucking dark. Yet an image floats above the Edge; it seems impervious. There is a pool of white underneath and around it, an oasis of contrast that moves as it moves. The image could be a simple mirage, but a mirage does not carry its own unmarked ground with it. And then I heard an odd, throaty rumble coming back to me. Mirages do not make sounds. Both Marart and I know that.

Marart has regained his balance and is hanging on to an unbroken line, which bends dangerously. But it is too late, for the blades of the fans beneath the clipper's skirting gently nick the salt. Marart's misplaced weight throws the clipper off-center and the fans dig into the crystals, leaving a worm's trail. The caresses of the fans cause the clipper to heel further and gravity tugs at him.

There is nothing Marart can do. If he falls, perhaps his suit will protect him from scraping wounds.

For a moment I think I see his face behind the thin visor of his helmet and I even imagine that he is smiling. Another mirage, perhaps, and I glance quickly to reassure myself that my clipper is sailing smoothly and the yellow blur still weaves in the distance. It paces us as we run along the Edge, half a kilometer to the east — another heat vision, like all the illusions that make up the Flats. But when I look back at Marart and his craft, several meters behind me now, the deck of his clipper is empty.

His clipper slowly drags to starboard and tips over onto its side. He is still hanging on. Then his mast reaches for the salt, brushes it, and the clipper is cartwheeling. Its plastic shell disintegrates, and the wreckage is a tangle of rigging lines, mast, and sail, all wrapped around shattered motors. And over the whine of the fans beneath my clipper and the snap of the sails above me, I imagine his screams. They are not loud, only forever, and they do not end even when my imagination's Dopplering has deepened their sounds to a low hum.

I stare past the whiteness of the Flats into the blackness of the Edge, and the mirage is still out there, flickering in the heat. I crowd on more sail, let out the jib lines, and feel the lurch as my speed increases. My clipper is close to instability, but I know I must go this fast to catch the mirage and slip into the oasis of the past that surrounds it. Marart's crumpled clipper falls farther and farther behind.

I think then of the Timing Race last year, when Marart and I watched Dannelle meet a mirage along the Edge. Her clipper flew behind the wavering image, then seemed to touch it before both flickered in the heat waves and slowly disappeared over the horizon. She had been transported into the past, the time of the machined mirages. Marart and I knew that, because we both had chased the mirages until they vanished. And when we stopped our clippers and walked from them, we knelt and touched the tracks the mirage had made in the salt. Illusions do not make tracks.

We walked in the shallow grooves of the thing's tracks until we came upon its skeleton, still glowing as the scorched metal cooled. A hundred-meter trail of scattered debris led to its huge tail, where the pilot sat. He was burned horribly, only his face unmarked beneath the helmet we lifted.

Marart and I buried the man from the past beside his machine and said little to each other as we walked back to our clippers. The machine was fueled by a sweet-smelling liquid we lifted to our nostrils. It was huge and made of metal. There was nothing like it in all the world. There had been nothing like it for centuries. Perhaps it was jolted out of its true time when Dannelle's clipper closed on it, Marart said as we walked. Perhaps Dannelle had taken its place in the far past, he whispered. A new machine joins the past, an old one must fall out. I said nothing. Dannelle had been my lover and now she was gone — gone farther than mere death.

The search groups never found Dannelle or her clipper. Missing, the groups concluded. Marart and I knew better; we knew the mirages were real — visions of the past — and pathways into that time.

We told no one and, instead, raced to touch a mirage so that *we* could sail into the past. Marart had tried to kill me today to reach the mirage first.

As I blink my eyes, forcing my mind to the present, I try to focus on the mirage. But it vanishes, leaving me alone. I do not slacken my sails, though I am in the lead. Marart's death has given me this heat and thus the right to race Henna in the finals.

I adjust the rigging lines, steering for the finish banner, which vibrates vaguely in the distance. The clipper shifts slightly. The fans' whine becomes louder for a second as the skirting lifts on the high side and then I am sailing smoothly again.

There are small hillocks here and there on the Flats, as well as long ditches that cross the expanse, going and coming from nowhere. I must watch for those, because there is no way I can beat into the wind, not in a clipper. I can run only before the wind, making sure it is constantly near my back. I can sail a beam reach, perhaps ninety degrees to the wind, but that is all. If I try to come closer to the wind, I will heel over and suffer Marart's fate. There is no keel on my clipper, as there would be on a true sailboat, no resistance from the water to keep me upright. That is why we sail here, where the land is level and relatively free of obstructions.

The power for the fans that keep the deck centimeters from the salt bed is within acceptable limits and the reserve battery is fully charged. My visor snaps up and out of the way at the touch of my fingers and I let the wind tear at my eyes.

A gust of wind to starboard touches my sails as I cross the finish banner, and the frictionless clipper skitters meters to port before I can regain control. In that instant I think of Marart and I wonder who will look for his body. It will not be me. Only lovers and friends go to reclaim the dead in the caldron of the Flats. I am neither.

We crouched around the heater in the tent, watching our breath billow and rubbing our palms together in front of the red coils. I finished one beer and reached into the kitbag behind me for another.

"The front is supposed to pass tonight and a high move in tomorrow," Henna said. "Lots of southerlies for the next three days." No one spoke. "That's what the meteorologist said. What's his name, the thin one?"

"Withers," someone answered from the other side of the heater. I couldn't see a face to connect with the voice. It didn't matter; I wasn't familiar with more than a handful of the pilots this year. Henna was one of the few I knew.

"Yes, Withers. On-the-mark forecast," Henna said, an edge to her voice. "He said straight winds today, no gusts."

Someone cleared his throat and I glanced up to see Marart's brother looking at me, his dark eyes making me uncomfortable. His name came to me slowly. Dallin, I remembered. "You were there, weren't you?" I gulped more beer and looked at my breath hanging in the air.

"Yes."

"What happened?" He was still flushed from going out to retrieve his brother's body.

"A line broke. He should have jumped, but he hung on instead," I said quickly.

"No gusts? No sudden gusts abeam?" Dallin asked.

I shook my head. I glanced up and Henna met my gaze. I shook my head again.

"I saw what made his clipper heel," Dallin said, looking over at Henna for a moment. I drained the last of my beer and reached for another. Bottles clinked together as I lengthened the row of empties. "I was behind you today, a kilometer or so back," he

206

said, looking at me again.

Had he seen the mirage, too? Had his brother told him what they really were?

"It was the wind. You know what the Flats are like. Wind comes from nowhere. You've seen the white devils out there. One got Marart," I said, my voice too loud for the tent. If he'd been that far behind us, he might believe *I* was the cause of Marart's death. From that distance, it might appear that I rammed Marart.

"Maybe," Dallin said, his eyes hating me.

Again I wondered if Dallin knew the truth. His brother had been obsessed with speed. He had believed the machines that had raced these Flats centuries ago moved hundreds of kilometers each hour. Joining the past would allow him to race in one of those machines, he had thought. He would not have let someone else beat him to that, not even his own brother. Dallin could *not* know the truth.

It was almost silent in the tent, only the ticking of the heater coils audible as they switched on again. "Say what you're thinking," I whispered.

Dallin went on slowly, his eyes looking at me all the while. "Maybe you ran against Marart out there today. Maybe that's what made him lose control. You've said often enough how badly you want the Timing Race. Maybe enough to foul someone's clipper to take the heat."

His words hung in the chilled air. I set the beer bottle beside me, wanting to smash a jagged neck free and cut him, afraid I would if I held it a moment longer.

"Are you accusing me of murder?" He shook his

207

head. He knew he had no proof. "File a fouling charge, then."

"No one else saw it. It would be just your word against mine."

"Why are you doing this?" I asked, the bitterness welling up in me. "I didn't harm your brother," I said, my voice tight in my throat. I could not tell him what had happened, that his brother had tried to kill *me*. Not without telling the truth of the mirages.

"I saw you out there, Paul. I saw you—"

"You saw nothing. Nothing that you could ever prove."

"You killed him, just as if you'd thrown him off his clipper yourself," Dallin said, his face reddening even more. "If you hadn't been so eager to—"

"You're more a fool than I thought," I said. "Keep your lies to yourself from now on." I pulled two beers from the kitbag and stood up. Dallin said something, but I didn't listen. Instead, I swept aside the tent flap and walked into the night.

The stars were outrageous. Every one seemed a pin through fabric, and no matter how many times I blinked, I could not make them sparkle. The air was cold and it hurt as I breathed it in.

As searingly hot as the days were here, the nights were just as bitterly cold. I hoped the water ballast in my clipper's tanks would not freeze again tonight.

Laughter reached me from somewhere far away. I turned and looked at the rows of white, bell-shaped tents that stretched into the darkness, each one lit from within. Shadows moved inside the canvas as the spectators played through the evening. The nearest spectator tent was two hundred meters away, separated from the pilots' tents by our encircling clippers.

I made it a practice never to walk into spectator territory during a Timing Race, for once they found out you were a pilot, they would pester you far into the dawn.

Timing Race. We ran our clippers across the Flats for sport and the spectators flocked to watch. If they were fortunate, they would see one of us die. I thought mildly of Marart, then of Dannelle, and I wished to be out there, running along the Edge, searching for her.

The dull noise from the tent behind me rose lightly, then fell again. I didn't turn, for I knew who was standing there.

"He was only saying what first came into his mind, Paul," Henna said, shivering in the cold as she moved beside me. "He and his brother were very close. He didn't mean what he said to you."

"Yes, he did."

"I've heard stories about mirages on the Flats, Paul," Henna said. I almost said something. Did she know? "It seems every year someone sees something odd out there. Maybe Dallin saw a heat mirage," she said. I breathed easier, but her words left me uncomfortable.

"Remember three years ago? That pilot from Oregon who swore he'd seen wagons crossing the Flats?" She paused and I could hear her rhythmic breathing. "And then Dannelle last year. She said she saw a blue blur that slid across the salt, trailing pieces of itself." Henna's voice was lost in the night. "I'm sorry, Paul. I didn't mean to say her name, it's—"

"Don't worry. I don't mind."

"You still believe she's alive, don't you, Paul?" She paused and I nodded, though I was sure she couldn't see the gesture. "Are you tired? Thinking of Marart?"

"He must have made a mistake." I desperately wanted to tell her the truth, that he had tried to kill me, but I couldn't.

"And you won't? Never?" There was something akin to laughter in her tone, something I didn't like.

"Perhaps I *am* tired," I said, rubbing my hands together, hearing the sound of rough skin over calluses. It sounded so much like the noise of handling rigging lines that for a moment I thought I saw Marart's visored smile in the dark.

"The moon will be up in half an hour," Henna said, sliding her hands between mine. Her hands were warmer, but just as weathered from sailing clippers. "I know, let's go to the Edge. We haven't been there in years. Let's watch it against the moon. It'll be fun. Paul?"

I looked at her face, but in the dim light I couldn't read it. We hadn't been lovers for two years now, not since I'd met Dannelle and walked away from Henna. Then I realized her reasons didn't matter; being alone tonight was not something I wanted. "Why not?" I laughed, suddenly hugging her, feeling her warmth through the coveralls we both wore. "Race you there. Last one sets up the recharge panels." I tugged at her sleeve. "Come on, Henna."

I walked to my clipper, reached it, and touched the smooth plastic deck, straightened the rubberized skirting so that it touched the ground. My clipper was long, six meters, and narrow through the bow and stern; it only vaguely looked like the bulbous hover-

210

crafts that lumbered along the waterways. Amidships, where the controls were clustered, it was barely wide enough to sit, perhaps kneel. The mast was up and the bright-green sail furled along the boom. Near the bow lay the spinnaker, ready to balloon when the clipper reached forty knots. The fan switches were under my fingers, and if I turned them on, the deck would lift its three centimeters.

I heard Henna behind me and she touched my arm. "No. No racing. Not tonight. Let's take the water truck instead." The electric truck was so slow, I thought; hauling our water from the mountains was all it could do. But the wind was out of the south by now, and would be again tomorrow. If we took our clippers, there would be no easy way to return, since it was difficult to beat upwind. So I nodded my head and whispered yes.

We took turns running the steering levers, giggling and shouting back and forth as we crawled across the Flats toward the Edge. For a moment I thought I saws a shape shift in the dark, but the crunch of the truck's balloon tires on the salt shattered the dream.

While Henna set up the heater and opened the food pouches she'd squirreled away in her coverall pockets, I set up the solar panel and pointed it toward the Cedar Mountains, where the sun would first show itself in the morning. With the main battery drained, we would have to wait until it was recharged before we could head back. Luckily, the final race was not until the day after next.

We sat, huddled beside the heater, eating crackers and fruit, drinking beer I'd taken from the tent. The moon was over the mountaintops to the east and was just beginning to lose its yellowness. But we paid more attention to the blackness that swallowed the salt flats a half kilometer ahead. We sat on a small rise, dirt somewhere beneath the ever-present layer of white salt, and looked down into the Edge. The line of black marked the bombs' blast radii. What targets the bombs had searched for were long lost, but there was a stump of a city a hundred thirty kilometers to the east, the sailplane pilots said. The blackness stretched all the way to it; only the mountaintops were spared.

Though the Edge was black, there were brief shimmers of light along the border—short bursts of color, like the waves of the northern lights. At times there seemed to be only one; other times the glimmers came in pairs. But they always appeared along the border, never deep within the Edge.

I decided they were glimpses of the past, the oases I chased. If it were daytime, the oases would look like bursts of color and light. I wondered whether I would see details if we were closer. Perhaps somewhere in those gleams was Dannelle.

"You're thinking about her again, Paul?" When I said nothing, she continued, her voice quiet. "I hated her, and you. Did you know that? When she disappeared last year I was glad it happened. Not now, not anymore—but I was bitter then."

"She's out there," I said, holding Henna's hand, feeling her warmth. She shook her head. "I've told no one what we really saw . . ." I continued, letting my voice trail off into the dark.

"Today, you mean?"

"No, when Dannelle vanished." Henna shook her

212

head again. "The destruction out there," I said, pointing to the Edge, "was unimaginable. The bombs were stronger than the sun itself. You've heard the stories. Thousands of them fell here, each one warping reality a small bit, until even space and time were changed. They fell for days. Even time rips eventually. Now there are ways into the past. Perhaps to the future, too." I said the words I'd often thought but never spoken, not even to Marart. I couldn't stop. "The strange lights on the Edge, the mirages we've all seen, are only oases of the past that are somehow visible. Imagine the power of the destruction and tell me it's not possible."

"You're insane, Paul," she said deliberately, but her accusation only made me more sure of myself. "Hallucinations, Paul. We see mirages because of the heat waves. That's all it is, the heat."

"I've touched a dead man from the past, from the time before the wars," I said. "Marart has, too. We found him in his machine after Dannelle disappeared through one of the time oases. Her presence jarred him loose, we thought."

"You believe she's down there somewhere, waiting for you? Is that why you killed Marart? To reach her before he did?" Her voice accused me of more than murder.

"He tried to keep me from the mirage and its oasis. He tried to force me onto some rocks, but he lost control. I swear it," I said, squeezing her hand tightly. "I can find her if I can catch one of the images and slip into its time oasis, just as she did. I know I can."

"You're obsessed with her, Paul. That's all." She did not believe me. I would have to take her to the

213

dead man's strange machine and that was impossible tonight. It was too far for the truck's worn batteries.

The blackness of the fused salt, the constant flickers of color, and the moonlight contrasted with one another. I could hear Henna exhale loudly. She touched me, her fingers light on my temples, as if she were trying to rub away the insanity that she thought was there.

"Dear Paul, don't torment yourself. Forget her and live your life." I didn't push away her hands, even though I saw Dannelle's face in my mind. I needed someone. That was why I'd told Henna all this. Dannelle would understand, I thought.

We made love three times that night, caressing each other with callused hands while we waited for our interest to return. I laid aside my memories for a while. Neither of us spoke, perhaps each afraid that more words would widen the gap between us. Even so, I couldn't keep my mind on what my body was doing.

Each time she cried out, each time I shouted with pleasure, I heard the faraway sound of Marart's agonized last cries as his clipper pulled him over the salt. But in the nightmare of my passion, the salt was fused, not jagged as it was on the Flats, and it seemed to take him forever to fall silent. Sliding on a sheet of glass, forever.

I sat at the table, shielded from the others by cloudlike curtains, and drank quickly from the glass. Voices from the rest of the huge tent reached me now and again. They were spectator voices. The woman at the bar had given me a bottle and a glass and found me this table in a corner. She'd once been a pilot, she

214

said, and understood I wanted privacy. I had smiled and tried to thank her, but she'd slipped back into the crush of spectators.

I needed to be away from the other pilots, to think; so I'd walked between the encircling clippers to spectator ground, their tents silver and noisy. A few had noticed me, but I hadn't stopped at their calls, instead pushing into this tent crowded with spectators and alcohol. As I drank to the bottom of the glass and refilled it, I kept imagining that I felt Henna's fingers on my back. It was difficult to push that image away and pull Dannelle's face into focus, but I did, and then drank again.

"They said you were here."

I looked up and saw Dallin standing beside the drifting cloth curtains. I didn't take my eyes from his, but I could tell spectators were watching.

"I didn't kill Marart. I told you what happened during the race."

"He told me everything," Dallin said, his voice dropping low. "The mirages. Dannelle. Even the man you buried out there on the Flats. I'm going to the Association, and I'm going to take them to that machine. Marart told me where it is."

"Listen to me," I said, gripping the glass tighter, feeling its solidness against my palm. "Marart tried to run me against some rocks. We were chasing a mirage and he tried to kill me. He wanted to reach it first. I didn't kill him. I told you that." Dallin reached inside his jacket and pulled out a long, thin knife.

"They'll know you were a murderer when they dig up that man out there," Dallin said. He moved to one side, brushing against the curtains, the knife pointed

215

at my face.

I threw the heavy glass at his eyes and when he jumped to the side, I leaped over the table and pushed him to the floor. He grunted as the breath went out of him and I had my hand wrapped in his hair, trying to pull his head back too far. But then he squirmed under me and I caught a glimpse of a freed hand, the knife still in its grasp.

Its blade slashed my shirt and the skin under it, but the pain didn't come. Then I had my hand around his wrist, and still kneeling astride his chest, I pushed his arm down, the knife with it. I noticed its edge was dark with my blood.

The noise in the back of his throat grew louder, then quieted, and I looked down at my hands, both twisted around his one. His wrist was at a strange angle and the knife's haft was still in his fingers. The blade was in his chest and froth welled up around its edges.

I felt the presence of spectators behind me and heard the movement of someone's feet on the wood floor and the quiet cough of someone in a far corner. Dallin's final, gentle exhalation seemed much louder.

He was dead, but somehow I was relieved. Now no one knew the truth of the mirages except myself and Henna. Yet as I took my hands from the still-warm one of Dallin, I felt a chill in the heat of the crowded tent and heard Henna's voice in my mind. She had warned me of insanity, told me to forget my obsession, and I had paid her no mind. A man was dead because I would not forget, and Henna could accuse me of one more thing: murder.

"We cannot race tomorrow. We'll have to call it off, Paul. You see that, don't you?"

I looked up at Henna, glanced down at my beer, and shook my head. There had been silence in the tent since I walked in. No one bothered to ask me about the Association's inquiry, not that it mattered. I would lie to the pilots, just as I had lied to the Association. I don't know why he attacked me, I had said, unable to tell them I was glad Dallin was dead.

"Two pilots dead, Paul. The spectators love you, did you know that? You give them exactly what they want," Henna said when I didn't answer.

"The Association cleared me."

"They know everything, do they?" she asked, staring at me.

"The Timing Race isn't canceled," I said, louder now.

"What did Dallin say to you?" she asked. "What did you and Dallin talk about?"

She knew without my having to say it. She believed my theories of the Edge now, that was plain.

"You buried a man out there, you're sure of it?" People stared at Henna, but no one spoke, not even to ask questions. "It wasn't a woman you two buried to hide an accident? You said Marart wanted speed. Could that really have been you, Paul? Perhaps Dannelle isn't what you're searching for. Perhaps you *know* where she is."

Everyone waited for an answer to her confusing questions and it was hard not to explode in denial. I stood and slipped through the tent flap, leaving it open behind me as I walked into the night.

217

I made my way to the clippers, found mine in the darkness, and touched it with one hand. The spectator tents glowed in the near distance.

"Paul, I'm sorry." It was Henna. I'd known she'd follow me. I moved my hand to indicate a place by the clipper's deck and she leaned against it.

"I didn't kill Dannelle," I said. "She's still alive somewhere, somewhen. Both Marart and I believed that."

"I was just frightened of what you'd become, Paul," she said, taking the beer from my hand and drinking deeply.

"I killed Dallin to keep him from telling the Association of the mirages."

"I know, Paul."

"You don't hate me? You must. I'm a murderer, Henna."

"I want to believe what you say about time and the Edge, but I can't," Henna said softly. "Not completely."

"It's true, Henna. Tomorrow you'll see that it's true. We can both touch the mirage and slip into the past. We can both go back."

"So we can both be with her, Paul? You left me for her, don't you remember?" She paused, drank beer again. My mouth was dry, but I wanted to stay clear. "Would you chase mirages for me, Paul? If it was I who vanished, would you be so obsessed?"

I thought of Dannelle and for the first time in a year, I could not see her face. I inhaled quickly and heard my breath rattle in my throat. I looked up and saw Henna smile, her teeth points in the light. Dannelle's clipper, its sails dark-blue, I could see, but

218

not her face. Henna's kept coming into focus.

"You loved me once, Paul. In the past," she said and smiled again. "You can love me again. I'm here now. Dannelle's not."

The temptation was strong—so strong. I remembered Henna's touch as we'd lain under the night sky beside the Edge, the time oases gleaming in the distance. She was alive and warm; Dannelle was only that centuries down the line of time.

"Let's go to the Edge again tonight," she said. "We can forget all this." It was as if she wanted to make love to me in front of Dannelle's memory—or ghost. It depended on what she believed.

I wanted Henna then, more than I'd ever wanted anyone. Her touch, her warmth, her soft words, even her callused hands. But somehow I managed to stand and push myself away from my clipper.

"No, Henna. I'm going out on the Flats tomorrow to find another mirage."

My rejection showed on her face. "You'll not forget her. You'll not call off the race. Tomorrow, then. And Paul," she said, so softly that I thought for a moment it was only the wind on my clipper's sail, "stay away from me—now, and in the race. I want the past now, too, Paul. Keep out of my way. Understand?"

She stood and walked into the darkness and I could think only of her face where Dannelle's was supposed to be.

I crouched next to my clipper, rolling the skirting down so that it touched the ground, making sure there were no gaps where the air could push through.

The mast was already up and the rigging lines snapped into place. Fabric rippled above me as the bright-green sails moved in the wind. When I turned on the fans and the deck lifted three centimeters, I would let the sail fill with wind and the clock would start.

I looked at the salt beneath my knees. It was smashed flat here from the constant footsteps, but if one went out into the caldron of the Flats, where there were no prints, it would crunch marvelously, sounding like shells underfoot. And it would glitter. It was difficult to see that when the clipper was reaching for sixty-five knots, but impossible to miss now. It was painful to look at.

"Are you set?" a voice behind me asked as I stood and stretched my legs. My coverall was white from the salt. I turned and saw Harmon, the Association timer. He held his timepiece close to his stomach, in both hands, as if it would leap from his grasp.

"Almost. Two more lines to check."

"Whenever you're ready, board your car and give me the signal." I nodded slightly. Like everyone from the Association, he called my clipper a car. Habit from long ago, I suppose.

I squinted into the sun and saw Henna's clipper fifty meters away, its sails a deep rust. Even that short distance away, it seemed suspended in midair, the shimmering heat waves below it, the hazy sky above. She was sitting in her cockpit, ready to start.

Gently, slowly, I crawled upon the deck of my clipper, careful not to snag any of the rigging lines with my feet. I maneuvered around the fan-intake vent and settled into the shallow cockpit. As soon as I had flipped the switches that engaged the fans, I pulled the mainsheet lines and heard the snap of the sail's fabric. The battery meters went down and I could hear the whine of the blades as the deck rose. The wind shoved the clipper aside, but I pulled the boom over and corrected. Harmon had started his timepiece by now, I knew, and I set course for the mirage of the Edge, seeing Henna's clipper from the corner of my eye, moving as I moved.

I kneel on the deck of my clipper, yanking desperately on the mainsheet lines, trying to pull them and spill the sails. In the distance, beyond the sails I so achingly stare at, I think I see the finish banner, its length distorted by the heat waves. Another kilometer and I will be safe.

Henna is still bearing down on me, her course pointed to an imaginary spot of collision. She, too, is pulling on rigging lines, readjusting hers as I readjust mine. It is as if there is a band between us that allows us to separate only so far and that tugs us together when it wants.

It has been a tight race. Several times we ran alongside each other, our decks only meters apart. I did not brush against her speeding clipper, nor did I see one of the mirages.

But now Henna is trying to kill me with her clipper. I cannot be sure, of course, but I think my rejection hurt her deeper than she would admit to me. She has not spoken to me since she walked away from my clipper and me last night. She must have planned this then. I glance toward her and see that she is still aiming her clipper at me. It cannot be accidental, this course. Why now, I wonder as I try to steer to starboard and toward the Edge? Why not in the middle of the Flats, where there were no witnesses?

Against the mountains in the far distance of the Edge. I see a blur that is different from the perpetual line of ground mirage. It dances and floats on the breeze at my back, though it is coming toward me, I realize, running directly into the wind. Every time I blink, it shifts shape and position. I rub my fingers at the corners of my eyes, but the blur remains. I realize that Henna is not trying to kill me. She only saw the mirage before I did and is heading for it.

I cannot take my eyes from it, not even to watch my instruments, because as I look, it grows larger. Then, all in one long moment, I can make it out. It is yellow, only a shade or two darker than the salt it carries beneath it as it crosses the blackened Edge. Long nosed, with dark wheels that rise half the height of the machine, its snout points toward me. No, toward Henna. It heads for her. As it becomes clearer in the hazy reflection from the salt, I hear its engine roaring and spitting sound in all directions. Then I see the pilot. He is all but invisible, hidden by the bulk of the machine so that only his head and neck can be seen. His machine is across the Edge now and on white salt, covering the kilometer between the Edge and us quickly.

I release the rigging lines to cover my ears against the sounds. How can he stand it? He must be insane from the pounding.

I hesitate, not knowing what to do. Do I force Henna to one side, as Marart tried to do to me, causing her to disappear in shards of plastic as Marart did? Or do I let her live, and lose my chance to join Dannelle's time? I cannot make up my mind, for although I've wanted Dannelle for so long, I cannot recall her face. Instead I seem to feel in the warm air that tears at my lips Henna's even warmer hands on my naked back as we lie on the salt at the Edge.

My thoughts are fused, just as the salt lies fused to the east. I do nothing, and that becomes my decision.

The mirage flickers one last time to the side and seems to touch her clipper, the distortion of its lines merging with her sails for a fraction of a second.

My hands are still off the rigging lines and Henna is pulling away from me, her course altered, the hard shape of her clipper shimmering in the reflected heat. She does not disappear, but I am sure she has slipped through the oasis of time and is even now in the past. I can still see her, of course, as I can see all the images from the past here on the Flats.

I try to follow her clipper, but as we near the Edge, my batteries register zero and I coast to a stop, my deck grinding in the salt as the sails still pull with the wind. She continues, the line of blue reflection widening beneath her keel. As I blink away the sweat from my eyes, her image flickers and finally vanishes in the heat waves rising from the blackened salt of the Edge.

The ground crews come toward me in the electric trucks. They will want to know what happened to Henna and I will have to tell them the truth. I know they will not believe me, just as Henna at first refused to listen. She is in the past now, but I am no closer to

223

the face I cannot recall.

I sit in the darkness and wait for dawn. The sail moves above me, the boom slides back and forth in its peculiar way, and I imagine I can hear my own heart beating.

Everyone from the Timing Race — the pilots, the spectators, even the Association — has long since left the Flats.

But I've stayed, living in a tent near this mountain spring, using the long days to sail my clipper along the Edge.

I tried to tell them what had happened, but they only looked at me quietly and said they'd consider banning me from the Timing Race next season. I don't care, really, for I can search as well on my own.

I believe I know why Henna had tried for the mirage and the past. I first thought it was because she wanted to see if I'd look for her, as I'd looked for Dannelle. But then I remembered her last words to me. She'd wanted to join the past, too, she'd said. Now I believe she went down the line of time to find Dannelle. Perhaps to kill her, as I'd killed Dallin. Perhaps to tell her that it was Henna I loved, to shatter her memories of me.

I sail the Edge every day, searching for both of them and the past. In my mind, they have merged into one; Henna's face flickers in my dreams, but I still remember Dannelle's name. It doesn't really matter which one I find first. They are simply two particles of the same desire.

The sun slips over the mountain behind me and I

feel its warmth drive away the chill of the desert night. As soon as the batteries are recharged, I will switch on the fans and pull the sails tight.

Perhaps today I will see one of their full-rigged clippers soaring above the fused ground of the Edge.

And when I find one of their mirages, I will sail alongside it to join its oasis of time. I will slip into the past, cross my own edge of desire, and relive my love. I will find one of them eventually. And in the blooming heat of the early morning, I shudder, feel the chill of anticipation, and smile as I look down into the mirage-haven of the Edge. Such destruction, and yet such beauty, she'd said, and she had been right.

THE SONGBIRDS OF PAIN

By Garry Kilworth

Tomorrow they would break her legs.

At first, every morning there were songbirds in the fire trees outside her hospital window, and every evening the frogs sang in the storm drains with choirs of bass voices. (Not when she woke or went to sleep: In her twilight world of pain there was no real sleep, just a clinging to the edge of a dream, an intermittent misting of the brain.) Then there came a time when the birds and frogs seemed to be singing from within her, deep within her flesh, her bones. The pitch of their notes was, on occasion, as sharp as thorns; and at other times, as dull as small hammer blows on a hollow skull. Her world was fully of the agony of their music: The songbirds of Brazil entered her blood and swam the channels of her body with slow wings. The tree frogs, the ground frogs, they also filled the long, narrow passages of her limbs, her breasts, and her mind with their melodies. If snakes could sing they would have been there, too, accompanying the cicadas and the grasshoppers; the rhythmic, ticking beetles; even the high-singing bats and the clicking lizards. She tried to remember the time when these songsters, these choral wonders of an exotic lands, were not part of her, were separate from her. There was a man, somewhere, who led her to this state. If she could remember . . .

Philip would indulge her, she knew, to the extent of his fortune. Anita's approach, however, was cautious because of the nature of her request. Even so, the amount of money involved was considerable and, as was his habit, he reached for the whiskey when he was thrown off balance. She had come to realize that it was not the alcohol that was the crutch but the need to hold something in his hand upon which he could concentrate while he recovered his composure. The worst was yet to come. She waited until he had poured his drink and was gripping the glass.

"Yes—" she mentioned the sum—"it's a lot of money, I know, but I'll give up a few things . . . my fur coat, this flat. . . ."

He looked up sharply. "The flat? Where will you live? You're not moving out of London. What do you want this money *for*?"

She hesitated before replying. It was difficult to tell someone you needed a great deal of money in order to have all your bones broken. It would sound ridiculous. Perhaps it *was* ridiculous.

"I'll have to go away . . . it's an operation. Don't look so alarmed. It's not that I'm sick or anything."

He frowned, rolling the crystal tumbler slowly between his palms. Anita wondered whether Philip's wife was aware of this trait: She liked to think she could read this man better than Marjorie could, but perhaps that was arrogance—conceit? Perhaps Marjorie was aware of more important supports than whiskey glasses. Like mistresses.

"Cosmetic surgery? But you're already beautiful. I like the way you are. Why should you want to change?"

"It's more than that, Philip. Something I can't really explain. . . . I'm twenty-six. In a few more years my present . . . looks will begin to fade. I need a beauty that will remain outstanding. It's all I have. I'm not clever like you. Nor do I have the kind of personality that Marjorie possesses. You both have a charisma that goes deeper than looks. You may think it's something superficial that I'm searching for, but I do need it. I want to make the *best* of myself. If I'm beautiful to begin with, then that just means that I need less improvement—but there is a great deal of me I want improved."

"Where will you go? Where is this place, the USA?"

She shook her head. Perhaps this was one time when he would refuse her adamantly. In which case she would have to bide her time, wait for another lover, just as wealthy, but more willing to indulge her.

Yet she knew she could not leave this man. She loved him much too deeply.

"Brazil. A town on the edge of the jungle called Algarez. There's a surgeon there . . . I would trust him. It's a difficult operation, but I know he's carried

229

it out on two other women. It was very successful."

"Brazil?" Again, the rolling of the glass, the slight frown of disapproval. She knew that his business interests would not allow him time to travel at this point in the calendar. She would have to go alone. "Do I know either of these women?"

"One of them. Sarah Shields."

"The actress. But my God, she was unrecognizable when she returned to society. I mean, she looked nothing like her former self—extremely beautiful, yes, but. . . ."

Anita suddenly wanted to knock the glass out of his hand.

Sometimes he lacked the understanding of which she knew he was capable.

". . . beautiful, *yes*, *but*. . . ." There was no *buts* to Anita. Everything was contained in one word. Beauty. She wanted it badly. *Real* beauty, not just a passable beauty. To be the most . . .

"Will you help me?" she asked simply.

He looked into her eyes, and suddenly he smiled. A wonderful, understanding smile, and she knew it would be all right. Philip was usually the most generous of men, but there was that protective shield around his heart, wineglass thin but resistant nonetheless, which she had to shatter gently at times. It was not just the large issues, like this, that revealed the fragile shell that encapsulated his *givingness*, but small things, too—like a trip to the art gallery or the reading of a poem to her while they lay in bed after making love. It was something to do with his fear of being manipulated, something concerned with defending that part of his ego that abhorred control.

She knew he needed her but not as much as she needed him—in fact her own need reached desperation point at times, and she resented the fact that his, though apparent, was not as consuming as her own. Anita thought suddenly of his wife. She had never been jealous of Marjorie. Anyone else, yes, but Marjorie was his wife and, more important, she came *before* Anita.

"When will you leave?" he asked.

"Next month," she replied.

Anita went into the kitchen to make some coffee while Philip finished his whiskey. As she made the coffee she considered the forthcoming trip. Travel was now one of her greatest enjoyments, although this had not always been the case. Brazil. She wondered whether she would like it there. She remembered her first visit abroad, how awful it had been. Normandy, as a young girl on a school exchange. It had been a depressing visit. The family she stayed with insisted on impressing her with trips to the war graves—rows and rows of white crosses. Strange, she thought, that men who had died in such chaos should be buried in neat, symmetrical lines, while conversely, men who had lived quiet, orderly lives—bankers, stockbrokers, insurance people—usually ended up in untidy graveyards, their headstones looking as if they had been planted by some blind, maladroit giant.

She shook off the thoughts of death. After all, it was not death that awaited her in Brazil, but fulfillment, albeit that the road to that end was paved with pain. She knew it was going to be hard, but it was a rebirth that was worth the agony she would have to endure. She hoped her mind was strong enough.

When Philip met her she had been a twenty-year-old shop assistant. He had persuaded her to take up a career in modeling so that she could travel with the small fashion house he financed and they could be together more often.

She was now twenty-six and wiser only in a world as seen through Philip's eyes. He had kept her closeted, comfortable, and happy for four years. Her opinions were secondhand and originally his. She realized this had created an insipid personality, but for the present she was satisfied with the status quo. Later, when she had lost him (as she was bound to do one day), perhaps she could develop her own identity.

Of Philip's former life, she knew only the surface details. He had married at twenty-five while in the process of clawing his way to the first ledge on the cliff of success. Success, in Philip's terms, was money and certain pleasures that went with it. He was a considerate lover and good to his wife in all but absolute fidelity. He was not a philanderer. Also he did not squander money on luxuries he did not really require, like yachts, cars, and swimming pools. He had one of everything he needed except . . . except women. The thought jarred when she reduced it to those terms. There was a certain greed associated with his wants that she generously connected with insecurity. The truth probably lay somewhere between those two character defects.

His had not been an easy climb, either. He had come from a poor background. Philip had since acquired considerable polish and was thought of by his contemporaries as an aristocratic businessman rather than working class—*nouveau riche*.

At the time Anita had met him, he had been thirty-two. He had given her a lift home after work at a store for which he supplied new fashions. Now she was making coffee for him following an evening at the theater and before he went home to his wife.

She took in the coffee, and they drank it in silence. They would not make love tonight. Sex was not the most important part of their relationship, in any case. Philip needed her more for the affection she gave him. Not that Marjorie was unaffectionate, but Anita had come to know that while Philip was a tough businessman, he was privately very sentimental and needed a great deal of emotional support. It provided the background softness to a life full of hard-bitten decisions. Neither woman was volatile or demonstrative. They were both warm and loyal, with loving dispositions.

It was not contrasts Philip required, but additions. In turn, he gave much—almost as much as either woman asked for—in both practical and emotional terms.

"I'll have to be getting home now," he said, after the coffee.

She nodded. "I know."

"I'm sorry. I'd like to stay tonight, but Marjorie's expecting me."

"It's all right, Philip, really it is. I'm fine. I've got a good book and the television if I need it. Please don't worry."

He kissed her gently on the brow, and she stood up and fetched his coat.

"I'll call you," he said, standing at the door.

"I'll be here." He never could say goodbye, always

233

using feeble excuses, like a just-remembered something or other, to prolong the final parting for the
night. Even a half-closed door was not a sure indication that he was on his way. He might turn at the last
minute, whip off his coat, and say, "Dammit, another
hour won't hurt. I'll say the car had a flat or
something."

"Go, Philip," she said. "Just *go*."

He shrugged huffily inside his overcoat and
stepped onto the landing. She closed the door and
then went into the living room to clear away the
coffee things. She carried them into the kitchen, but
as she placed the tray on the working surface, her arm
knocked over the percolator, which was still on. Hot
coffee splashed onto her leg, and the pain sent her
reeling backward.

"Philip!" she cried.

She inspected herself. There was a red weal the size
of a handprint on her thigh, as if she had been
slapped hard.

Philip. Damn him. He was never there when he was
needed most. That was one of the disadvantages of
being a kept woman. The partner was not on call.
Christ that hurts, she thought. She put her leg under
the cold water tap and turned it on. The water would
bring down her skin temperature. Afterward, she felt
a little better and took several aspirin before crawling
into bed. Funny, she thought, lying in bed, when she
was a child they said the worst thing one could do
with a burn was put cold water on it. A dry bandage
was the recommended treatment. Now, *they*, whoever
they were, had decided to reverse the treatment completely. The world was controlled by whims. The last

thing she remembered before she fell asleep was that her leg still hurt her.

The flight to Brasilia was long and uncomfortable, but Anita was excited, not only by the thought of the impending operation, but by the idea of being in South America.

She made her visits during the next day and took in the nightlife of the city in the evening. There was no real enjoyment in it for her though, because she wanted to share it all with Philip, and he was several thousand miles away.

She telephoned him, but the instrument had always been impersonal to her. She could not feel close to him, even while she was listening to his vaguely distorted voice.

"Philip . . . it's Anita."

An echo of her voice followed each word and then a long, deep silence in which it seemed to her that the ears of the world were tuned in to their private conversation.

". . . lo, darling . . . are you?" Parts of his speech were lost to her. It was a distressing business. She wanted to reach out and touch him, not exchange banalities over thousands of miles. Damn, what was that clicking? She could not hear him properly.

"Fine, everything's fine," she said.

It sounded hollow, flat. There was more of the same.

"Look after yourself," he finished, after a very unsatisfactory five minutes. When she replaced the receiver she felt further away from him than before the call had begun. Hell, it was supposed to bring them closer, not emphasize the vast distance that separated them. She needed him desperately. If she had asked him, he would have come running, but there was no real excuse — not one of which he would approve. Just a longing for his company, which was almost a physical hurt inside her.

The flight to the hospital, over the dark-green back of prehistoric jungles, was short but not uneventful.

They flew low enough in the small aircraft for her to study the moody rivers, the sudden clearings studded with huts, the forests pressing down a personal night beneath their impenetrable layers of foliage. Down there were big cats, deadly snakes, spiders the size of soup plates, and alligators with skins like tank tracks.

On landing, she went straight to the hospital. It was a small, white building on the outskirts of the town, surrounded by gardens with trees of brilliant hues. The color of the blossoms was so light and buoyant, it seemed that only the buried roots held the splendid trees to the earth: Should the roots be severed, they would rise slowly like balloons, to take her up into the atmosphere.

Anita's fanciful thoughts, she knew, stemmed from her desire to steer herself away from considering the forthcoming operation. When she was confronted by the surgeon, however, she knew she would have to face up to the ordeal. His office was on the second floor. He had switched off his air conditioner and flung windows and balcony doors open wide, letting in the smell of vegetation. She could see out, over the balcony and beyond the hospital gardens. The light seemed to gather near the edge of the dark jungle, as if the forest perimeter was a dam to hold back the day, to stop its bright wave rolling in to defile the old trees and ancient, overgrown temples.

The surgeon spoke; his words, perhaps subconsciously, were timed exactly to coincide with the metronomic clicking of the auxiliary overhead fan.

"You realize," he said, "there will be a great deal of pain."

He was an elderly American with a soft accent and gentle eyes, but she had difficulty in not looking down at his hands. Those narrow fingers, as white as driftwood with continual scrubbing, would soon be cracking her bones. They were strong-looking hands, and the arms to which they were joined, powerful. Many limbs had been purposefully broken with cold, calculated accuracy, by those hands.

"We can only give you drugs up to a certain point. The whole operation is a long business — a series of operations in fact — and we don't want to send you out a morphine addict."

She nodded. "I understand."

What sort of instruments are used? she wanted to ask, but was too afraid of the answer to actually do so.

She imagined ugly steel clamps, vises, and mechanical hammers that were fitted with a precision more suited to a factory jig than a medical instrument. This is the way we break your bones. *We screw this here, that there — can you feel the cold metal against your skin? The plates gripping the bones? — then, once we have lined it up and in position — whap! — down comes the weight between the guide blocks and* crack! *goes the bone. Easy, isn't it?*

"Of course, once we're finished with you, you will be . . . ah, even more beautiful than you can imagine."

"That's what I want. I don't care about the pain so long as the result is good."

"Not *good* but *breathtaking*. We'll straighten out any defects in the limbs, give you a jawline that Cleopatra would envy, small feet, slender hands. We'll also graft a little flesh here and there. Take away any excess. The eyes, we can do much with the eyes. And we'll have to break those fingers, one or two of them . . . am I being too blunt?"

"No, no." She had paled, she knew, at the word *break*. The other words were fine. She could take terms like *straighten the limbs* — but *break* had a force behind it that shook her confidence.

"I'll be all right," she said. "It must be the journey, the heat or something. Please don't worry. Please go on."

Her body was alive with feeling, as if electricity were coursing through her veins instead of blood. She concentrated on his words as he began to describe what her experience would be, to ensure, he said, that she knew *exactly* what to expect. If she wished, she could leave now, and there would be no charge.

Outside the window, the birds were singing, and she concentrated not on his descriptions of the forthcoming mutilations of her body but on their songs.

At first the pain was a patchy, dull feeling, its location in her body specific to certain areas, like her

238

forearms, which were the first to be broken. An aching that was difficult but not impossible to bear.

At night, when she was left alone, she could feel the pain throbbing and pulsing in the various parts of her limbs. Later, it developed a sharpness and spread like a field fire through her whole anatomy, until there was no pinpointing its source.

The pain was her, she was the pain. It reached a pitch and intensity that filled her with a terror she had never before thought possible, could not have imagined in her worst nightmares. It had shape and form and had become a tangible thing that had banished her psyche, had taken over completely her whole being. There was nothing inside her skin but the beast pain: no heart, no brain, no flesh, no bones, no soul. Just the beast.

It was *unbearable*, and she refused to bear it. She tried, with all her willpower, to remove it from her body. It was then that the pain began to sing to her. It called in the birds from beneath their waxen leaves, the fabric blossoms: It summoned the night singers, the small, green tree frogs and the booming bulls from their mudbank trumpets; it persuaded the chit-chat lizards to enter in, and the insects to abandon the bladed grasses for its sake. When it had gathered together its choirs, the beast pain sang to her. It sang unholy hymns with mouths of needle teeth, and the birds, frogs, and insects sang its song. Gradually, over the many days, she felt the sharp sweetness of their music giving her a new awareness, lifting her to a new, higher plane of experience, until there came a time when she was dependent upon their presence.

Tomorrow they would break her legs. She lay back

in her bed, unable to move her head because of the clamps on her jaw. Her arms were completely healed. The plaster had left them pale and thin, with her skin flaking off, but the doctor assured her they would soon look normal. Better than normal, of course. Then her jaw had been reshaped. That was *almost* healed.

The surgeon was insistent she wait for her legs to be remodeled, even though she told him she wanted the process hurried so that she could get back to Philip. *Her legs.*

She knew the worst pain was yet to come. Then, of course, there were the minor operations: her nose, fingers, toes, and ears. (Afterward she could wear her hair shorter. Would not need to cover those ugly ears, which would then be beautiful.) The surgeon had also mentioned scraping away some of the bone above her eyes, where there were slight bulges. (She had never noticed them, but he had obviously done so.) Also there were her shoulder blades to adjust—the scapu-lae—she was even beginning to learn the Latin names. . . .

Sweet pain! What delicious strains came from its small mouths. Sing to me, she whispered, *sing*! She needed more and more.

"The hands haven't gone too well; we're going to have to rework them," he said.

She smiled, as much as the wire brace would allow.

"If you have to."

"You're a brave woman."

"I try to be," she replied, drifting off into her other world, the *real* world, where she became herself. Her actual *self*.

In there, deep inside, lay the quintessential spark of being, where she was pure *Anita*. To reach that spark, it was necessary to use an agent — drugs, medication, will, faith, religion, or perhaps *pain*. Pain was her vehicle to that interior world, that inscape that made the rest of life seem a wasteland of experience. There was the power, the energy of birth. The cold release of death. Heady. Unequivocally the center of the universe. So strange to find that all else revolved around her. That nothing existed that was not derived from her. Even Philip. She *was* the sun, the moon, the stars, the earth. She was void, she was matter, she was light.

Anita and her pain.

"How do you feel?" asked the surgeon.

She smiled. "I really do feel like a new woman. How do I look?"

"See for yourself. . . ." He indicated the mirror on the wall, but she had already studied herself for hours before the mirror in her room. The scars were now invisible, the blemishes and bruises gone. Blue-black skin had been replaced by her normal cream complexion. And now? Now her features were . . . breathtaking, yes. Her whole body was absolutely perfect in its proportions. This was what she had desired for so many years. Beauty, absolute.

"I'm very pleased," she said. "I really haven't the words to express my thanks."

He held up a hand. "I've been adequately rewarded," he said. "We don't do it for love of beauty — although I admit to being proud of my art. And I must congratulate you on your courage. You withstood the pain with as much bravery as I've ever seen."

She shrugged. "It isn't something I'd like to go through again," she lied, "but I think it's been worth it. It *has* been worth it," she hastily amended.

They shook hands.

"You're a beautiful woman," he said, in a voice that suggested he had forgotten he had created her.

On the drive away, she barely looked at the trees, still dripping with colors. Their blooms no longer interested her. Nor did the birds upon their branches. She had her own colors, her own songbirds.

Philip was waiting by the exit of the airport arrival lounge. She saw him from the far side of the room.

He was looking directly at her, and she realized that he did not recognize her. He looked away and began searching the faces of the other passengers.

She began walking toward him. Twice more he looked at her, as if expecting a sign from her to tell him she was Anita, then back to the other passengers.

She noticed his expression was expectant but calm. He thought he had no need to be anxious. Anita was supposed to declare herself. As she drew closer she *almost* wavered in her purpose.

Her heart flooded with emotion. God, he was her *life*. Never would she have the same feelings for any other man. He was everything to her. Philip. Even the name was enough to fill her heart with the desire, the passion, the tender feelings of love.

She needed him, wanted him above all else except. . . .

She studied his eyes, his face, his quizzical expression as she passed him and then went through the exit, her feelings choking her. She was leaving him. She wanted him desperately, but she was leaving him — and the delicious pain, the emotional agony, was exquisite. She nurtured the hurt inside her, listening to the music that ran through her veins. This was beauty: the delight, the ecstasy of spiritual pain, even sweeter than a physical hurt. Her songbirds would be with her till death, and her indulgence in the music they created washed through her whole being and made her complete, made the whole of existence complete, for everyone — even Philip.

THE CHANGED MAN AND
THE KING OF WORDS

By Orson Scott Card

Once there was a man who loved his son more than life. Once there was a boy who loved his father more than death.

They are not the same story, not really. But I can't tell you one without telling you the other.

The man was Dr. Alvin Bevis, and the boy was his son, Joseph, and the only woman that either of them loved was Connie, who in 1977 married Alvin, with hope and joy, and in 1978 gave birth to Joe on the brink of death and adored them both accordingly. It was an affectionate family. This made it almost certain that they would come to grief.

Connie could have no more children after Joe. She shouldn't even have had *him*. Her doctor called her a

245

damn fool for refusing to abort him in the fourth month when the problems began. "He'll be born retarded. You'll die in labor." To which she answered, "I'll have one child, or I won't believe that I ever lived." In her seventh month they took Joe out of her, womb and all. He was scrawny and little, and the doctor told her to expect him to be mentally deficient and physically uncoordinated. Connie nodded and ignored him. She was lucky. She had Joe, alive, and silently she said to any who pitied her, *I am more a woman than any of you barren ones who still have to worry about the phases of the moon.*

Neither Alvin nor Connie ever believed Joe would be retarded. And soon enough it was clear that he wasn't. He walked at eight months. He talked at twelve months. He had his alphabet at eighteen months. He could read at a second-grade level by the time he was three. He was inquisitive, demanding, independent, disobedient, and exquisitely beautiful, with a shock of copper-colored hair and a face as smooth and deep as a coldwater pool.

His parents watched him devour learning and were sometimes hard pressed to feed him with what he needed. *He will be a great man*, they both whispered to each other in the secret conversations of night. It made them proud; it made them afraid to know that his learning and his safety had, by chance or the grand design of things, been entrusted to them.

Out of all the variety the Bevises offered their son in the first few years of his life, Joe became obsessed with stories. He would bring books and insist that Connie or Alvin read to him, but if it was not a storybook, he quickly ran and got another, until at

246

last they were reading a story. Then he sat imprisoned by the chain of events as the tale unfolded, saying nothing until the story was over. Again and again "Once upon a time," or "There once was a," or "One day the king sent out a proclamation," until Alvin and Connie had every storybook in the house practically memorized. Fairy tales were Joe's favorites, but as time passed, he graduated to movies and contemporary stories and even history.

The problem was not the thirst for tales, however. The conflict began because Joe had to live out his stories. He would get up in the morning and announce that Mommy was Mama Bear, Daddy was Papa Bear, and he was Baby Bear. When he was angry, he would be Goldilocks and run away. Other mornings Daddy would be Rumpelstiltskin, Mommy would be the Farmer's Daughter, and Joe would be the King. Joe was Hansel, Mommy was Gretel, and Alvin was the Wicked Witch.

"Why can't I be Hansel's and Gretel's father?" Alvin asked. He resented being the Wicked Witch. Not that he thought it *meant* anything. He told himself it merely annoyed him to have his son constantly assigning him dialogue and action for the day's activities. Alvin never knew from one hour to the next who he was going to be in his own home.

After a time, mild annoyance gave way to open irritation; if it was a phase Joe was going through, it ought surely to have ended by now. Alvin finally suggested that the boy be taken to a child psychologist. The doctor said it was a phase.

"Which means that sooner or later he'll get over it?" Alvin asked. "Or that you just can't figure out what's going on?"

"Both," said the psychologist cheerfully. "You'll just have to live with it."

But Alvin did not like living with it. He wanted his son to call him Daddy. He *was* the father, after all. Why should he have to put up with his child, no matter how bright the boy was, assigning him silly roles to play whenever he came home? Alvin put his foot down. He refused to answer to any name but Father. And after a little anger and a lot of repeated attempts, Joe finally stopped trying to get his father to play a part. Indeed, as far as Alvin knew, Joe entirely stopped acting out stories.

It was not so, of course, Joe simply acted them out with Connie after Alvin had gone for the day to cut up DNA and put it back together creatively. That was how Joe learned to hide things from his father. He wasn't *lying*; he was just biding his time. Joe was sure that if only he found good enough stories, Daddy would play again.

So when Daddy was home, Joe did not act out stories. Instead he and his father played number and word games, studied elementary Spanish as an introduction to Latin, plinked out simple programs on the Atari, and laughed and romped until Mommy came in and told her boys to calm down before the roof fell in on them. *This is being a father*, Alvin told himself. *I am a good father.* And it was true. It was true, even though every now and then Joe would ask his mother hopefully, "Do you think that Daddy will want to be in *this* story?"

"Daddy just doesn't like to pretend. He likes your stories, but not acting them out."

In 1983 Joe turned five and entered school; that same year Dr. Bevis created a bacterium that lived on acid precipitation and neutralized it. In 1987 Joe left school, because he knew more than any of his teachers; at precisely that time Dr. Bevis began earning royalties on commercial breeding of his bacterium for spot cleanup in acidized bodies of water. The university suddenly became terrified that he might retire and live on his income and take his name away from the school. So he was given a laboratory and twenty assistants and secretaries and an administrative assistant, and from then on Dr. Bevis could pretty well do what he liked with his time.

What he liked was to make sure the research was still going on as carefully and methodically as was proper, and in directions that he approved of. Then he went home and became the faculty of one for his son's very private academy.

It was an idyllic time for Alvin.

It was hell for Joe.

Joe loved his father, mind you. Joe played at learning, and they had a wonderful time, reading *The Praise of Folly* in the original Latin, duplicating great experiments, and then devising experiments of their own—too many things to list. Enough to say that Alvin had never had a graduate student so quick to grasp new ideas, so eager to devise newer ones of his own. How could Alvin have known that Joe was starving to death before his eyes?

For with Father home, Joe and Mother could not play.

Before Alvin had taken him out of school, Joe used to read books with his mother. All day at home she would read *Jane Eyre*, and Joe would read it in school, hiding it behind copies of *Friends and Neighbors*. Homer, Chaucer, Shakespeare, Twain, Mitchell, Galsworthy, Elswyth Thane. And then in those precious hours after school let out and before Alvin came home from work they would be Ashley and Scarlett, Tibby and Julian, Huck and Jim, Walter and Griselde, Odysseus and Circe. Joe no longer assigned the parts the way he did when he was little. They both knew what book they were reading, and they would live within the milieu of that book. Each had to guess from the other's behavior what role had been chosen that particular day; it was a triumphant moment when at last Connie would dare to venture Joe's name for the day, or Joe call Mother by hers. In all the years of playing the games, never once did they choose to be the same person; never once did they fail to figure out what role the other played.

Now Alvin was home, and that game was over. No more stolen moments of reading during school. Father frowned on stories. History, yes; lies and poses, no. And so while Alvin thought that joy had finally come, for Joe and Connie joy was dead.

Their life became one of allusion, dropping phrases to each other out of books, playing subtle characters without ever allowing themselves to utter the other's name. So perfectly did they perform that Alvin never knew what was happening. Just now and then he'd realize that something was going on that he didn't understand.

"What sort of weather is this for January?" Alvin said one day, looking out the window at heavy rain.

"Fine," said Joe, and then, thinking of "The Mer-

250

chant's Tale," he smiled at his mother. "In May we climb trees."

"What?" Alvin asked. "What does that have to do with anything?"

"I just like tree climbing."

"It all depends," said Connie, "on whether the sun dazzles your eyes."

When Connie left the room, Joe asked an innocuous question about teleology, and Alvin put the previous exchange completely out of his mind.

Or rather tried to put it out of his mind. He was no fool. Though Joe and Connie were very subtle, Alvin gradually realized he did not speak the native language of his own home. He was well enough read to catch a reference or two. Turning into swine. Sprinkling dust. "Frankly, I don't give a damn." Remarks that didn't quite fit into the conversation, phrases that seemed strangely resonant. And as he grew more aware of his wife's and his son's private language, the more isolated he felt. His lessons with Joe began to seem not exciting but hollow, as if they were both acting a role. Taking parts in a story. The story of the loving father-teacher and the dutiful, brilliant student-son. It had been the best time of Alvin's life, better than any life he had created in the lab, but that was when he had believed it. Now it was just a play. His son's real life was somewhere else.

I didn't like playing the parts he gave me, years ago, Alvin thought. *Does he like playing the part that I have given him?*

"You've gone as far as I can take you," Alvin said at breakfast one day, "in everything, except biology of course. So I'll guide your studies in biology, and for everything else I'm hiring advanced graduate students in various fields at the university. A different one each day."

Joe's eyes went deep and distant. "You won't be my teacher anymore?"

"Can't teach you what I don't know," Alvin said. And he went back to the lab. Went back and with delicate cruelty tore apart a dozen cells and made them into something other than themselves, whether they would or not.

Back at home, Joe and Connie looked at each other in puzzlement. Joe was thirteen. He was getting tall and felt shy and awkward before his mother. They had been three years without stories together. With Father there, they had played at being prisoners, passing messages under the guard's very nose. Now there was no guard, and without the need for secrecy there was no message anymore. Joe took to going outside and reading or playing obsessively at the computer; more doors were locked in the Bevis home than had ever been locked before.

Joe dreamed terrifying, gentle nightmares, dreamed of the same thing, over and over; the setting was different, but always the story was the same. He dreamed of being on a boat, and the gunwale began to crumble wherever he touched it, and he tried to warn his parents, but they wouldn't listen, they leaned, it broke away under their hands, and they fell into the sea, drowning. He dreamed that he was bound up in a web, tied like a spider's victim, but the spider never, never, never came to taste of him, left him there to dessicate in helpless bondage, though he cried out and struggled. How could he explain such

252

dreams to his parents? He remembered Joseph in Genesis, who spoke too much of dreams; remembered Cassandra; remembered Iocaste, who thought to slay her child for fear of oracles. *I am caught up in a story*, Joe thought, *from which I cannot escape. Each change is a fall; each fall tears me from myself. If I cannot be the people of the tales, who am I then?*

Life was normal enough for all that. Breakfast lunch dinner, sleep wake sleep, work earn spend own, use break fix. All the cycles of ordinary life played out despite the shadow of inevitable ends. One day Alvin and his son were in a bookstore, the Gryphon, which had the complete Penguin Classics. Alvin was browsing through the titles to see what might be of some use when he noticed Joe was no longer following him.

His son, all the slender five feet nine inches of him, was standing half the store away, bent in avid concentration over something on the counter. Alvin felt a terrible yearning for his son. He was so beautiful, and yet somehow in these dozen and one years of Joe's life, Alvin had lost him. Now Joe was nearing manhood, and very soon it would be too late. *When did he cease to be mine?* Alvin wondered. *When did he become so much his mother's son? Why must he be as beautiful as she, and yet have the mind he has? He is Apollo*, Alvin said to himself.

And in that moment he knew what he had lost. By calling his son Apollo, he had told himself what he had taken from his son. A connection between stories the child acted out and his knowledge of who he was.

The connection was so real, it was almost tangible, and yet Alvin could not put it into words, could not bear the knowledge, and so, and so, and so—

Just as he was sure he had the truth of things, it slipped away. Without words, his memory could not hold it, lost the understanding the moment it came. *I knew it all, and I have already forgotten.* Angry at himself, Alvin strode to his son and realized that Joe was not doing anything intelligent at all. He had a deck of tarot cards spread before him. He was doing a reading.

"Cross my palms with silver," said Alvin. He thought he was making a joke, but his anger spoke too loudly in his voice. Joe looked up with shame on his face. Alvin cringed inside himself. *Just by speaking to you, I wound you.* Alvin wanted to apologize, but he had no strategy for that; so he tried to affirm that it had been a joke by making another. "Discovering the secrets of the universe?"

Joe half-smiled and quickly gathered up the cards and put them away.

"No," Alvin said. "No, you were interested; you don't have to put them away."

"It's just nonsense," Joe said.

You're lying, Alvin thought.

"All the meanings are so vague, they could fit just about anything." Joe laughed mirthlessly.

"You looked pretty interested."

"I was just, you know, wondering how to program a computer for this, wondering whether I could do a program that would make it make some sense. Not just the random fall of the cards, you know. A way to make it respond to who a person really is. Cut

254

through all the—"

"Yes?"

"Just wondering."

"Cut through all the—?"

"Stories we tell ourselves. All the lies that we believe about ourselves. About who we really are."

Something didn't ring true in the boy's words, Alvin knew. Something was wrong. And because in Alvin's world nothing could long exist unexplained, he decided the boy seemed awkward because his father had made him ashamed of his own curiosity. *I am ashamed that I have made you ashamed*, Alvin thought. *So I will buy you the cards.*

"I'll buy the cards. And the book you were looking at."

"No, Dad," said Joe.

"No, it's all right. Why not? Play around with the computer. See if you can turn this nonsense into something. What the hell, you might come up with some good graphics and sell the program for a bundle." Alvin laughed. So did Joe. Even Joe's *laugh* was a lie.

What Alvin didn't know was this: Joe was not ashamed. Joe was merely afraid. For he had laid out the cards as the book instructed, but he had not needed the explanations, had not needed the names of the faces. He had known their names at once, had known their faces. It was Creon who held the sword and the scales. Ophelia, naked, wreathed in green, with man and falcon, bull and lion around. Ophelia, who danced in her madness. And I was once the boy with the starflower in the sixth cup, giving it to my child-mother, when gifts were possible between us.

255

The cards were not dice, they were names, and he laid them out in stories, drawing them in order from the deck in a pattern that he knew was largely the story of his life. All the names that he had borne were in these cards, and all the shapes of past and future dwelt here, waiting to be dealt. It was this that frightened him. He had been deprived of stories for so long, his own story of father, mother, son was so fragile now that he was madly grasping at anything; Father mocked, but Joe looked at the story of the cards, and he believed. *I do not want to take these home. It puts myself wrapped in a silk in my own hands.* "Please don't," he said to his father.

But Alvin, who knew better, bought them anyway, hoping to please his son.

Joe stayed away from the cards for a whole day. He had only touched them the once; surely he need not toy with this fear again. It was irrational, mere wish fulfillment, Joe told himself. *The cards mean nothing. They are not to be feared. I can touch them and learn no truth from them.* And yet all his rationalism, all his certainty that the cards were meaningless, were, he knew, merely lies he was telling to persuade himself to try the cards again, and this time seriously.

"What did you bring *those* home for?" Mother asked in the other room.

Father said nothing. Joe knew from the silence that Father did not want to make any explanation that might be overheard.

"They're silly," said Mother. "I thought you were a scientist and a skeptic. I thought you didn't believe in things like this."

"It was just a lark," Father lied. "I bought them for Joe to plink around with. He's thinking of doing a computer program to make the cards respond somehow to people's personalities. The boy has a right to play now and then."

And in the family room, where the toy computer sat mute on the shelf, Joe tried not to think of Odysseus walking away from the eight cups, treading the lip of the ocean's basin, his back turned to the wine. *Forty-eight kilobytes and two little disks. This isn't computer enough for what I mean to do*, Joe thought. *I will not do it, of course. But with Father's computer from his office upstairs, with the hard disk and the right type of interface, perhaps there is space and time enough for all the operations. Of course I will not do it. I do not care to do it. I do not dare to do it.*

At two in the morning he got up from his bed, where he could not sleep, went downstairs, and began to program the graphics of the tarot deck upon the screen. But in each picture he made changes, for he knew that the artist, gifted as he was, had made mistakes. Had not understood that the Page of Cups was a buffoon with a giant phallus, from which flowed the sea. Had not known that the Queen of Swords was a statue and it was her throne that was alive, an angel groaning in agony at the stone burden she had to bear. The child at the gate of ten stars was being eaten by the old man's dogs. The man hanging upside down with crossed legs and peace upon his face, he wore no halo; his hair was afire. And the Queen of Pentacles had just given birth to a bloody star, whose father was not the King of Pentacles, that poor cuckold.

And as the pictures and their stories came to him, he began to hear the echoes of all the other stories he had read. Cassandra, Queen of Swords, flung her bladed words, and people batted them out of the air like flies, when if they had only caught them and used them, they would not have met the future unarmed. For a moment Odysseus bound to the mast was the hanged man; in the right circumstances, Macbeth could show up in the ever-trusting Page of Cups, or crush himself under the ambitious Queen of Pentacles, Queen of Coins if she crossed him. The cards held tales of power, tales of pain, in the invisible threads that bound them to one another. Invisible threads, but Joe knew they were there, and he had to make the pictures right, make the program right, so that he could find true stories when he read the cards.

Through the night he labored until each picture was right; the job was only begun when he fell asleep at last. His parents were worried on finding him there in the morning, but they hadn't the heart to waken him. When he awoke, he was alone in the house, and he began again immediately, drawing the cards on the TV screen, storing them in the computer's memory; as for his own memory, he needed no help to recall them all, for he knew their names and their stories and was beginning to understand how their names changed every time they came together.

By evening it was done, along with a brief randomizer program that dealt the cards. The pictures were right. The names were right. But this time when the computer spread the cards before him — This is you, this covers you, this crosses you — it was meaningless. The computer could not do what hands could do. It could not understand and unconsciously deal the cards. It was not a randomizer program that was needed at all, for the shuffling of the tarot was not done by chance.

"May I tinker a little with your computer?" Joe asked.

"The hard disk?" Father looked doubtful. "I don't want you to open it, Joe. I don't want to try to come up with another ten thousand dollars this week if something goes wrong." Behind his words was a worry: *This business with the tarot cards has gone far enough, and I'm sorry I bought them for you, and I don't want you to use the computer, especially if it would make this obsession any stronger.*

"Just an interface, Father. You don't use the parallel port anyway, and I can put it back afterward."

"The Atari and the hard disk aren't even compatible.

"I know," said Joe.

But in the end there really couldn't be much argument. Joe knew computers better than Alvin did, and they both knew that what Joe took apart, Joe could put together. It took days of tinkering with hardware and plinking at the program. During that time Joe did nothing else. In the beginning he tried to distract himself. At lunch he told Mother about books they ought to read; at dinner he spoke to Father about Newton and Einstein until Alvin had to remind him that he was a biologist, not a mathematician. No one was fooled by these attempts at breaking the obsession. The tarot program drew Joe back

259

after every meal, after every interruption, until at last he began to refuse meals and ignore the interruptions entirely.

"You have to eat. You can't die for this silly game," said Mother.

Joe said nothing. She set a sandwich by him, and he ate some of it.

"Joe, this has gone far enough. Get yourself under control," said Father.

Joe didn't look up. "I'm under control," he said, and he went on working.

After six days Alvin came and stood between Joe and the television set. "This nonsense will end now," Alvin said. "You are behaving like a boy with serious problems. The most obvious cure is to disconnect the computer, which I will do if you do not stop working on this absurd program at once. We try to give you freedom, Joe, but when you do this to us and to yourself, then—"

"That's all right," said Joe. "I've mostly finished it anyway." He got up and went to bed and slept for fourteen hours.

Alvin was relieved. "I thought he was losing his mind."

Connie was more worried than ever. "What do you think he'll do if it doesn't work?"

"Work? How could it work? Work at what? Cross my palm with silver and I'll tell your future."

"Haven't you been *listening* to him?"

"He hasn't said a word in days."

"He believes in what he's doing. He thinks his program will tell the truth."

Alvin laughed. "Maybe your doctor, what's-his-name, maybe he was right. Maybe there was brain damage after all."

Connie looked at him in horror. "God, Alvin."

"A joke, for Christ's sake."

"It wasn't funny."

They didn't talk about it, but in the middle of the night, at different times, each of them got up and went into Joe's room to look at him in his sleep.

Who are you? Connie asked silently. *What are you going to do if this project of yours is a failure? What are you going to do if it succeeds?*

Alvin, however, just nodded. He refused to be worried. Phases and stages of life. Children go through times of madness as they grow.

Be a lunatic thirteen-year-old, Joe, if you must. You'll return to reality soon enough. You're my son, and I know that you'll prefer reality in the long run.

The next evening Joe insisted that his father help him test the program. "It won't work on me," Alvin said. "I don't believe in it. It's like faith healing and taking vitamin C for colds. It never works on skeptics."

Connie stood small near the refrigerator. Alvin noticed the way she seemed to retreat from the conversation.

"Did you try it?" Alvin asked her.

She nodded.

"Mom did it four times for me," Joe said gravely.

"Couldn't get it right the first time?" Father asked. It was a joke.

"Got it right every time," Joe said.

Alvin looked at Connie. She met his gaze at first, but then looked away in—what? Fear? Shame? Em-

261

barrassment? Alvin couldn't tell. But he sensed that something painful had happened while he was at work. "Should I do it?" Alvin asked her.

"No," Connie whispered.

"Please," Joe said. "How can I test it if you won't help? I can't tell if it's right or wrong unless I know the people doing it."

"What kind of fortuneteller are you?" Alvin asked. "You're supposed to be able to tell the future of strangers."

"I don't tell the future," Joe said. "The program just tells the truth."

"Ah, truth!" said Alvin. "Truth about what?"

"Who you really are."

"Am I in disguise?"

"It tells your names. It tells your story. Ask Mother if it doesn't."

"Joe," Alvin said, "I'll play this little game with you. But don't expect me to regard it as *true*. I'll do almost anything for you, Joe, but I won't lie for you."

"I know."

"Just so you understand."

"I understand."

Alvin sat down at the keyboard. From the kitchen came a sound like the whine a cringing hound makes, back in its throat. It was Connie, and she was terrified. Her fear, whatever caused it, was contagious. Alvin shuddered and then ridiculed himself for letting this upset him. He was in control, and it was absurd to be afraid. He wouldn't be snowed by his own son.

"What do I do?"

"Just type things in."

"What things?"

"Whatever comes to mind."

"Words? Numbers? How do I know what to write if you don't tell me?"

"It doesn't matter what you write. Just so you write whatever you feel like writing."

I don't feel like writing anything, Alvin thought. *I don't feel like humoring this nonsense another moment.* But he could not say so, not to Joe; he had to be the patient father, giving this absurdity a fair chance. He began to come up with numbers, with words. But after a few moments there was no randomness, no free association in his choice. It was not in Alvin's nature to let chance guide his choices. Instead he began reciting on the keyboard the long strings of genetic-code information on his most recent bacterial subjects, fragments of names, fragments of numeric data, progressing in order through the DNA. He knew as he did it that he was cheating his son, that Joe wanted something of himself. But he told himself, *What could be more a part of me than something I made?*

"Enough?" he asked Joe.

Joe shrugged. "Do you think it is?"

"I could have done five words and you would have been satisfied?"

"If you think you're through, you're through," Joe said quietly.

"Oh, you're very good at this," Alvin said. "Even the hocus-pocus."

"You're through then?"

"Yes."

Joe started the program running. He leaned back

and waited. He could sense his father's impatience, and he found himself relishing the wait. The whirring and clicking of the disk drive. And then the cards began appearing on the screen. This is you. This covers you. This crosses you. This is above you, below you, before you, behind you. Your foundation and your house, your death and your name. Joe waited for what had come before, what had come so predictably, the stories that had flooded in upon him when he read for his mother and for himself a dozen times before. But the stories did not come. Because the cards were the same. Over and over again, the King of Swords.

Joe looked at it and understood at once. Father had lied. Father had consciously controlled his input, had ordered it in some way that told the cards that they were being forced. The program had not failed. Father simply would not be read. The King of Swords, by himself, was power, as all the Kings were power. The King of Pentacles was the power of money, the power of the bribe. The King of Wands was the power of life, the power to make new. The King of Cups was the power of negation and obliteration, the power of murder and sleep. And the King of Swords was the power of words that others would believe. Swords could say, "I will kill you," and be believed, and so be obeyed. Swords could say, "I love you," and be believed, and so be adored. Swords could lie. And all his father had given him was lies. What Alvin didn't know was that even the choice of lies told the truth.

"Edmund," said Joe. Edmund was the lying bastard in *King Lear*.

"What?" asked Father.

"We are only what nature makes us. And nothing more."

"You're getting this from the cards?"

Joe looked at his father, expressing nothing.

"It's all the same card," said Alvin.

"I know," said Joe.

"What's this supposed to be?"

"A waste of time," said Joe. Then he got up and walked out of the room.

Alvin sat there, looking at the little tarot cards laid out on the screen. As he watched, the display changed, each card in turn being surrounded by a thin line and then blown up large, nearly filling the screen. The King of Swords every time. With the point of his sword coming out of his mouth, and his hands clutching at his groin. *Surely*, Alvin thought, *that was not what was drawn on the Waite deck.*

Connie stood near the kitchen doorway, leaning on the refrigerator. "And that's all?" she asked.

"Should there be more?" Alvin asked.

"God," she said.

"What happened with you?"

"Nothing," she said, walking calmly out of the room. Alvin heard her rush up the stairs. And he wondered how things got out of control like this.

Alvin could not make up his mind how to feel about his son's project. It was silly, and Alvin wanted nothing to do with it, wished he'd never bought the cards for him. For days on end Alvin would stay at the laboratory until late at night and rush back again in the morning without so much as eating breakfast with his family. Then, exhausted from lack of sleep, he would get up late, come downstairs, and pretend for the whole day that nothing unusual was going on. On such days he discussed Joe's readings with him, or his own genetic experiments; sometimes, when the artificial cheer had been maintained long enough to be believed, Alvin would even discuss Joe's tarot program. It was at such times that Alvin offered to provide Joe with introductions, to get him better computers to work with, to advise him on the strategy of development and publication. Afterward Alvin always regretted having helped Joe, because what Joe was doing was a shameful waste of a brilliant mind. It also did not make Joe love him any more.

Yet as time passed, Alvin realized that other people were taking Joe seriously. A group of psychologists administered batteries of tests to hundreds of subjects—who had also put random data into Joe's program. When Joe interpreted the tarot readouts for these people, the correlation was statistically significant. Joe himself rejected those results, because the psychological tests were probably invalid measurements themselves. More important to him was the months of work in clinics, doing readings with people the doctors knew intimately. Even the most skeptical of the participating psychologists had to admit that Joe knew things about people that he could not possibly know. And most of the psychologists said openly that Joe not only confirmed much that they already knew but also provided brilliant new insights. "It's like stepping into my patient's mind," one of them told Alvin.

"My son is brilliant, Dr. Fryer, and I want him to succeed, but surely this mumbo-jumbo can't be more than luck."

Dr. Fryer only smiled and took a sip of wine. "Joe tells me that you have never submitted to the test yourself."

Alvin almost argued, but it *was* true. He never had *submitted*, even though he went through the motions. "I've seen it in action," Alvin said.

"Have you? Have you seen his results with someone you know well?"

Alvin shook his head, then smiled. "I figured that since I didn't believe in it, it wouldn't work around me."

"It isn't magic."

"It isn't science, either," said Alvin.

"No, you're right. Not science at all. But just because it isn't science doesn't mean it isn't true."

"Either it's science or it isn't."

"What a clear world you live in," said Dr. Fryer. "All the lines neatly drawn. We've run double-blind tests on his program, Dr. Bevis. Without knowing it, he has analyzed data taken from the same patient on different days, under different circumstances; the patient has even been given different instructions in some of the samples, so that it wasn't random. And you know what happened?"

Alvin knew but did not say so.

"Not only did his program read substantially the same for all the different random inputs for the same patient, but the program also spotted the ringers. Easily. And then it turned out that the ringers were a consistent result for the woman who wrote the test we

267

happened to use for the non-random input. Even when it shouldn't have worked, it worked."

"Very impressive," said Alvin, sounding as unimpressed as he could.

"It *is* impressive."

"I don't know about that," said Alvin. "So the cards are consistent. How do we know that they *mean* anything, or that what they mean is *true*?"

"Hasn't it occurred to you that your *son* is why it's true?"

Alvin tapped his spoon on the tablecloth, providing a muffled rhythm.

"Your son's computer program objectifies random input. But only your son can read it. To me that says that it's his *mind* that makes his method work, not his program. If we could figure out what's going on inside your son's head, Dr. Bevis, then his method would be science. Until then it's an art. But whether it is art or science, he tells the truth."

"Forgive me for what might seem a slight to your profession," said Alvin, "but how in God's name do *you* know whether what he says is true?"

Dr. Fryer smiled and cocked his head. "Because I can't conceive of it being wrong. We can't test his interpretations the way we tested his program. I've tried to find objective tests. For instance, whether his findings agree with my notes. But my notes mean nothing, because until your son reads my patients, I really don't understand them. And after he reads them, I can't conceive of any other view of them. Before you dismiss me as hopelessly subjective, remember please, Dr. Bevis, that I have every reason to fear and fight against your son's work. It undoes everything that I have believed in. It undermines my own life's work. And Joe is just like you. He doesn't think psychology is a science, either. Forgive *me* for what might seem a slight to your son, but he is troubled and cold and difficult to work with. I don't like him much. So why do I believe him?"

"That's your problem, isn't it?"

"On the contrary, Dr. Bevis. Everyone who's seen what Joe does, believes it. Except for you. I think that most definitely makes it *your* problem."

Dr. Fryer was wrong. Not everyone believed Joe.

"No," said Connie.

"No what?" asked Alvin. It was breakfast. Joe hadn't come downstairs yet. Alvin and Connie hadn't said a word since "Here's the eggs" and "Thanks."

Connie was drawing paths with her fork through the yolk stains on her plate. "Don't do another reading with Joe."

"I wasn't planning on it."

"Dr. Fryer told you to believe it, didn't he?" She put her fork down.

"But I didn't believe Dr. Fryer."

Connie got up from the table and began washing the dishes. Alvin watched her as she rattled the plates to make as much noise as possible. Nothing was normal anymore. Connie was angry as she washed the dishes. There was a dishwasher, but she was scrubbing everything by hand. Nothing was as it should be. Alvin tried to figure out why he felt such dread.

"You will do a reading with Joe," said Connie,

269

"*because* you don't believe Dr. Fryer. You always insist on verifying everything for yourself. If you believe, you must question your belief. If you doubt, you doubt your own disbelief. Am I not right?"

"No." *Yes.*

"And I'm telling you this once to have faith in your doubt. There is no truth whatever in his God-*damned* tarot."

In all these years of marriage, Alvin could not remember Connie using such coarse language. But then she hadn't said *god-damn*; she had said God-*damned*, with all the theological overtones.

"I mean," she went on, filling the silence, "I mean how can anyone take this seriously? The card he calls Strength — a woman closing a lion's mouth, yes, fine, but then he makes up a God-*damned* story about it, how the lion wanted her baby and she *fed it to him.*" She looked at Alvin with fear. "It's sick, isn't it?"

"He said that?"

"And the Devil, forcing the lovers to stay together. He's supposed to be the firstborn child, chaining Adam and Eve together. That's why Iocaste and Laios tried to kill Oedipus. Because they hated each other, and the baby would force them to stay together. But then they stayed together anyway because of shame at what they had done to an innocent child. And then they told everyone that asinine lie about the oracle and her prophecy."

"He's read too many books."

Connie trembled. "If he does a reading of you, I'm afraid of what will happen."

"If he feeds me crap like that, Connie, I'll just bite my lip. No fights, I promise."

She touched his chest. Not his shirt, his chest. It felt as if her finger burned right through the cloth. "I'm not worried that you'll fight," she said. "I'm afraid that you'll believe him."

"Why would I believe him?"

"We don't live in the Tower, Alvin!"

"Of course we don't."

"I'm not Iocaste, Alvin!"

"Of course you aren't."

"Don't believe him. Don't believe anything he says."

"Connie, don't get so upset." Again: "Why would I believe him?"

She shook her head and walked out of the room. The water was still running in the sink. She hadn't said a word. But her answer rang in the room as if she had spoken: "Because it's true."

Alvin tried to sort it out for hours. Oedipus and Iocaste. Adam, Eve, and the Devil. The mother feeding her baby to the lion. As Dr. Fryer had said, it isn't the cards, it isn't the program, it's Joe. Joe and the stories in his head. Is there a story in the world that Joe hasn't read? All the tales that man has told himself, all the visions of the world, and Joe knew them. Knew and believed them. Joe the repository of all the world's lies, and now he was telling the lies back, and they believed him, every one of them believed him.

No matter how hard Alvin tried to treat this nonsense with the contempt it deserved, one thing kept coming back to him. Joe's program had known that Alvin was lying, that Alvin was playing games, not telling the truth. Joe's program was valid at least that far. *If his method can pass that negative test, how can I call myself a scientist if I disbelieve it before I've given it the* positive test *as well?*

That night while Joe was watching *M*A*S*H* reruns, Alvin came into the family room to talk to him. It always startled Alvin to see his son watching normal television shows, especially old ones from Alvin's own youth. The same boy who had read *Ulysses* and made sense of it without reading a single commentary, and he was laughing out loud at the television.

It was only after he had sat beside his son and watched for a while that Alvin realized that Joe was not laughing at the places where the laugh track did. He was not laughing at the jokes. He was laughing at Hawkeye himself.

"What was so funny?" asked Alvin.

"Hawkeye," said Joe.

"He was being serious."

"I know," said Joe. "But he's so sure he's *right*, and everybody believes him. Don't you think that's funny?"

As a matter of fact, no, I don't. "I want to give it another try, Joe," said Alvin.

Even though it was an abrupt change of subject, Joe understood at once, as if he had long been waiting for his father to speak. They got into the car, and Alvin drove them to the university. The computer people immediately made one of the full-color terminals available. This time Alvin allowed himself to be truly random, not thinking at all about what he was

272

choosing, avoiding any meaning as he typed. When he was sick of typing, he looked at Joe for permission to be through. Joe shrugged. Alvin entered one more set of letters and then said, "Done."

Alvin entered a single command that told the computer to start analyzing the input, and father and son sat together to watch the story unfold.

After a seemingly eternal wait, in which neither of them said a word, a picture of a card appeared on the screen.

"This is you," said Joe. It was the King of Swords.

"What does it mean?" asked Alvin.

"Very little by itself."

"Why is the sword coming out of his mouth?"

"Because he kills by the words of his mouth."

Father nodded. "And why is he holding his crotch?"

"I don't know."

"I thought you knew," said Father.

"I don't know until I see the other cards." Joe pressed the return key, and a new card almost completely covered the old one. A thin blue line appeared around it, and then it was blown up to fill the screen. It was Judgment, an angel blowing a trumpet, awakening the dead, who were gray with corruption, standing in their graves. "This covers you," said Joe.

"What does it mean?"

"It's how you spend your life. Judging the dead."

"Like God? You're saying I think I'm God?"

"It's what you do, Father," said Joe. "You judge everything. You're a scientist. I can't help what the cards say."

"I study life."

"You break life down into its pieces. Then you make your judgment. Only when it's all in fragments like the flesh of the dead."

Alvin tried to hear anger or bitterness in Joe's voice, but Joe was calm, matter-of-fact, for all the world like a doctor with a good bedside manner. Or like a historian telling the simple truth.

Joe pressed the key, and on the small display another card appeared, again on top of the first two, but horizontally. "This crosses you," said Joe. And the card was outlined in blue, and zoomed close. It was the Devil.

"What does it mean, crossing me?"

"Your enemy, your obstacle. The son of Laios and Iocaste."

Alvin remembered that Connie had mentioned Iocaste. "How similar is this to what you told Connie?" he asked.

Joe looked at him impassively. "How can I know after only three cards?"

Alvin waved him to go on.

A card above. "This crowns you." The Two of Wands, a man holding the world in his hands, staring off into the distance, with two small saplings growing out of the stone parapet beside him. "The crown is what you think you are, the story you tell yourself about yourself. Lifegiver, the God of Genesis, the Prince whose kiss awakens Sleeping Beauty and Snow White."

A card below. "This is beneath you, what you most fear to become." A man lying on the ground, ten swords piercing him in a row. He did not bleed.

"I've never lain awake at night afraid that someone

274

would stab me to death."

Joe looked at him placidly. "But, Father, I told you, swords are words as often as not. What you fear is death at the hands of storytellers. According to the cards, you're the sort of man who would have killed the messenger who brought bad news."

According to the cards, or according to you? But Alvin held his anger and said nothing.

A card to the right. "This is behind you, the story of your past." A man in a sword-studded boat, poling the craft upstream, a woman and child sitting bowed in front of him. "Hansel and Gretel sent into the sea in a leaky boat."

"It doesn't look like a brother and sister," said Alvin. "It looks like a mother and child."

"Ah," said Joe. A card to the left. "This is before you, where you know your course will lead." A sarcophagus with a knight sculpted in stone upon it, a bird resting on his head.

Death, thought Alvin. Always a safe prediction. And yet not safe at all. The cards themselves seemed malevolent. They all depicted situations that cried out with agony or fear. That was the gimmick, Alvin decided. Potent enough pictures will seem to be important whether they really mean anything or not. Heavy with meaning like a pregnant woman, they can be made to bear anything.

"It isn't death," said Joe.

Alvin was startled to have his thoughts so appropriately interrupted.

"It's a monument after you're dead. With your words engraved on it and above it. Blue Homer. Jesus. Mahomet. To have your words read like scrip-

275

ture."

And for the first time Alvin was genuinely frightened by what his son had found. Not that this future frightened him. Hadn't he forbidden himself to hope for it, he wanted it so much? No, what he feared was the way he felt himself say, silently, *Yes, yes, this is True. I will not be flattered into belief*, he said to himself. But underneath every layer of doubt that he built between himself and the cards he believed. Whatever Joe told him, he would believe, and so he denied belief now, not because of disbelief but because he was afraid. Perhaps that was why he had doubted from the start.

Next the computer placed a card in the lower right-hand corner. "This is your house." It was the Tower, broken by lightning, a man and a woman falling from it, surrounded by tears of flame.

A card directly above it. "This answers you." A man under a tree, beside a stream, with a hand coming from a small cloud, giving him a cup. "Elijah by the brook, and the ravens feed him."

And above that a man walking away from a stack of eight cups, with a pole and traveling cloak. The pole is a wand, with leaves growing from it. The cups are arranged so that a space is left where a ninth cup had been. "This saves you."

And then, at the top of the vertical file of four cards, Death. "This ends it." A bishop, a woman, and a child kneeling before Death on a horse. The horse is trampling the corpse of a man who had been a king. Beside the man lie his crown and a golden sword. In the distance a ship is foundering in a swift river. The sun is rising between pillars in the east. And Death holds a leafy wand in his hand, with a sheaf of wheat bound to it at the top. A banner of life over the corpse of the king. "This ends it," said Joe definitively.

Alvin waited, looking at the cards, waiting for Joe to explain it. But Joe did not explain. He just gazed at the monitor and then suddenly got to his feet. "Thank you, Father," he said. "It's all clear now."

"To you it's clear," Alvin said.

"Yes," said Joe. "Thank you very much for not lying this time." Then Joe made as if to leave.

"Hey, wait," Alvin said. "Aren't you going to explain it to me?"

"No," said Joe.

"Why not?"

"You wouldn't believe me."

Alvin was not about to admit to anyone, least of all himself, that he did believe. "I still want to know. I'm curious. Can't I be curious?"

Joe studied his father's face. "I told Mother, and she hasn't spoken a natural word to me since."

So it was not Alvin's imagination. The tarot program had driven a wedge between Connie and Joe. He'd been right. "I'll speak a natural word or two every day. I promise," Alvin said.

"That's what I'm afraid of," Joe said.

"Son," Alvin said, "Dr. Fryer told me that the stories you tell, the way you put things together, is the closest thing to truth about people that he's ever heard. Even if I don't believe it, don't I have the right to hear the truth?"

"I don't know if it *is* the truth. Or if there is such a thing."

"There is. The way things *are*, that's truth."

"But how *are* things, with people? What causes me to feel the way I do or act the way I do? Hormones? Parents? Social patterns? All the causes or purposes of all our acts are just stories we tell ourselves, stories we believe or disbelieve, changing all the time. But still we live, still we act, and all those acts have *some* kind of cause. The patterns all fit together into a web that connects everyone who's ever lived with everyone else. And every new person changes the web, adds to it, changes the connections, makes it all different. That's what I find with this program, how you believe you fit into the web."

"Not how I *really* fit?"

Joe shrugged. "How can I know? How can I measure it? I discover the stories that you believe most secretly, the stories that control your acts. But the very telling of the story changes the way you believe. Moves some things into the open, changes who you *are*. I undo my work by doing it."

"Then undo your work with me, and tell me the truth."

"I don't want to."

"Why not?"

"Because I'm in your story."

Alvin spoke then more honestly than he ever meant to. "Then for God's sake tell me the story, because I don't know who the hell you are."

Joe walked back to his chair and sat down. "I am Goneril and Regan, because you made me act out the lie that you needed to hear. I am Oedipus, because you pinned my ankles together and left me exposed on the hillside to save your own future."

"I have loved you more than life."

"You were always afraid of me, Father. Like Lear, afraid that I wouldn't care for you when I was still vigorous and you were enfeebled by age. Like Laios, terrified that my power would overshadow you. So you took *control*; you put me out of my place."

"I gave years to educating you—"

"Educating me in order to make me forever your shadow, your student. When the only thing that I really loved was the one thing that would free me from you—all the stories."

"Damnable stupid fictions."

"No more stupid than the fiction *you* believe. Your story of little cells and DNA, your story that there is such a thing as reality that can be objectively perceived. God, what an idea, to see with inhuman eyes, without interpretation. That's exactly how stones see, without interpretation, because without interpretation there isn't any *sight*."

"I think I know that much at least," Alvin said, trying to feel as contemptuous as he sounded. "I never said I was objective."

"*Scientific* was the word. What could be verified was scientific. That was all that you would ever let me study, what could be verified. The trouble is, Father, that nothing in the world that matters at all is verifiable. What makes us who we are is forever tenuous, fragile, the web of a spider eaten and remade every day. I can never see out of your eyes. Yet I can never see any other way than through the eyes of every storyteller who ever taught me how to see. That was what you did to me, Father. You forbade me to hear any storyteller but you. It was *your* reality I had to surrender to. *Your* fiction I had to believe."

Alvin felt his past slipping out from under him. "If I had known those games of make-believe were so important to you, I wouldn't have—"

"You knew they were that important to me," Joe said coldly. "Why else would you have bothered to forbid me? But my mother dipped me into the water, all but my heel, and I got all the power you tried to keep from me. You see, Mother was not Griselde. She wouldn't kill her children for her husband's sake. When you exiled me, you exiled her. We lived the stories together as long as we were free."

"What do you mean?"

"Until you came home to teach me. We were free until then. We acted out all the stories that we could. Without you."

It conjured for Alvin the ridiculous image of Connie playing Goldilocks and the Three Bears day after day for years. He laughed in spite of himself, laughed sharply, for only a moment.

Joe took the laugh all wrong. Or perhaps took it exactly right. He took his father by the wrist and gripped him so tightly that Alvin grew afraid. Joe was stronger than Alvin had thought. "Grendel feels the touch of Beowulf on his hand," Joe whispered, "and he thinks, Perhaps I should have stayed at home tonight. Perhaps I am not hungry after all."

Alvin tried for a moment to pull his arm away but could not. *What have I done to you, Joe?* he shouted inside himself. Then he relaxed his arm and surrendered to the tale. "Tell me my story from the cards," he said. "Please."

Without letting go of his father's arm, Joe began, "You are Lear, and your kingdom is great. Your whole life is shaped so that you will live forever in stone, in memory. Your dream is to create life. You thought I would be such life, as malleable as the little worlds you make from DNA. But from the moment I was born you were afraid of me. I couldn't be taken apart and recombined like all your little animals. And you were afraid that I would steal the swords from your sepulcher. You were afraid that you would live on as Joseph Bevis's father, instead of me forever being Alvin Bevis's son."

"I was jealous of my child," said Alvin, trying to sound skeptical.

"Like the father rat that devours his babies because he knows that someday they will challenge his supremacy, yes. It's the oldest pattern in the world, a tale older than teeth."

"Go on, this is quite fascinating." *I refuse to care.*

"All the storytellers know how this tale ends. Every time a father tries to change the future by controlling his children, it ends the same. Either the children lie, like Goneril and Regan, and pretend to be what he made them, or the children tell the truth, like Cordelia, and the father casts them out. I tried to tell the truth, but then together Mother and I lied to you. It was so much easier, and it kept me alive. She was Grim the Fisher, and she saved me alive."

Iocaste and Laios and Oedipus. "I see where this is going," Alvin said. "I thought you were bright enough not to believe in that Freudian nonsense about the Oedipus complex."

"Freud thought he was telling the story of all

281

mankind when he was only telling his own. Just because the story of Oedipus isn't true for everyone doesn't mean that it isn't true for me. But don't worry, Father. I don't have to kill you in the forest in order to take possession of your throne."

"I'm not worried." It was a lie. It was a truthful understatement.

"Laios died only because he would not let his son pass along the road."

"Pass along any road you please."

"And I am the Devil. You and Mother were in Eden until I came. Because of me you were cast out. And now you're in hell."

"How neatly it all fits."

"For you to achieve your dream, you had to kill me with your story. When I lay there with your blades in my back, only then could you be sure that your sepulcher was safe. When you exiled me in a boat I could not live in, only then could you be safe, you thought. But I am the Horn Child, and the boat bore me quickly across the sea to my true kingdom."

"This isn't anything coming from the computer," said Alvin. "This is just you being a normal resentful teen-ager. Just a phase that everyone goes through."

Joe's grip on Alvin's arm only tightened. "I didn't die, I didn't wither, I have my power now, and you're not safe. Your house is broken, and you and Mother are being thrown from it to your destruction, and you know it. Why did you come to me, except that you knew you were being destroyed?"

Again Alvin tried to find a way to fend off Joe's story with ridicule. This time he could not. Joe had pierced through shield and armor and cloven him, neck to heart. "In the name of God, Joe, how do we end it all?" He barely kept from shouting.

Joe relaxed his grip on Alvin's arm at last. The blood began to flow again, painfully; Alvin fancied he could measure it passing through his calibrated arteries.

"Two ways," said Joe. "There is one way you can save yourself."

Alvin looked at the cards on the screen. "Exile."

"Just leave. Just go away for a while. Let us alone for a while. Let me pass you by, stop trying to rule, stop trying to force your story on me, and then after a while we can see what's changed."

"Oh, excellent. A son divorcing his father. Not too likely."

"Or death. As the deliverer. As the fulfillment of your dream. If you die now, you defeat me. As Laios destroyed Oedipus at last."

Alvin stood up to leave. "This is rank melodrama. Nobody's going to die because of this."

"Then why can't you stop trembling?" asked Joe.

"Because I'm angry, that's why," Alvin said. "I'm angry at the way you choose to look at me. I love you more than any other father I know loves his son, and this is the way you choose to view it. How sharper than a serpent's tooth—"

"How sharper than a serpent's tooth it is to have a thankless child. Away, away!"

"Lear, isn't it? You gave me the script, and now I'm saying the goddamn lines."

Joe smiled a strange, sphinxlike smile. "It's a good exit line, though, isn't it?"

"Joe, I'm not going to leave, and I'm not going to

drop dead, either. You've told me a lot. Like you said, not the truth, not *reality*, but the way you see things. That helps, to know how you see things."

Joe shook his head in despair. "Father, you don't understand. It was *you* who put those cards up on the screen. Not I. My reading is completely different. Completely different, but no better."

"If I'm the King of Swords, who are you?"

"The Hanged Man," Joe said.

Alvin shook his head. "What an ugly world you choose to live in."

"Not neat and pretty like yours, not bound about by rules the way yours is. Laws and principles, theories and hypotheses, may they cover your eyes and keep you happy."

"Joe, I think you need help," said Alvin.

"Don't we all," said Joe.

"So do I. A family counselor maybe. I think we need outside help."

"I've told you what you can do."

"I'm not going to run away from this, Joe, no matter how much you want me to."

"You already have. You've been running away for months. These are *your* cards, Father, not mine."

"Joe, I want to help you out of this—unhappiness."

Joe frowned. "Father, don't you understand? The Hanged Man is smiling. The Hanged Man has won."

Alvin did not go home. He couldn't face Connie right now, did not want to try to explain what he felt about what Joe had told him. So he went to the laboratory and lost himself for a time in reading records of what was happening with the different subject organisms. Some good results. If it all held up, Alvin Bevis would have taken mankind a long way toward being able to read the DNA chain. There was a Nobel in it. More important still, there was real change. *I will have changed the world*, he thought. And then there came into his mind the picture of the man holding the world in his hands, looking off into the distance. The Two of Wands. His dream. Joe was right about that. Right about Alvin's longing for a monument to last forever.

And in a moment of unusual clarity Alvin saw that Joe was right about everything. Wasn't Alvin even now doing just what the cards called for him to do to save himself, going into hiding with the Eight of Cups? His house was breaking down, all was being undone, and he was setting out on a long journey that would lead him to solitude. Greatness, but solitude.

There was one card that Joe hadn't worked into his story, however. The Four of Cups. "This answers you," he had said. The hand of God coming from a cloud. Elijah by the brook. *If God were to whisper to me, what would He say?*

He would say, Alvin thought, that there is something profoundly wrong, something circular in all that Joe has done. He has synthesized things that no other mind in the world could have brought together meaningfully. He is, as Dr. Fryer said, touching on the borders of Truth. But, by God, there is something wrong, something he has overlooked. Not a *mistake*, exactly. Simply a place where Joe has not put two true

285

things together in his own life: Stories make us who we are; the tarot program identifies the stories we believe; by hearing the tale of the tarot, we have changed who we are; therefore—

Therefore, no one knows how much of Joe's tarot story is believed because it is true, and how much becomes true because it is believed. Joe is not a scientist. Joe is a tale-teller. But the gifted, powerful teller of tales soon lives in the world he has created, for as more and more people believe him, his tales become true.

We do not have to be the family of Laios. I do not have to play at being Lear. I can say no to this story, and make it false. Not that Joe could tell any other story, because this is the one that he believes. But I can change what he believes by changing what the cards say, and I can change what the cards say by being someone else.

King of Swords. Imposing my will on others, making them live in the world that my words created. And now my son, too, doing the same. But I can change, and so can he, and then perhaps his brilliance, his insights can shape a better world than the sick one he is making us live in.

And as he grew more excited, Alvin felt himself fill with light, as if the cup had poured into him from the cloud. He believed, in fact, that he had already changed. That he was already something other than what Joe said he was.

The telephone rang. Rang twice, three times, before Alvin reached out to answer it. It was Connie.

"Alvin?" she asked in a small voice.

"Connie," he said.

286

"Alvin, Joe called me." She sounded lost, distant.

"Did he? Don't worry, Connie, everything's going to be fine."

"Oh, I know," Connie said. "I finally figured it out. It's the thing that Helen never figured out. It's the thing that Iocaste never had the guts to do. Enid knew it, though. Enid could do it. I love you, Alvin." She hung up.

Alvin sat with his hand on the phone for thirty seconds. That's how long it took him to realize that Connie sounded *sleepy*. That Connie was trying to change the cards, too. By killing herself.

All the way home in the car, Alvin was afraid that he was going crazy. He kept warning himself to drive carefully, not to take chances. He wouldn't be able to save Connie if he had an accident on the way. And then there would come a voice that sounded like Joe's, whispering, That's the story you tell yourself, but the truth is you're driving slowly and carefully, hoping she will die so everything will be simple again. It's the best solution, Connie has solved it all, and you're being *slow* so she can succeed, but telling yourself you're being *careful* so you can live with yourself after she's dead.

No, said Alvin again and again, pushing on the accelerator, weaving through the traffic, then forcing himself to slow down, not to kill himself to save two seconds. Sleeping pills weren't *that* fast. And maybe he was wrong; maybe she hadn't taken pills. Or maybe he was thinking that in order to slow himself down so that Connie would die and everything would be simple again —

Shut up, he told himself. *Just get there*, he told himself.

He got there, fumbled with the key, and burst inside. "Connie!" he shouted.

Joe was standing in the archway between the kitchen and the family room.

"It's all right," Joe said. "I got here when she was on the phone to you. I forced her to vomit, and most of the pills hadn't even dissolved yet."

"She's awake?"

"More or less."

Joe stepped aside, and Alvin walked into the family room. Connie sat on a chair, looking catatonic. But as he came nearer, she turned away, which at once hurt him and relieved him. At least she was not hopelessly insane. So it was not too late for change.

"Joe," Alvin said, still looking at Connie, "I've been thinking. About the reading."

Joe stood behind him, saying nothing.

"I believe it. You told the truth. The whole thing, just as you said."

Still Joe did not answer. *Well, what can he say, anyway?* Alvin asked himself. *Nothing. At least he's listening.* "Joe, you told the truth. I really screwed up the family. I've had to have the whole thing my way, and it really screwed things up. Do you hear me, Connie? I'm telling both of you, I agree with Joe about the past. But not the future. There's nothing magical about those cards. They don't tell the future. They just tell the outcome of the pattern, the way things will end if the pattern isn't changed. But we can change it, don't you see? That's what Connie was trying to do with the pills, change the way things turn out. Well, *I'm* the one who can really change, by changing me. Can you see that? I'm changed already. As if I drank from the cup that came to me out of the cloud, Joe. I don't have to control things the way I did. It's all going to be better now. We can build up from, up from—"

The ashes, those were the next words. But they were the wrong words, Alvin could sense that. All his words were wrong. It had seemed true in the lab, when he thought of it; now it sounded dishonest. Desperate. Ashes in his mouth. He turned around to Joe. His son was not listening silently. Joe's face was contorted with rage, his hands trembling, tears streaming down his cheeks.

As soon as Alvin looked at him, Joe screamed at him. "You can't just let it be, can you! You have to do it again and again and again, don't you!"

Oh, I see, Alvin thought. *By wanting to change things, I was just making them more the same. Trying to control the world they live in. I didn't think it through well enough. God played a dirty trick on me, giving me that cup from the cloud.*

"I'm sorry," Alvin said.

"No!" Joe shouted. "There's nothing you can say!"

"You're right," Alvin said, trying to calm Joe. "I should just have—"

"Don't say *anything*!" Joe screamed, his face red.

"I won't, I won't," said Alvin. "I won't say an-other—"

"Nothing! Nothing! Nothing!"

"I'm just agreeing with you, that's—"

Joe lunged forward and screamed it in his father's

face. "God damn you, don't talk at all!"

"I see," said Alvin, suddenly realizing. "I see — as long as I try to put it in words, I'm forcing my view of things on the rest of you, and if I—"

There were no words left for Joe to say. He had tried every word he knew that might silence his father, but none would. Where words fall, there remains the act. The only thing close at hand was a heavy glass dish on the side table. Joe did not mean to grab it, did not mean to strike his father across the head with it. He only meant his father to be still. But all his incantations had failed, and still his father spoke, still his father stood in the way, refusing to let him pass, and so he smashed him across the head with the glass dish.

But it was the dish that broke, not his father's head. And the fragment of glass in Joe's hand kept right on going after the blow, followed through with the stroke, and the sharp edge of the glass cut neatly through the fleshy, bloody, windy part of Alvin's throat. All the way through, severing the carotid artery, the veins, and above all the trachea, so that no more air flowed through Alvin's larynx. Alvin was wordless as he fell backward, spraying blood from his throat, clutching at the pieces of glass imbedded in the side of his face.

"Uh-oh," said Connie in a high and childish voice.

Alvin lay on his back on the floor, his head propped up on the front edge of the couch. He felt a terrible throbbing in his throat and a strange silence in his ears where the blood no longer flowed. He had not known how noisy the blood in the head could be, until now, and now he could not tell anyone. He

290

could only lie there, not moving, not turning his head, watching.

He watched as Connie stared at his throat and slowly tore at her hair; he watched as Joe carefully and methodically pushed the bloody piece of glass into his right eye and then into his left. *I see now*, said Alvin silently. *Sorry I didn't understand before. You found the answer to the riddle that devoured us, my Oedipus. I'm just not good at riddles, I'm afraid.*

400 BOYS

By Marc Laidlaw

We sit and feel Fun City die. Two stories above our basement, at street level, something big is stomping apartment pyramids flat. We can feel the lives blinking out like smashed bulbs; you don't need second sight to see through other eyes at a time like this. I get flashes of fear and sudden pain, but none last long. The paperback drops from my hands, and I blow my candle out.

We are the Brothers, a team of twelve. There were twenty-two yesterday, but not everyone made it to the basement in time. Our slicker, Slash, is on a crate loading and reloading his gun with its one and only silver bullet. Crybaby Jaguar is kneeling in the corner on his old blanket, sobbing like a maniac; for once he has a good reason. My best Brother, Jade, keeps spinning the cylinders of the holotube in search of stations, but all he gets is static that sounds like screaming turned inside out. It's a lot like the screaming in our minds, which won't fade except as it gets squelched voice by voice.

Slash goes, "Jade, turn that thing off or I'll short-cirk it."

He is our leader, our slicker. His lips are gray, his mouth too wide where a Soooooot scalpel opened his cheeks. He has a lisp.

Jade shrugs and shuts down the tube, but the sounds we hear instead are no better. Faraway pounding footsteps, shouts from the sky, even monster laughter. It seems to be passing away from us, deeper into Fun City.

"They'll be gone in no time," Jade goes.

"You think you know everything," goes Vave O'Claw, dissecting an alarm clock with one chrome finger the way some kids pick their noses. "You don't even know what they are—"

"I saw 'em," goes Jade. "Croak and I. Right, Croak?"

I nod without a sound. There's no tongue in my mouth. I only croaked after my free fix-up, which I got for mouthing badsense to a Controller cognibot when I was twelve.

Jade and I went out last night and climbed an empty pyramid to see what we could see. Past River-run Boulevard the world was burning bright, and I had to look away. Jade kept staring and said he saw wild giants running with the glow. Then I heard a thousand guitar strings snapping, and Jade said the giants had ripped up Big Bridge by the roots and thrown it at the moon. I looked up and saw a black arch spinning end over end, cables twanging as it flipped up and up through shredded smoke and never fell back—or not while we waited, which was not long.

"Whatever it is could be here for good," goes Slash, twisting his mouth in the middle as he grins. "Might never leave."

Crybaby stops snorting long enough to say, "Nuh-never?"

"Why should they? Looks like they came a long way to get to Fun City, doesn't it? Maybe we have a whole new team on our hands, Brothers."

"Just what we need," goes Jade. "Don't ask me to smash with 'em, though. My blade's not big enough. If the Controllers couldn't keep 'em from crashing through, what could we do?"

Slash cocks his head. "Jade, dear Brother, listen close. If I ask you to smash, you smash. If I ask you to jump from a hive, you jump. Or find another team. You know I only ask these things to keep your life interesting."

"Interesting enough," my best Brother grumbles.

"Hey!" goes Crybaby. He's bigger and older than any of us but doesn't have the brains of a ten-year-old. "Listen!"

We listen.

"Don't hear nothin'," goes Skag.

"Yeah! Nuh-nuthin'. They made away."

He spoke too soon. Next thing we know there is thunder in the wall, the concrete crawls underfoot, and the ceiling rains. I dive under a table with Jade.

The thunder fades to a whisper. Afterward there is real silence.

"You okay, Croak?" Jade goes. I nod and look into the basement for the other Brothers. I can tell by the team spirit in the room that no one is hurt.

In the next instant we let out a twelve-part gasp.

295

There's natural light in the basement. Where from?

Looking out from under the table, I catch a parting shot of the moon two stories and more above us. The last shock had split the old tenement hive open to the sky. Floors and ceilings layer the sides of a fissure; water pipes cross in the air like metal webs; the floppy head of a mattress spills foam on us.

The moon vanishes into boiling black smoke. It is the same smoke we saw washing over the city yesterday, when the stars were sputtering like flares around a traffic wreck. Lady Death's perfume comes creeping down with it.

Slash straddles the crack that runs through the center of the room.

He tucks his gun into his pocket. The silver of its only bullet was mixed with some of Slash's blood. He saves it for the Sooooot who gave him his grin, a certain slicker named HiLo.

"Okay, team," he goes. "Let's get out of here pronto."

Vave and Jade rip away the boards from the door. The basement was rigged for security, to keep us safe when things got bad in Fun City. Vave shielded the walls with baffles so when Controller cognibots came scanning for hideaways, they picked up plumbing and an empty room. Never a scoop of us.

Beyond the door the stairs tilt up at a crazy slant; it's nothing we cannot manage. I look back at the basement as we head up, because I had been getting to think of it as home.

We were there when the Controllers came looking for war recruits. They thought we were just the right age.

"Come out, come out, wherever in free!" they yelled. When they came hunting, we did our trick and disappeared.

That was in the last of the calendar days, when everyone was yelling:

"Hey! This is it! World War Last!"

What they told us about the war could be squeezed into Vave's pinky tip, which he had hollowed out for explosive darts. They still wanted us to fight in it. The deal was, we would get a free trip to the moon for training at Base English, then we would zip back to Earth charged up and ready to go-go-go. The Sino-Sovs were hatching wars like eggs, one after another, down south. The place got so hot that we could see the skies that way glowing white some nights, then yellow in the day.

Federal Control had sealed our continental city tight in a see-through blister: Nothing but air and light got in or out without a password. Vave was sure when he saw the yellow glow that the SinoSovs had launched something fierce against the invisible curtain, something that was strong enough to get through.

Quiet as queegs we creep to the Strip. Our bloc covers Fifty-sixth to Eighty-eighth between Westland and Chico. The streetlights are busted like every window in all the buildings and the crashed cars. Garbage and bodies are spilled all over.

"Aw, skud," goes Vave.

Crybaby starts bawling.

"Keep looking, Croak," goes Slash to me. "Get it all."

I want to look away, but I have to store this for

297

later. I almost cry because my ma and my real brother are dead. I put *that* away and get it all down. Slash lets me keep track of the Brothers.

At the Federal Pylon, where they control the programmable parts and people of Fun City, Mister Fixer snipped my tongue and started on the other end.

He did not live to finish the job. A team brigade of Quazis and Moofs, led by my Brothers, sprang me free.

That takes teamwork. I know the Controllers said otherwise, said that we were smash-crazy subverts like the Anarcanes, with no pledge to Fun City. But if you ever listened to them, salt your ears. Teams never smashed unless they had to. When life pinched in Fun City, there was nowhere to jump but sideways into the next bloc. Enter with no invitation and . . . things worked out.

I catch a shine of silver down the Strip. A cognibot is stalled with scanners down, no use to the shaveheads who sit in the Pylon and watch the streets.

I point it out, thinking there can't be many shaveheads left.

"No more law," goes Jade.

"Nothing in our way," goes Slash.

We start down the Strip. On our way past the cog, Vave stops to unbolt the laser nipples on its turret. Hooked to battery packs, they will make slick snappers.

We grab flashlights from busted monster marts. For a while we look into the ruins, but that gets nasty fast. We stick to finding our way through the fallen mountains that used to be pyramids and block-long hives. It takes a long time.

There is fresh paint on the walls that still stand, dripping red-black like it might never dry. The stench of fresh death blows at us from center city.

Another alley cat pissed our bloc.

I wonder about survivors. When we send our minds out into the ruins, we don't feel a thing. There were never many people here when times were good. Most of the hives emptied out in the fever years, when the oldies died and the kiddykids, untouched by disease, got closer together and learned to share their power.

It keeps getting darker, hotter; the smell gets worse. Bodies staring from windows make me glad I never looked for Ma or my brother. We gather canned food, keeping ultraquiet. The Strip has never seen such a dead night. Teams were always roving, smashing, throwing clean-fun free-for-alls. Now there's only us.

We cross through bloc after bloc: Bennies, Silks, Quazis, Mannies, and Angels. No one. If any teams are alive they are in hideaways unknown; if they hid out overground they are as dead as the rest.

We wait for the telltale psychic tug—like a whisper in the pit of your belly—that another team gives. There is nothing but death in the night.

"Rest tight, teams," Jade goes.

"Wait," goes Slash.

We stop at two hundred sixty-fifth in the Snubnose bloc. Looking down the Strip, I see someone sitting high on a heap of ruined cement. He shakes his head and puts up his hands.

"Well, well," goes Slash.

The doob starts down the heap. He is so weak he

tumbles and avalanches the rest of the way to the street. We surround him, and he looks up into the black zero of Slash's gun.

"Hiya, HiLo," Slash goes. He has on a grin he must have saved with the silver bullet. It runs all the way back to his ears. "How's Soooooots?"

HiLo doesn't look so slick. His red-and-black lightning-bolt suit is shredded and stained, the collar torn off for a bandage around one wrist. The left lens of his dark owlrims is shattered, and his buzzcut is scraped to nothing.

HiLo doesn't say a word. He stares up into the gun and waits for the trigger to snap, the last little sound he will ever hear. We are waiting, too.

There's one big tear dripping from the shattered lens, washing HiLo's grimy cheek. Slash laughs. Then he lowers the gun and says, "Not tonight."

HiLo does not even twitch.

Down the Strip, a gas main blows up and paints us all in orange light.

We all start laughing. It's funny, I guess. HiLo's smile is silent.

Slash jerks HiLo to his feet. "I got other stuff under my skin, slicker. You look like runover skud. Where's your team?"

HiLo looks at the ground and shakes his head slowly.

"Slicker," he goes, "we got flattened. No other way to put it." A stream of tears follows the first; he clears them away. "There's no Soooooots left."

"There's you," goes Slash, putting a hand on Hi-Lo's shoulder.

"Can't be a slicker without a team."

"Sure you can. What happened?"

HiLo looks down the street. "New team took our bloc," he goes. "They're giants, Slash — I know it sounds crazy."

"No," goes Jade, "I seen 'em."

HiLo goes, "We heard them coming, but if we had seen them I would never have told the Soooooots to stand tight. Thought there was a chance we could hold our own, but we got smeared.

"They *threw* us. Some of my buds flew higher than the Pylon. These boys . . . incredible boys. Now Four hundredth is full of them. They glow and shiver like the lights when you get clubbed and fade out."

Vave goes, "Sounds like chiller-dillers."

"If I thought they were only boys I wouldn't be scared, Brother," goes HiLo. "But there's more to them. We tried to psych them out, and it almost worked. They're made out of that kind of stuff: It looks real, and it will cut you up, but when you go at it with your mind it buzzes away like bees. There weren't enough of us to do much. And we weren't ready for them. I only got away because NimbleJax knocked me cold and stuffed me under a transport.

"When I got up it was over. I followed the Strip. Thought some teams might be roving, but there's nobody. Could be in hideaways. I was afraid to check. Most teams would squelch me before I said word one."

"It's hard alone, different with a team behind you," goes Slash. "How many hideaways do you know?"

"Maybe six. Had a line on JipJaps, but not for sure. I know where to find Zips, Kingpins, Gerlz, Myrmies, Sledges. We could get to the Galrog bloc

301

fast through the subtunnels."

Slash turns to me. "What have we got?"

I pull out the beat-up list and hand it to Jade, who reads it. "JipJaps, Sledges, Drummers, A-V-Marias, Chix, Chogs, Dannies. If any of them are still alive, they would know others."

"True," goes Slash.

Jade nudges me. "Wonder if this new team has got a name."

He knows I like spelling things out. I grin and take back the list, pull out a pencil, and put down FOUR HUNDRED BOYS.

"Cause they took Four hundredth," Jade goes. I nod, but that is not all. Somewhere I think I read about Boys knocking down the world, torturing grannies. It seems like something these Boys would do.

Down the street the moon comes up through smoke, making it the color of rust. Big chunks are missing.

"We'll smash em," goes Vave.

The sight of the moon makes us sad and scared at the same time. I remember how it had been perfect and round as a pearl on jewelrymart velvet, beautiful and brighter than streetlights even when the worst smogs dyed it brown. Even that brown was better than this chipped-away bloody red. Looks like it was used for target practice. Maybe those Boys tossed the Bridge at Base English.

"Our bloc is gone," goes HiLo. "I want those Boys. It'll be those doobs or me."

"We're with you," goes Slash. "Let's move fast. Cut into pairs, Brothers. We're gonna hit some hideaways.

Jade, Croak, you come with me and HiLo. We'll see if those Galrogs will listen to sense."

Slash tells the other Brothers where to look and where to check back.

We say good-bye. We find the stairs to the nearest subtunnel and go down into lobbies full of shadow, where bodies lie waiting for the last train.

We race rats down the tunnel. They are meaner and fatter than ever, but our lights hold them back.

"Still got that wicked blade?" goes Slash.

"This baby?" HiLo swings his good arm, and a scalpel blade drops into his hand.

Slash's eyes frost over, and his mouth tightens.

"May need it," he goes.

"Right, Brother." HiLo makes the blade disappear.

I see that is how it has to be.

We pass a few more lobbies before going up and out. We've moved faster than we could have on ground; now we are close to the low end of Fun City.

"This way." HiLo points past broken hives. I see codes scripted on the rubbled walls: Galrog signals?

"Wait," goes Jade. "I'm starved."

There is a liquor store a block away. We lift the door and twist it open, easy as breaking an arm. Nothing moves inside or on the street as our lights glide over rows of bottles. Broken glass snaps under our sneakers. The place smells drunk, and I'm getting that way from breathing. We find chips and candy bars that have survived under a counter, and we gulp them down in the doorway.

"So where's the Galrog hideaway?" goes Jade, finishing a Fifth Avenue bar.

Just then we feel that little deep tug. This one

whispers death. A team is letting us know that it has us surrounded.

HiLo goes, "Duck back."

"No," goes Slash. "No more hiding."

We go slow to the door and look through. Shadows peel from the walls and streak from alley mouths. We're sealed tight.

"Keep your blades back, Brothers."

I never smashed with Galrogs; I see why Slash kept us away. They are tanked out with daystars, snappers, guns, and glory-stix. Even unarmed they would be fierce, with their fire-painted eyes, chopped topknots a dozen colors, and rainbow geometrics tattooed across their faces. Most are dressed in black; all are on razor-toed roller skates.

Their feelings are masked from us behind a mesh of silent threats.

A low voice: "Come out if you plan to keep breathing."

We move out, keeping together as the girls close tight. Jade raises his flashlight, but a Galrog with blue-triangled cheeks and purple-blond topknot kicks it from his hand. It goes spinning a crazy beam through his dark. There is not a scratch on Jade's fingers. I keep my own light low.

A big Galrog rolls up. She looks like a cognibot slung with battery packs, wires running up and down her arms and through her afro, where she's hung tin bells and shards of glass. She has a laser turret strapped to her head and a snapper in each hand.

She checks me and Jade over and out, then turns toward the slickers.

"Slicker HiLo and Slicker Slash," she goes. "Cute

304

match, but I thought Soooooots were hot for girlies."

"Keep it short, Bala," goes Slash. "The blocs are smashed."

"So I see." She smiles with black, acid-etched teeth. "Hevvies got stomped next door, and we got a new playground."

"Have fun playing for a day or two," goes HiLo. "The ones who squelched them are coming back for you."

"Buildings squashed them. The end of the ramming world has been and gone. Where were you?"

"There's a new team playing in Fun City," HiLo goes.

Bala's eyes turn to slits. "Ganging on us now, huh? That's a getoff."

"The Four Hundred Boys," goes Jade.

"Enough to keep you busy!" She laughs and skates a half-circle. "Maybe."

"They're taking Fun City for their bloc—maybe all of it. They don't play fair. Those Boys never heard of clean fun."

"Skud," she goes, and shakes her hair so tin bells shiver. "You blew cirks, kids."

Slash knows that she is listening. "We're calling all teams, Bala. We gotta save our skins now, and that means we need to find more hideaways, let more slickers know what's up. Are you in or out?"

HiLo goes, "They smashed the Soooooots in thirty seconds flat."

A shock wave passes down the street like the tail end of a whiplash from center city. It catches us all by surprise and our guards go down; Galrogs, Brothers,

Sooooooot—we are all afraid of those wreckers. It unites us just like that.

When the shock passes we look at one another with wide eyes.

All the unspoken Galrog threats are gone. We have to hang together.

"Let's take these kids home," goes Bala.

"Yeah, Mommy!"

With a whisper of skates, the Galrogs take off. Our well-armed escort leads us through a maze of skate trails cleared in rubble.

"Boys, huh?" I hear Bala say to the other slickers. "We thought different."

"What did you think?"

"Gods," Bala goes.

"Gods!"

"God-things, mind-stuff. Old Mother looked into her mirror and saw a bonfire made out of cities. Remember before the blister tore? There were wars in the south, weirdbombs going off like firecrackers. Who knows what kind of stuff was cooking in all that blaze?

"Old Mother said it was the end of the world, time for the ones outside to come through the cracks. They scooped all that energy and molded it into mass. Then they started scaring up storms, smashing. Where better to smash than Fun City?"

"End of the world?" goes HiLo. "Then why are we still here?"

Bala laughs. "You doob, how did you ever get to be a slicker? Nothing ever ends. Nothing."

In ten minutes we come to a monster-mart pyramid with its lower mirror windows put back together in jigsaw shards.

Bala gives a short whistle, and double doors swing wide.

In we go.

The first thing I see are boxes of supplies heaped in the aisles, cookstoves burning, cots, and piles of blankets. I also spot a few people who can't be Galrogs—like babies and a few grownups.

"We've been taking in survivors," goes Bala. "Old Mother said that we should." She shrugs.

Old Mother is ancient, I have heard. She lived through the plagues and came out on the side of the teams. She must be upstairs, staring in her mirror, mumbling.

Slash and HiLo look at each other. I cannot tell what they are thinking. Slash turns to me and Jade.

"Okay, Brothers, we've got work to do. Stick around."

"Got anywhere to sleep?" Jade goes. The sight of all those cots and blankets made both of us feel tired.

Bala points at a dead escalator. "Show them the way, Shell."

The Galrog with a blond topknot that's streaked purple speeds down one aisle and leaps the first four steps of the escalator. She runs to the top without skipping a stroke and grins down from above.

"She's an angel," goes Jade.

There are more Galrogs at the top. Some girls are snoring along the walls.

Shell cocks her hips and laughs. "Never seen Brothers in a monstermart before."

"Aw, my ma used to shop here," goes Jade. He checks her up and over.

"What'd she buy? Your daddy?"

Jade sticks his thumb through his fist and wiggles it with a big grin. The other girls laugh but not Shell. Her blue eyes darken and her cheeks redden under the blue triangles. I grab Jade's arm.

"Don't waste it," goes another Galrog.

"I'll take the tip off for you," goes Shell, and flashes a blade. "Nice and neat."

I tug Jade's arm, and he drops it.

"Come on, grab blankets," goes Shell. "You can bed over there."

We take our blankets to a corner, wrap up, and fall asleep close together. I dream of smoke.

It is still dark when Slash wakes us.

"Come on, Brothers, lots of work to do."

Things have taken off, we see. The Galrogs know the hideaways of more teams than we ever heard of, some from outside Fun City. Runners have been at it all night, and things are busy now.

From uptown and downtown in a wide circle around Four hundredth, they have called all who can come.

The false night of smoke goes on and on, no telling how long. It is still dark when Fun City starts moving.

Over hive and under street, by sewer, strip, and alleyway, we close in tourniquet-tight on Four hundredth, where Soooooots ran a clean-fun bloc. From First to One thousandth, Bayview Street to Riverrun Boulevard, the rubble scatters and the subtunnels swarm as Fun City moves. Brothers and Galrogs are joined by Ratbeaters, Drummers, Myrmies, and Kingpins, from Piltdown, Renfrew, and the Up-

308

perhand Hills. The Diablos cruise down with Chogs and Cholos, Sledges and Trimtones, JipJaps and A-V-Marias. Tints, Chix, RockoBoys, Gerlz, Floods, Zips, and Zaps. More than I can remember.

It is a single team, the Fun City team, and all the names mean the same thing.

We Brothers walk shoulder to shoulder, with the last Soooooot among us.

Up the substairs we march to a blasted black surface. It looks like the end of the world, but we are still alive. I can hardly breathe for a minute, but I keep walking and let my anger boil.

Up ahead of us the Four Hundred Boys quiet down to a furnace roar.

By Three hundred ninety-fifth we have scattered through cross streets into the Boys' bloc.

When we reach Three hundred ninety-eighth fire flares from hives ahead. There is a sound like a skyscraper taking its first step. A scream echoes high between the towers and falls to the street.

At the next corner, I see an arm stretched out under rubble. Around the wrist the cuff is jagged black and red.

"Go to it," goes HiLo.

We step onto Four hundredth and stare forever. I'll never forget.

The streets we knew are gone. The concrete has been pulverized to gravel and dust, cracked up from underneath. Pyramid hives are baby volcano cones that hack smoke, ooze fire, and burn black scars in the broken earth. Towers hulk around the spitting volcanoes like buildings warming themselves under the blanked-out sky.

Were the Four Hundred Boys building a new city? If so, it would be much worse than death.

Past the fires we can see the rest of Fun City. We feel the team on all sides, a pulse of life connecting us, one breath.

HiLo has seen some of this before, but not all. He sheds no tears tonight.

He walks out ahead of us to stand black against the flames. He throws back his head and screams:

"Heeeeeey!"

A cone erupts between the monster buildings. It drowns him out; so he shouts even louder.

"Hey, you Four Hundred Boys!"

Shattered streetlights pop half to life. Over my head one explodes with a flash.

"This is our bloc, Four Hundred Boys!"

Galrogs and Trimtones beat on overturned cars. It gets my blood going.

"So you knocked in our hives, you Boys. So you raped our city."

Our world. I think of the moon, and my eyes sting.

"So what?"

The streetlights black out. The earth shudders. The cones roar and vomit hot blood all over those buildings; I hear it sizzle as it drips.

Thunder talks among the towers.

"I bet you will never grow UP!"

Here they come.

All at once there are more buildings in the street. I had thought they were new buildings, but they are *big* Boys. Four hundred at least.

"Stay cool," goes Slash.

The Four Hundred Boys thunder into our streets.

310

We move back through shadows into hiding places only we can reach.

The first Boys swing chains with links the size of skating rinks. Off come the tops of some nearby hives. The Boys cannot quite get at us from up there, but they can cover us with rubble.

They look seven or eight years old for all their size, and there is still baby pudge on their long, sweaty faces. Their eyes have a vicious shine like boys that age get when they are pulling the legs off a bug—laughing wild but freaked and frightened by what they see their own hands doing. They look double deadly because of that. They are on fire under their skin, fever yellow.

They look more frightened than us. Fear is gone from the one team. We reach out at them as they charge, sending our power from all sides. We chant, but I do not know if there are any words; it is a cry. It might mean, "Take us if you can, Boys; take us at our size."

I feel as if I have touched a cold, yellow blaze of fever; it sickens me, but the pain lets me know how real it is. I find strength in that; we all do. We hold onto the fire, sucking it away, sending it down through our feet into the earth.

The Boys start grinning and squinting. They seem to be squeezing inside out. The closest ones start shrinking, dropping down to size with every step.

We keep on sucking and spitting the fever. The fire passes through us. Our howling synchronizes.

The Boys keep getting smaller all the time, smaller and dimmer. Little kids never know when to stop. Even when they are burned out, they keep going.

As we fall back the first Boy comes down to size. One minute he is taller than the hives; then he hardly fills the street. A dozen of his shrinking pals fill in on either side. They whip their chains and shriek at the sky like screaming cutouts against the downtown fires.

They break past HiLo in the middle of the street and head for us. Now they are twice our size . . . now just right.

This I can handle.

"Smash!" yells Slash.

One Boy charges me with a wicked black curve I can't see till it's whispering in my ear. I duck fast and come up faster where he doesn't expect me.

He goes down soft and heavy, dead. The sick, yellow light throbs out with his blood, fades on the street.

I spin to see Jade knocked down by a Boy with an ax. There is nothing I can do but stare as the black blade swings high.

Shrill whistle. Wheels whirring.

A body sails into the Boy and flattens him out with a footful of razors and ballbearings. Purple-blond topknot and a big grin. The Galrog skips high and stomps his hatchet hand into cement, leaving stiff fingers curling around mashed greenish blood and bones.

Shell laughs at Jade and takes off.

I run over and yank him to his feet. Two Boys back away into a dark alley that lights up as they go in. We start after, but they have already been fixed by Quazis and Drummers lying in wait.

Jade and I turn away.

HiLo still stares down the street. One Boy has stood tall, stronger than the rest and more resistant to our power. He raps a massive club in his hand.

"Come on, slicker," HiLo calls. *"You remember me, don't you?"*

The biggest of the Boys comes down, eating up the streets. We concentrate on draining him, but he shrinks more slowly than the others.

His club slams the ground. Boom! Me and some Galrogs land on our asses. The club creases a hive, and cement sprays over us, glass sings through the air.

HiLo does not move. He waits with red-and-black lightning bolts serene, both hands empty.

The big slicker swings again, but now his head only reaches to the fifth floor of an Rx. HiLo ducks as the club streaks over and turns a storefront window into dust.

The Soooooot's scalpel glints into his hand. He throws himself at the Boy's ankle and grabs on tight.

He slashes twice. The Boy screams like a cat. Neatest hamstringing you ever saw.

The screaming Boy staggers and kicks out hard enough to flip HiLo across the street into the metal cage of a shop window. HiLo lands in a heap of impossible angles and does not move again.

Slash cries out. His gun shouts louder. One blood-silver shot. It leaves a shining line in the smoky air.

The Boy falls over and scratches the cement till his huge fingertips bleed. His mouth gapes wide as a manhole, his eyes stare like the broken windows all around. His pupils are slit like a poison snake's, his face long and dark, hook-nosed.

God or boy, he is dead. Like some of us.

Five Drummers climb over the corpse for the next round, but with their slickie dead the Boys are not up to it. The volcanoes belch as though they too are giving up.

The survivors stand glowing in the middle of their bloc. A few start crying, and that is a sound I cannot spell. It makes Crybaby start up. He sits down in cement, sobbing through his fingers. His tears are the color of an oil rainbow on wet asphalt.

We keep on sucking up the fever glow, grounding it all in the earth.

The Boys cry louder, out of pain. They start tearing at each other, running in spirals, and a few leap into the lava that streams from the pyramids.

The glow shrieks out of control, out of our hands, gathering between the Boys with its last strength — ready to pounce.

It leaps upward, a hot snake screaming into the clouds.

Then the Boys drop dead and never move again.

A hole in the ceiling of smoke. The dark-blue sky peeks through, turning pale as the smoke thins. The Boys' last scream dies out in the dawn.

The sun looks bruised, but there it is. Hiya up there!

"Let's get to it," goes Slash. "Lots of cleanup ahead." He has been crying. I guess he loved HiLo like a Brother. I wish I could say something.

We help one another up. Slap shoulders and watch the sun come out gold and orange and blazing white. I don't have to tell you it looks good, teams.

SEVENTH SENSE

By Robert Haisty

We unsnap our seat belts and lean back. I am hoping for two things: to get away from the gray Chicago rain and to finish my report for the Baltimore meeting. But by the time we reach cruising altitude I'm sure neither is going to happen. There's no break in the clouds, and already I know the old guy in the window seat is going to be a talker.

I halfway expected it — as soon as I saw him plop through the forward cabin door, hold out his boarding pass to the blond stewardess, and say something that made her dimple sweetly. It's that feeling you get when there are at least fifteen empty seats in front of you, but you know, sure as prunes, he's going to walk past every one of them and stop at your row with a little smile, and you were saving that seat in case Miss Galaxy came by.

He isn't really *doing* anything — just sitting there. Why do I find myself staring at him? On closer study, he doesn't even look so old; it's just that he seems archaic, somehow—and cautious. Imagine a thoroughly circumspect turtle eyeing over his shoulder the galloping approach of a half-grown Great Dane puppy.

He nods, grins. "You travel much?"

"Not a whole lot," I mumble halfheartedly. "Do you?"

"Oh, yes indeed. I'm on the move constantly."

He sits quietly then, and I optimistically begin sorting out my notes for the report. But as soon as the stewardess has dropped off a gin and tonic for him and a vodka martini for me—and a faint, wistful scent of orange blossoms for both of us—he lowers his seatback, turns toward me, and starts. "Yeah," he says with an ironic chuckle that there could have been any question about it, "I travel all right."

He has a voice that sounds deceptively unobtrusive, quiet even; yet it carries handily above the roar of the engines—not an easy man to ignore. And immediately, as if he were the Ancient Mariner and I, the Wedding Guest, I find myself putting my papers aside to listen to him.

"I'll tell you this: When you make as many towns a year as I do, you get so you can taste things in the wind. You pick up on all kinds of stuff. I once read: 'The constant traveler grasps propositions too subtle to describe. Too fleeting to hold. He knows things others do not.' "

"Like what?" I know I rolled my eyes disbelievingly toward the heavens before I could stop myself. But he doesn't pay any attention to that, or to my question.

"I've come to realize it gradually," he says.

"Through God knows how many thousand lonely breakfasts, up too early for the body to respond; trying to come back to life on coffee too strong, pale eggs too runny, with too much black pepper, and the morning paper. Then out of the red-clothed breakfast grill and into the city, still sleeping in the morning haze all cities seem to gather. Thirty years of it hasn't stopped that gnawing in the gut of a morning. That's the loneliest time there is. Not the nights. At night, people draw together. You get a feeling of order. We've conquered the night with soft electric lights and whiskey sours. Old travelers get together in quiet little bars and wear the night away. We don't say much. We don't really have to."

The Constant Traveler stops talking and pulls an orange out of his pocket, digging a stubby thumb into the peel. The aroma makes me think of the stewardess, and I wish I had ordered two drinks. He offers me part of his orange, and involuntarily I start to reach for it, then draw back.

"Hey!" he says. "Were you born like that?"

"Like — ?"

"With three fingers." He leans forward to look across at my left side. "On each hand?"

"Yes, as a matter of fact I was. Sure."

"Well I'll be. Cause you any problems?"

"No. No, of course not."

"Well," he says, laughing, "long as you're not a piano player."

"No problem there. I'm what you call tone deaf." I shouldn't have said it, because instantly his eyes dart to my ears, and I know he is studying them now.

He starts to say something else but apparently

thinks better of it. Instead he forces himself to gaze at his knees and says: "Well, I'll be double-dipped damned."

I try again to withdraw to my papers, but it isn't easy.

"Now then," he says, "you travel around some, don't you? Haven't you noticed the difference lately?"

"The difference in what?"

"The feeling. In the air."

I shake my head. "What does it feel like?" I shouldn't have asked.

"Listen," he says. "Not long ago I was in New Orleans. It was the end of summer, actually—one of those muggy nights you can't stir with a stick. And we were sitting out on a veranda bar, listening to the mournful honks of the riverboats, trying to drink ourselves out of a mood we didn't like, but getting worse into it instead. Anyway, here's the story:

"There were four of us at the table. Ralph Turner and Bill Ryan—they're copies of me, though we don't really look a lot alike. But we all have graying, thinning hair and what I guess you'd call travel-worn faces. The other guy was new to me. His name was Frank Burgeston, and there was kind of a keenness about him. As tall as Ralph, he was powerfully built and in excellent physical condition. He had a longish face, but it wasn't thin. His eyes, behind horn-rimmed glasses, seemed to burn with a restless energy. And my offhand remark that night triggered something in them.

" 'I get a funny feeling,' I had said, breaking a long silence that ensued after we finished ordering drinks, 'that something's going to happen pretty soon.'

" 'So you feel it, too,' Bill said dryly, lighting a cigarette.

"Old Ralph drew long and hard on his pipe, then cupped it in his hands as he let the smoke slowly roll out. For the first time in ten years I suddenly had the desire to smoke again. Ralph poked at the pipe with a matchstick, sending a small aromatic cloud across the table. He glanced up quickly when a slight breeze shook the strings of red and yellow paper lanterns hanging in shallow parabolas above the tables. Ralph looked across at Bill, then quickly back down to the checkered tablecloth, a little embarrassed at what he was saying: 'Yeah. Me too. I can't seem to shake the damned thing.'

"But it was Frank's eyes, and the *way* he said what he did that set my backbone crawling. 'I can tell you a little more about it,' he said flatly. 'You aren't the only ones, you know. I got the same thing in Cleveland, St. Louis — all over.'

" 'Earthquake?' I said. 'Brushfire war?'

"Frank shook his head slowly. 'No,' he said. We were silent for a while. Then I shoved my chair back and stretched my legs straight out in front of me, wiggling my toes inside my shoes to get some blood flowing. 'Aaaaggghhh,' I said. 'Come on, you guys. What the hell's the matter with us? So we think we all have some kind of premonition. So what? You know we just talked ourselves into it — with the help of the goddamned humidity. Or maybe because the market is so lousy.'

"The drinks arrived then, and there was another long silence. When Frank finally spoke he gave me another bout of gooseflesh, though all he said was,

319

'I'm afraid there's more to it than that.'

"He turned away from us then, to gaze for a moment through the open door as the bartender inside deftly capped a tray of drinks with cherries and lemon twists. Our eyes shifted automatically to catch the play of ripples along a pair of long, finely turned thighs in black net as the cocktail waitress executed a little dip that turned into a smooth, practiced lifting of the heavy tray when she straightened. Then she moved out on her next sortie. Was it really just my imagination that the mood of the whole place was quiet, and heavy, and waiting?

"Frank seemed uncomfortable about what he had just said, as if he had revealed more than he intended. Yet I had the distinct impression he wanted to tell us something else. But he kept watching the rhythmic swings of the waitress, and to change the subject he said, 'There's some beautiful bilateral symmetry for you.' He turned back to the table. 'Do you guys know, one of the top textbooks in the world on crystallography uses a full-page color photo of the sexiest bikini model you ever saw to illustrate bilateral symmetry? That's what I call forward thinking.'

" 'Jesus! You spend your time reading about crystallography?'

" 'It is one of the things,' Frank said, 'that interest me. Fascinating, in fact.'

" 'I'll tell you what fascinates me.' Bill chuckled. 'Ralph, when she comes back, let's ask her if she's bilateral.'

"Everybody laughed, but our mood would not stay up. It drifted, like a curled leaf floating on a pond — blown first out, in aimless patterns, then back, then out again. We sat for a time, pensive.

" 'I think we drink too much, and too late at night,' Ralph said. 'Bad for the liver, you know. Back in Milwaukee they say, *Dir ist wohl eine Laus über die Leber gelaufen.*'

" 'A louse must have walked across your liver.' Frank echoed, smiling for the first time that night. But then, falling back into his deep mood, he shook his head again. 'Look around this place. Now, you can say it's their livers, or too many positive ions in the air, or the phase of the moon—but there's not a person in here that doesn't act like doomsday.'

" 'Yeah sure,' Bill grunted. 'Let's say that it must be the ions.'

" 'Or,' Frank replied, a little sharply, 'let's say it isn't.' He hesitated a minute, then said, 'Listen, let me tell you something that happened a few years back. See, I used to play trumpet in a pretty good symphony orchestra. Well, after the concerts there would always be a reception for the guest artist. And one night—after a particularly good performance—a stranger at the party dropped a verbal bomb.

" 'I remember he was a short, heavyset man with dark, bushy hair and quick brown eyes. New in town, he had been invited by a neighbor, and he certainly had not intended to stir up a hornet's nest. He simply remarked that, yes, the performance had been brilliant, and wasn't it unfortunate that the piano was a little out of tune.'

" 'Is that all?' Bill asked, like the rest of us listening, more than a little puzzled by Frank's tale.

" 'All! You wouldn't believe how upset musicians can get over something like that. He might as well

321

have said the conductor couldn't keep time. So the thing grew and grew, and there were two armed camps: those who said the piano had been in perfect tune and those who said, come to think of it, they had noticed it was a little off. Finally somebody remembered the tape recording of the concert, and the tapes were put through an elaborate analysis with oscilloscopes and tone generators.'

" 'All that, just to—'

" 'It was important to us! Anyway, the results bore out the stranger's contention. Several notes *had* been out of tune, but so slightly it was generally regarded as an incredible feat that human ears had detected them.'

"Frank paused then for a long sip of his drink. By reflex, we all reached for our glasses, swirling the remaining bits of ice gently before we drank. High to our left a tiny point of light came into view and moved steadily through the bright stars until, crossing in front and continuing westward away from us, it appeared for a while to be stationary, then it was lost in the background. Probably a 707. It was so high we heard nothing of it, only the faint sounds of trucks in the distance; then a boat. I wondered again about the point of Frank's story. Everything is moving in its proper course. I mused. Why do we look for witches among the milkmaids?

"Then Frank replaced his glass on the table and sat with the tips of his fingers touching. 'At the time the tapes were being analyzed,' he said, 'we were also checking out the stranger. What we discovered was that the man was an incredibly skillful lip-reader. And that he had been totally deaf since early childhood.'

" 'What!' we all shouted at once.

" 'Well, I can tell you, we asked the same thing,' Frank said. 'Besides that, we were mad as hell because we thought he had been playing a stupid joke on us. But you know, when we confronted him, he was completely shocked. He said he hadn't realized we were not aware of the problem with the piano. We asked him how, then, in God's name, he had known the piano was out of tune. "Why," he said, surprised we should ask, "I saw it in your faces." '

" 'Jesus!' Bill gulped. 'Who ever heard of anything like—'

" 'I learned a lot from that man,' Frank said. 'A lot. He showed me how there are many inputs to our senses that don't register in our conscious minds but show up in other ways. The main thing is to develop confidence in what you perceive. It's more than intuition. Intuition is like smelling. This is more like *tasting*. It's knowing—a sensation of being aware.'

" 'And you think we're sensing the integrated reading from thousands of faces with . . . an awareness . . . that something is not right?' Ralph asked quietly, almost as if he'd been afraid to voice it.

" 'Why don't we go ahead and say it,' Frank replied flatly. 'What we're talking about is the end of the world—at least the world as we know it. You know, there's been a group somewhere hollering about it ever since man learned to talk. Now nobody anywhere is saying a thing. Because this time it's for real.'

"We nodded, shuffled around in our chairs. 'Yeah,' Frank agreed. 'That's about it. But you feel so damn foolish coming right out and trying to talk about it.

Do you see a giant fireball, or what?'

" 'No. Nothing like that. I think—I know—they're on their way. An invasion. I don't even think there'll be much violence. Just such superior beings . . . it won't be our world any longer.'

"Well, I remember we didn't say much after that, but shortly finished our drinks and went up to what was—for me, at any rate—a restless night. I was glad to get back on the road. And I really don't know what made me want to talk about it today. After all, nothing's happened."

The Constant Traveler's story has filled most of the flight. We must be just minutes out of Baltimore. I glance at my watch. It's about ten minutes. "How long ago was all that?" I ask him as I collect my papers.

"Oh, let's see . . . New Orleans . . . it must have been three or four months."

"Well, that was quite a night you guys had, huh?" I grin at him.

"Yeah. Yeah, I guess it was." He looks a little sheepish.

I finish gathering my things and snap the case shut. Outside it looks completely black. We must be in some heavy clouds, but the flight has actually been very smooth. Better get my jacket down; they're just about ready to call the approach.

I hate landing in the rain, especially at night. It's like being thrown out of the womb at the wrong time. I hate the smell of wet coats; having to stand in a little pocket of people under a roof that's too small; the *schish*ing sound the tires make on the water. All the lights are smeared.

324

And of course the baggage is taking longer. He waits with the ease of habit. The others are shifting their feet, turning at every new noise, checking their watches. Finally our bags come down.

"Say, do you want to share a cab?" he asks. "They'll be hard to come by tonight."

"No, thanks. I'm renting a car. Not staying in the city."

"Oh, okay." He seems disappointed.

"Can I drop you somewhere?" I ask, a little more kindly.

He waves negative with a palm vertical. "Wouldn't want to take you out of your way."

"Come on." We lift our suitcases at the same time and turn down the long corridor to the transportation area. "I'd be glad to have the company."

The little hotel where he is staying is several blocks off the main route. It's an old section, pretty run down, but it feels comfortable. There are a few islands like this one left in every city, and these old salesmen know them all.

It is still raining—cold and steady. He turns his collar up, pulls the checkered travel hat down tighter, thanks me again, and dashes for the front door. There is a quick shaft of light, making silver wires of the raindrops, and he's gone. In a few minutes he'll be at Old Fashioneds, surrounded by the red-amber glow of antique polished mahogany; warm, out of the rain.

I stop to light a cigarette, hold the smoke deep for a minute, then direct a slow, thin stream at the windshield wipers before I pull back out into the street. I have had an uncomfortable feeling about it for quite

325

a while, and now I'm sure. They *do* sense it. They don't know we are here, of course, but they know something is. And they're definitely not ready for our migration. *If we come in now they will damage themselves trying to resist*.

It may be a struggle for me to convince the rest of the Encroach Team, but they've got to be convinced. We certainly have no wish to destroy this planet or any of the beings on it. But if Encroach debates too long, it'll all be over. At best, we'll barely be able to get word back to leader Twelve in time to stop them. Miserable communications lag! Will we ever break the *c*-cubed velocity barrier? It's a good thing we decided to have a final meeting—and that group from Cappadocia finally agreed to come. With Encroach so scattered and not allowed to use normal communications channels, I'd never be able to get an agreement in time to stop the migration.

As it is, maybe I won't have too much trouble. After all, what is one cycle to us? But think what one hundred seventy-two of their years can do for them. They really do have a remarkable degree of perception already—even, as he said, a rudimentary awareness sense, though they do not seem to understand the Schuman resonances at all. It's even possible we could wait for two cycles. In any case, it would be unthinkable to do it now.

The group from New Zealand does not agree. Neither does the one from Galápagos. Some of the others are undecided. It's definitely not going to be easy. And the time we're losing!

"I never heard of such a thing. Are you questioning whether we can handle them? When have we ever had any trouble controlling the Originals?" There is much nodding of agreement with New Zealand.

"After all, we had a full report from Exploration before anything was planned." One of the Central European groups is heard from. "This is no time to be calling it off. Too late anyway."

"With all due credit to Exploration," I tell them, "they have not encountered this degree of development in our other galaxies. It simply is not obvious on a casual encounter. There is real sensitivity here. They are beyond accommodation."

"And in another cycle or two they may be beyond anything," Galápagos retorts. "I don't think we have a choice. There's no place else to go. You know how long it took us to find this planet. We certainly can't risk being burned out with no place to—"

"What risk?" I interrupt. "They are not progressing faster than we are, certainly. We'll be able to come in next cycle if we have to. And I'm convinced they will be able to accept us by then. It should be interesting; they are so much like us in many ways. Take away their extra finger, their peculiar ear structure, and they're even ahead of us in certain things. The sounds they call music, for example—"

"We agree with Central USA." The African groups stand up. "We've seen it too. There is no question of their sensitivity. It must be allowed to develop before we approach them. They must be able to understand—to accept us."

"Agreed!" shouts Far North.

"If we are going to call it off," Encroach Leader

says, "it has to be done immediately. Let's have the vote now."

"I think you're imagining things," Galápagos mutters. "And I'll tell you something else. Disengagement won't be trivial."

Galápagos was right about that. We carried the vote, though it was closer than I had expected. But it has taken until Friday to work out the details of the disengagement. I am thoroughly tired by the time I finally get to the airport.

He is there. The Constant Traveler. He lifts the arm resting on the bar a couple of inches in greeting. "Hello, Traveler," I tell him. "Is this a coincidence, or is somebody following somebody?"

He grins, showing the wide gap in his front teeth. "Pure, plain coincidence. Happens all the time, believe me."

"Well"—I signal for a beer—"I don't know about that."

"Oh, yes," he assures me. "When you've traveled more you'll know what I mean. You keep running into the same people."

"How was your stay?" I reach for the beer.

"Great. Made a couple of good sales. Hey! How about that market? Up nearly sixty points this week."

"Yeah!" Suddenly I am not so tired anymore. "Interesting, isn't it."

"Interesting, hell. It means about three thousand bucks to me. Say, what flight are you on? Going back to Chicago?"

"No. Another direction."

"Too bad," he says, just before he drains the glass and pops it down on the bar with a loud, long sigh of pleasure. "Sorry I won't be having your company." He slides easily off the stool and picks up his case. "But I'll see you again somewhere. Better run. I got a plane to catch."

I watch him walk out into the main corridor, then angle off to the left and merge into the stream of shoulders, heads, and assorted luggage moving to the flight gates. I am sorry to see him go. He's like part of the furnishings. But just before he said good-bye there was an instant when he looked at me, wanting to say something—and in that instant he, a superbly trained professional, knew he had violated security. He is a machine-tool salesman like I am a Xeninian sheepherder!

That story of his—fantastic. It bought them one hundred seventy-two years, anyway. But there was no Frank. And no Bill. And no Ralph, or New Orleans bar. There was a light in the sky, all right. Was there really a deaf man? Perhaps.

LUNATIC BRIDGE

By Pat Cadigan

"There's divorce and there's divorce," said Nelson Nelson. "You ever been divorced, Deadpan?"

I lit a cigarette, using the time to decide if NN were asking me an honest question or just gassing. I had no doubt the old fox could have wormed his way into my personal data; most employers can. And he was a great one for asking questions he already knew the answers to. He'd told me once he did it because he was interested in other people's realities.

"No," I said after a bit.

"Certain philosophers say real divorce is rare because few people ever make truly solid connections with each other."

"Philosophers?" I tapped my cigarette over the suckhole in the low desk between us and shifted around uncomfortably on my couch. NN's practice of conducting business in a reclining position had become tiresome and the vulgar gold lamé was making me itch all over. "So who are the philosophers of divorce?"

NN looked wise. "The other members of my Restaurant-of-the-Month Club, actually. We suppered in the Jet Stream last night and the subject came up with the cranberry souffle."

"You discussed a case?"

NN's forehead puckered. His eyebrows were nonexistent these days, which made a frown one of his more peculiar expressions. "Don't be absurd, Allie. Someone else brought the subject up. I listened."

"Did you hear anything that would help me?"

"Hard to say. I'm old enough to have seen several swings of the togetherness pendulum. For a few years, everyone's getting Two'd and Three'd and Gang'd. Then suddenly everyone's an island again, nobody wants to be committed to anyone else. But regardless of what people think they want, they clump. They can't help it. Even outcasts align with other outcasts. Nobody wants to be completely outside the tribe."

I said nothing and scratched my rash. Sooner or later, NN would find his way to the point.

"Take an extreme case of clumping gone to bond," he went on in his listen-to-this-you-could-learn-something voice. "You remember the LadyBug Twins from a few years back?"

I nodded, still scratching away. "They were big news when I was in training in J. Walter Tech."

"They were big news everywhere in the mindplay business. We were all wiggling to see how that one would come out and what precedents it would set."

I remembered the two identical women grinning

332

from holo tanks almost hourly. The resemblance was strictly manufactured and they'd decided that it wasn't enough to seal their friendship. They'd wanted their brainwaves synchronized as well and the request had taken them into court—some kind of free will/civil rights problem. No one wanted to rule on the case until a sharp lawyer pointed out that their petition was interpretable as a desire for a particular brand of psychosis, which meant they were entitled to psychomimics' licenses, just like anyone else. The LadyBugs had faded out of the public fishbowl quickly after that. The last anyone had heard of them, they were still happily thinking alike.

"Don't tell me," I said, sitting up. "The LadyBugs have split up, one of them wants to be a ballet dancer and I'm supposed to pathos-find her."

NN gave me one of his looks. "You get some funny ideas, Deadpan. The LadyBugs are still happy as sandbags and loony as Klein bottles. You follow contemporary composers?"

"Not on purpose. Why?"

He thumbed a button on his couch frame. Music came up out of the walls and floated down from the ceiling. "Recognize this?"

"Sure. That's the Poconos Movement from *Transcontinental Elopement*. Jord Coor and Revien Lam."

NN looked satisfied for no reason I could readily think of. *Transcontinental Elopement* was hardly an obscure piece of music in spite of the fact that it was 408 hours long. You were supposed to listen to it all in one sitting, but who has seventeen days to spare for uninterrupted music? Seventeen days was allegedly how long it had taken Coor and Lam to go from one edge of the continent to the other by a rambling overland route, composing as they went. The novelty of its length had contributed to its popularity at first — the *Transcontinental Elopement* listening party became the event of the hour, with people camping out in suites, following the journey on 360° holo. Real purists hired overland transportation and recreated the trip while those with less stamina or spare time took it in doses. The Poconos Movement was one of the more favored doses, all frisky piccolos and galloping guitars. You wouldn't have thought piccolos could describe the Poconos so well, but they did.

"Still with me, Deadpan?"

"Oh, sure." I squirmed into another position, scratching my left calf with my right foot and clawing at my ribs. "I always liked the Coor and Lam stuff."

NN turned the volume down a little. "Likewise. It has great spirit, isn't it so? Coor and Lam produced a fine body of work together, right up until two years ago, when they went their separate ways."

"Yah. Which one hired me?"

"Coor." NN raised himself on one elbow. "And if you don't stop that scratching, I'm going to have you flayed alive to save you the trouble. What in *hell* is wrong with you?"

"I'm allergic to this goddam gold lamé." I stood up, trying to scratch everywhere at once. My overblouse clung to me, snapping with static when I pulled it away from the slight potbelly I'd been too lazy to exercise off. Fusion power we licked; static cling has us on the ropes. It's a funny world.

"Here." Nelson Nelson produced a small tube and tossed it to me. "Suddenly everyone's allergic to gold lamé. I had Lindbloom in here about a thrillseeking assignment and she could barely hold still."

Well, that sounded like Lindbloom, gold lamé or no gold lamé. Most thrillseekers have a tendency to prowl when not hunting a kick in someone's brain. All mindplayers seem to end up acting out. Dreamfeeders wander around looking absent, belljarrers are usually secluded somewhere if they aren't on a job and neurosis-peddlers bounce off the walls. Cackling. I wasn't quite sure what effect pathosfinding was having on me, except I'd noticed lately that I'd taken to sightreading the Emotional Index of the odd stranger here and there.

"Better?" NN asked as I swabbed cool blue jelly on my arms.

"Much. What is this stuff?"

"Home remedy. Take it with you."

"Maybe I ought to leave it here. For next time." I glanced at the couch.

"Deadpan, I'm hurt. You're sneering at the future I looked forward to in the dear, dead days of my youth."

"Pardon?"

"Gold lamé. Back when I was a kid, they promised us a clean, glorious future of prosperity where positively everything would be covered with gold lamé. They stopped making the stuff forty years ago and now I have to have it specially manufactured. But I figure I'm entitled."

I pulled up one loose pantleg and smeared his home remedy on my thigh. "Tell me about Jord Coor. And I wasn't sneering."

"There's not much for *me* to tell you; I put all the

335

information in your data bank and you were too sneering. Coor's trying to put himself together for a solo career and having a bad time of it. The six-month hiatus he took after the split has stretched into a year and a half and he's feeling desperate."

"He waited a year and a half before hiring a pathosfinder?"

"Some people have to take the long way home just so they know they've been somewhere."

"Is he really ready to try it alone?"

"*He* says. That's something you'll have to determine."

"What about his ex-partner?"

"Out of sight but traceable. Part of their separation agreement was a clause promising a certain amount of cooperation in any future individual endeavors, musical or otherwise."

"Was their split really that amiable?"

"Who knows? Divorce is a funny thing."

"But they weren't married. Or were they? I don't keep up on celebrity statistics."

NN's forehead puckered again. I couldn't wait for his eyebrows to grow back. He did some odd things and I had yet to figure what it was he was acting out. "Maybe not in the conventional sense. But they worked mind-to-mind for ten years. What do you think that means but marriage? More than marriage. Follow?"

I nodded.

"So if you look up Revien Lam for some reason, don't hook in with both of them. Don't put them in a composing situation together."

"But they don't want to compose together."

"Who said so?" NN snapped. "Did I say so?" He shook his head. "Deadpan, the thing you gotta remember about divorced people is when they have a real crisis, they think about jumping right back into the old situation, even if that's the worst thing they could do, and it usually is. The whole music world would love to see them together again and they don't really want to be back together. Which, paradoxically, gives them common ground and pushes them closer together. Follow that?"

"Yah." I finished applying jelly to my other leg. "And I didn't sneer. They don't call me Deadpan Allie and lie."

"You sneered, woman. Inside if not outside. I could tell." He cut off the music and put the Bolshoi Ballet on the ceiling holo by way of dismissing me and having the last word. "It's a mutually wished-for and consummated divorce, Deadpan. Leave it that way."

Fandango sneaked up behind me and propped her chin on my shoulder. "Hi. I'm your two-headed transplant."

I kept staring at the read-out screen. "I'm not going to encourage you."

She tickled me under the chin with one of her dreadlocks. The damnedest things come back into style. "Why are you researching the LadyBugs?"

"I'm looking at a case of extreme togetherness that worked. Or has yet to fail, I'm not sure which." I pushed back from my desk and went down the three steps into the living room to flop on the couch.

337

Fandango tagged after me, pausing at the bar near the steps to dial up a couple of birch beers.

"You think there's a difference?" she said, handing me a glass before she climbed into the pouch chair to the right of the couch. "Between something that works and something that has yet to fail?"

"Glad you asked." I waved at the coffeetable. *Full Day*, another Coor and Lam composition, came on softly. This one was only twenty-four hours long, looped for continuous play. "According to a tract I read by one of the leading experts on human relationships—who also happens to be a member of NN's Restaurant-of-the-Month Club—there are three main theories on the patterns that two-person bondings of any nature follow."

Fandango turned her bloodstone eyes on me. The bloodstones were new. With the dreadlocks, they made her look like a cross between a werewolf and a witch-doctor. I didn't mention it to her. She'd have just gone and added fangs for effect. "Let's hear it. I know you're itching to tell me."

"Don't use that expression. One theory says a two-way partnership that lasts until the death of one or both partners never reached its ultimate peak and thus never got the chance to deteriorate. Another theory says that all partnerships end before the actual split. In the last stage, there are two sets of elements thrown together behind a facade of unity." I put my birch beer down on the coffeetable. If I was going to get rid of my potbelly, I couldn't be pouring birch beer into it. "The third theory states that all partnerships are illusions. One personality dominates and absorbs the other. I guess the LadyBugs would be a rather extreme example, in a way."

"The LadyBugs are loono and have licenses to prove it," Fandango said, with not a little disdain.

"Then there are all the variations on those theories. The most interesting one postulates that whatever happens between two people, a third entity is created which can, in some cases, attain such definition and strength as to be a different person."

Fandango finished her birch beer and hung out of the chair to set the glass on the carpet. "And what does all this tell you?"

"It tells me experts probably work alone." I stared at the meditation maze on the ceiling. Researching the LadyBugs, I decided, was the wrong approach. They weren't partners, not the way Coors and Lam had been. Congruence wasn't necessarily complement.

"Turn up the music, will you?" Fandango said, sinking down a little more in the chair. "It just entered my circadian peak."

I obliged her. Only her head was visible in the pouch chair now. I'd never cared for the idea of being swallowed by a piece of furniture, no matter how comfortable it was supposed to be, but then, it wasn't my chair anyway. Fandango had dragged it over to my apartment from her place. That was the advantage of living at the agency — you could get out of your apartment and take it with you.

The LadyBugs were still grinning from the console in my work area above the living room. I abandoned the maze and wandered back to my desk to punch for Jord Coor's entry. He was an emphatically plain man with a wide face and long, straight black hair. His eyes were the same flat black, onyx biogems according to his data. The overall effect was *blah*, as though his life's ambition was to pass unnoticed. Not the acter-outer type, which probably meant there was more than the usual amount of energy pent up behind that broad forehead. If he ran just loosely to form, he was prone to what I thought of as the creative tantrum, as well as bursts of creativity alternating with blocks. His being half a team had probably masked a lot of that.

After awhile, I punched for Revien Lam's picture. The screen swallowed Coor and delivered his ex-partner's image with an electronic burp. Time for another tune-up. Revien Lam seemed to have tried to make himself as different from Coor as possible. He'd had a bleachout, hair and all. Against his color, or lack of it, the sapphire eyes were startling. His features were pointy where Coor's were blunted, the face almost an inverted triangle. Only the knobs of his jawbone kept him from looking too pixie-ish.

Just for the hell of it, I shrank Lam's picture and recalled Coor's, putting them side by side. They stared at me and I stared back. Art makes strange mindfellows. It was hard to imagine the two of them hooked in together, Coor through the left eye and Lam through the right, working both in real time and the eternal Now of mind-time. A rather trippy experience.

And a very long trip at that. Ten years of continual mind-to-mind contact was a lot more intimate than two people should have been with each other, as far as I was concerned. They had to be a couple of pretty rugged individualists to have kept themselves sorted out.

"Rugged individualist," I said aloud.

"What?" asked Fandango, coming out of her musical trance.

I looked over my shoulder at her. "I said, 'Rugged individualist.' "

She waved at the coffee table, lowering the music. "Who?"

"Just a thought. Go back to your rhapsody and forget I said anything." I turned back to the screen and stared at the ex-collaborators some more.

If you stare at something long enough, sometimes it will begin to look wrong. Lam's picture was on the right and Coor's was on the left and the arrangement was making me uncomfortable to the point of irritation. I tried looking at them with my right eye covered and then my left, but I'd never been that good at isolating my visual fields without mechanical help. Feeding an image into one hemisphere of the brain alone can sometimes give you a different perspective on something, but all I was getting out of the effort was more uncomfortable.

When I switched the pictures around, I felt a lot better, even both eyes open. Aesthetically, the new arrangement was more pleasing though I was damned if I could have said why. I sat back and put my heels up on the desk, gazing at the pictures through the V-frame of my legs. The system had placed Lam's picture on the right when I'd called for Coor's. Maybe if I'd made the placement myself I'd have liked it better? I shook my head. That wasn't it and I knew it. I rested my gaze on the dividing line between the pictures for several seconds and then nearly fell out of the chair.

The resemblance between them was so marked I felt like an ass for not having seen it immediately. It wasn't exactly a physical resemblance and yet it was. The similarity lay in their expressions, especially in the eye and mouth areas—the same things that make the long-married look alike. I had the screen enlarge those portions and remove the distinguishing coloration.

I marveled. It was almost possible to forget which features belonged to which man. Just for the hell of it, I patched Coor's eyes and mouth into Lam's face and vice versa. My system wasn't programmed for fine detail graphics and the result was crude, but not unreasonable.

"And what does that tell you, Dr. Frankenstein?" Fandango called, hanging out of the chair to see what I was doing.

"Take a nap," I said and punched for pictures of Coor and Lam as they had been prior to becoming collaborators, careful to keep Lam on the left and Coor on the right.

The youthfulness of their faces startled me. I checked the dates. The pictures were fourteen years old, which made it something close to two years before they'd met. At twenty, Coor had that I'm-an-adult-I-know-things look to him while the seventeen-year-old Lam appeared to be the sort of twink you could sell a perpetual motion machine to.

I made more enlargements of their features and side-by-sided them one at a time. There was a definite similarity of expression around their eyes, as though they might have been looking at things in the same way, literally. They'd just had to meet and discover it.

I punched up pictures from three years later. A year into the partnership, Lam had dyed himself black with red accents. The struggle for differentiation had already begun.

Forward another three years. The haunted look of Lam's opal eyes was reflected by Coor's. I went to my auxiliary screen and called up a list of their compositions for that time. *The Freak Parade, Persimmon Dances, The Abstruse Pillow*. I listened to short excerpts from each one on my phones. It was easy to hear the conflict, but they'd conflicted so well together.

I jumped ahead to their last full year together. Coor looked weary and Lam looked crazed. By then it must have required incredible effort to keep from merging. Lam had been in the first stage of his bleach job and it struck me that his decision to be bleached this time instead of dyed was probably a strong statement of his perception of what was happening between himself and his partner. And there was Coor, looking the same as always, making a statement by making no statement.

I leaned my elbows on the desk and looked from one face to the other. If I'd been shown all the pictures and then been asked to guess which man had hired me, I'd have probably picked Lam, not Coor.

And what about Lam? I punched for any available data. There wasn't much—some vital statistics, a facsimile of the separation agreement, and his last known address, two years out of date. Probably safe to assume he'd given up music entirely. Considering how he'd been pulling away for ten years, it was in character—another and final way to differentiate himself from Coor, a pattern of behavior he was locked into for good.

"And what does all *this* tell you?" said a voice in my ear. Fandango had crept up behind me again. Served me right for having my work area in an open space just off my living room.

"It tells me some people gain freedom by trading one form of bondage for another."

"Yah? You don't have to tell *me* that. I'm a neurosis-peddler, remember?"

"Well, you asked." I frowned at the screen. "I think my basic problem here is just training someone to be a unit after being half a team for ten years."

Fandango looked at the screen and wagged her dreadlocks. "Ah, they never should have broken up."

"That's a matter of opinion," I said, amused. "An opinion that my client's been struggling against. Maybe Lam, too, for all I know."

"Sorry. I guess I can say it because I won't be doing the dirty work. But speaking as a member of the listening audience—" she made a face, which, considering the way she looked, was actually quite an accomplishment. "I don't know." She pulled one foot high up on her thigh in a sloppy but limber half-lotus and absentmindedly massaged her sole. "Maybe I don't know what I'm talking. All I do is make people wash their hands a lot and associate sex with the color orange. But maybe it's better to be half of something wonderful than a whole nothing at all."

"It hasn't been determined that Jord Coor is nothing on his own yet," I said a little sharply. "If it had, I wouldn't be on this job."

"Yah. But maybe this kind of mindplay only postpones having to admit something like the truth, huh?" She bounced back to the pouch chair, dreadlocks flying, and hopped in.

"Thanks for the moral support," I said.

"Anytime." She turned the music up again.

"This part of Massachusetts used to be such a mess that they put a 200-year ban on external construction even after they cleaned it up. It'll be another eighty-four years before you see anything but naked landscape, if then." Jord Coor's square face was impassive in the near twilight. I wasn't sure that I hadn't met someone even more deadpan than I was. He pointed to the horizon. "Those low hills are called monadnocks, according to the locals. About half of them are occupied, hollowed out, like this one." He tapped his foot on the soft dirt.

"Pretty," I said.

He almost smiled. "For centuries, nobody knew that. It was all defaced with factories, ugly little industrial towns. Poison all over the place, in everything. I've seen pictures." A small wind pushed a strand of hair over the lower half of his face and he tossed his head to remove it. The motion put us unexpectedly eye to eye. The onyxes were like two bottomless holes.

"I thought this would be the ideal place to hide out, weather the first of the separation. Really go underground, in a place that was also coming back into its own."

A chill crept into the air as the sun slid closer to the

lumpy line of monadnocks. Jord waved at the manhole we'd climbed out of earlier and I nodded. The hole led down to an uncomfortably small (for me) elevator that took us back into the big empty chamber at the top of the stacked rooms he persisted in calling a house.

We went down to the living room, which was five times larger than it had to be, considering what he used it for—namely, very little. A designer who apparently went to a lot of parties had shaped it so that it was punctuated with conversation areas and gathering spots all around an off-center bar. It all had an untouched, still-not-broken-in look. Jord just wasn't ready to make himself at home and that wasn't a good sign.

He wasn't ready to begin work either; he was treating me like a guest, or maybe an insurance agent, anything but a pathosfinder. Not that clients ever start pouring their hearts and minds out the moment I hit their turf. The first meeting was always uncomfortable, but Jord Coor's avoidance was among the highest I'd come up against. He sat me in one of the nooks around the bar and dispensed birch beer and chitchat until I was bloated and more knowledgeable about north-central Massachusetts than I could ever have wanted to be. I let him run. Eventually he was going to blurt out something having to do with the reason I was there and that would give both of us the momentum to go to work. Best for him to make the first move.

When it came, it came without preamble. He looked up at me from his fourth glass of birch beer and said, "I just want it back."

346

"It?"

"Whatever it was I had before I met Revien. Sometimes I can almost feel it. It's almost there. But it's like stepping forward and finding the floor suddenly gone. Nothing there, just emptiness. And I realize all those years with Revien—I've come away half an artist." He set his glass on a small shelf by his elbow. "That's how it feels, anyway. I've been changed."

"Did you expect that you wouldn't be?"

"Changed, certainly." His face hardened. "Changed but not diminished. Not shortchanged. Apparently what we added to the partnership we subtracted from ourselves. Or what I added to the partnership I subtracted from myself. I don't know about Revien." He blinked. "And you'd think I *would* know, wouldn't you. Ten years in and out of each other's heads, you'd think we had no secrets." He stared past me. "But we were only half hooked in. That was close enough. Early on, we went all the way just to try it. Only twice, though. It was too much. Felt so strange, as though we were asleep, dreaming, and discovered there was someone else dreaming the same dream." His gaze slid over to me. "You ever feel that way with a client?"

"Mindplayers are specially trained not to get loose and runny around the borders, though most people don't have problems keeping self divided from nonself. It sounds like an effect peculiar to your relationship."

He nodded slowly. "Perhaps it was."

"Who first brought up the idea of separating?"

He took a deep, uncomfortable breath. "I don't

347

know if it's a matter of an idea that came up. More like a sub-theme that was always there and evolved into being the main melody. We were always pulling apart as much as pulling toward each other." He frowned, wobbling between a hasty retreat from the subject and a headlong plunge into the problem.

"This might be a good time for the first session," I said casually. "While it's at the top of your mind."

He licked his lips, preparing an objection.

"It doesn't get any easier," I added.

His smile was sudden and unexpectedly warm. "No, I don't suppose it does, does it?"

The studio was a strange room, windowless and just big enough to keep a claustrophobe from stampeding. The acoustical walls and ceiling caught even the brush of our feet on the carpet and the whisper of our clothes and seemed to focus on them, making each noise into a significant sound before it was gone. In the center of the room, a marvelously restored barrel-house upright piano stood back to back with a techno-crazy chunk of synthesizer bristling with wires and stepladdered with keyboards, as though inviting comparison and choice.

"A synthesizer won't always do the job," Jord said as I touched the rich old wood of the piano. "Sometimes there's no substitute for the real instrument." One hand hovered over the yellowed keys, his fingers falling into position for a chord. Then he looked up at me. "What made you choose cat's-eye?"

"I found them interesting."

"Look toward the light." He lifted my chin and

studied my eyes. "Revien would like eyes like those. They shimmer. The same way he does."

I pulled away from him gently. "Revien shimmers?"

"It's hard to explain."

"Then don't explain. Show me." I went over to my system stacked by the far wall and began putting the eight components together. I could feel him watching, unspoken objections and excuses piling up between us, thickening the air.

"This is smaller than most of the systems I've seen," he said suddenly, from just behind me. I had just enough presence not to jump. After you've been pathosfinding awhile, you get to where you can not only sense an Emotional Index without looking but also judge a client's physical position relative to yourself. I hadn't thought one could come up behind me without my knowing.

"My agency developed this model," I told him, keeping busy with the connections so he wouldn't know he'd startled me. "This one's only for pathosfinding and enhancement, which is why there's so little to it. Your last pathosfinder probably had a standard, multi-purpose system."

He made a skeptical sounding noise. "Revien and I used a composing box. It wasn't a lot bigger than this. Are you sure it'll do the job?"

I was grinning on the inside. "Back at the agency, we've got a system the size of a small canyon. You have to let it eat your head to use it. It does a job and a half, just about anything by way of mindplay, but it wouldn't do anything more for us than this does. Which is to provide a medium for the meeting of our minds. It works, but only as well as we do. You know

349

how it is with machines."

He moved around to my right, frowning at the assembly. It looked like a model of a building designed by an architect with recurring Cubist nightmares. "Revien used to call our composing box the lunatic bridge."

"Why?" I asked, pulling some flat pictures out of a drawer.

"We'd send a piece of ourselves down the wire into the box and the pieces would fuse into the lunatic that composed the music."

I didn't raise my eyebrows. "Interesting way to look at it. Did you—do you—see it that way?"

"A lunatic on a bridge?" He wouldn't let the smile come, attempting to out-deadpan me. "I tried not to. Try not to." He looked at the pictures I was holding.

"This is something my agency developed strictly for musicians. Some are flat photos, others are repros of old paintings. You take a good look at them and tell me what you hear. Are you more comfortable lying down or sitting up?"

"Lying down. I'll get some mats out of the storeroom."

"Just one. I'll sit up, if that's all right."

I pushed the chair at the synthesizer over while he fetched a mat and went about molding it into a contour for himself.

He almost froze on the first picture, but we'd built up too much momentum and it carried him into the exercise whether he liked it or not. But he took his time with the photo of a man and a woman in the middle of a glitzy blow-out. The woman was Lindbloom, several years younger, before she'd started dyeing herself midnight blue. Even in plain flesh-tone she was striking, which may have contributed to his stalling. People like to stare at Lindbloom.

"A lot of laughter and chatter around those two," he said at last. "An old Coor and Lam piece playing in the background, very old. One of our first. He's caught between nostalgia and looking ahead to the possibilities, mainly with the woman. She doesn't think in terms of past or future, it's all a big Now to her. When she gets far enough from one experience, it's like it happened to someone else. She's timeless and that's her strength. He isn't, and that's his weakness."

For someone who had been slow to begin, he'd made a strong start. I went on to the next picture, a low aerial view of some half-above-ground homes in Colorado, with Pike's Peak taking up the background.

"Wind," he said after awhile. "Rustling. The air is colder than usual for the season. No birds singing. There's a far away machine sound; no one could identify it even if they could hear it. They're all dug in, hiding, and they don't make a sound."

He barely hesitated on the third picture, a repro of a Magritte, a man with an apple obscuring his face. "He's trying to talk but the fruit muffles him. All that comes out are these 'mmf-mmf' sounds."

The Magritte was the real breaker; he went quickly through the other nine pictures. By the time he finished, he was agitated and antsy, ready either to get started or beg off for the night. I pulled the connections out of the system drawer and untangled with wires.

"Give me your eyes," I said, kneeling down beside him. Obediently, he popped them into my cupped hand. I put the system connections to his empty eyelids and let them crawl in to engage the optic nerves. I had programmed a tonal exercise for him instead of the usual color or pattern building. Judging from the way he sagged on the mat, it seemed to have been the right choice.

I took half a minute to examine his eyes. They were almost brand new and well taken care of, which was a good sign. I put them in the lefthand compartment of the solution jar, breathed myself into near-trance and then popped out my own eyes.

I had intended to let him feel my presence gradually, to avoid contact-shock but he seemed to have been waiting for me. At the first taste of me, he drew me in with a smoothness born of years of working mind-to-mind with someone else. I hadn't expected him to receive me as easily as he had his former partner. Old responses live long, die hard, and frequently leave a troublesome corpse. But that was normal trouble.

There was no visual. Absolutely no visual at all and that wasn't normal trouble. My mind translated the lack into the dark of eyelessness. The urge to visualize was almost overpowering but I managed to check it. The tonal exercise was still running and that was my next surprise. Most people hear bell-like sounds when you hook them into a tonal. Jord Coor's reaction was something completely new to me.

He heard seagulls. Very musical seagulls—their cries complemented and harmonized the way they never really would have in the outside world. It wasn't at all unpleasant but in the sightless night of his perspective, it was rather spooky. I prodded gently, thinking that perhaps he'd been waiting for a sign from me before he turned on the pictures.

Sea? I asked. Actually, I wasn't sure whether I'd thought *sea* or *see* at him.

A secret sea, he answered without disturbing the gulls. I caught undertones of surf, a whispering rhythm and the not-quite-voice of the wind fading in and out. A perfect sound-picture, waiting for someone to add sight.

Do you never visualize? I asked. Carefully. Deadpan outside, deadpan inside.

It's the sound that matters. Or is it just pretty pictures you want, holo matinees? The last word came out more like *hollow* matinees.

It's a matter of what you *want*, I told him. The cries of the seagulls died away as the exercise came to an end. We let it go. His presence grew stronger, becoming a pressure in the darkness, filling all the space around my own self. New sounds began, all the pleasurable sounds he could remember, footsteps on a hard surface, people humming, the sharp clang of metal on metal, whispers, whistles, whales. His inner ear had remixed them into a harmoniousness that hadn't been there when he'd first heard them.

Some would say all this is music in itself, he said. *But it isn't. It needs translation. Interpretation.*

A tumble of conventional music drowned out the sounds. Shreds and snatches of various things, including old Coor and Lam compositions passed through me, as though he were trying to find the frequency at which I'd vibrate.

I felt for his Emotional Index. He was in a sort of performance mode. I let him go on throwing music while I did a gradual spread, sliding around him and into his terrain. It was exceedingly strange without visuals, but not unpleasant. Texture began to mix with sound and I had a sudden, vivid physical impression of him standing with his eyes closed, listening. What he was listening for I couldn't quite tell—the music within that would be sparked by the sounds without, or perhaps the elusive music of the subconscious spheres. I couldn't even make out whether this was a memory of something he'd done or the image he held of himself in the act of composing. His mind was stew, everything melting into and flavoring everything else, much more so than I'd found in many of my other clients. Stew is a wonderful thing, free of the over-compartmentalization and learned behavior that can (and does) cripple more than one artist. But stew could be too thick and formless, a mass in which ideas lost definition and coherence and ultimately dissolved, leaving behind only a hint of what they might have once been, just old seasonings boiled out and gone dead. Jord Coor was nowhere near this state, much to my relief.

I kept coming across abrupt, intense concepts and ideas sticking up like barbs—barbs and bait combined. The temptation to supply the missing visual element was nearly overwhelming. Trying to move around the barbs rather than directly into them was impossible; I'd come to depend on visualization the same way I'd depended on my physical sight. I sank down deeper into his terrain, careful not to probe too hard, looking for some sign of suppression.

It was like sinking blindfolded into a sensory stimulation tank. Very sensual man, this Jord Coor. The undertones said he'd just never been terribly taken by the visual experience. He was not an habitual admirer of sunsets or scenery, his earlier bit of showing me the Massachusetts countryside notwithstanding. Most of his concentration had always been on the auditory and, after that, the tactile.

He answered my question before I asked it. *Revien. He liked pictures. Always Revien. He supplied the pictures, if that's what you're looking for.*

I was still troubled. There should have been pictorial memories stashed about here and there, pictures of Revien's pictures, but I couldn't find them. Either Jord had buried them that deep or — highly unlikely, I thought — Revien Lam had taken them with him in an act of mindwipe. (And if so, had the mindwipe been forcible — or submitted to? Or, even more disturbingly, had Jord forced them on his partner? Expulsion? It was almost too much to think about.)

I went deeper into his sensory terrain. Not much effort on my part now; he was drawing me down in a movement that felt much like an embrace. The sensations became more intense, taking on a sort of insistence. Sensory offerings, all fragments wanting completion. I began to get that besieged feeling I always got when a client was trying too hard.

Easy, I told him.

Mild wave of surprise from him. *But it's always this way.*

You're coming and going in all directions. Do you have a focus?

His mind immediately went to Revien Lam. I felt it

rather than saw it, but there was no doubt as to whom he was thinking of. A memory of what it had been to share his presence, intense but dreamlike, something that might have happened only in his own imagination. And now a sensation of stretching out, reaching across a distance that might have been the span of a table or the emptiness of a universe, reaching for con

fall

fall

falling, plummeting down a long tunnel and nothing nothing nothing nothing

tact.

In the distortion of mind-time, it was over before it had begun. I might have lost consciousness. It seemed that way. I found myself at rest far above the terrain I'd been delving, in the upper, superficial layers of his sense-memory. His energy level was markedly diminished.

Always, he said. *Always like that. Without him.*

I reached down into him again but his mind was drifting now. It was like pushing into layer after layer of silk streamers floating in mid-air, and about as substantial. I could receive no clear impression of anything except fatigue. Quitting time.

Just before I withdrew, it came to me, a wisp from a wisp, an actual visual that lasted for half a thought-beat, if that long.

Revien Lam, at last and of course. With a wire winding out from under one eyelid like the trail of a dark tear.

Jord Coor was more than happy to have me leave

356

him alone. I wheeled my equipment down to the big, emptyish guest room (taking the ramps instead of that box of an elevator) and plugged into the long-term eidetic fixer. Reviewing a session so quickly—or rather, reliving it—isn't always the wisest thing to do in terms of wear and tear on the psyche, but I had to study this one.

It didn't take long for hindsight to kick in and show me what had been wrong with the whole mission in the first place. He had drawn me in so quickly on first contact that I hadn't consciously noticed—there had been no personality/identity barriers to pass through, not even so much as a mild mental fence.

Why hadn't I noticed, I wondered. Had I just assumed they'd been there the way they were in every other mind?

My professional reflexes spoke up, maddeningly in the voice of Nelson Nelson.

Think about it, Allie. Those barriers would have proved an inconvenience to him and Lam. My brain helpfully provided the image of NN's office, picturing him in recline behind his desk. I began to get a psychosomatic itch. Gold lamé. *And maybe that's your key, Deadpan. Help him build up his barriers again—help him by helping him resist your help.*

I'd never gone mind-to-mind with the old fox so it was rather unsettling (and infuriating) to find I'd given him a position in my brain as a persona for self-dialog.

Which just goes to show you, he/I went on, *that the most affecting contact isn't always mind-to-mind, is it, kid?*

I disengaged in a hurry, itching to get away from

357

him.

I let a day go by before the next session, hoping the breathing space would allow us both to regroup. But when we hooked in again, it was more of the same, more stew, more chaos, that long reach toward something followed by the fall and the weightlessness, drifty mind-state of exhausted semi-consciousness, or quasi-consciousness, or something.

"The blank spot," Jord said after we unhooked. He was lying on the mat in the studio, blinking at the ceiling. "The place where I used to compose. Nothing there any more."

I had no intention of accepting that, but after three more sessions, I began to think I was licked. It was astounding just how little information I was getting from him, mental stew notwithstanding. Most people's minds teem with associations, memories, and all the rest of the mental furniture and decoration that accrues during a lifetime. His seemed to be all put away or suppressed—I could receive only the briefest of impressions concerning episodes in his past that didn't involve Revien Lam. Did he really expect me to believe that for ten years there had been nothing in his life but composing with his partner? In another few sessions, he might have convinced us both. Except that would have meant Big Obsession and there was none of that unmistakable, dangerous flavor in his mind.

Still, the only visual I could get from him was that same image of Revien Lam. Sometimes it was as static as the flat pictures I had showed him for *What*

Do You Hear? Other times it was alive, the movements barely discernible, dreamlike but still there.

It was that lone visual that gave me the idea to try what I did. Nelson Nelson would have advised against it and five days before, I wouldn't have considered it myself. But we were falling into a feedback loop. If I could not shift him away from the idea of Revien Lam as a missing part of himself, then perhaps Lam—the Lam in his mind—could serve to trigger new reactions.

"Just one eye this time," I said, when we began the fifth session.

He looked up at me from the mat. That studied expressionlessness left his face like a mask melting away, leaving behind naked panic.

"Why?" His voice seemed to crackle.

"It could be helpful to use a method you're accustomed to."

He almost flinched from the wire I offered him and for a moment I thought he would refuse. Then he took the connection, removed his eye himself, and held it out to me.

I'd known this would be a very difficult type of session but even so, I wasn't prepared for the bizarreness of it. It was something like being awake and asleep at the same time, only much more so. More like being only partially in existence. I had to adjust my concentration radically and I wasn't sure that I hadn't asked too much of my mind. I might not have managed at all if it hadn't been for Jord Coor himself.

He fell easily into our configuration, his mind coming alive—*really* coming alive. He had no problem at all with the mix of textures. Mind and real world spilled over into each other for him, each one feeding the other. Now he could generate visuals, picking up little bits from his right eye. I saw myself as he saw me, a sort of professional mechanism sitting in a chair, as composed as could be. The visual of Revien Lam oozed over into the real world and shimmered in and out of being around me, a cross between an hallucination and a ghost. Sometimes it faded out of existence on its own; sometimes Coor blotted it out. But the feel of him was always there — or rather, the feel that was the lack of him.

There was never any point of actual stability or equilibrium; he teetered back and forth between perceiving the outside world and then the inside of his mind as dominant. The remaining eye remmed occasionally with waking dreams cannibalized from actual visual and the mind. A keyboard that seemed to be a hybrid of the piano and the synthesizer spread out before us, an hallucinatory horizon. The keys sank as ghost hands danced on them. I couldn't tell whose hands they were; the music itself was mostly inaudible.

Something new? I asked.

You can't hear it, either? The right eye fixed on me momentarily. *I think it might be something Revien and I were working on before we . . . went.*

Can you turn up the volume?

But the keyboard was already gone. There was a sensation of movement forward, acceleration, and then the real world paled. An image of Jord Coor appeared with his back to me, walking away.

Jord?

He paused and turned toward me slightly.

Where are we going?

The corner of his mouth twitched so realistically I almost forgot I was seeing a mental image. Very briefly, I had a glimpse of his face in the outer world, duplicating the movement.

Jord?

He began walking again. I traveled along in his wake, undecided as to whether I wanted to catch up with him. He kept glancing over his shoulder at me, always the left shoulder, his eye hard and too bright. We were moving through a landscape that I couldn't quite make out, except that it felt bleak and barren, a wasteland or badland, an image out of some old dream.

Eventually, I felt us descending. The landscape darkened and rose up canyonlike. No stew here; everything was locked away behind rock. Nothing grew here. You could wander around in it for the rest of your life with empty hands.

The landscape leveled off after awhile and I could discern a lighter area ahead. The end of the wasteland, I thought. So basic and literal. I should have expected it in this man.

I was covering my bemusement at this when I realized the man himself was gone—or at least, his mental image of himself was missing, though a good portion of his concentration remained, urging me forward. I didn't like the feel of it—no words, nothing like a mental signal, just an urging that was not quite a push. But I went. There was no firm reason to pull back yet and I was curious. The undertones barely registered, as though he had managed to vanish and remain at the same time.

Abruptly, I was standing at the edge of an abyss. I waited. Light was coming up from somewhere.

Jord?

Far away, I caught a slight movement. Jord Coor and I faced each other across the chasm. His head was a blur. I looked around, trying to find some way to reach him.

Then the light grew brighter and I saw he was walking toward me on empty air.

No, not air; a bridge that formed itself under him with each step. Lunatic bridge.

Halfway across, he stopped. There was a long, frozen moment when nothing happened and it seemed as though nothing would, ever again. I leaned forward and saw him clearly for the first time. The right side of his body was blank.

With no more thought than anyone would have given to an act of blind instinct, he yanked me to him.

It would have taken a lot more magnetism than he had to eat me alive but it was still a bumpy experience. Rather than pull back against him, I rushed down, through and out the other side. His realized half brushed me like tentacles, not quick enough to latch on and incorporate me. Disappointment followed in cold waves as I kept moving, back up the wire to break the link.

"I *am* sorry," he said for the fourth or fifth time.

"It's all right," I told him while I puttered around with the system. I still felt off-balance, with a psychosomatic brown-out in my right eye. It hadn't really been such a close call; subconsciously, I'd probably been prepared for an attempt at absorption. Still, it's rattling to have someone try to merge with you, change you into a stranger. "You didn't hurt me."

Jord fisted his left eye in a childlike way. "I knew you weren't Revien, I really did. I knew it the whole time, but I was going to take you anyway." He drew his legs up and rested his chin on his knees. "I guess I've been incomplete for so long, I'll take anyone." No more of that careful expressionlessness now; all masks were off for good. He looked forlorn. I'd seen that look before, on clients who had just realized how alone they really are in their own heads.

"He's got it, you know," he said. "Revien. He's got the other half of me. He *is* the other half of me now."

We do indeed adore our delusions, I thought as I tested the connection he'd used. I didn't tell him he was mistaken. I could have talked at him for the rest of the day and most of the night and maybe have made him admit he might possibly be mistaken, that he'd only atrophied and he really was complete if unused to working alone. And then the next time we hooked in, it would be the same thing all over again. I was going to have to demonstrate it to him—or rather, get him to demonstrate it to himself.

But the only way I could do that was to get a different perspective on him and the old partnership—and that was something only Revien Lam could give me.

Nelson Nelson was grumpy about it. Or perhaps he was just irritated at having to interrupt his viewing of

363

the Bolshoi to take my call. It amazed me that anyone could watch *Swan Lake* and *Coppelia* so often without tiring. Seeing him through his ceiling holo was unsettling; it felt like I was going to drop down on him and mash him into his itchy gold lamé.

"Sure I can find Revien Lam for you. It'll take a little while so you might want to take that time to work with your client a little more."

"NN, the man tried to eat me. He's close to pathological in his insistence that Revien Lam either has half of his ability or *is* half of his ability. I've got to feel things from Lam's point of view."

"Feel *what* things?"

"The partnership. As it was. All I can get from Coor is an absence of something and he tried to fill the absence with me."

"You really think that's going to help you?"

"It's more information than I can get from Coor and that's *got* to be helpful."

NN actually harrumphed. "Seems to me any pathosfinder worth her neurons ought to be able to probe someone skillfully enough to get all the information she needs."

I teetered on the edge of a tirade about having to work with a client who sincerely believed a good portion of himself was actually somebody else. Apparently no one had ever tried to eat NN. Who would have wanted to actually *be* that old fox, anyway? "Any pathosfinder worth her neurons also knows when to back off from her client and find her data elsewhere," I said evenly. "My man's on the defensive. The only way I can reach him effectively—and with minimal trauma—is to show him I've got the information he's hiding from himself. And the only way I can get it is from Revien Lam."

We stared at each other through our respective screens. To be fair, I think I had the upper hand, literally — it's hard to stare someone down when you're lying flat on your back.

"I'll have Lam's location for you in a couple of hours. What are you going to tell Coor?"

"I'll think of something. The truth is always good," I said and switched off before he could object.

Actually, I had no intention of telling Coor the truth, or at least not the whole truth. A lie would have been pointless and cruel, since he'd have felt Lam's impression when we hooked in again. I ended up telling him I was giving us both a couple days' thinking space. He surprised me by being disappointed and apprehensive rather than relieved. It wasn't until I was on my way to upstate New York that I realized he'd just gotten used to having me around. Sometimes it doesn't do a lonely person any good to keep him company.

It wasn't so surprising that Revien Lam had chosen to alight in an area not terribly far from his ex-collaborator. But while Jord Coor was living completely alone in an underground enclosure, Lam had opted for the Park.

I'd heard of the Park, though I'd never been there before. It was a sort of continuously running circus/picnic/freakshow/camp for those who didn't want the party to end. The Park population, which varied from week to week, roamed freely over a few hundred acres of weather-shielded countryside, eating, sleeping and playing as the spirit moved them. There were no clocks, no calendars and few rules. Violence was punishable by immediate, permanent expulsion but other than that, the Park people did as they pleased. It was probably the best way to lose all touch with reality short of buying a psychosis. A lot of people tried to lose themselves in the Park for just that reason. Some could and some couldn't; the rest, the hard-core Park People, would have been lost anywhere. The Park just kept them from cluttering up the rest of the world.

I wondered what Revien Lam's motivation had been for signing himself into the land of silk and funny. Whatever it was, I was willing to bet it had something to do with his wanting contact with a lot of people on a superficial level. Ten years of extreme intimacy was the sort of thing that could give a person a real appreciation for the superficial.

My first glimpse of the Park was shortly after dawn from the air, in the backseat of a flyer while the pilot snored behind the stick. Tents and pavilions dotted the rolling green landscape while people streamed among and around them like small currents of confetti. The Park wasn't an easy place to find someone but NN's office had contacted a guide for me, to help me find Revien Lam. I wondered, though, how I was supposed to find the guide.

The pilot snored through the landing, leaving me to unload my own equipment at the front gates of the Park. People accumulated along the flimsy fence to watch me, drifting over like colorful bits of cloth blown by an idle wind. It was an amazingly quiet audience—no chatter, no laughter, hardly a whisper. The faces, most of them dyed or polished or both, weren't exactly solemn. A few of them looked apprehensive, some even envious (of what, I wondered). Most of them had what I could already identify as a 'Park Look', as distinct as the sound of a regional accent in a voice. Had Revien Lam traded in his likeness to Jord Coor for a facial uniform?

I wheeled my equipment up to an ornate little kiosk at the entrance. There was no one inside, no bell to ring for service and no indication that I should either wait for someone to take charge of me or just go in myself. I looked left and right at my audience lining the fence. They stared back, unmoved. I thought of cows. Finally, a man with a stiff fringe of apple-red hair detached himself from the watchers on my right and ambled over. He almost stopped, his gold starburst eyes looking me and my equipment over critically. Somehow, I failed to measure up as anything sufficiently interesting to make him stop.

"Excuse me," I called after him.

He turned in slow motion without actually ceasing to wander away.

"How do I go about finding someone in here?"

His expression said I was sixteen different kinds of fools. "You look around." He moved into a loose gaggle of men and women on their way to a tall green tent.

No one else along the fence showed any inclination to come forward and offer any hints, suggestions, or even idle conversation. I moved my equipment further inside the Park, trying not to feel overly conspicuous. A laughing group of people playing some kind of game with big balloons materialized out of no-where and surrounded me, allowing me to be part of their playing field briefly before they skipped away, shedding one of their balloons as they went. It bounced gently at my feet and I picked it up.

"That was an invitation," said a female voice behind me. I turned around.

You see it all, eventually; all the ways people play with their bodies. Dye-jobs, bleach-jobs, certain kinds of transplants, alterations that border on muti-lation. You see people displaying just about anything of themselves, but this was something that could have been an image straight out of someone's troubled brain, come down the wires of a mindplay system and into the outer world to be made flesh. At least, sort of.

She let me stare at her. From a distance, I might have thought she was wearing a very close-fitting helmet that ended a few inches above her eyebrows, with some long strands of hair hanging out from underneath. But up close, it was too easy to see that her skull was made of glass.

Well, not real glass, of course, but something transparent. It was nauseating and fascinating all at once. There are certain kinds of minds I refuse to enter and I was fairly sure this was one of them.

"I was a pathosfinder once," she said.

Surprise number two. "You must be my guide." It would be hard not to choke NN for this when I saw him again.

"I'd have known you were a pathosfinder anyway. Just by that look on your face. All pathosfinders get that look. Even the ones named Deadpan Allie."

"What look is that?"

"Like you're trying to see through solid objects." She caressed her transparent skull with her fingers. "Watch out. This is what you're headed for."

I wondered if she were punning.

"It's what you're really after, you know. Letting everyone dip into your head, dipping into everyone else's. What makes you think anyone'll have need or desire for you in here?"

"I thought my office explained."

She put her hands in the pockets of her loose, wrinkled pants. "They did."

I could have sworn her brain changed color, flushed. "Then you do know where I can find Revien Lam."

"In a way. Once we get to him, you'll have to figure out how to find him on your own."

I nodded, thinking she must have been a pretty lousy pathosfinder.

Her lips stretched in a hard smile. "Only because of the telepathy. Mindplaying activated it, since you didn't ask." She patted her skull again delicately, as though she were smoothing her hair. "I'm used to receiving thoughts. It's made me a different person. Many different people." Her right lobe swelled slightly. "Do you know how many people you are? Or have you stopped counting?" She frowned. "Oh. Haven't started yet. Well. Never mind. I'll take you to Revien Lam. He's one of the tent people. It's a long walk."

An hour later, I knew for certain she hadn't been gassing when she'd said that. I plodded after her, struggling with my system, and reading Emotional

Indices at random (including some of the balloonatics, who reappeared twice more to make an invitation). There were a lot of anxious people in the Park, from what I could tell just by sight. It was catching; I could feel it beginning to chew at me around the edges. Glass-Skull (I realized belatedly she'd never told me her name) seemed unaffected by it, for all of her telepathy. She marched through the groups lounging on the grass or milling around aimlessly or spilling in and out of the carnival-colored tents which apparently dispensed food, toys, and other kinds of amusements, just for the asking. The daily charge for living in the Park had to be something past phenomenal.

My guide didn't slow down until we reached the shore of a small lake in the center of a lightly wooded area. On the other side, I saw a collection of the usual multi-colored tents with the standard multi-colored people passing in and out of them in the eternal quest for diversion. Glass-Skull gazed at them across the quiet water while I shifted from one tired foot to the other.

"Would you like me to tell you what you're thinking?" she asked without looking at me.

I shrugged.

She laughed and led me along a dirt path around the pond, pausing again at the outskirts of the tent grouping.

"Which one is he in?" I asked, since she didn't seem disposed to go any farther.

"The largest one," she said, pointing to a red tent trimmed with gold braid and tassels. "It's a sort of dormitory, so you won't have any privacy. Except, of course, in your own mind. A luxury some of us wouldn't be able to stand even if we were capable of having it." She put her hand on my arm as I was about to wheel my equipment forward. The contact was electric; I felt my mind jump in response. Being touched by a telepath is always a jolt.

"You can go on by yourself. Some can't." She let go and stepped back, and I was relieved to have her pressure fade from my brain.

The tent wasn't exactly crowded but there was an aroma of healthy bodies, or a healthy aroma of bodies, that made the air heavy and close. It reminded me less of a dormitory than it did of some kind of ward, one abandoned by its keepers. I left my equipment just inside the entrance and took a walk around, stepping over the people strewn about. Two men and a woman invited me to join what seemed to be a complicated game of marbles (played, I noticed undelightedly, with biogem eyes) and burst into high laughter when I declined. A baby-faced woman with wiry, metallic hair and silver eyes pressed an orange into my hand. I dropped it into my pocket and maneuvered between a man who was tattooing something upside-down on his naked chest and the woman who was dictating it to him.

I knew him immediately. His natural skin tone was just beginning to return from the bleaching, but his flesh still looked tight and stretched, too delicate for exposure to direct sunlight. He was lying on a scatter of pillows as though he'd been tossed there, head thrown back and eyes closed, a funny little smile on his mouth. I squatted down next to him.

"Revien Lam?" I had to say his name twice before

371

he raised his head slowly and looked at me.

My first thought was that he'd had a stroke. The two sides of his face seemed to have little to do with each other. Each eye perceived me independently, traveling over my face in separate patterns. Then he covered his right eye and said, "Do you know me?" The words came out with effort — *Do. You. Know. Me.*

"Not exactly. I know Jord Coor."

"Ah." He covered his left eye, surveyed me briefly with the right, and then went back to looking at me with his left again. And then I knew. I moved up on his left side and put my lips close to his ear.

"When did you have it cut?"

"Cut." His mouth worked silently. I'd have to be more specific.

"When did you have your corpus callosum severed?"

"Cut. Cut. Three months after Jord cut. After we cut ourselves apart." The words came a little easier now, as though he were getting back into the practice of speaking out loud. His head turned slightly and the sapphire eye glittered at me. "You are?"

"I'm a pathosfinder working for Jord Coor."

He turned his head all the way toward me and looked at me with his right eye again. "Music," he said, and began humming.

"You've had your visual fields rechanneled, too, haven't you?"

He went back to the left eye. "Completely divided. Right up the middle. What the hell, it's company."

"Company?" I had a queasy feeling I knew what he meant.

"Company. Not so lonely in here with the two halves. See, completely divided but not *so* completely. One final cord, one spinal cord still. I can feel each other."

"Is there someplace we can go to talk?"

He waved one hand clumsily. "I live here. Nobody cares."

"I'd like to delve you, if you'd give permission."

"Permission." He nodded. "But can't go outside—skin. After dark, all right. But really, nobody cares in here."

"Would you be willing to hook in with me?"

He frowned and went to his right eye. "Repeat?"

He must have been one of those people whose verbal and comprehension skills were spread over both hemispheres like birdshot. "Would you be willing to hook into my system with me—" I pointed to it over by the tent entrance. "Meet me mind-to-mind."

Back to the left eye. "Which mind did you want to meet?"

"Either. Both, if possible."

That funny little smile again. It was a composite smile from two different faces. "Do our best. Haven't been delved since the split, never before without Jord, eye to eye. To eye."

As it were. I went to get my system.

Nobody paid much attention to me while I set things up, including Revien Lam. He went back to daydreaming or dozing or whatever it was he did with his hemispheres. As soon as I was ready to go, however, I found myself with a sudden dilemma. Did

I hook in with him one eye at a time or both together? I considered asking him and then decided not to. Depending on which hemisphere took the question, the answer might be different. I went for the left eye first, removing it for him and plugging him into the same tonal exercise I'd used on Coor.

I put my hands up to my own eyes and paused. Now, what about me? Should I use both eyes or just one—and if only one, *which* one? I ended up removing both. Since I had nearly no idea of what I was going to find in there, it was probably best to go at it with all my concentration.

The tones translated to this half of his brain as a human voice singing syllables. His own voice, interestingly enough. The visualization was weak and fuzzy but I could make out the image of himself as a creature with a great big head and a negligible body. The head was stretched and distorted at the top, too wide, forcing the eyes to look in two different directions. The left eye was bigger than the right.

It got so lonely, he said, and the words were completely clear, almost firm enough to be tangible. *I never knew it could be that lonely. A peculiar thing. The nature of attachment and disconnection.* The top of his head stretched wider. *One and one equal one, sooner or later. Couldn't let that happen, we knew it. Merge into one person and we'd never sort him from me. But so* lonely. *Now I feel the ghost of his essence—or the essence of his ghost.*

I cast around some but I couldn't feel it in all the fuzzy vagueness.

Other side, he said.

I unplugged just long enough to switch the connection to his right eye and give that side a minute with the tonal. Then I went back down the wires.

It really was like entering a different mind. The personality barrier here was thicker and similar to, but not the same as, the one I'd gone through when he'd been hooked in through his left eye.

The moment I pushed through, I heard them—seagulls. The same ones, singing the tones. I lost my equilibrium and found myself sprawled belly down on sand, the damp grains rough against me. The sunlight was nearly blinding. A very well realized wave licked at me.

Revien?

The tonal faded away and the beach went with it. I pulled myself together just as the abyss formed. Lam had me floating disembodied over it, like a dream observer.

Whose abyss is this? I asked the empty air.

Ours, came the answer from below me.

The image was absurdist, impossible. A chasm could not have just one side or a bridge that connected the side with itself. My inner eyes crossed, uncrossed, crossed again; then the visual steadied down, translating into a Moebius strip. A composite of Coor and Lam was standing on it.

This is where I live now, the composite said, touching Coor's dark hair on the left side and pressing Lam's cheek on the right. *Hidden away like the bastard child I am. I'm even still composing music, but he can't get at it.* Just beyond the composite, a pale image of Revien Lam shimmered in and out of existence; Lam's awareness leaking through from the other side via the spinal cord connection. (Final cord, he'd called it at first, I remembered.)

Why can't he get at the music? I asked.

Other side. Have to send it to the other side for it to come out.

But if Coor's composing ability is really here, you should be able to express music using this side alone.

Not outwardly. The ability to express is not what he left here. Only the ability to compose.

And your own ability to compose? Is that here, too? There was no answer. *Lam's ability*, I clarified.

Yes.

Then you're not two opposite halves rejoined. You're the same side, superimposed. You're congruent, not complemented.

The composite wavered. *Coor is the complement to Lam. The congruent is complement.*

No, I said reasonably. *If you were hooked in through opposite eyes*—I stopped. I'd forgotten that in a normal, undivided brain, the optic nerves fed equally into both hemispheres, not right into right and left into left, the way they did in Lam's mutilated organ. The notion that maybe Coor wasn't deluded about Lam having a portion of himself began to creep up on me and I wondered belatedly what would have happened if I'd hooked into Coor through his right eye rather than his composing eye.

I was moving forward to examine the composite more closely when the visual cracked like a whip. For something like an eternity or thought-beat, everything was jumbled and whirling. Then it all came back into ultra-sharp focus and I was standing on the edge of the abyss, where I'd been in Jord Coor's mind. No more Moebius strip—there was a real bridge across the chasm with three figures on it: the composite, Revien Lam and Jord Coor. The real Jord Coor, blank on the right side, no delusory presence. He was right there with us, in the Park, in the tent, in Revien Lam's mind. Somehow, for whatever reason, he'd tracked me down and sneaked up on me again.

Withdrawal and disconnection would take too long. I rushed toward them, but even as I did, it was already happening. They each had hold of the composite and were pulling at it, stretching it like heat-softened rubber. The whole visual shuddered and bucked, pushing me back away from the bridge.

This is between us! Jord said hostilely, and I wasn't sure whom he was talking to.

You have no right! Lam hurled repulsion at him and somehow managed to draw him closer. *Mine now! Mine!*

You stole it!

You forced me to take it! You gave it up willingly!

I strained toward the bridge and they almost merged in their joint effort to knock me away. I backed off quickly.

You're part of me now, whether you wanted it or not, whether I wanted it or not! Lam said.

I have a right to be whole!

The composite between them was becoming a shapeless blob.

You refused to be whole. You gave away, Lam said.

Not gave. You just couldn't give back. You sucked it all without giving in return!

You wanted to be part of me, the better to love yourself!

Then that's how it is, Jord said. *We've both been after the same thing all along—you want me and I want me.*

The composite suddenly swelled and enveloped them. A million images spewed from the bridge, scenes from their respective pasts, now juxtaposed, double exposures. I pulled back even further. There was just one figure on the bridge now; its body kept shimmering and changing. Sometimes it was all Coor, then all Lam, then various mixtures of the two, Lam dominant, Coor dominant, both equal. Shimmer, melt, change.

I withdrew, put my eyes back in and without looking at the two limp bodies still hooked into my system, went outside and vomited into the neat, short, emerald grass.

"I did warn you," Glass-Skull said. She wiped my face with a damp rag. "You can go on by yourself. Some can't. Even so, how many different people are you?"

I looked up at her from where I was sitting, still trying to pull myself together enough to call NN and ask him if this meant my license had just been voided.

She smiled. "Go ahead, think about it. A little bit of one mind here, a little of another there . . ."

I had an intense, swift impression of a whole world of people hooking in with each other, unhooking, changing partners to hook in again, myself among them, and all the little bits left behind, the little bits carried away in exchange, the things that stay with you once you've touched another mind with your own.

"Transformed," Glass-Skull said. "Modified. You're polluted, stained, dyed, altered. And you will never be the same." She rubbed her head gently. "This is what you're heading for." I swear I saw her brain writhe in its transparent case.

I leaned forward and vomited again.

NN visited me every day in the hospital. He always showed up at mealtimes, relentlessly cheerful, applying the nutrient patch to my arm himself and chattering away about only the most innocuous things. He didn't bring up what had happened until I reached the point where I could keep down somewhat substantial fluids, but he was very brisk and all business when he did. I was about to have my noontime frappe when he lit on the edge of my bed and said, "You know, in a way, it's always been true that we're made of all the lives we've ever touched."

Nausea rose in me and I set the frappe aside. "Thanks. You've made my day."

"Now, now, Allie." NN picked up the tumbler and stirred the contents with the straw. "Just what is it about that idea that you find so revolting? Is it really so bad?"

"Every time a mindplayer pushes through those barriers of personality and identity, something is weakened in both the mindplayer and the client. We're losing the individual; we're getting homogenized. Someday, everyone will be everyone else. It'll be like *that*." I pointed at the frappe and burped.

"If you play that back, you'll realize how hysterical it sounds. Do you really feel like you're losing yourself? You're as Allie as you ever were. Maybe not so Deadpan at the moment, but we'll make allowances for trauma, and that's all it is, you know. You saw something bizarre happen to a couple of weak people and you were in mind-to-mind contact with them when it happened. Watching that kind of unnatural act — being forced to take part in it, even — that would put anyone off their feed." He tried to offer me the frappe and I pushed it away, burping again.

"*Allie*. Think straight for a minute. As a personal favor to me. When Coor and Lam merged, did they try to incorporate you?"

"Coor tried to eat me once, you know that."

"Ah, but when he got hold of Lam, did he make a grab at you?"

"No."

"Well, that's it, then."

"Yah, that's it. I'm already part of both of them. And vice versa."

"*Not* the same." NN moved closer to me, edging the frappe up to my mouth. "Look, maybe it's not pretty, but it's what they really wanted. Like the LadyBugs. They tried to run from it and they couldn't. Face it — some people have to be part of somebody else. Maybe they've always had to be each other and you really had nothing to do with it."

I remembered the resemblance between them, present before they'd even met. "Made for each other," I muttered.

"Coor and Lam, sure." NN tapped my lips with the straw.

Coor and Lam. Coor . . . and Lam? Unbidden, it popped into my head. Coor and Lam. Coeur et

L'Ame.

"Heart and Soul," I said aloud.

"What?" NN frowned. His eyebrows were just beginning to fill in again.

"Nothing. Just an old song from a few hundred years ago."

"Song is gone but the memory lingers on, eh, Allie?"

"Not exactly."

" 'Not exactly.' Deadpan goes hysterical, then cryptic. You probably wouldn't even tell me the truth as to whether you've been divorced or not."

"Sure I've been divorced," I said sourly. "Hundreds of times, from all the clients I've ever had."

"Don't start that again."

I opened my mouth to tell him I was divorcing him, too, but he shoved the straw between my lips.

"Suck," he said, and I did.

TALES OF TERROR AND POSSESSION

MAMA (1247, $3.50)
by Ruby Jean Jensen
Once upon a time there lived a sweet little dolly, but her one beaded glass eye gleamed with mischief and evil. If Dorrie could have read her dolly's thoughts, she would have run for her life— for her dear little dolly only had killing on her mind.

JACK-IN-THE-BOX (1892, $3.95)
by William W. Johnstone
Any other little girl would have cringed in horror at the sight of the clown with the insane eyes. But as Nora's wide eyes mirrored the grotesque wooden face her pink lips were curving into the same malicious smile.

ROCKABYE BABY (1470, $3.50)
by Stephen Gresham
Mr. Macready—such a nice old man—knew all about the children of Granite Heights: their names, houses, even the nights their parents were away. And when he put on his white nurse's uniform and smeared his lips with blood-red lipstick, they were happy to let him through the door—although they always stared a bit at his clear plastic gloves.

TWICE BLESSED (1766, $3.75)
by Patricia Wallace
Side by side, isolated from human contact, Kerri and Galen thrived. Soon their innocent eyes became twin mirrors of evil. And their souls became one—in their dark powers of destruction and death . . .

HOME SWEET HOME (1571, $3.50)
by Ruby Jean Jensen
Two weeks in the mountains would be the perfect vacation for a little boy. But Timmy didn't think so. The other children stared at him with a terror all their own, until Timmy realized there was no escaping the deadly welcome of . . . *Home Sweet Home.*

Available wherever paperbacks are sold, or order direct from the Publisher. Send cover price plus 50¢ per copy for mailing and handling to Zebra Books, Dept. 2050, 475 Park Avenue South, New York, N.Y. 10016. Residents of New York, New Jersey and Pennsylvania must include sales tax. DO NOT SEND CASH.

ASHES
by William W. Johnstone

OUT OF THE ASHES (1137, $3.50)

Ben Raines hadn't looked forward to the War, but he knew it was coming. After the balloons went up, Ben was one of the survivors, fighting his way across the country, searching for his family, and leading a band of new pioneers attempting to bring America OUT OF THE ASHES.

FIRE IN THE ASHES (1310, $3.50)

It's 1999 and the world as we know it no longer exists. Ben Raines, leader of the Resistance, must regroup his rebels and prep them for bloody guerrilla war. But are they ready to face an even fiercer foe—the human mutants threatening to overpower the world!

ANARCHY IN THE ASHES (1387, $3.50)

Out of the smoldering nuclear wreckage of World War III, Ben Raines has emerged as the strong leader the Resistance needs. When Sam Hartline, the mercenary, joins forces with an invading army of Russians, Ben and his people raise a bloody banner of defiance to defend earth's last bastion of freedom.

BLOOD IN THE ASHES (1537, $3.50)

As Raines and his rugged band of followers search for land that has escaped radiation, the insidious group known as The Ninth Order rises up to destroy them. In a savage battle to the death, it is the fate of America itself that hangs in the balance!

ALONE IN THE ASHES (1721, $3.50)

In this hellish new world there are human animals and Ben Raines—famed soldier and survival expert—soon becomes their hunted prey. He desperately tries to stay one step ahead of death, but no one can survive ALONE IN THE ASHES.

Available wherever paperbacks are sold, or order direct from the Publisher. Send cover price plus 50¢ per copy for mailing and handling to Zebra Books, Dept. 2050, 475 Park Avenue South, New York, N.Y. 10016. Residents of New York, New Jersey and Pennsylvania must include sales tax. DO NOT SEND CASH.